Praise for No. 1 *New York*
bestselling author

NORA ROBERTS

"Her stories have fueled the dreams
of twenty-five million readers."
—*Entertainment Weekly*

"Roberts is indeed a word artist, painting her story
and her characters with vitality and verve."
—*Los Angeles Daily News*

"Roberts creates exceptional characters who...
live on in the reader's imagination and heart."
—*Publishers Weekly*

"Roberts has a warm feel for her characters
and an eye for the evocative detail."
—*Chicago Tribune*

"Roberts...is at the top of her game."
—*People* magazine

"Roberts' bestselling novels are
some of the best in the romance genre."
—*USA TODAY*

NORA ROBERTS

No. 1 *New York Times* bestselling author
Nora Roberts is "a word artist, painting her
story and characters with vitality and verve,"
according to the *Los Angeles Daily News.* She
has published over a hundred novels, and her work
has been optioned and made into films, excerpted
in *Good Housekeeping* and has been translated into
over twenty-five different languages and published
all over the world.

In addition to her amazing success in mainstream,
Nora has a large and loyal category romance
audience, which took her to their hearts in 1981
with her very first book.

With over 127 million copies of her books in
print worldwide and a total of sixty-nine
New York Times bestsellers as of 2001, thirteen
of them reaching No. 1, she is truly a publishing
phenomenon.

NORA ROBERTS

The Name of The Game

Harlequin Mills & Boon

First Published 1988
First Australian Paperback Edition 2005
ISBN 0 733 56241 8

THE NAME OF THE GAME © 1998 by Nora Roberts
Philippine Copyright 1988
Australian Copyright 1988
New Zealand Copyright 1988

Published by
Harlequin Mills & Boon
3 Gibbes Street
CHATSWOOD NSW 2067
AUSTRALIA

Printed and bound in Australia by
McPherson's Printing Group

To Faye Ashley.
Now you'll have to leave me the bracelet.

One

"Marge Whittier, this is your chance to win *ten thousand dollars*. Are you ready?"

Marge Whittier, a forty-eight-year-old schoolteacher and grandmother of two from Kansas City squirmed in her chair. The lights were on, the drum was rolling and the possibility of her being sick was building. "Yes, I'm ready."

"Good luck, Marge. The clock will start with your first pick. Begin."

Marge swallowed a lump of panic, shuddered with excitement and chose number six. Her sixty seconds began to dwindle, and the tension grew as she and her celebrity partner picked their brains for the right answers. They leaped over such questions as who founded psychoanalysis and how many yards in a mile, then came to a screeching halt. What element do all organic compounds contain?

Marge went pale, and her lips quivered. She was an English teacher and a bit of a history and movie buff, but science wasn't her long suit. She looked pleadingly at her partner, who was better known for her wit than for her wisdom. Precious seconds ticked away. As they fumbled, the buzzer sounded. Ten thousand dollars flowed through Marge's sweaty fingers.

The studio audience groaned their disappointment.

"Too bad, Marge." John Jay Johnson, the tall, sleekly polished host, laid a sympathetic hand on her shoulder. His rich, rolling voice expressed just the right combination of disappointment and hope. "You were so close. But with eight correct answers you add another eight hundred dollars to your total. An impressive one." He smiled at the camera. "We'll be back after this break to total up Marge's winnings and to give you the correct answer to the stumper. Stay with us."

The music was cued. John Jay kept his avuncular smile handy. He used the timed ninety-second break to come on to the pretty celebrity panelist.

"Pompous jerk," Johanna muttered. The pity was that she was too aware his smooth looks and slick manner were keeping *Trivia Alert* up in the ratings. As producer, she'd learned to accept John Jay as part of the set. She checked the second hand of her watch before walking over to the losers. Putting on a smile of her own, she commiserated and congratulated as she eased them along. She needed them in camera range for the finish.

"Coming up on five," she announced, and signaled for applause and music. "And cue."

John Jay, his arm around Marge and his three-thousand-dollar caps gleaming, closed the show.

They were one big happy family as the assistant director shut off his stopwatch. "That's a wrap."

Kiki Wilson, Marge's partner and the current star of a popular situation comedy, chatted a few moments longer with Marge in a way that would have the schoolteacher remembering her warmly for years to come. When Kiki rose, her smile was still firmly in place as she walked the few steps to John Jay.

"If you ever pull something like that again," she said quietly, "you'll need a paramedic."

Knowing she was referring to his quick—and, if he did say so, clever—hand maneuver just before the end of the break, John Jay smiled. "Just part of the service. About that drink, sweetheart..."

"Kiki." In a smooth move that didn't appear nearly as rushed and harassed as it was, Johanna swung over and scooted the actress away. "I want to thank you again for agreeing to do the show. I know how hectic your schedule must be."

Johanna's warm voice and soothing manner brought Kiki's blood pressure down slightly. "I enjoyed it." Kiki pulled out a cigarette and tapped it absently against an enameled case. "It's a cute show, moves fast. And God knows the exposure never hurts."

Though Johanna didn't smoke, she carried a small gold lighter. Pulling it out, she lit Kiki's cigarette. "You were wonderful. I hope you'll consider coming back."

Kiki blew out smoke and regarded Johanna. The lady knew her job, Kiki admitted. Even though she looked like some cuddly little model for shampoo or yogurt. It had been a long day, but the catered dinner break had been first-class, the studio audience generous with their applause. In any case, her agent had told her that *Trivia Alert* was *the* up-and-coming game show of the year. Considering that, and the fact that Kiki had a good sense of humor, she smiled.

"I just might. You've got a good crew, with one notable exception."

Johanna didn't have to turn to know where Kiki's narrowed gaze had landed. With John Jay it was either love or disgust, with little middle ground. "I have to apologize for any annoyance."

"Don't bother. There are plenty of jerks in the business." Kiki studied Johanna again. Quite a face, she decided, even with the minimal makeup. "I'm surprised you don't have a few fang marks."

Johanna smiled. "I have very thick skin."

Anyone who knew her would have attested to that. Johanna Patterson might have looked soft and creamy, but she had the energy of an Amazon. For eighteen months she had slaved, hustled and bargained to get and keep *Trivia Alert* on the air. She wasn't a novice in the entertainment business, and that made her all the more aware that behind the scenes and in the boardrooms it was still a man's world.

That would change eventually, but eventually was too long a wait. Johanna wasn't patient enough to wait for doors to open. When she wanted something badly enough, she gave them a push. For that she was willing to make certain adjustments herself. The business of entertainment was no mystery to her; nor were the deals, the concessions or the compromises. As long as the end product was quality, it didn't matter.

She'd had to swallow pride and sacrifice a principle or two to get her baby off and running. For example, it wasn't her name, but her father's logo that flashed importantly at the end of the show: Carl W. Patterson Productions

His was the name the network brass related to, and his was the one they trusted. So she used it—grudgingly—then ran things her way.

Thus far, the uneasy marriage was into its second year and holding its own. Johanna knew the business—and her father—too well to take for granted that it would continue.

So she worked hard, tying up loose ends, hammering out solutions to problems and delegating carefully what couldn't be handled personally. The success or failure of the show wouldn't make or break her, financially or professionally, but she had more than money and reputation tied up with it. She had her hopes and her self-esteem.

The studio audience had been cleared. A few technicians remained on the set, either gossiping or tidying up last-minute business. It was just past eight o'clock, and moving into hour fourteen for Johanna.

"Bill, do you have the dupes?" She accepted the copies of the day's tape from her editor. Five shows were produced and recorded in one full-day session. Five costume changes for the celebrity panelists—Johanna had a policy against referring to them as guest stars. Five wardrobe trips for John Jay, who insisted on a change from underwear out for each show. His natty suits and coordinated ties would be sent back to the Beverly Hills tailor who provided them free in exchange for the plug at the end of each show.

His job was over, but Johanna's was just beginning. The tapes would be reviewed, edited and carefully timed. Johanna would oversee each step. There would be mail to go through, letters from home viewers who hoped to be chosen as contestants, more letters from people who disagreed with certain answers. She'd go head-to-head with her research coordinator to check facts and select new questions for upcoming shows. Though she couldn't personally interview and screen each potential contestant, she would go over her contestant coordinator's selections.

The game-show scandals of the fifties were long over, but no one wanted a repeat of them. Standards and Practices was very strict, their rules and regulations very clear. Johanna made it a habit never to relax her own, and to check each detail herself.

When screened contestants arrived at the studio for a day's taping, they were turned over to staff members who sequestered them from the crew, the audience and their prospective partners. They were entertained and soothed, literally cut off from the show until their turn came to participate.

Questions were locked in a safe. Only Johanna and her personal assistant had the combination.

Then, of course, there were the celebrities to deal with. They would want their favorite flowers and choice of beverage in their dressing rooms. Some would go with the flow and make her life easier, and others would be difficult just to show they were important. She knew—and they knew she knew—that most of them appeared on morning game shows not for the money or the fun but for the exposure. They were plugging series and specials, placating their networks or scrambling to keep their face familiar to the public.

Fortunately, a good percentage of them had fun once the ball was rolling. There were still more, however, who required pampering, cajoling and flattery. She was willing, as long as they helped her keep her show on the air. When a woman had grown up with artistic temperaments and the wheeling and dealing of the entertainment business, very little surprised her.

"Johanna."

Regretfully Johanna put her fantasy of a hot bath and a foot massage on hold. "Yes, Beth?" She slipped the tapes into her oversize tote and waited for her assistant. Bethany Landman was young, sharp and energetic. Just now she seemed to be bubbling over. "Make it good. My feet are killing me."

"It's good." A bouncy dark contrast to Johanna's cool blond looks, Bethany gripped her clipboard and all but danced. "We've got him."

Johanna secured the tote on the shoulder of her slim violet-blue jacket. "Who have we got and what are we going to do with him?"

"Sam Weaver." Beth caught her lower lip between her teeth as she grinned. "And I can think of a lot of things we could do with him."

The fact that Bethany was still innocent enough to be impressed by a hard body and tough good looks made Johanna feel old and cynical. More, it made her feel as though she'd been born that way. Sam Weaver was every woman's dream. Johanna wouldn't have denied him his talent, but she was long past the point where sexy eyes and a cocky grin made her pulse flutter. "Why don't you give me the most plausible?"

"Johanna, you have no romance in your soul."

"No, I don't. Can we do this walking, Beth? I want to see if the sky's still there."

"You read that Sam Weaver's done his first TV spot?"

"A miniseries," Johanna added as they wound down the studio corridor.

"They aren't calling it a miniseries. Promotion calls it a four-hour movie event."

"I love Hollywood."

With a chuckle, Bethany shifted her clipboard. "Anyway, I took a chance and contacted his agent. The movie's on our network."

Johanna pushed open the studio door and breathed in the air. Though it was Burbank air and therefore far from fresh, it was welcome. "I'm beginning to see the master plan."

"The agent was very noncommittal, but..."

Johanna stretched her shoulders, then searched for her keys. "I think I'm going to like this *but*."

"I just got a call from upstairs. They want him to do it. We'll have to run the shows the week before the movie and give him time to plug it every day." She paused just long enough to give Johanna a chance to nod. "With that guarantee they'll put on the pressure and we've got him."

"Sam Weaver," Johanna murmured. There was no denying his drawing power. Being tall, lanky and handsome in a rough sort of way didn't hurt, but he had more than that. A bit part in a feature film five, maybe six years before had been a springboard. He'd been top-billed and hot box office ever since. It was more than likely he'd be a pain in the neck to work with, but it might be worth it. She thought of the millions of televisions across the country, and the ratings. It would definitely be worth it.

"Good work, Beth. Let's get it firmed up."

"As good as done." Bethany stood by the spiffy little Mercedes as Johanna climbed in. "Will you fire me if I drool?"

"Absolutely." Johanna flashed a grin as she turned the key. "See you in the morning." She drove the car out of the lot like a bullet. Sam Weaver, she thought as she turned the radio up and let the wind whip her hair. Not a bad catch, she decided. Not bad at all.

Sam felt like a fish with a hook through his mouth, and he didn't enjoy the sensation. He slumped in his agent's overstuffed chair, his long, booted legs stretched out and a pained scowl on the face women loved to love.

"Good Lord, Marv. A game show? Why don't you tell me to dress like a banana and do a commercial?"

Marvin Jablonski chomped a candied almond, his current substitute for cigarettes. He admitted to being forty-three, which made him a decade older than his client. He was trim and dressed with a subtle flair that spoke of wealth and confidence. When his office had consisted of a phone booth and a briefcase, he'd dressed the same. He knew how vital illusions were in this town. Just as he knew it was vital to keep a client happy while you were manipulating him.

"I thought it was too much to expect that you'd be open-minded."

Sam recognized the touch of hurt in Marv's tone—the poor, self-sacrificing agent, just trying to do his job. Marv was far from poor and he'd never been into personal sacrifice. But it worked. With something like a sigh, Sam rose and paced the length of Marv's glitzy Century City office. "I was open-minded when I agreed to do the talk-show circuit."

Sam's easy baritone carried a hint of his native rural Virginia, but his reputation in Los Angeles wasn't that of a country gentleman. As he paced, his long-legged stride made the observer think of a man who knew exactly where he was going.

And so he did, Marv thought. Otherwise, as a selective and very successful theatrical agent he would never have taken the struggling young actor on six years before. Instinct, Marv was wont to say, was every bit as important as the power breakfast. "Promotion's part of the business, Sam."

"Yeah, and I'll do my bit. But a game show? How is guessing

what's behind door number three going to boost the ratings for *Roses?*''

''There aren't any doors on *Trivia.*''

''Thank God.''

Marv let the sarcasm pass. He was one of the few in the business who knew that Sam Weaver could be maneuvered with words like *responsibility* and *obligation.* ''And it'll boost the ratings because millions of sets are tuned in to that half-hour spot five days a week. People love games, Sam. They like to play, they like to watch and they like to see other people walk out with a free lunch. I've got miles of facts and figures, but let's just say that most of those sets are controlled by women.'' His smile spread easily, shifting his trim, gray-flecked mustache. ''Women, Sam, the ones who buy the bulk of the products the sponsors are hyping. And that fizzy little soft drink that's the major sponsor for *Roses* also buys time on *Trivia.* The network likes that, Sam. Keeps things in the family.''

''That's fine.'' Sam hooked his thumbs in the pockets of his jeans. ''But we both know I didn't take the TV deal to sell soda pop.''

Marv smiled and ran a hand over his hair. His new toupee was a work of art. ''Why did you take the deal?''

''You know why. The script was gold. We needed the four hours to do it right. A two-hour feature would have meant hacking it to bits.''

''So you used TV.'' Marv closed his fingers together lightly, as if he were shutting a trap. ''Now TV wants to use you. It's only fair, Sam.''

Fair was another word Sam had a weakness for.

A short four-letter epithet was Sam's opinion. Then he said nothing as he stared out at his agent's lofty view of the city. He wasn't so many years off the pavement that he'd forgotten what it felt like to have the heat bake through his sneakers and frustration run through his blood. Marv had taken a chance on him. A calculated risk, but a risk nonetheless. Sam believed in paying his dues. But he hated making a fool of himself.

''I don't like to play games,'' he muttered, ''unless I set the rules.''

Marv ignored the buzzer on his desk; it was the prerogative of a man in demand. "You talking politics or the show?"

"Sounds to me like they've been lumped together."

Marv only smiled again. "You're a sharp boy, Sam."

Sam turned his head just a fraction. Marv had been hit by the power of those eyes before. They were one of the reasons he'd signed an unknown when he'd been in a position to refuse the business of well-established luminaries. The eyes were big, heavy lidded and blue. Electric blue, with the power of a lightning bolt. Intense, like his long-boned, narrow face and firm mouth. The chin wasn't so much cleft as sculpted. The kind of chin that looked as though it could take a punch. The nose was a bit crooked, because it had.

California sun had tanned the skin a deep brown and added the interest of faint lines. The kind that made a woman shiver, imagining the experiences that had etched them there. There was a mystery about his face that appealed to females, and a toughness that drew approval from other men. His hair was dark and left long enough to go its own way.

It wasn't a face for a poster in a teenager's room, but it was the kind that haunted a woman's secret dreams.

"How much choice do I have on this?" Sam asked.

"Next to none." Because he knew his client, Marv decided it was time to bare the truth. "Your contract with the network ties you to promotion work. We could get around it, but it wouldn't be good for you, this project or any future ones."

Sam didn't give a damn if it was good for him. He rarely did. But the project was important. "When?"

"Two weeks from today, I'll move the paperwork through. Keep it in perspective, Sam. It's one day out of your life."

"Yeah." One day, he thought, could hardly make much difference. And it wasn't easy to forget that a decade before he'd have considered an offer to do a game show as much of a miracle as manna from heaven. "Marv..." He paused at the door. "If I make an ass out of myself, I'm going to dump Krazy Glue on your hairpiece."

It was strange that two people could have business in the same building, often ride the same elevator, but never cross paths. Sam didn't make the trip from Malibu to his agent's office often. Now that his career was on the rise he was usually tied up in rehearsals, script meetings or location shoots. When he had a few weeks, as he did now, he didn't waste it battling L.A.'s traffic or closing himself up inside Century City's impressive walls. He preferred the seclusion of his ranch.

Johanna, on the other hand, made the trip to her Century City office daily. She hadn't taken a personal vacation in two years, and she put in an average of sixty hours a week on her show. If anyone had tagged her as a workaholic she would have shrugged off the label. Work wasn't an illness, as far as Johanna was concerned; it was a means to an end. The long hours and dedication justified her success. She was determined that no one accuse her of riding on Carl Patterson's coattails.

The offices maintained by *Trivia*'s staff were comfortable but understated. Her own was large enough to prevent her from feeling claustrophobic and practical enough to make the statement that this was a place of business. She arrived like clockwork at eight-thirty, broke for lunch only if it included a meeting, then worked straight through until she was finished. Besides her almost maternal devotion to *Trivia*, she had another concept on the back burner. A word game this time, an idea that was nearly refined enough to take to the network brass.

Now she had her jacket slung over her chair and her nose buried in a week's worth of potential questions passed on to her by Research. She had to get close to the words because she refused to wear the reading glasses she needed.

"Johanna?"

With little more than a grunt, Johanna continued to read. "Did you know Howdy Doody had a twin brother?"

"We were never close," Bethany said apologetically.

"Double Doody," Johanna informed her with a nod. "I think it's a great one for the speed round. Did you catch today's show?"

"Most of it."

"I really think we should try to lure Hank Loman back. Soap stars are a big draw."

"Speaking of big draws..." Bethany set a stack of papers on

Johanna's desk. "Here's the contract for Sam Weaver. I thought you'd like to look it over before I run it up to his agent."

"Fine." She shuffled papers before drawing the contract close enough to focus on it. "Let's send him a tape of the show."

"The usual fruit and cheese for the dressing room?"

"Um-hmm. Is the coffee machine fixed?"

"Just."

"Good." She took a casual glance at her watch. It was a simple affair with a black leather band. The diamond-encrusted one her father's secretary had picked out for her last birthday was still in its box. "Listen, you go on to lunch. I'll run these up."

"Johanna, you're forgetting how to delegate again."

"No, I'm just delegating me." Rising, she shook the creases out of her pale rose jacket. After picking up the remote channel changer from her desk, she aimed it at the television across the room. Both picture and sound winked off. "Are you still seeing that struggling screenwriter?"

"Every chance I get."

Johanna grinned as she shrugged into her jacket. "Then you'd better hurry. This afternoon we need to brainstorm over the home viewer's contest. I want that rolling by next month." She picked up the contracts and slipped them and a cassette into a leather portfolio. "Oh, and make a note for me to slap John Jay's wrist, will you? He charged a case of champagne to the show again."

Bethany wrote that down enthusiastically and in capital letters. "Glad to do it."

Johanna chuckled as she swung out the door. "Results of the contestant screening by three," she continued. "That tech's wife—Randy's wife—she's in Cedars of Lebanon for minor surgery. Send flowers." Johanna grinned over her shoulder. "Who says I can't delegate?"

On the ride up in the elevator, Johanna smiled to herself. She was lucky to have Beth, she thought, though she could already foresee the time when her assistant would be moving up and out. Brains and talent rarely settled for someone else's dream. She liked to think she'd proved that theory for herself. In any case, Johanna had Beth now, and with the rest of her bright young staff,

Johanna was on her way to establishing her own niche in the competitive world of daytime television.

If she could get her new concept as far as a pilot, she had no doubt she could sell it. Then maybe a daytime drama, something with as much action as heartache. That story was already in its beginning stages. In addition to that, she was determined to have a nighttime version of *Trivia* syndicated to the independents. She was already on the way to achieving her five-year goal of forming her own production company.

As the elevator rose, Johanna automatically smoothed down her hair and straightened the hem of her jacket. Appearances, she knew, were as important as talent.

When the doors opened, she was satisfied that she looked brisk and professional. She passed through the wide glass doors into Jablonski's offices. He didn't believe in understatement. There were huge Chinese-red urns filled with feathers and fans. A sculpture of what might have been a human torso gleamed in brushed brass. The carpet was an unrelieved white and, Johanna's practical mind thought, must be the devil to keep clean.

Wide chairs in black and red leather were arranged beside glass tables. Trade magazines and the day's papers were set in neat piles. The setup told her Jablonski didn't mind keeping clients waiting.

The desks in the reception area followed the theme in glossy red and black. Johanna saw an attractive brunette seated at one. Perched on the corner of the desk and leaning close to the brunette was Sam Weaver. Johanna's brow lifted only slightly.

She wasn't surprised to see him flirting with one of the staff. Indeed, she expected that kind of thing from him and others like him. After all, her father had had an affair with every secretary, receptionist and assistant who had ever worked for him.

He'd been the tall, dark and handsome type, too, she thought. Still was. Her only real surprise at running into Sam Weaver was that he was one of that rare breed of actor who actually looked better in the flesh than on the screen.

He packed a punch, an immediate one.

Snug jeans suited him, she acknowledged, as did the plain cotton shirt of a working man. No gold flashed, no diamonds winked.

He didn't need them, Johanna decided. A man who could look at the receptionist the way Sam was looking at that brunette didn't need artifice to draw attention to him.

"She's beautiful, Gloria." Sam bent closer to the snapshots the receptionist was showing off. From Johanna's angle it looked as though he were whispering endearments. "You're lucky."

"She's six months old today." Gloria smiled down at the photograph of her daughter, then up at Sam. "I was lucky Mr. Jablonski gave me such a liberal maternity leave, and it's nice to be back at work, but boy, I miss her already."

"She looks like you."

The brunette's cheeks flushed with pride and pleasure. "You think so?"

"Sure. Look at that chin." Sam tapped a finger on Gloria's chin. He wasn't just being kind. The truth was, he'd always gotten a kick out of kids. "I bet she keeps you busy."

"You wouldn't believe—" The still-new mother might have been off and running if she hadn't glanced up and seen Johanna. Embarrassed, she slid the pictures into her drawer. Mr. Jablonski had been generous and understanding, but she didn't think he'd care to have her spending her first day back on the job showing off her daughter. "Good afternoon. May I help you?"

With a slight inclination of her head, Johanna crossed the room. As she did, Sam swiveled on the desk and watched her. He didn't quite do a double take, but damn near.

She was beautiful. He wasn't immune to beauty, though he was often surrounded by it. At first glance she might have been taken for one of the hordes of slim and leggy California blondes who haunted the beaches and adorned glossy posters. Her skin was gold—not bronzed, but a very pale and lovely gold. It set off the smoky blond hair that fluffed out to tease the shoulders of her jacket. Her face was oval, the classic shape given drama by prominent cheekbones and a full mouth. Her eyes, delicately shaded with rose and violet, were the clear blue of a mountain lake.

She was sexy. Subtly sexy. He was used to that in women as well. Maybe it was the way she moved, the way she carried herself inside the long loose jacket and straight skirt, that made her seem so special. Her shoes were ivory and low-heeled. He found himself noticing even them and the small, narrow feet they covered.

She didn't even glance at him, and he was glad. It gave him the chance to stare at her, to absorb the sight of her, before she recognized him and spoiled the moment.

"I have a delivery for Mr. Jablonski."

Even her voice was perfect, Sam decided. Soft, smooth, just edging toward cool.

"I'll be happy to take it." Gloria gave her most cooperative smile.

Johanna unzipped her portfolio and took out the contracts and tape. She still didn't look at Sam, though she was very aware he was staring. "These are the Weaver contracts and a tape of *Trivia Alert*."

"Oh, well—"

Sam cut her off neatly. "Why don't you take them in to him, Gloria? I'll wait."

Gloria opened her mouth, then shut it again to clear her throat as she rose. "All right. If you'd just give me a moment," she said to Johanna, then headed down the corridor.

"Do you work for the show?" Sam asked her.

"Yes." Johanna gave him a small and purposefully disinterested smile. "Are you a fan, Mr.—?"

She didn't recognize him. Sam had a moment to be both surprised and disconcerted before he saw the humor of it and grinned. "It's Sam." He held out a hand, trapping her into an introduction.

"Johanna," she told him, and accepted the handshake. His easy reaction made her feel petty. She was on the verge of explaining when she realized he hadn't released her hand. His was hard and strong. Like his face, like his voice. It was her reaction to them, her quick and intensely personal reaction to them, that drove her to continue the pretense and blame it on him.

"Do you work for Mr. Jablonski?"

Sam grinned again. It was a fast, crooked grin that warned a woman not to trust him. "In a manner of speaking. What do you do on the show?"

"A little of this, a little of that," she said, truthfully enough. "Don't let me keep you."

"I'd rather you did." But he released her hand because she was tugging at it. "Would you like to have lunch?"

Her brow lifted. Five minutes ago he'd been cuddling up to the brunette; now he was inviting the first woman who came along to lunch. Typical. "Sorry. I'm booked."

"For how long?"

"Long enough." Johanna glanced past him to the receptionist.

"Mr. Jablonski will have the contracts signed and returned to Ms. Patterson by tomorrow afternoon."

"Thank you." Johanna shifted her portfolio and turned. Sam laid a hand on her arm and waited until she looked back at him. "See you."

She smiled at him, again disinterestedly, before she walked away. She was chuckling when she reached the elevators, unaware that she'd tucked the hand he'd held into her pocket.

Sam watched her until she'd turned the corner. "You know, Gloria," he said, half to himself, "I think I'm going to enjoy playing this game after all."

Two

On the day of a taping, Johanna was always on the set by nine. It wasn't that she didn't trust her staff. She did. She simply trusted herself more. Besides, last week they'd had a few mechanical glitches with the moving set that swung the contestants and their counters stage center for play, then off again for the championship round. Small problems like that could delay taping anywhere from five minutes to two hours. By checking everything through personally beforehand, she sweetened the odds.

All the lights on the display board had to be tested, and the dressing rooms had to be primped and fresh coffee and cookies arranged for the prospective contestants.

They weren't due until one, but experience told Johanna that most would arrive early so they could chew their nails in the studio. Soothing them was one job she gladly delegated. The celebrities were also due at one so they could do a run-through and still have plenty of time for hair, makeup and wardrobe.

John Jay would arrive at two to complain about the suits that had been selected for him. Then he would close himself in his dressing room to sulk before his makeup call. When he was suited up, powdered and sprayed he would emerge, ready to shine for the cameras. Johanna had learned to ignore his artistic temperament—for the most part—and to tolerate the rest. There was no arguing with his popularity quotient. It was largely due to him that the line would form outside the studio for tickets for the day's taping.

Johanna checked off her duties one by one, then double-checked everyone else's. Over the years, efficiency had grown from a habit to an obsession. At noon she downed something that resembled a shrimp salad. The taping should start at three and, if God was in his heaven, be over by eight.

Fortunately, the female celebrity was a repeater who had done *Trivia* at least a dozen times, along with numerous other game shows. That gave Johanna one less headache. She hadn't given Sam Weaver a thought.

So she told herself.

When he arrived, she would turn him and his entourage over to Bethany. It would give her assistant a thrill and keep God's gift to women out of her hair.

She only hoped he could handle the game. The questions were fun, for the most part, but they weren't always easy. More than once she'd had a celebrity grumble and complain because an inability to answer had made him or her look stupid. Johanna made it a policy to see that each show's batch of questions contained the obvious and amusing, as well as the challenging.

It wouldn't be her fault if Sam Weaver turned out to have an empty head. He would only have to smile to gain the audience's forgiveness.

She remembered the way he'd smiled at her when she'd asked if he worked for Jablonski. Yes, that was all it would take to make every woman at home and in the studio turn to putty—except her, of course.

"Check the bell." Johanna stood in the middle of the set and directed her sound technician. At her signal the bright, cheery beep of the winning bell rang. "And the buzzer." The flat drone of the loser sounded. "Bring up the lights in the winner's circle." She nodded in satisfaction as the bulbs flashed.

"The contestants?"

"Sequestered." Bethany checked her clipboard. "We have the accountant from Venice returning from last week. He's a three-game winner. First challenger's a housewife from Ohio in town visiting her sister. Nervous as hell."

"Okay, see if you can help Dottie keep them calm. I'll give the dressing rooms a last check."

Mentally calculating her time as she went, Johanna scooted down the corridor. Her female celebrity was Marsha Tuckett, a comfortable, motherly type who was part of the ensemble of a family series in its third year. A nice contrast for Sam Weaver, she thought. Johanna made sure there were fresh pink roses on the dressing table and plenty of club soda on ice. Satisfied the room was in order, she walked across the narrow hall to the next room.

Because she hadn't thought roses appropriate for Sam Weaver, she'd settled on a nice leafy fern for the corner. As a matter of course she checked the lights, plumped the pillows on the narrow daybed and made certain the towels were fresh and plentiful. A last look showed her nothing he could find fault with. Carelessly she stole a mint from the bowl on the table and popped it into her mouth, then turned.

He was in the doorway.

"Hello again." He'd already decided to make it his business to find her, but he hadn't expected to be quite so lucky. He stepped into the room and dropped a garment bag negligently over a chair.

Johanna pushed the candy into the corner of her mouth. The dressing room was small, but she couldn't recall feeling trapped in it before. "Mr. Weaver." She put on her best at-your-service smile as she offered a hand.

"It's Sam. Remember?" He took her hand and stepped just close enough to make her uncomfortable. They both knew it wasn't an accident.

"Of course. Sam. We're all delighted you could join us. We'll have our run-through shortly. In the meantime, you can let me or one of the staff know if you need anything." She looked past him, puzzled. "Are you alone?"

"Was I supposed to bring someone?"

"No." Where was his secretary, his assistant, his gofer? His current lover?

"According to my instructions, all I needed was five changes. Casual. Will this do to start?"

She studied the navy crewneck and the buff-colored slacks as though it mattered. "You look fine."

She'd known who he was all along, Sam thought. He wasn't so much annoyed as curious. And she wasn't comfortable with him now. That was something else to think about. Making a woman comfortable wasn't always a goal. After reaching for a mint himself, he rested a hip against the dressing table. It was a move that brought him just a little closer. Her lipstick had worn off, he noticed. He found the generous and unpainted shape of her mouth appealing.

"I watched the tape you sent."

"Good. You'll have more fun if you're familiar with the format. Make yourself comfortable." She spoke quickly but not hurriedly. That was training. But she wanted out, and she wanted out now. That was instinct. "One of the staff will be along to take you to Makeup."

"I also read credits." He blocked the door in an offhand way. "I noticed that a Johanna Patterson is executive producer. You?"

"Yes." Damn it, he was making her jittery. She couldn't remember the last time anyone had been able to make her nervous. Cool, controlled and capable. Anyone who knew her would have given that description. She glanced deliberately at her watch. "I'm sorry I can't stay and chat, but we're on a schedule."

He didn't budge. "Most producers don't hand-deliver contracts."

She smiled. Though on the surface it was sweet, he saw the ice underneath and wondered at it. "I'm not most producers."

"I won't argue with that." It was more than attraction now, it was a puzzle that had to be solved. He'd managed to resist any number of women, but he'd never been able to resist a puzzle. "Since we missed lunch before, how about dinner?"

"I'm sorry. I'm—"

"Booked. Yeah, so you said." He tilted his head just a bit, as if to study her from a new angle. It was more than the fact that he was used to women being available. It was the fact that she seemed bound and determined to brush him off, and not very tactfully. "You're not wearing any rings."

"You're observant."

"Involved?"

"With what?"

He had to laugh. His ego wasn't so inflated that he couldn't take no for an answer. He simply preferred a reason for it. "What's the problem, Johanna? Didn't you like my last movie?"

"Sorry. I missed it," she lied, smiling. "Now if you'll excuse me, I've got a show to see to."

He was still standing at the door, but this time she brushed past him. And against him. Both felt a jolt, unexpected and tingling.

Annoyed, Johanna kept walking.

Intrigued, Sam kept watching.

She had to admit, he was a pro. By the middle of the taping of the first show, Sam had gotten in a casual and very competent plug for his new miniseries *No Roses for Sarah*. So effective, that Johanna knew she'd tune in herself. The sponsors and the network brass would be delighted. He'd charmed his partner, the mother of two from Columbus, who had walked onto the set so tense that her voice had come out in squeaks. He'd even managed to answer a few questions correctly.

It was hard not to be impressed, though she worked at it. When the lights were on and the tape was rolling he was the embodiment of that elusive and too often casually used word: *star*. John Jay's posturing and flashing incisors shifted to the background.

Not all entertainers were at ease in front of a live audience. He was. Johanna noted that he was able to turn on just the right amount of enthusiasm and enjoyment when the cameras were rolling, but also that he played to the studio audience during breaks by joking with his competitor and occasionally answering a question someone shouted out at him.

He even seemed to be genuinely pleased when his partner won five hundred in cash in the bonus speed round.

Even if he was just putting on a good face, Johanna couldn't fault him for it. Five hundred dollars meant a great deal to the mother of two from Columbus. Just as much as her moment in the sun with a celebrated heartthrob.

"We've got a very tight game going here, folks." John Jay smiled importantly at the camera. "This final question will determine today's champion, who will then go to the winner's circle and try for ten thousand dollars. Hands on your buzzers." He drew the card from the slot on his dais. "And the final question, for the championship, is...who created Winnie the Pooh?"

Sam's finger was quick on the trigger. The woman from Columbus looked at him pleadingly. John Jay called for a dramatic silence.

"A. A. Milne."

"Ladies and gentlemen, we have a new champion!"

As the cheers got louder and his partner threw her arms around his neck, Sam caught Johanna's look of surprise. It was easy to read her mind and come up with the fact that she didn't see him as a man who could read and remember storybooks—especially not classic children's books.

John Jay said the official goodbyes to the accountant from Venice and broke for a commercial. Sam had to all but carry his partner to the winner's circle. As he settled back in his chair, he glanced at Johanna.

"How'm I doing?"

"Sixty seconds," she said, but her voice was friendlier because she saw he was holding his partner's hand to calm her.

When the minute was up, John Jay managed to make the woman twice as nervous as he ran down the rules and the possibilities. The clock started on the first question. They weren't so difficult, Sam realized. It was the pressure that made them hard. He wasn't immune to it himself. He really wanted her to win. When he saw she was beginning to fumble, he blanked out the lights and the camera the way he did during any important scene. The rules said he could answer only two questions for her. Once he did, letting her keep her viselike grip on his hand, she was over the hump.

There were ten seconds left when John Jay, his voice pitched to the correct level of excitement, posed the last question. "Where was Napoleon's final defeat?"

She knew it. Of course she knew it. The problem was to get the word out. Sam inched forward in the impossibly uncomfortable swivel chair and all but willed her to spit out the word.

"Waterloo!" she shouted, beating the buzzer by a heartbeat. Above their heads, *$10,000* began to flash in bold red lights. His partner screamed, kissed him full on the mouth, then screamed again. While they were breaking for a commercial, Sam was holding her head between her knees and telling her to take deep breaths.

"Mrs. Cook?" Johanna knelt down beside them and monitored the woman's pulse. This wasn't the first time a contestant had reacted so radically. "Are you going to be all right?"

"I won. I won ten thousand dollars."

"Congratulations." Johanna lifted the woman's head far enough to be certain it was merely a case of hyperventilation. "We're going to take a fifteen-minute break. Would you like to lie down?"

"No. I'm sorry." Mrs. Cook's color was coming back. "I'm all right."

"Why don't you go with Beth? She'll get you some water."

"Okay. I'm fine, really." Too excited to be embarrassed, Mrs. Cook managed to stand, with Johanna taking one arm and Sam the other. "It's just that I've never won anything before. My husband didn't even come. He took the kids to the beach."

"You'll have a wonderful surprise for him," Johanna said soothingly, and kept walking. "Take a little breather, then you can start thinking about how you're going to spend that money."

"Ten thousand dollars," Mrs. Cook said faintly as she was passed over to Beth.

"Do you get a lot of fainters?" Sam asked.

"Our share. Once we had to stop taping because a construction worker slid right out of his seat during the speed round." She watched a moment longer until she was satisfied Bethany had Mrs. Cook under control. "Thanks. You acted quickly."

"No problem. I've had some practice."

She thought of women fainting at his feet. "I'll bet. There'll be cold drinks and fresh fruit in your dressing room. As long as Mrs. Cook's recovered, we'll start the tape in ten minutes."

He took her arm before she could move away. "If it wasn't my last movie, what is it?"

"What is what?"

"All these little barbs I feel sticking into my heart. You have a problem with me being here?"

"Of course not. We're thrilled to have you."

"Not we. You."

"I'm thrilled to have you here," she corrected, wishing he didn't make it a habit to stand almost on top of her. Her low heels brought her eyes level with his mouth. She discovered it wasn't the most comfortable view. "This series of contests, like your movie, will be shown during the May sweeps. What could be better?''

''A friendly conversation, over dinner.''

''You're persistent, Mr. Weaver.''

''I'm puzzled, Ms. Patterson.''

Her lips very nearly twitched. There was something cute about the way he drawled her last name. ''A simple no shouldn't puzzle a man who obviously thinks so well on his feet.'' Deliberately she looked at her watch. ''Half your break's up. You'd better change.''

Because things ran smoothly, they were able to tape three shows before the dinner break. Johanna began to have fantasies about finishing on time. She kept them to herself, knowing how easy it was to jinx success. The dinner spread wasn't elaborate, but it was plentiful. Johanna didn't believe in pinching pennies over such minor matters as food. She wanted to keep her celebrities happy and her contestants at ease.

During the break she didn't sit, but grabbed a plate and a few essentials and kept herself available. The audience had been cleared, and new ticketholders would be allowed in for the two final tapings. All she had to do was avoid any crises, keep the energy level up and make certain John Jay didn't proposition any of the females on set.

With the first in mind, Johanna kept her eyes on the new challenger, a young woman from Orange County who appeared to be about six months pregnant.

''Problem?''

She'd forgotten that her other prerequisite had been to avoid Sam Weaver. Reminding herself to keep the celebrities happy, she turned to him as she plucked a small chilled shrimp from her plate. ''No, why?''

''You don't relax, do you?'' Without expecting an answer, he chose a slim carrot stick from her plate. ''I've noticed you're watching Audrey like a hawk.''

She wasn't surprised that he already knew the expectant mother by her first name. ''Just being cautious.'' She bit into the shrimp and unbent enough to smile at him. After all, the day was nearly over. "During one of my early shows we had an expectant mother go into labor in the winner's circle. It's not an experience you forget."

"What did she have?" he asked, testing.

"A boy." Her smile became more generous as her eyes met his. It was one of her best memories. "By the time she was half-way to the hospital the staff had a pool going." She swallowed the last of the shrimp. "I won."

So she liked to bet. He'd keep that in mind. "I don't think you have to worry about Audrey. She's not due until the first part of August." He caught Johanna's curious look. "I asked," he explained. "Now, can I ask you a question? Professional," he added when he sensed her withdrawal.

"Of course."

"How often do you have to wind John Jay up?"

She had to laugh, and she didn't bother to object when he snitched a cube of cheddar from her plate. "Wind down's more like it. He's harmless, really. Only he thinks he's irresistible."

"He told me the two of you were...cozy."

"Really?" She glanced briefly over in the show's host's direction. The haughty look was so casual and innate that Sam grinned. "He's also an optimist."

He was glad to hear it. Very glad. "Well, he does his job. Somehow he manages to hit the note between cheerleader and father confessor."

Covering her personal opinion with her professional one was an old habit. To her, entertainment was first and last a business. "Actually, we're lucky to have him. He hosted another show about five years back, so he's not only familiar but also has a strong appeal to the home viewer."

"Are you going to eat that sandwich?"

Without answering, Johanna took half of the roast-beef-and-Swiss and handed it to him. "Are you enjoying yourself so far?"

"More than I'd expected." He took a bite. So she had a taste for hot mustard. He was fond of spice himself, and in more than food. "Will you be offended if I tell you I kicked a bit about doing it?"

"No. I'm the first to admit that the show isn't Shakespeare, but it serves its purpose.'' Leaning against a wall, she watched one of the crew heap on a second helping. ''What have you found appealing about it?''

He avoided the obvious answer. Her. The one he gave was equally true. ''I got a kick out of seeing those people win. Of course, I developed a soft spot for Mrs. Cook. Why do you do it?''

She avoided several possible answers. The one she settled on was true enough. ''I enjoy it.'' When he offered her his glass of sparkling water and lime, she accepted without thinking. She was relaxed, optimistic about the rest of the day and, though she didn't realize it, comfortable in his company.

''I hesitate to point this out, but it looks like we're having dinner after all.''

She looked at him again, slowly, gauging him and her reaction to him. If she'd had a different background, different memories, fewer disillusionments, she would have been flattered. More, she would have been tempted. He had a way of looking at her as though they were alone; as though, if they'd been in a room with hundreds of other people, he would have picked her, and only her, out.

Trick of the trade, she told herself, disliking her own cynicism.

''Isn't it handy we got that out of the way?'' She handed him back his glass.

''Yeah. It should make it easier for us to do it again.''

Casually she signaled to the crew to begin clearing up. ''I don't want to rush you, but we'll start taping again in fifteen minutes.''

''I never miss my cue.'' He shifted his body just enough to prevent her from walking by him. He had the moves, Johanna thought. Very smooth. Very slick. ''I get the impression you like to play games, Johanna.''

There was a dare in his voice. She caught it, and was trapped. Though her voice was cool again, she stood her ground and met his gaze. ''Depends on the stakes.''

''Okay, how's this? If I win the next two games you'll have dinner with me. I set the time and the place.''

''I don't like those stakes.''

''I haven't finished. If I lose I come back on the show within six months. No fee.'' That had her attention, he noted, pleased with himself. He hadn't misjudged her dedication to her show or her weakness for a dare.

"Within six months,'' she repeated, studying him to assess whether he could be trusted. Not an inch, she decided, on many matters. But she didn't see him as a man to welch on a bet.

"Deal?'' He made his voice deliberately challenging as he held out a hand.

It was too good a bet to turn down. His eyes were too mocking to ignore. "Deal.'' She set her palm against his, then removed it and stepped away. "Ten minutes, Mr. Weaver.''

Johanna had a very bad feeling when Sam and his teammate took the first game. Since the conception of the show, she'd had a strict personal policy against rooting for either side. It didn't matter that no one could read her thoughts. She knew them, and prejudice of any kind was unprofessional. She certainly would never have imagined herself actually rooting against a certain team. She did now.

It was because she wanted him back on the show, she told herself when the last taping of the day began. The producer, not the woman, had made the bet. It was ridiculous to think that she was afraid, even uneasy, about having a meal with him. That would only be a small annoyance—like a spoonful of bad-tasting medicine.

But she stood behind camera two and cheered inwardly when he opposing team took the lead.

He didn't show nerves. Sam was much too skilled an actor to show nerves in front of a camera. But they dogged him. It was the principle, he told himself. That was the only reason he was so determined to win and make Johanna pay the price. He certainly wasn't infatuated. He'd been around too long to be infatuated just because a woman was beautiful. And aloof, his mind added. And contrary and stubborn. And damn sexy.

He wasn't infatuated. He just hated to lose.

By the beginning of the final round, the two teams were neck and neck. The studio audience was loud and raucous, the contestants wired. Johanna's stomach was in knots. When Sam turned and winked at her during the commercial break she nearly bared her teeth.

Positions jockeyed back and forth. Professionally Johanna knew that when the show aired it would pull the television audience in. That was, after all, the name of the game. Personally, she'd hoped for a landslide, however boring.

When the final question came up, she held her breath. Sam was quick to push the button, but his partner was quicker. He nearly swore. The expectant mother from Orange County had more than her own fate in her hands.

"Surrender, Dorothy!" she shouted. When the lights went on, Sam took her face in his hands and kissed her. Hard. Audrey would be able to dine out on the moment for months. Sam kept his arm around her as they walked toward the winner's circle. Once she was settled, he strolled casually over to Johanna and bent closer to her ear.

"Saturday night, seven. I'll pick you up."

She only nodded. It was hard to speak when your teeth were clenched.

Johanna found several vital tasks to perform after the taping was completed. She did not, as was her habit, say a personal thank-you to both guest stars. That job was handed over to Bethany. She made herself scarce for thirty minutes so that she could be sure Sam Weaver was off and out of her hair. Until Saturday.

She couldn't quite drum up the job-well-done mood the end of the day usually brought her. Instead she made a list of details to see to the following day that would keep her occupied from the time she got up until she crawled back home again. Business as usual, she told herself, and broke the tip off her pencil.

"Everybody's happy," Beth told her. "The questions we didn't use in the speed round are locked back in the safe. The contestants we didn't get to are ready and willing to come back next week. Your dupes." She handed Johanna the tapes. "We've got some great shows. Especially the last one. Even the techs were getting into it. They loved Sam." Bethany pushed back a lock of hair. "And you know how jaded techs can be. Anyway, it's nice to know that besides being gorgeous and sexy he's got some smarts.''

Johanna grunted and dropped the tapes in her carryall.

Bethany tilted her head. ''I was going to ask you if you wanted to take some of the leftover fruit home, but it looks more like you'd prefer raw meat.''

''It's been a long day.''

''Uh-huh.'' Beth knew her boss better. Johanna had pulled a roll of antacids out of her bag and had popped two of them. A sure sign of trouble. ''Want to have a drink and talk about it?''

Johanna had never made it a habit to confide in anyone. There simply hadn't been enough people in her life she could trust. Johanna knew Beth. Her assistant was young and energetic, but she was also trustworthy. She was also the closest thing Johanna had ever had to a foul-weather friend.

''I'll pass on the drink, but how about walking me out to my car?''

''Sure.''

The sun hadn't set. Johanna found something reassuring about that after having been inside all day. She'd put the top down, she thought, and take the drive home through the Hills fast. Maybe a bit recklessly. She had a taste for the reckless, a taste she usually controlled. It came from her father. But tonight it might do her good to give in to it for a little while.

''What did you think of Sam Weaver?''

Bethany cocked a brow. ''Before or after I stopped drooling?''

''After.''

''I liked him,'' she said simply. ''He didn't expect the red carpet, he wasn't condescending and he wasn't snickering behind his hand at the contestants.''

''Those are all negative virtues,'' Johanna pointed out.

''Okay, I liked the way he joked around with the crew. And the way he signed autographs as though he wanted to instead of acting as though he were granting a favor.'' She didn't add that she'd asked for one herself. ''He acted like somebody without making sure everybody remembered that *somebody* was in all capital letters.''

"Interestingly said," Johanna murmured. "Are you still keeping that little book with the list of celebrity panelists?"

Beth colored a bit. She was in the business, but that didn't stop her from being a fan. "Yeah. Sam gets five stars."

Johanna's lips twitched a bit at her assistant's top rating. "I guess I should be relieved to hear it. I'm having dinner with him on Saturday."

Bethany's mouth went into the O position. There were stars in her eyes. She simply couldn't help it. "Wow."

"It's confidential."

"Okay," Bethany said, and Johanna knew she was as good as her word. "Johanna, I know you were raised in the business and Cary Grant probably bounced you on his knee, but doesn't it give you a tingle?"

"It gives me a pain," Johanna stated bluntly as she pulled open her car door. "Actors aren't my type."

"Too general."

"Okay, blue-eyed lanky actors with a drawl aren't my type."

"You're sick, Johanna. Very, very sick. You want me to go as proxy?"

She chuckled as she lowered herself into the car. "No. I can handle Sam Weaver."

"Lucky you. Listen, not to pry or anything..."

"But?"

"You will remember the details? I might want to write a book or something."

"Go home, Beth." The engine sprang to life as she twisted the key. Yes, she definitely wanted power and speed tonight.

"Okay, just let me know if he always smells so good. I can live on that."

Shaking her head, Johanna roared out of the lot. She hadn't been interested enough to notice what Sam Weaver had smelled like.

Like a man, her memory informed her. He'd smelled very much like a man.

Three

It was only dinner. Nothing to worry about. Certainly nothing, after several days to put it in perspective, to be annoyed about. They would no doubt go to one of L.A.'s flashier restaurants, where Sam could see and be seen. Between the pâté and the double chocolate mousse he would greet and chat with the other glamorous types who patronized that kind of eatery.

Meat houses, her second stepmother had called such places. Not because of the menu but because of the flesh exposed. Darlene had been one of the most honest and least affected of her father's attachments.

If she wanted to stretch a point, Johanna could consider it a business dinner. She found she wanted to stretch a point. She could tolerate this, as she had tolerated many other meals, as a part of the game everyone who wanted to remain part of the business learned to play. Since it was business, she would be charming and chatty, even gracious, until it was over and she could close the door on the entire episode.

She didn't like persistent men.

She didn't like men with reputations.

She didn't like Sam Weaver.

That was before the flowers arrived.

Johanna had spent Saturday morning gardening and half-hoping Sam Weaver wouldn't find her address. He hadn't called to ask her for it or to confirm plans. Waiting for him to do just that had left her jumpy and out of sorts all week. That was just one more sin to lay at his door.

It was her habit whenever she worked outside to take her cordless phone with her. Business could crop up even on weekends. Today, however, she pretended to have forgotten it and spent a warm and pleasant morning tending a plot of columbine.

This was her respite, even her vice, in a way. The flowers she planted were nurtured and cared for. They rewarded her by renewing themselves year after year. Their continuity soothed her. This, as was the case in other areas of her life, was something she'd done with her own hands. Whatever rewards she reaped, whatever failures she suffered, were her own.

The flowers lasted. The people in her life rarely did.

Her jeans were scruffy at the knees and her hands stained with mulch when the delivery man pulled up. Johanna shaded her eyes as she rose.

"Miz Patterson?"

"Yes."

"Sign here, please." The deliveryman met her halfway across her lawn, handing her first his clipboard and then a long white box embossed with a florist's name and tied with a red satin ribbon. "Nice garden you got there," he said with a tip of his hat as he climbed back into the truck.

She was a sucker for flowers. Without waiting to go in and wash up, Johanna opened the box. They were roses. Not a dozen red or two dozen pink, but one long-stemmed sample of every color she'd ever seen, from the purest white to the deepest red, and all the pinks and golds between. Charmed, she lowered her face to the box to draw in their scent.

Heady. Roses were always heady, lush and unashamedly sensual.

It wasn't her birthday. In any case, her father—or rather her father's secretary—wasn't imaginative enough to have thought of such a sweet and charming gift. Though her fingertips were soiled, she pulled open the card that had come with the box. I don't know your favorite color. Yet. Sam.

She wanted to shrug it off. Pretty gestures came so easily to some. It would have taken only a casual order to an assistant to have them delivered. How well she knew it. So he'd found her, she thought with a shrug as she started back across the lawn. The deal was still on, and she'd live up to her end of it.

She tried, really tried, to set them aside and go back to work on the buds she'd planted herself. But she couldn't dismiss the roses, didn't have the heart to dampen her own pleasure. She was smiling when she sniffed the flowers again. Smiling still when she went into the house to arrange them.

He hadn't looked forward to an evening quite so much in a long time. It was easy to compare it to a winning poker hand or a successful day at the track. He'd never cared half as much for the purse as for the winning. He'd have preferred to think of it in those terms, but the truth was that he was looking forward to spending a few hours in Johanna Patterson's company.

Maybe he was intrigued because she was so disinterested. Sam took a turn sharp and fast while the radio blared through the open windows. What man didn't appreciate a challenge? If she'd taken him at his word on their first meeting, they might have enjoyed a pleasant lunch and an easy hour. He'd never know if that would have been the end of it. The fact that she'd refused, and had continued to refuse, only made him more determined to wear her down.

Women came easily to him. Too easily. Sam wouldn't deny he'd gone through a stage when he'd taken advantage of that. But his background, and what many might have considered the rather quaint and traditional values that had gone into it, had surfaced again.

The press could beat the drum of his romantic adventures all they liked. The truth was, he *was* a romantic. Rolling from one bed to the next had never been his style.

There were two Sam Weavers. One was intensely private, guarded about matters like family and relationships, the things that really mattered. The other was an actor, a realist who accepted that the price of fame was public consumption. He gave interviews, didn't bother to dodge the paparazzi and was always willing to sign an autograph. He'd learned to shrug off whatever reports were exaggerations or outright lies. They were the public Sam's problem. The private one couldn't have cared less.

He wondered, given what he now knew about Johanna Patterson's background, which Sam Weaver she would understand.

She was the only child of the respected producer Carl Patterson, the product of his first, and reportedly most tempestuous marriage.

Her mother had disappeared or, as some reports put it, "gone into seclusion," after the marriage had failed. Johanna had grown up in the luxury of Beverly Hills, had attended the best schools. Some rumors stated that she adored her father, others that there was no love lost between them. In either case, she was the only offspring Patterson had after four marriages and numerous affairs.

He was surprised that she lived back in the Hills. He'd expected some slick condo in the city or a wing in her father's Beverly Hills estate. The sharp professional woman he'd met seemed out of place so far from the action. He was more surprised when he found the house.

It was tiny. Like a dollhouse, but without the gingerbread. Hardly more than a cabin, it was rustic and sturdy, with the wood unpainted and the panes of glass sparkling in the evening sun. There wasn't much land before the trees and the hills took it over. What was there was uneven and rocky. To compensate—more, to enhance it—flowers and budding vines were everywhere. The dashing little Mercedes parked in the driveway looked as though it had been left there by mistake.

Hands in pockets, he stood beside his own car and looked again. She didn't have any close neighbors, and the view was nothing to write home about, but it seemed as though she'd carved out her own corner of the mountainside. He knew about that. Appreciated it.

When he reached the door, he caught the scent of sweet peas. His mother planted them each spring, outside the kitchen windows. Johanna opened the door and found him smiling.

"Brigadoon," he said, and watched her polite smile turn to an expression of puzzlement. "I was trying to think what your place reminded me of. Brigadoon. Like it's only here once every hundred years."

Damn him, she thought, feeling almost resigned. She'd barely managed to put the roses in perspective and here he was, charming her again. "I wasn't sure you'd find it."

"I have a good sense of direction. Most of the time." He glanced toward the flowers that flanked both sides of her house. "From the looks of things, the roses were overkill."

"No." It would have been petty not to let him know they'd

pleased her. "It was sweet of you to send them." He wasn't wearing a dinner suit, but a breezy linen shirt and pleated slacks. Johanna was glad she'd guessed right when she'd bypassed glitz for the subtler lines of a slim-skirted white dress. "If you'd like to come in a minute, I'll get my jacket."

He did, though he thought it would be a shame to cover up her arms and shoulders. The living room was small enough to be cozy. She'd arranged deep chairs by a white bricked fireplace and had added dozens of pillows. It made Sam think that when Johanna was finished with work she liked to take off her shoes and snuggle in.

"This isn't what I expected."

"No?" She pulled on a sizzling tomato-red jacket. "I like it."

"I didn't say I didn't like it, I said it wasn't what I expected." He noted his roses had been given a place of honor on the mantel, tucked prettily in a clear, widemouthed vase that glinted at the bottom with colored pebbles. "Do you have a favorite?"

She glanced at the roses. "No. I just like flowers." The clusters of rubies at her ears glinted as she adjusted them. "Shall we go?"

"In a minute." He crossed to her, noticing with some interest the way she stiffened up. Despite it, he took her hand. "Are you going to be a good sport about this?"

She let out a little sigh. "I've thought about it."

"And?" It was the easy curving of his lips that made her relax.

"I decided I might as well."

"Are you hungry?"

"Some."

"Mind a bit of a ride?"

Curious, she tilted her head. "No, I suppose not."

"Good." He kept her hand in his as they walked outside.

She should have known he was up to something. They didn't drive into the city as she'd expected. Rather than comment, Johanna let the conversation flow as she wondered how to handle him. Actors were a tricky bunch. They knew how to set the stage, how to read their lines, how to put on whatever face was most appropriate to the situation. At the moment, it seemed Sam had chosen to be the casually friendly companion a woman could relax with. Johanna wasn't ready to give him an inch.

He drove fast, just faster than the law allowed and just under the edge of safety. Even when they left the freeway for a road that was rough and sparsely populated, he continued at the same steady clip.

"Mind if I ask where we're going?"

Sam negotiated a lazy turn. He'd wondered how long it would take before she asked. "To dinner."

Johanna turned to study the landscape. The land rolled by, wide and dusty. "Something over an open fire?"

He smiled. She'd used her haughty tone again, and damned if he didn't enjoy hearing it. "No, I thought we'd eat at my place."

His place. The thought of dining privately with him didn't alarm her. She was too confident of her ability to handle whatever situation cropped up. She was more curious about the fact that he would have a *place* this far from the glitz. "You have a cave?"

Because there was amusement in her voice now, his smile widened. "I can do a little better than that. I only eat in restaurants when it's necessary."

"Why?"

"Because you end up doing business, or being stared at. I wasn't in the mood for either tonight." Pebbles spit from under the tires as he turned to drive through a plain wooden gate.

"That's part of the game, isn't it?"

"Sure, but there has to be a reason to play it." He whizzed by a pretty white house with blue shutters, giving two blasts of his horn. "My foreman and his family live there. If he knows its me he won't come looking for trespassers."

They passed barns and sheds, and she was surprised that they looked as though they had a purpose other than a decorative one. She spotted paddocks with split-rail fencing and dark, rich dirt. A dog—or what sounded like a pair of them—began to bark.

The road forked, and then she saw the ranch house. It, too, was white, but the shutters were gray and the three chimneys it boasted were brick weathered to a dusky rose. It was low and spreading, shaped like an H turned on its side. For all its size, it didn't overpower. There were rockers on the porch, sturdy wooden ones that gave the impression that someone sat in them often. Window boxes had been freshly painted a bright, sassy red. Tumbling out of them were pansies and bushy impatiens. Though the air here was hot and dry, they were thriving and well tended.

Johanna stepped out of the car to turn a slow circle. It certainly looked like a working ranch. "Quite a place."

"I like it," he said, mimicking her earlier remark.

She acknowledged that with a quick, though cautious, smile. "It must be inconvenient to commute."

"I keep a place in L.A." He shrugged it off as though it were no more than a storage closet. "The best thing about finishing a film is being able to come back here and dig in for a while. Before I got hooked on acting, I'd wanted to come west and work on a ranch." He took her arm as they walked up the two wooden steps to the porch. They creaked. For some reason, Johanna found that endearing. "I was lucky enough to do both."

She glanced at the pansies, with their arrogant Alice-in-Wonderland faces. "Do you raise cattle?"

"Horses." He'd left the door unlocked. It was a habit he'd grown up with. "I bought the place about three years ago. Convinced my accountant that it'd be a great tax shelter. It made him feel better."

The hardwood floors were polished to a high gloss, scattered with hand-hooked rugs in muted pastels. In the entrance a collection of pewter—bowls, spoons, mugs, even a dented candlestick—was arranged on a waist-high table. The early twilight crept through the windows.

It had a good feel, a solid feel. Though she would never had admitted it out loud, Johanna had always felt strongly that houses had their own personalities. She'd selected her own house because it had made her feel warm and comfortable. She'd left her father's because it had been possessive and dishonest.

"Do you get to stay here often?" she asked him.

"Not often enough." He glanced around at the walls, which he'd painted himself. The house, like his career, was something he never took for granted. Though he'd never known poverty, he'd been taught to appreciate security, and that nothing replaced sweat for earning it. "Would you like a drink, or would you rather go for dinner?"

"Dinner," she said firmly. She knew better than to drink, socially or otherwise, on an empty stomach.

"I was hoping you'd say that." In the casual way he had, he took her hand and led her down the hall. The wing of the house ran straight. At the end it opened up into a large country kitchen. Copper pots hung from hooks over a center island. The room was flanked by counters and cabinets on one side and a small stone hearth on the other. A ribbon of windows gave an open view of dusk settling over a brick terrace and a mosaic pool. She'd thought to find a servant or two busily preparing the evening meal. Instead, all she found was the scent of cooking.

"It smells wonderful."

"Good." Scooping up two hot pads, Sam bent down to the oven. "I left it on warm." He drew out a casserole of bubbly lasagna.

Food wasn't something that usually excited her, but now the scent alone drew her over to his side. How long had it been since she'd seen someone take a homemade meal out of an oven? "It looks wonderful, too."

"My mother always told me food tastes better if it looks good." He picked up a long loaf of Italian bread and began slicing.

"You didn't cook this."

"Why not?" He glanced over his shoulder, amused that she was frowning again. She looked so thoughtful that he was tempted to run a fingertip down the faint line that formed between her brows. "Cooking's a very manageable skill if you approach it properly and have the right incentive."

Johanna stuck with carryout or prepackaged microwave meals. "And you have both?"

"I wanted to be an actor, but I didn't have any desire to be a starving actor." He poured garlic butter over the bread, set the oven, then slid it in. "After I came to California, I kicked around from audition to audition and from greasy spoon to greasy spoon. A couple of months of that and I called home and asked my mother for some recipes. She's a great cook." Sam drew the cork from a bottle of wine, then set it aside to breathe. "Anyway, it

took me a lot less time to figure out how to sauté trout than it did
for me to get a memorable part.''

"Now that you've had a number of memorable parts, what's
your incentive?''

"To cook?'' He shrugged and took a leafy spinach salad from
the refrigerator. "I like it. We're about ready here. You want to
grab the wine? I thought we'd eat outside.''

The trouble with Hollywood, Johanna thought as she followed
him out, was that things were never what they seemed. She'd been
sure she had Sam Weaver pegged. But the man she'd assessed
and dismissed wouldn't have copied recipes from his mother.

Nor was he the type, she thought as she set the wine down,
who would have prepared a charming dinner for two, alfresco,
with pretty blue stoneware plates and thick yellow candles. It was
every bit as friendly as it was romantic. The romance she'd expected, and she knew just how to discourage it. The offer of
friendship was another matter.

"Light those candles, will you?'' He glanced around briefly,
checking the way a man did when he was already certain things
were just as he wanted them to be. "I'll get the rest.''

Johanna watched him go back inside. Did someone who walked
like that, she wondered—as though he were heading toward a
shoot-out—really prepare spinach salad? She struck a match and
held it to the wick of the first candle. Apparently so. There were
more important things to lie about than cooking. She held the
match to the second candle, then deliberately blew it out. She
wouldn't have called avoiding three on a match superstitious. Just
practical.

She heard the music he put on, something low and bluesy, with
a lot of sax. While he brought out the rest of the meal, she poured
the wine.

His instincts had been right, Sam thought as they settled at the
wicker table. He'd been on the verge of making dinner reserva-
tions at some tony restaurant when he'd pulled back. He'd cooked
for women before, but never here. He never brought anyone to
the ranch, because the ranch was home. Private. Off limits to the
press and the public, it was both refuge and sanctuary from a
world he was a voluntary member of—when he chose to be. At

the time, he hadn't been sure why he'd wanted to break his own rule with Johanna. Now he began to understand.

At the ranch he could be himself—no pretenses, no roles. Here he was Sam Weaver from Virginia, and here he was most comfortable. He didn't have to be *on* here. And he wanted to be himself with Johanna.

She wasn't without pretenses, he mused as he watched her. Not entirely. Unless he missed his guess, most of her resentment had faded, but not her distrust. He'd already decided to ease his curiosity and find the reason for it.

Maybe she'd been stung in an affair that had gone sour. Broken hearts often mended jaggedly. If she had been betrayed by a man she'd cared for and trusted, it would be logical that she would put up some defences. It might take some time before he could wear them down, but he had a feeling it would be worth it. He'd start with what he believed was the focus of her life: her work.

"Were you happy with the taping the other day?"

"More than." She was too fair-minded not to give him his due. "You were really good, not just as far as the answers went, but overall. A lot of times you can have people zip right through the questions and be a dead bore." She broke off a piece of bread, then nibbled at the crust. He'd hit the right tone. It was always easy for her to relax when the subject was business. "And, of course, it was a coup to have you."

"I'm flattered."

She studied him again with those cool blue eyes. "I doubt it would be that easy to flatter you."

"An actor always wants to be wanted. Well, to a point, anyway," he added with another quick grin. "Do you know how many game shows I've turned down in the last couple of days?"

She smiled and sipped her wine. "Oh, I could hazard a guess."

"How'd you get into it? Producing?"

"Heredity." Her lips tightened only briefly. After taking a second sip, she set her glass down. "I guess you could say I like pulling the strings."

"You'd have learned young with Carl Patterson as your father." He saw it, very briefly but very clearly. More than resentment, less than pain. "He's produced some of the best, and most

successful television shows, as well as an impressive number of
features. Being second-generation can be a strain, I imagine.''

"You get past it." The lasagna was cheesy and rich with spices.
Johanna concentrated on it. "This really is terrific. Your mother's
recipe?''

"With some variations." So her father was off limits. He could
respect that—for now. "How about the show itself? How did that
get started?''

"With the flu." At ease again, she smiled and took another
bite.

"Care to elaborate?''

"I had the flu, a nasty bout of it, a couple of years ago. I had
to stay in bed for a week, and since it hurt my eyes to read, I lay
there hour after hour and watched television. The game shows
hooked me." She didn't object when he topped off her glass. The
wine was very mellow and dry, and she knew her limit right down
to the swallow. "You get involved, you know, in the games, and
the people playing them. After a while you start rooting for them,
tensing up in an effort to help them. When someone wins, the
vicarious thrill is automatic. And then you have the advantage of
almost always being smarter at home, because there's no pressure.
That's a nice smug feeling.''

He watched her as she spoke. She was animated now, the way
she'd been while she'd rushed around the set making sure things
fell into place. "So after your bout with the flu you decided to
produce one.''

"More or less." She could remember running into the brick
wall of the network brass and ultimately having to appeal to her
father. "In any case, I had the concept, and the experience in
producing. I'd done a couple of documentaries for public television and had worked on a prime-time special. With a little string-
pulling, we got a pilot done. Now we're only a couple of ratings
points from being on top. I'm waiting for the go-ahead to start
evening syndication.''

"What happens then?''

"The demographics open. You get the kids who've finished
their homework, the business crowd who want to put their feet up

for a half hour. You up the ante. Give away some cars, bigger bucks.''

She was surprised to discover she'd cleared her plate. Usually she ate a few bites, then ended up picking at the rest, impatient for the meal—and the time sitting down—to be over.

"Want some more?''

"No. Thanks." She picked up her wine as she studied him. "I know I lost the bet, but it looks as though I got the best part of the deal.''

"Not from where I'm sitting.''

The shades came down. Just like that. One compliment, however offhand, and she pulled back. Seeing it, Sam rose and offered a hand. "Want to walk? There's enough moonlight.''

There was no point in being ungracious, Johanna told herself. She hated it when she became prickly over something unimportant. "All right. The only ranches I've ever seen have been on the back lot.''

He bundled up the last of the bread, then handed it to her. "We'll go by the pond. You can feed the ducks.''

"You have ducks?''

"Several overfed ducks." He slipped an arm around her shoulders to steer her. She smelled like the evening they walked through, quiet and promising. "I like looking at them in the morning.''

"Your Jake in *Half-Breed* would have eaten them for breakfast.''

"So you did see my last movie.''

She took a quick nip at the tip of her tongue. "Oh, was that your last one?''

"Too late. You've already boosted my ego.''

When she looked at him, his smile was appealing and too easy to respond to. *He* was too easy to respond to. In self-defense she looked back at the house.

"It's lovely from out here, too. You live all alone?''

"I like a little solitude now and then. Of course, I've got a few hands who look after things while I'm working, and Mae comes in a couple times a week to scoop at the dust.'' His hand slipped down to take hers. "My family comes out a few times a year and shakes everything up."

"Your parents visit you here?"

"Them, my brother, my two sisters, their families. Assorted cousins. The Weavers are a large and loud bunch."

"I see." But she didn't. She could only imagine. And envy. "They must be proud of you."

"They were always supportive, even when they thought I was crazy."

The pond was almost a quarter mile from the house, but the going was easy. It was obvious he walked the path often. She caught the scent of citrus, then the stronger scent of water. The moonlight struck it, highlighting the grass which had been left to grow ankle-high. Sensing an audience, several brown and speckled ducks paddled over to the water's edge.

"I've never had the nerve to come out here empty-handed," he told her. "I think they'd follow me home."

Johanna opened the linen cloth and broke off a crust of bread. It didn't even hit the water before it was gobbled up. She laughed; it was a low, delighted sound deep in her throat. Immediately she tore off another piece and, tossing this one farther out, watched a drake zoom in on it.

"I've always wanted to watch them from underneath so I could see their feet scramble." She continued to break off and toss. Ducks pursued the bread in groups and squabbled over it with bad-tempered quacks and competitive pecks. "My mother and I used to go out and feed the ducks. We'd give them silly names, then see if we could tell them apart the next time."

She caught herself, amazed that the memory had surfaced, stunned that she'd shared it. Her hand closed into a fist over the bread.

"There was a pond about five miles away when I was a kid," Sam said, as if he hadn't noticed her change in mood. "We used to ride our bikes to it during the summer, after we'd stolen a pack of crackers or whatever from the kitchen. We'd toss it out for the ducks—and a couple of pushy swans—and accidentally fall in as often as possible." He glanced out over the water. "Looks like someone's had a family."

She followed his gaze and saw a brown duck gliding along, trailed by a long shadow. As it came closer, Johanna saw that the shadow wasn't a shadow, it was fluffy ducklings. "Oh, aren't they sweet?" She crouched down for a closer look, forgetting about the hem of her skirt. The babies followed Mama on their evening swim, straight as an arrow. "I wish there was more light," she murmured.

"Come back when there is."

Johanna tilted her head up. In the moonlight his face was stronger, more attractive, than it had a right to be. The eyes, eyes that invariably drew women in, were as dark as the water. And, as with the water, Johanna didn't know what lay beneath the surface. Turning away again, she continued shredding the bread and tossing it.

He liked the way her hair haloed around her face, stopping just inches from her shoulders. A man could fill his hands with it. It would be soft, like the hand she rarely offered but he continued to take. It would carry that same subtle scent.

Her skin would be like that, on the back of her neck beneath all that heavy blond hair. He had an urge to touch it now, to skim his fingers over it and see if she trembled.

The ducks stopped their chatter when the last of the bread was consumed. A few hopefuls hung around the edge of the pond for a minute longer, then, satisfied the treat was done, glided away. Into the sudden silence came a night bird's song, and the rustle of a rabbit running into the brush.

"It's a lovely spot," she said, rising and brushing the crumbs from her fingers. "I can see why you like it so much."

"I want you to come back."

It was said very simply, so it shouldn't have meant so much. Johanna didn't back away, because that would have been admitting it did. If her heart was beating a little faster, she could pretend otherwise. She reminded herself that things often seemed more important in the moonlight than they did in the day.

"We had a bet. I lost." She said it lightly, already aware that the tone wouldn't matter. "But that's been paid up tonight."

"This has nothing to do with bets or games." He touched her hair as he'd wanted to. "I want you to come back."

She should have been able to shrug it off, to nip it before whatever was beginning to grow would blossom. It wasn't as easy as it should have been to dredge up the cool smile and the careless refusal. She looked at him, really looked at him, and could think of only one thing to say.

"Why?"

His lips curved. She watched the smile move slowly over his face, the angles shifting, the shadows playing. "Damned if I know. But when you do come back, maybe we'll both have an answer. Meanwhile, why don't we get this one question out of the way?"

He leaned toward her. She'd told herself she didn't want to be kissed. She wouldn't like it. She wasn't a demonstrative person, and for her a kiss wasn't merely a touching of lips. Even though she'd grown up in a world where a kiss was nothing more than a handshake—and often less binding—to her it was a personal thing that meant affection, trust, warmth.

She'd told herself she wouldn't be kissed. But that had been before the moonlight and the bird's song. That had been before he'd touched her.

Her eyes were wary. He saw that even as he brushed his lips lightly over hers. He'd meant it to be light, casual, hardly more than a peace offering. She was so cool and lovely, and so firmly on guard, that he'd been unable to resist.

An easy kiss. A friendly kiss. That was where he'd meant to begin and end it. That was before he'd tasted her.

He drew back, not quite sure of his footing. He hadn't been prepared for whatever had rushed into him, not for the punch of it. With the water lapping beside them, he stared down at her. Moonlight was on her face, and he touched her cheek where the light played. She didn't move. He couldn't know that her own stunned reaction had left her rooted to the spot.

He touched her again, drawing his fingers back through her hair until they gripped it. Still she didn't move. But when his lips came to hers again, hard, hungry, she met passion with passion.

She'd never wanted it to be like this. Desire raced through her, pushing her to keep pace with it. His mouth ran along her jaw, across her face, making her shiver with pleasure, but she twisted until their lips joined again.

A craving she'd never known she had...a dream she'd never allowed into her waking hours...that was what he was. Wherever his hands touched, they lingered, as if he couldn't get enough. Lost in the first wave of pleasure, she pressed against him.

No, he couldn't get enough. He pulled her head back and deepened the kiss. She tasted like the night, dark, haunted. The thin silk under her jacket teased and shifted until he had to force back the urge to tear it away. He wanted her, all of her. There, in the tall, damp grass, he wanted to discover all her secrets and make them his own.

She was breathless when they drew apart. That frightened her. Caution and control had been hard-learned lessons, and she always, without exception, applied them to all the areas of her life. She'd lost them both in the flash of an instant, in the brush of his lips.

She had to remember what he was: an artist, both in his craft and with his women. More, she had to remember what *she* was. There was no room in her life for reckless passion in the moonlight.

He reached for her again, just to trace his knuckles along her cheek. Because even that affected her, she moved aside.

"This isn't the answer for either of us." She didn't like hearing the strain in her own voice, or the lingering huskiness he'd caused.

"It was a lot more than I bargained for," he admitted. The defenses were going up again. He took her hand before she could withdraw behind them completely. "I felt something the first time I saw you. Now I begin to see why."

"Lust at first sight?"

"Damn it, Johanna."

She'd hated herself the moment she'd said it, but she couldn't back down. If she backed down, she'd give in. "Let's let it go, Sam. I'll be honest and say that was more than nice, but I'm just not interested in the sequel."

Anger stirred. He knew his own temper well enough to take things slow. He'd never decked a woman. Yet. "What are you interested in?"

She recognized barely restrained fury when she heard it. It was almost a relief. If he'd been kind, if he'd been the least bit persuasive, she would have crumbled. "My job." She tried for a smile and almost managed it. "That's really enough complications for me."

"Lady, anybody who can kiss like that is just asking for complications."

She hadn't known she could kiss like that. She certainly hadn't known she'd wanted to. And what was even more unnerving was that she wanted to kiss him again. "I suppose that's a compliment. Shall we just say it was an interesting evening and leave it at that?"

"No."

"That's the best I can do."

He touched her hair again. It wasn't a testing gesture this time, it was a possessive one. "Okay. You'll learn as you go along."

She couldn't pretend to be amused, because he was frightening her. It wasn't a fear that he would drag her to the ground and finish what they'd both started, but it was a fear that he would prove to be stronger-willed and much more determined than she.

Stay out of his way, her mind warned her. And get started on it now.

"It was much too nice an evening to end it with an argument. I appreciate the meal and the walk. Now it's getting late, and since it's a long drive, we should be going."

"All right." He was much too annoyed to fight with her. Better, he thought, that he do exactly as she asked, then reevaluate the situation. Turning homeward, he reached out to guide her so that she wouldn't stumble. When she jerked at his touch, he smiled again, and most of his annoyance left him.

"The longest trips are often the most eventful, don't you think?"

She thought it best to leave that question unanswered.

Four

"Just how many cases of Diet Zing do we have?" Johanna waited for Bethany to run down her list.

"Considering what the crew pinched, about a hundred and fifty cases. We're square on the porto-vacs and the gift certificates and, of course, the encyclopedias." Bethany turned over the list of parting gifts. Though she thought it odd that Johanna was staring out the window rather than checking off her own list, she didn't comment. "About the home viewers' contest," Bethany began.

"Hmmm?"

"The home viewers' contest?"

"Oh." Johanna swore at herself, then pulled her gaze away from the window and her mind away from Sam Weaver. Daydreaming was always a waste of time, but it was a sin during office hours. "I want to get that nailed down this morning." She unlocked the top drawer of her desk and pulled out a file. "I have several potential questions. Research put in a lot of extra time on it last week. The idea is to have John Jay announce a different one every day, somewhere during the program." She glanced down the list again to satisfy herself. "I don't want him to do it at the same time every day, particularly not at the beginning. If we're going to draw people in, I want them to watch all day, all week. Is the deal on the car set?"

"Almost. We're going with the American product and tying it in with the drawing the week of the Fourth of July."

"Fine, but I want two."

"Two what?"

"Two cars, Beth. Watch *Trivia Alert* and win." She smiled a bit and tapped the end of her pencil on the desk. "Two luxury cars. One should be a convertible. People in Omaha with two kids don't usually buy convertibles. Let's make it a red one, at least for the ads. We'll have the full-sized car in white and John Jay in a blue suit.''

"Hit them over the head with patriotism?"

"Something like that. See if we can bring the total value up to fifty thousand.''

"Sure.'' Bethany blew her bangs away from her eyes. "I'll use charm. And if that doesn't work I'll use Mongo the enforcer.''

"Use the ratings,'' Johanna suggested. "I want a big ad in the *TV Guide* and the Sunday supplements. Black and white for the guide, color for the supplements.'' She waited while Bethany made her notes. "The ten-second spot at ten is already set. We'll tape it as soon as the cars are delivered. We have to pick five questions from the list.'' She handed Bethany a copy. "And the list doesn't go out of this office.''

Bethany skimmed down. "Where did Betty meet the leader of the pack?'' Lips pursed, she glanced up. "Betty who?''

"Brush up on your girl groups. Early-sixties rock and roll.''

Bethany merely made a face. "These are pretty tough.''

That was exactly what she'd wanted to hear. "They're worth fifty thousand.''

Giving a quiet murmur of agreement, she checked another question. "Johanna, how could anyone know how many witches were burned at the stake in Salem?''

"None.'' Sitting back, Johanna ran the pencil through her fingers. "They were hanged.''

"Oh. Well, so far I'm batting a thousand.'' When Johanna's phone rang, Bethany took another hard look at the questions.

"Mr. Weaver's on the line, Ms. Patterson.''

Johanna opened her mouth and was surprised when nothing came out.

"Ms. Patterson?''

"What? Oh, tell Mr. Weaver I'm in a meeting.''

When she hung up, Beth glanced over. "I wouldn't have minded waiting.''

"I doubt he's calling to discuss the show.'' Telling herself to dismiss it, Johanna picked up her list and made her eyes focus. "What do you think about number six?''

"I don't know that answer, either. Johanna...'' Outgoing and candid herself, Bethany nonetheless understood and respected her boss's restraint. "Did everything go okay the other night?"

It would have been foolish to pretend to misunderstand. "It went fine. Very pleasant." Johanna dug into her pocket for a roll of antacids. "I'm leaning toward numbers one, four, six, nine and thirteen."

Beth looked at each one, decided she might have an inkling about question thirteen, then nodded. "Let's go for them." She handed the list back so that Johanna could lock them up. "Could we pretend we're out of the office, maybe at home with our feet up and a nice bottle of wine already half-gone?"

Johanna turned the key and pocketed it. "Do you have a problem, Beth?"

"No, but I'd swear you did."

"I'm fine." Johanna began to stack and straighten papers on her desk. "We had a friendly dinner, some pleasant conversation, and that was that. I have no idea why Sam's calling me at the office, but I don't have time to chat with him."

"I didn't mention Sam," Bethany pointed out. "You did. I only mentioned a problem." She smiled sympathetically. "I get the feeling they're the same thing."

Johanna rose and, with her hands in the deep pockets of her skirt, walked to the window. "He just can't get it through his head that I'm not interested."

"Are you? Not interested, I mean," Bethany supplied when Johanna turned her head.

"I don't want to be interested. It's the same thing."

"No. If you weren't interested you'd be able to smile, maybe pat him on the head and say thanks but no thanks. Not wanting to be interested means you are and you get around it by avoiding phone calls and making excuses."

Johanna pushed a thumb into the ivy geranium hanging in a basket at her window. The soil was moist. She'd watered it herself that morning. "How did you get to be an expert?"

"Unfortunately, most of it comes from observation rather than execution. He seems like a nice guy, Johanna."

"Maybe, but I don't have room for men right now, and less than none for actors."

"That's a hard line."

"It's a hard town."

Bethany wasn't willing to buy that. True, she'd only lived in L.A. for three years, but it still fascinated her. To her it remained the town where dreams could be chased and caught. "I hope you're not going to break my heart and tell me he's a jerk."

"No." With a reluctant smile, Johanna turned again. "No, he's not a jerk. Actually, you're right, he's a very nice guy, charming, easy to talk to—" She caught herself. "For an actor."

"He makes my insides tingle," Bethany confessed, unashamed and artless.

Mine, too, Johanna thought. Which was precisely why she wasn't going to see him again. "You're supposed to be concentrating on your screenwriter," she said briskly, then stopped when she saw Beth's expression. "Trouble?"

"He dumped me." She shrugged her shoulders in an unconcerned gesture. Johanna only had to look at Beth's eyes to see how much she was hurting. "It's no big deal, really. We weren't serious."

Maybe he wasn't, Johanna thought with a mixture of sympathy and resignation. "I'm sorry. Everyone has spats, Beth."

Bethany understood that, had even expected it. She hadn't expected deceit. "We went a little beyond that. It's better this way, really it is. I thought he was interested in me, you know, but when I found out he was more interested in my position—" She caught herself, swore silently, then smiled. "Doesn't matter. He was just one of the many toads you have to go through to find the prince."

"What about your position?" It never took Johanna long to put two and two together. Screenwriter, assistant producer. Toss in ambition and it added up perfectly. "Did he want you to hawk a script?"

Uncomfortable, Bethany shifted. "Not exactly."

"Spit it out, Beth."

"All right. He had the idea that I could influence you to influence your father to produce his screenplay. When I told him it wouldn't work, he got mad, then I got mad, and one thing led to another." She didn't add that it had been ugly. She didn't have to.

"I see." Why were there so many creeps in this world? Johanna wondered. So many users. "I am sorry, Beth."

"Bruises fade," Beth said easily, though she was aware hers would last a long time. "Besides, I've got the satisfaction of hoping he sells nothing but commercial jingles for the next ten or twenty years."

"Do yourself a favor," Johanna advised her. "Fall in love with an insurance salesman." She glanced toward the door as her secretary popped a head in.

"Telegram, Ms. Patterson."

With a murmured thank-you, Johanna took it. Stupid, she told herself as her fingers tensed on the paper. It had been almost twenty-five years since she'd gotten that brief and heartbreaking telegram from her mother. She hadn't even been old enough to read it herself. Shoving back the memory, she tore the envelope open.

I can be as stubborn as you. Sam.

Johanna scowled at the single line, read it twice, then crumpled it into a ball. But instead of tossing it in the wastebasket, she shoved it into her pocket.

"Bad news?" Bethany asked.

"A weak threat," Johanna said, picking up her remote. "The show's starting."

The damn woman was making him crazy. Sam groomed the mare, who'd been bred only hours before to his prize stud. She was still skittish and prone to nip. High-strung, pedigreed and temperamental, she reminded Sam of Johanna. That made him smile, if a bit grimly. He didn't think Johanna would appreciate being compared to a horse, not even a purebred.

She hadn't returned one of his calls. *Miss Patterson is unavailable. Miss Patterson is in a meeting.*

Miss Patterson is avoiding you like the plague.

He was beginning to feel like a gawky teenager with a crush on the class princess. More than once he'd told himself to write her off, to find some less complicated woman to spend an evening with.

The mare turned her head and took aim at his shoulder. Sam

merely shifted out of range and continued to stroke and soothe. He didn't want to spend the evening with a less complicated woman. He wanted to spend it with Johanna. Just a test, he told himself, to see if whatever had happened by the pond would happen again. And if it did, what the hell was he going to do about it?

He was better off not seeing her again. A man had a lot more freedom when he cluttered up his life with many women than when he found himself concentrating on only one. He wasn't trying to concentrate on her, he reminded himself. He just couldn't get her out of his head.

What secrets did she have tucked away inside her? He had to find out.

When she'd kissed him...there had been no secrets there. She'd been open, passionate and as honest as a man could hope for. It hadn't been ordinary. He knew what it was to kiss a woman for pleasure, for obligation or because the script called for it. That moment with Johanna had been nothing so simple as pleasure, and it had been nothing so casual as obligation. The reaction—his *and* hers—hadn't been in any script.

She'd been as stunned as he was, and as unnerved. Didn't she want to know why?

The hell with what she wanted, Sam decided as he shut the stall door. *He* had to know why. Whether she wanted to or not, Johanna was going along for the ride.

She was beat. Johanna downed two aspirin and a carton of yogurt at her kitchen sink. Her afternoon had been taken up by back-to-back meetings, and though she should have been celebrating the nighttime syndication of *Trivia*, she'd opted for a quiet evening at home. She'd have to set up a party for the crew next week. They deserved it. And she'd see that Beth got a raise. For tonight, she didn't want to think about production meetings or sponsors. Her flowers needed tending.

The sun was warm on her face and arms as she walked outside to her garden. The roses that climbed the trellis along the side of the house needed pinching off. Snapdragons and hollyhocks needed weeding. Some of the taller and heavier-bloomed plants would require staking. Pleased with the scents and colors, she dug in.

She'd spent many quiet afternoons with the gardener on her father's estate, learning the names of the plants and the care they required. He'd let her have a plot of her own and had shown her how to turn soil and plant seeds, how to separate at the roots and prune. She'd learned how to blend plants for color, texture, height and flowering periods from him. On rainy days, or during cold snaps, he'd let her explore the greenhouse, where fragile seedlings had been nursed or exotic bulbs forced for early blooming.

The scents there had never been forgotten, the sultriness, the heat, even the damp smell of watered soil. He'd been a kind man, a little stoop-shouldered and thick through the middle. During one brief fantasy she'd imagined he was her father and they'd gone into business together.

She hadn't known until she'd heard him talking with another servant that he'd felt sorry for her.

All the servants had felt sorry for her—the little girl who was only brought out and paraded at her father's whim. She'd had a three-story dollhouse, a tea set of English china and a white fur coat. There had been ballet lessons and piano lessons and French taught by a private tutor. Other little girls would have dreamed of having what Johanna had only had to lift a hand for.

At six, her picture had been splashed across the press. She'd worn a red velvet dress that had skimmed her ankles and a tiny diamond tiara as flower girl at her father's second wedding. A Hollywood princess.

The bride had been an Italian actress who enjoyed having tantrums. Her father had spent a good deal of that two-year union on the Italian Riviera. Johanna had spent most of it in the gardens of his Beverly Hills estate.

There had been a scandal and a mudslinging divorce. The actress had kept the Italian Villa, and her father had had a blistering affair with the lead in his next production. Johanna, at age eight, had already developed a cool and all-too-adult view of relationships.

She preferred her flowers. She didn't like wearing gloves. She felt that she got a better sense of the soil and the fragile roots with

her hands uncovered. When she managed to squeeze in time for
a manicure, she was usually met with shock and dismay. As a
matter of routine, Johanna kept her nails clipped short and didn't
bother with enamel.

Unfeminine. That was what Lydia had called her. Lydia had
been one of her father's more vocal and longer-lasting distractions.
Lydia had been palely beautiful and unceasingly selfish. Fortunately, she hadn't wanted to marry Carl Patterson any more than
he had wanted to marry her.

*Send the girl to the nuns in Switzerland, darling. Nothing like
nuns for teaching a girl a little femininity and grace.*

Johanna, at twelve, had lived in terror that she would be sent
away, but Lydia had been replaced before she'd managed to pressure Carl into paying the tuition.

Unfeminine. The word still cropped up in Johanna's head from
time to time. She usually ignored it; she'd found her own style of
womanhood. But now and again, like an old scar, the word caused
an itch.

On her hands and knees, she brushed through her patio dahlias,
back to the freesia that would bloom in another few weeks. With
care and precision, she pulled out any weeds that had had the
audacity to sprout. It had been a dry spring, and after testing the
soil she decided she'd give everything a good soak before calling
it a day.

She heard the car but didn't bother to glance up, because she
expected it to drive by. When it didn't, Johanna had just enough
time to look around before Sam swung out of the driver's side.

She said nothing and remained kneeling, speechless.

He was furious. The long drive from his ranch had given him
plenty of time to work on his temper. Here he was chasing after
some cool-eyed go-to-hell blonde and all he could think of when
he saw her was how she'd looked in the moonlight.

It was dusk now, the light soft and tenuous. She was kneeling
in front of a bank of flowers like some pagan virgin sacrifice. She
didn't rise, and her hands were stained with soil and grass. The
air smelled like sin, dark and rich.

"Why the hell do you have a secretary and an answering machine if you don't intend to answer messages?"

"I've been busy."

"What you are is rude."

She hated that. Hated knowing it was true. "I'm sorry." She put on her coolest and most professional smile. "The show's going into syndication and I've been tied up with meetings and paperwork. Was there something important?"

"You know damn well it's important."

She spent the next ten seconds carefully wiping the worst of the dirt from her hands onto her jeans and staring at his boots. "If there's a problem with your contract—"

"Cut it, Johanna. We've done our business. That's over."

She looked at him then. "Yes, that's right."

He stuck his hands in his pockets. If he'd had them free much longer he might have throttled her. "I don't like feeling like a fool."

"I'm sure you don't." She rose, careful to keep an arm's length of distance between them. "I'm losing the light, Sam. If there's nothing else..." The rest of the words slid down her throat when he grabbed her by her shirtfront.

"You're going to turn away from me once too often," he said quietly. Much too quietly. "I've always considered myself fairly even-tempered. Seems I was wrong."

"Your temperament's not my problem."

"The hell it isn't." To prove his point, he yanked her against him. Her hands came up automatically for balance and defense. But his mouth was already on hers.

There was no testing kiss this time, no friendly overture. There was only the outpouring of urgency and demand that had clawed inside him for days. She didn't struggle. He hated to think of what he might have done if she had. Instead, she went very still, and for a moment nearly fooled them both into thinking she was unaffected.

Then she moaned. The sound went from her mouth into his, filled with surrender and despair. Before the sound had died her arms were around him, her fingers digging into his shoulders.

Twilight deepened, cooling the air, but she felt only the heat from his body as she pressed against him. He smelled of horses and leather. Dazed, she thought that the scent must be part of some deeply buried fantasy. Knight on white charger. But she didn't want to be rescued. Like a fool, she'd thought she could escape, from him, from herself. It only took a moment to show her how firmly she was already bound.

He brushed his mouth across her face, drawing in the taste, the softness. Her lips skimmed his jaw as she, too, searched for more. He tightened his arms around her. He'd thought he'd understood what it was to ache for a woman. Nothing had ever come close to this. He hurt everywhere, with a pain more erotic than anything he'd ever imagined. The more he touched, the more he hurt. The more he hurt, the more he was driven to touch.

"I want you, Johanna." His hands were in her hair now, as if he couldn't trust them to wander over her again. "I haven't been able to stop thinking about you for days. For nights. I want to be with you. Now."

She wanted it, too. A shudder ran through her as she clung to him. She wanted him. She wanted to let go of her control, of her caution, and just feel—the way he could make her feel. Somehow she already knew that he could bring her things she'd never believed in. Once he did, she'd never be the same.

For a moment longer, she held on. Regret, more than she'd ever known, replaced desire as she drew away. With an effort she managed a smile as she glanced at the smudges on his shoulders. "My hands were dirty."

He took them both. "Let's go inside."

"No." Gently she drew her hands from his. "It wouldn't work, Sam. *We* wouldn't work."

"Why?"

"Because I wouldn't want it to. I wouldn't let it work."

He took her chin in his hand. "Bull."

"I wouldn't." She wrapped her fingers around his wrist. The pulse was fast there, as fast as her own. "I'm attracted to you, I won't deny that. But it can't lead anywhere."

"It already has."

"Then it can't lead any farther. Believe me when I say I'm sorry, but we're both better off facing up to it now."

"I'm sorry, too, but I can't accept it." He moved his hand to her cheek in a gesture that pierced her with its tenderness. "If you're expecting me to walk away and leave you alone, you're going to be disappointed.''

She took a deep breath and met his eyes squarely. "I'm not going to sleep with you."

His brow lifted. "Now, or ever?"

The last thing she'd expected to do was laugh, but the chuckle bubbled out. "Good night, Sam."

"Hold on. We're not finished." There was amusement in his voice as he gestured toward her front steps. "Why don't we sit down? It's a nice night." When she hesitated, he lifted his hands, palms out. "No contact."

"All right." She wasn't completely at ease with it but felt perhaps she owed them both that much. "Would you like a drink?"

"What have you got?"

"This morning's coffee."

"I'll skip it, thanks." He settled comfortably next to her, hip to hip. "I do like your place, Johanna," he began, wondering if he would be able to understand her better through it. "It's quiet, private, well looked-after. How long have you had it?"

"About five years."

"Did you plant all this?"

"Yes."

"What are those?"

She looked over to the edge of one of her borders. "Soapwort."

"Ugly name for such a pretty thing." The little pink flowers looked delicate, but he could see that they spread exactly as they chose. "You know, it occurs to me that we don't know each other very well." He leaned back against the next step, stretching his legs out. Johanna thought he looked very much at home.

"No," she said cautiously. "I suppose we don't."

"You believe in dating?"

She hooked her hands around her knees and smiled. "It's a nice occupation for teenagers."

"You don't figure adults can pull it off?"

On guard again, she moved her shoulders. "Most people I know have lovers, not boyfriends."

"And you don't have either."

"I like it that way."

The way she said it made him glance back at the little pink flowers again. "Why don't we shoot for another term, like companion?" He turned to study her profile. "We could try being companions for a while. That's an easy, uncomplicated term. No strings."

It sounded that way, but she knew better. "I meant what I said before."

"I'm sure you did." He crossed his feet at the ankles. "That's why I figured you wouldn't be afraid to get to know me better."

"I'm not afraid," she said immediately, showing him that he'd hit the right button.

"Good. There's a benefit Friday night at the Beverly Wilshire. I'll pick you up at seven."

"I don't—"

"You support raising funds for the homeless, don't you?"

"Of course I do, but—"

"And since you're not afraid, it wouldn't bother you to be my companion. It's formal," he continued smoothly. "I don't care much for that kind of evening myself, but it's for a good cause."

"I appreciate the offer, but I simply couldn't manage to get home from work and change in time for a formal function at the Wilshire by seven." And that, she thought, should be the end of that.

"All right, I'll pick you up at your office. That way we can make it seven-thirty."

She let out a huge breath, then shifted so that she could look at him directly. "Sam, why are you trying to maneuver me this way?"

"Johanna..." He took her hand and kissed her fingers, too quickly for her to object. "I can maneuver much better than this."

"I'll just bet."

Delighted, he grinned. "I love it when you use that tone. It's so proper. Makes me want to muss you up."

"You didn't answer my question."

"Which question? Oh, that one," he finished when she narrowed her eyes. "I'm not trying to maneuver you, I'm trying to make a date with you. No, not a date," he corrected. "No dates for adults. We can't call it a meeting, that's too businesslike. How about encounter? You like encounter?''

"I don't think so."

"One thing I've found out about you already, Johanna, is that you're a hard woman to please." He stretched out again with a sigh. "But that's all right. I can sit right here until you come up with the right choice of words. Stars are coming out."

Involuntarily she glanced up. She often sat out by herself in the evening. She'd been content to look at the stars alone. Somehow the night seemed more appealing with him there, and that worried her. Depending on someone else for your contentment was a big mistake.

"It's getting chilly," she murmured.

"Are you asking me in?"

She smiled, then rested her elbow on her knee. "It's not that chilly." They were silent for a moment. Then the silence was broken by a nighthawk. "Why aren't you down in the city at some club being seen with some up-and-coming actress with lots of teeth?"

As if he were thinking it through, Sam rested his elbows on the back of the step. "I don't know. Why aren't you down in the city at some club being seen with some hotshot director with a perfect tan?"

Still pouting a bit, she kept her head still but shifted her gaze over to him. "I asked you first."

"I love acting," he said after a moment. His voice was so calm and serious that she turned her head again. "I really love it when it all comes together—the script, the moves, the crew. And I don't mind being paid well for it, either. I've got a couple of weeks before we start shooting. Once we do, there are going to be a lot of very long and very demanding days. I don't want to waste the little time I have in a club." He touched her hair. They both remembered he'd promised there would be no contact, but she didn't object. "Are you going to come back and feed my ducks, Johanna?"

It was a mistake, she told herself as she smiled at him. A stupid one. At least she was making it with her eyes open. "I think I can make it Friday night, if you don't mind leaving the benefit a bit early. I'll have put in a full day at the office.''

''Seven-thirty, at your office?''

''Fine. No strings?''

''Deal.''

The minute he leaned toward her, she held up a hand. ''Don't kiss me, Sam.''

He backed off, not without effort. ''Now, or ever?''

She rose and brushed off the seat of her jeans. ''Now, anyway. I'll see you tomorrow.''

''Johanna.'' She paused at the top of the steps and looked back. ''Nothing,'' he told her. ''I just wanted to look at you again. Night.''

''Drive carefully. It's a long trip.''

He threw her a grin over his shoulder. ''It's getting shorter all the time.''

Five

By five-thirty the offices were like a tomb. Johanna was happy enough to have an extra hour to herself. Paperwork that never seemed to diminish during the normal working day could be gotten through in an uninterrupted hour. Questions for Monday's taping had been chosen and checked, but Johanna took the time to go over them herself to be certain they were as entertaining as they were educational.

She answered a pile of memos, read and signed letters and approved a stack of bills. The beauty of game shows, she thought as she worked, was that they were cheap to produce. In a big week they could give away over fifty thousand dollars and still come in at a fraction of the cost of a thirty-minute situation comedy.

She was still determined to get her other concept on the air, and was ready to make her pitch for the pilot so that when things clicked the show could debut in the fall. And they would click, Johanna promised herself. One more success, one more solid success, and her own production company could begin its struggle for survival.

Garden Variety Productions. She could already see the logo. Within two years others would see it, as well. And remember it.

She'd continue to do the games, of course, but she'd begin to expand her own horizons, as well. A daytime drama, a couple of prime-time movies, a weekly series. She could already see it building, step by step. But for now she had to concentrate on getting through the rest of the day. And the evening.

After her desk was cleared, Johanna brought out her secret. She'd hidden the bag in her bottom drawer, behind the office stationery. There'd been enough commotion over her bringing an evening dress to the office. Now Johanna pulled the box from the bag, opened it, then read the instructions through twice. It didn't seem that complicated. She'd make it an adventure, she told herself, even if it was silly. She'd told herself it was silly even as she'd let the clerk talk her into buying them.

Johanna set her equipment in orderly lines, with the instructions handy, then examined her hands, back, then palms. The clerk hadn't been wrong about her nails being a mess. And what was wrong with trying something new? Johanna picked up the first fake fingernail and began to file it. She tested it often, placing it on her short, unpainted thumbnail until she was satisfied that the length wasn't extravagant. Only nine more to go, she thought, and began to attack the rest.

As she worked, she slipped out of her shoes and curled her legs under her. It was a position she never would have permitted herself to take if anyone had been in the office. Alone, she switched to it without thinking. Once she had ten uniformly filed nails on her blotter, she went on to the next stage.

The instructions told her it was easy, quick and neat. Johanna peeled off the adhesive and pressed it against her nail. Easy. With the tweezers she carefully caught the tip of the backing and began to peel it off. The adhesive rolled into a ball. Patiently Johanna removed it and tried again. The third time she managed to make it stick. Pleased, she picked up the first nail and aligned it carefully over her own. After pressing down, she examined the result.

It didn't look like her thumb, but it was rather elegant. After she painted it with the Shell-Pink Fizz enamel the clerk had sold her, no one would know the difference.

It took her twenty minutes to complete one hand, and she had to resort to digging out her reading glasses—something else she never would have done unless completely alone. She was swearing at the clerk, at herself and at the manufacturer when the phone rang. Johanna hit line one and popped the nail off her index finger.

"Johanna Patterson," she said between her teeth.

"It's John Jay, honey. I'm so glad you're a workaholic."

Johanna glared at her naked index finger. "What is it?"

"I've got a teeny little problem, sweetheart, and need you to come to my rescue." When she said nothing, he cleared his throat. "Listen, it seems my credit card's at the limit and I'm in a bit of an embarrassment. Would you mind talking to the manager here at Chasen's? He says he knows you.''

"Put him on.'' Disgusted, she ran her hand through her hair and popped off another nail. It took less than two minutes to squeeze John Jay out of his embarrassment. After she hung up the phone, Johanna looked at her hand. Two of the nails she'd meticulously placed were gone, and her fingers were smeared with adhesive. Letting out a long breath, she began to remove the rest.

She was an intelligent, capable woman, she reminded herself. She was a hop and a skip away from being thirty and she held down a complex and demanding job. She was also probably the only woman in the country who couldn't attach fake nails.

The hell with it. She dumped everything, including the bottle of enamel, into the trash.

She did what she could with her hair in the women's lounge. Then, because she was feeling unfeminine and klutzy, she went dramatic with her makeup. Dressed only in thigh-high stockings and tap pants, she unzipped the garment bag. She'd only worn the gown once before, a year ago. It was strapless and clingy, a far cry from her usual style. With a shrug, Johanna stepped into it, and shimmied it up, then fought to reach the zipper. She swore again and wondered why she'd allowed herself to be talked into going out at all. Once the dress was secured, she tried to see as much of herself as possible in the waist-high mirrors.

It was a good fit, she decided as she turned to the side. And the color—which, she remembered grimly, would have matched the enamel now in the trash—was flattering. Though she couldn't see it, the hem skimmed her knees in the front, then graduated down to full-length in the back. Johanna changed her everyday earrings for pearl-and-diamond circles, then clasped on a matching choker.

As good as it gets, she thought, and zipped her office clothes in the bag. She'd have her secretary send them to the cleaners on Monday. With the bag slung over her arm, she started back to her office. She'd been wise to have Sam meet her here, Johanna decided. Not only did it make it less like a date, there was the added security that she'd have to be dropped off back in the parking garage so that she could drive herself home.

The coward's way. She shrugged her shoulders with a touch of annoyance as she walked. The safe way, she corrected. Whatever she was feeling for Sam was a little too fast and a little too intense. Having an affair wasn't in her plans, professionally or personally. She'd simply lived through too many of her father's.

Her life would never be like his.

As far as Sam Weaver was concerned, she would be sensible, cautious and, above all, in complete control of the situation.

Oh, God, he looked wonderful.

He was standing in her office by the window, his hands in the pockets of his tux and his thoughts on something she couldn't see. Pleasure, hardly comfortable, slammed into her. If she'd believed in happily-ever-afters, she would have believed in him.

He hadn't heard her, but he'd been thinking about her hard enough, deeply enough, that he'd known the moment she'd stepped into the doorway. He turned, and his image of her dissolved and reassembled.

She looked so fragile with her hair swept up off her neck and her shoulders bare. The business-first office had suited the woman he'd first met. The pretty garden and isolated house had suited the woman who'd laughed with him beside the pond. But this was a new Johanna, one who seemed too delicate to touch.

As ridiculous as it made him feel, he had to catch his breath. "I thought you'd skipped out."

"No." When she realized her knuckles were turning white clutching her summer bag, she relaxed them. "I was changing." Because she wanted badly to act natural, she made herself move to the closet. "I'm sorry if I'm a bit behind. I got caught up. Work," she said, and with a quick glance made certain the fiasco of plastic nails and polish was out of sight.

"You look wonderful, Johanna."

"Thanks." She shut the closet door, trying to take the compliment with the same ease with which it was given. "So do you. I'm ready whenever you are."

"I need another minute." He crossed to her, catching the quick surprise in her eyes just before he covered her bare shoulders with his hands and kissed her. He lingered over the kiss, struggling to keep the pressure light, the demand minimal. "Just wanted to see if you were real," he murmured.

She was real, all right, so real that she could feel her own blood pumping hot and quick. "We should go."

"I'd rather stay here and neck. Well, maybe some other time," he added when he saw her brow lift. With her hand in his, he started out of the office toward the elevators. "Listen, if this is really boring we could leave early. Take a drive."

"Hollywood galas are never boring." She said it so dryly that he laughed.

"You don't like them."

"I don't often find it necessary to attend them." She stepped into the elevator as the door opened.

"It's hard to be a part of a world and ignore it at the same time."

"No, it's not." She'd been doing it for years. "Some of us do better behind the scenes. I saw one of the early ads for your miniseries," she continued, changing the subject before he had a chance to probe. "It looked good, very classy, very sexy."

"That's marketing," he said dismissively as the elevator reached the underground parking garage. "It's not really sexy. It's romantic. There's a difference."

There was indeed, but it surprised her that he knew it. "When you've got your shirt off and your chest is gleaming, people think sex."

"Is that all it takes?" He opened the passenger door of his car. "I can be out of this cummerbund in under five seconds."

She swung her legs into the car. "Thanks, but I've already seen your chest. Why television?" she asked when he'd joined her. "At this point in your career, I mean."

"Because the majority of people won't sit still in a theater for four hours, and I wanted to do this movie. The small screen's more personal, more intimate, and so was this script." The car's engine echoed in the nearly empty garage as he backed up and began to drive out. "The character of Sarah is so fragile, so tragic. She's so absolutely trusting and naive. It knocked me out the way Lauren pulled it off," he added, referring to his co-star. "She really found the essence of that innocence."

And, according to the press, he and Lauren had had as many love scenes away from the cameras as they had in front of them. It would be wise, Johanna reminded herself, to remember that. "It's not usual to hear an actor talk about a character other than his own."

"Luke's a bastard," Sam said simply as he stopped at a light. "An opportunist, a womanizer and a heel. A very charming, glib-tongued one."

"Did you capture his essence?"

He studied Johanna before the light changed. "You'll have to watch and tell me."

Deliberately she turned away. "What's your next project?"

"It's a comedy."

"I didn't know you did comedy."

"Obviously you missed my tour de force as the Raisin Crunch man a few years ago."

The chuckle welled up. "I'm embarrassed to say I did."

"That's all right. I'm embarrassed to say I didn't. That was right before I did the Mano cologne commercials. 'What woman can resist a man who smells like a man?'"

She would have laughed again if she hadn't remembered her own reaction to everything about him, including his scent. "Well, no one can say you haven't paid your dues."

"I like to think I have, and I'm also aware that the Mano campaign got me a reading for *Undercover*."

She was sure it had. Johanna hadn't missed those particular ads. In them, Sam had been blood-pumpingly sexy, intensely male and cocky enough to make a woman's mouth water. His character in *Undercover* had been precisely the same, but with an underlying depth that had surprised both the audience and the critics.

"Those kind of breaks don't happen very often," she said aloud. "When they do, they're usually deserved."

"Well..." He drew the word out. "I think that was a compliment."

She shrugged. "I've never said you weren't good at what you do."

"Maybe we could turn that around and say the problem from

the outset has been that I am." She said nothing, but he thought that was answer enough.

Her brow creased a bit as they drove up to the well-lit limousine-adorned Beverly Wilshire. "Looks like quite a crowd."

"We can still go back to your office and neck."

She gave him a brief, very bland look as one of the uniformed staff opened her door. The moment she was on the curb, strobe lights and cameras flashed.

She hated that. She didn't have the words to explain even to herself how much she hated it. With a gesture that could be taken for one of aloofness rather than panic, she turned away. Sam slipped an arm around her and by doing so caused a dozen more flashes.

"They hound you less if you smile and cooperate," he murmured in her ear.

"Mr. Weaver! Mr. Weaver! What can you tell us about your upcoming television miniseries?"

Sam aimed his answer at the crowd of reporters and personalized it with a smile even as he started to walk. "With a quality script and a cast that includes Lauren Spencer, I think it speaks for itself."

"Is your engagement to Miss Spencer off?"

"It was never on."

One of the reporters got close enough to grab Johanna's arm. "Could we have your name, Miss?"

"Patterson," she said, and shook him off.

"Carl Patterson's girl," she heard someone in the crowd say. "That's the old man's daughter. Ms. Patterson, is it true your father's marriage is on the rocks? How do you feel about him being linked with a woman half his age?"

Saying nothing, Johanna swept through the front doors into the lobby.

"Sorry." Sam kept his arm around her. She was trembling a bit with what he took for anger.

"You had nothing to do with it." She only needed a moment, she thought, to calm down. Yes, there was anger, but there was also that stomach-churning distress that swooped down on her whenever she was confronted with cameras and demanding questions about her father. It had happened before and would happen again, as long as she was the daughter of Carl W. Patterson.

"You want to slip into the bar and get a drink? Sit in a dark corner for a minute?"

"No. No, really, I'm fine." As the tension eased, she smiled up at him. "I'd hate to go through that as often as you must."

"It's part of the job." But he lifted her chin with a finger. "Are you sure you're okay?"

"Of course. I think I'll just—"

But her plans for a brief escape were scotched when several people walked over to greet Sam.

She knew them, some by sight, others by reputation. Sam's co-star in his last feature was with her husband and happily pregnant with her first child. The elite of the press who had been permitted inside took the photo opportunity.

As they inched their way to the ballroom, others came by to renew an acquaintance or be introduced. Through her father she knew a great many of them herself. There were cheeks to be kissed, hugs to be given, hands to be shaken. A veteran actor with a silver mane of hair and a face that still graced billboards squeezed her. With an affection she felt for few, Johanna hugged him back. She'd never forgotten how he had come up to her room and entertained her with stories long ago, during one of her father's parties.

"Uncle Max, you're even more handsome than ever."

His laugh was low and gravelly as he kept his arm around her. "Jo-Jo. Looking at you makes me feel old."

"You'll never be old."

"Mary will want to see you," he said, speaking of his longtime and only wife. "She's run off with a safari to the ladies' room." He kissed her cheek again, then turned to size up Sam. "So you've finally broken down and taken on an actor. At least you've chosen a good one. I've admired your work."

"Thank you." After six years in the business, Sam had thought he was immune to being starstruck. "It's an honor to meet you, Mr. Heddison," he said, and he meant it. "I've seen everything you've ever done."

"Little Jo-Jo always had taste. I'd like to work with you some-time. Not many of this generation I'd say that to."

"Tell me when and where."

With his eyes narrowed, Max gave a slow nod. "I've a script I've been considering. Maybe I'll send it along and let you have a look. Jo-Jo, I'd like to see your pretty face more often." He kissed her again, then strode off to find his wife.

"I believe you're speechless," Johanna commented when Sam only continued to watch Max's back.

"There's not another actor alive I admire more than Max Hed-dison. He doesn't socialize much, and the couple of times I've seen him I didn't have the nerve to wangle an introduction."

"You, shy?"

"Intimidated is a mild way to put it."

Johanna took his hand again, touched that he could be. "He's the kindest man I know. Once for my birthday he gave me a puppy. My father was furious—he hates dogs—but he couldn't say anything because it was from Uncle Max."

"Jo-Jo?"

She shot him a look. "Uncle Max is the only one who has ever, or who will ever, call me that."

"I like it." He ran a finger down her nose. "It makes me won-der how you'd look in pigtails and a straw hat. Oh, God." She saw his expression change from one of amusement to resignation just before he was enveloped by slim white arms.

"Oh, Sam, I just can't believe how long it's been." The woman with the gypsy mane of red curls turned her face just enough to let the camera get her best side. "Darling, where *have* you been hiding?"

"Here and there." He managed, with considerable skill, to un-tangle himself. "How are you, Toni?"

"Well, how do I look?" She threw back her magnificent head and laughed. Johanna noted that her dress was cut to the lowest degree that the law would allow. "I've been so terribly busy I've lost touch. I've just started filming and could barely fit this little event into my schedule. It's so boring not being able to see friends."

"Johanna Patterson, Toni DuMonde."

"It's nice to meet you." Johanna knew DuMonde's reputation as a mediocre actress who traded more on sex appeal than talent. She'd married well twice, and both husbands had boosted her career.

"Any friend of Sam's—" she began, then stopped. "You aren't Carl's daughter, are you?" Before Johanna could answer, she threw her head back again, making sure her hair cascaded as she laughed. "What a riot! Darling, I've just been dying to meet you!" Placing a hand on Johanna's shoulder, she scanned the room. Her eyes, sharp and tawny, skimmed over minor celebrities, smiled at those worth noticing and narrowed when focused on a rival. When she found her objective, her smile turned up several hundred kilowatts. Johanna noticed the flashy diamond on her left hand as she signaled.

"This is such a happy coincidence," Toni continued. "I'm sure you'll understand how very delighted I am. Sweetheart, look who I found."

Johanna looked at her father as Toni snuggled against him. The move was calculated so that the diamond on her finger winked hard and cold and in plain sight.

"Johanna, I didn't realize you were attending." Carl brushed his cheek against hers, as he would have with any of his hundreds of acquaintances.

He was a tall man, with broad shoulders and a flat stomach. He'd allowed his face to line because he had a fear of going under the knife, even cosmetically. But he'd never permitted his body to sag. At fifty-five, Carl W. Patterson was in his prime. Women were as drawn to him now as they had been thirty years before. Perhaps more, as power added to his sex appeal.

"You're looking well," Johanna told him. Sam noted that there was none of the warmth here that there had been when she'd greeted Max Heddison. "Carl Patterson, Sam Weaver."

"A pleasure." Carl took Sam's hand in his hefty, well-manicured one. "I've kept my eye on your career. Word is you're starting a film with Berlitz soon. We go back a ways."

"I'm looking forward to it."

"Isn't this cozy?" Toni put in, clipping her free hand through Sam's arm. "The four of us running into each other this way.

We'll have to get a table together, won't we, Carl? After all, I'll want to get to know your daughter, now that we're going to be family.''

Johanna didn't freeze. She didn't even react. By this time she was past being surprised by her father. "Congratulations." She winced only slightly when a camera flashed, catching the four of them together.

"We haven't set the date yet." Toni beamed up at Carl. "But we plan to make it soon—well, as soon as a few minor matters are taken care of.''

Which would be the legal disposal of his fourth wife, Johanna surmised. Fortunately, she was no longer affected by the whims or variable presence of stepmothers. "I'm sure you'll be very happy.''

"We intend to be." Carl patted Toni's hand, looking at her rather than at his daughter.

"Do let's get a table, Carl, and have a drink to celebrate." Toni kept a casual grip on both men. So casual that it was barely noticeable when Sam removed her hand and took Johanna's. Hers was ice-cold and rigid.

"I'm sorry, we can't stay long." Sam's smile was charming and faintly apologetic.

"Oh, pooh, you've time for one quick drink before this place turns into a zoo." Toni trailed her fingertips up Carl's arm. "Darling, you'll have to insist.''

"No need to insist." She wouldn't be ill, Johanna told herself. She wouldn't even be upset. Neither did she smile as she looked up at her father. "The least I can do is drink to your happiness.''

"Wonderful." Toni thought it more than wonderful to be seen with a man as important as Carl and a man as attractive as Sam at the same time. "Now, Johanna darling, you mustn't believe all those naughty things you must have read about Sam and me. You know how people in this town love to talk." She turned to be escorted inside and shot a smile over her shoulder, daring Johanna not to believe every word.

"Why in the hell are you doing this?" Sam demanded.

"Because it's part of the game." Chin up, Johanna stepped into the ballroom.

*   *   *

The room was full of babble. It glittered as such events are meant to, and it would make excellent copy in *People*. It would raise a great deal of money—a hundred, perhaps a hundred and fifty thousand dollars—while making the evening worth the price of the meal. And the food was lavish.

She didn't eat. Johanna barely noticed what was placed in front of her, though Toni cooed over each course and made noises about calories. The ring on her hand flashed triumphantly every time she moved her fingers. She made coy little remarks about Sam behaving like a gentleman with her almost-stepdaughter, giggled delightedly about having a daughter the same age as herself and snuggled kisses on Carl's cheek when she wasn't flirting elsewhere.

He was dazzled by her. Johanna sipped champagne and watched her father preen whenever the redhead stroked his ego. She'd never known him to be dazzled by a woman before. Desirous, covetous, infuriated, but never dazzled.

"Just a teeny bit more," Toni said when Carl poured more wine. "You know how silly I get when I drink too much." She shot him an intimate look that promised she could get a great deal more than silly. "Isn't this a wild crowd?" She waved cheerily to someone at another table. "God, what a hideous dress. All those diamonds don't make up for plain bad taste, do they? Sam, darling, I heard Lauren's seeing some French race-car driver. Did she break your heart?"

"No," he said flatly, and shifted away when she patted his knee.

"That's because you always do the heartbreaking. Be very careful with this man, Johanna dear, better women than I have shed a tear over him."

"I'm certain," Johanna said sweetly, and sipped more champagne.

"Tell me, why haven't you had your daddy put you in the movies?" Toni gave her a cool woman-to-woman look over her glass.

"I don't act."

"What do you do?"

"Johanna produces daytime television," Carl put in. "The latest reports that crossed my desk were excellent, by the way."

"Thank you."

"Evening syndication is moving forward?"

"Yes, we just finalized it. I would have sent you a memo, but I thought you were out of town."

"We just spent two weeks on the most dismal location shoot in Arizona." Toni patted Carl's hand. "Thank God Carl was there to be sure I wasn't worn to a frazzle. Sam, I've heard the most marvelous things about your television thing. That'll be aired in a couple of weeks, won't it?"

He smiled at her again and nodded. He knew she'd tested for the part of Sarah and had yet to forgive him for not pulling strings to get it for her.

"We really should do a movie together, with Carl producing."

When hell freezes over, Sam thought. "I really hate to cut this short, but Johanna and I are already late." He rose before anyone could protest and offered a hand. "A pleasure meeting you, Mr. Patterson, and my compliments on your finest production." Taking Johanna by the hand, he grinned at Toni. "Don't ever change, darling."

"Good night," Johanna said to her father. "Best wishes." She didn't object to Sam's supporting arm as he guided her out of the ballroom. "You didn't have to cut your evening short on my account," she began.

"I didn't cut it short, and I'm not leaving only on your account. I don't like socializing with piranhas like Toni." He drew out the claim check for his car and handed it to the boy on the curb. "Besides, you look like you could use some fresh air."

"I'm not drunk."

"No, but you were heading there."

"I never get drunk, because I don't like to be out of control."

Truer words had never been spoken, he was certain. "Fine, but I'm going to get you something to eat anyway." He handed the boy who brought his car a twenty and ushered Johanna in himself. "Could you handle a burger?"

"I'm not hungry."

Stubborn, he thought, and just this side of sulking. "Okay, I want a burger."

She started to snap and realized just in time that she was being nasty. "Sam, I appreciate it, but I really don't want anything. Why don't you just drop me off so I can get my car?"

"You had five glasses of wine. I counted." He'd nursed one the moment he'd seen what kind of mood she was in. "I'm driving you home—after we eat."

"I can't leave my car in town."

"I'll have someone drop it off to you tomorrow."

"That's too much trouble. I can—"

"Johanna..." He pulled over to the curb and waited until she looked at him. "Let me be a friend, okay?"

She shut her eyes, wanting badly to do something else she never allowed herself. To cry, hard and long and for no reason at all. "Thanks. I guess I could use some food and some air."

In his tux, Sam ran into a bright fast-food restaurant, ordered burgers, fries and coffee, signed half a dozen autographs and ran out again. "Life's rarely simple anymore," he told Johanna as he tucked the bag between her feet. "The little girl behind the counter wanted to pay for them, and I know damn well she stuck her phone number in the bag. She must have been all of nineteen."

"You should have let me go in."

"We all have our crosses to bear." He headed out. "Johanna, I don't make it a habit to pay attention to what's said about me in print—unless it's a review—but I'd like to make an exception and tell you that Toni and I were never together."

"Sam, it's none of my business."

"Whether you think it's your business or not, I'd like you to believe me. If you've already got a picture of her and me, it's bad enough. When you add that to the fact that she's apparently going to marry your father, it's ludicrous."

Johanna opened her eyes and studied him as he drove. It hadn't occurred to her before. She'd been too wrapped up in her own thoughts and feelings to notice. But she saw it now. "She embarrassed you. I'm sorry."

"I just didn't like her implying—" Implying, hell, he thought. She'd practically taken out an ad. "I'd feel better if you understood there'd never been anything between us." He wanted to say more but found it difficult to say what he thought about the woman who was going to become a part of Johanna's family. "Anyway, it wasn't quite the evening I had in mind."

In a little while he pulled up at the crest of a hill. Below, spread out like a game of lights, was the Los Angeles Basin. He put the top down. Far off in the distance she heard the call of a coyote.

"We're not dressed for burgers, but I got plenty of napkins." He reached down for the bag and the back of his hand brushed her calf. "Johanna, I have to tell you something."

"What?"

"You have incredible legs."

"Give me a hamburger, Sam," she said, and took off her shoes. "Smells better than the veal medallions."

"Is that what we had?"

"No, that's what you didn't have. Here's the ketchup." He passed her a handful of little plastic bags, then waited until he was satisfied she was eating. If he'd ever seen anyone more miserable than Johanna had been at that pretty, flower-bedecked table with stars glittering in every corner, he couldn't remember. The worst of it was that she'd been struggling to be valiant about it.

"Want to talk about it?" When she only shrugged, he pressed a little harder. "I take it you didn't know your father was planning to get married again."

"I didn't know he was planning to get divorced again. He doesn't check these things through with me."

"Are you fond of your current stepmother?"

"My father's current wife," she corrected automatically, which told him a great deal. "I don't know, I've only met her a couple of times. I think she moved back to New York a few weeks ago. I was just surprised because he doesn't usually stack one marriage on top of the other. Generally there's a space of a year or two between legal contracts."

"He'll have a few months to get to know Toni better. He could change his mind."

"I'm sure he knows exactly what she is. One thing Carl isn't is stupid."

"Sometimes if you tell someone when you're angry with them it loosens things up."

"I'm not angry with him, not really."

He brushed his knuckles along her cheek. "Hurt?"

She shook her head, unable to trust herself to speak for a moment. "He lives his own life. He always has. And that makes it easier for me to live mine."

"You know, I had some real matches with my father." He shook the bag of fries, urging them on her.

"Did you?"

"God, did we fight." With a laugh, Sam opened his coffee and began to sip. "The Weavers have tempers. We like to yell. I think I spent most of the years between fifteen and twenty going head-to-head with my old man. I mean, just because I plowed the car through Greenley's fence was no reason to confiscate my license for six weeks, was it?"

"I imagine Greenley thought it was. Did you ever get your own way?"

"I figure that was about seventy-five, twenty-five, with him holding the lion's share. I probably got as much as I did because he was busy yelling at my brother or one of my sisters."

"It must be different, having a big family. I always imagined..."

"What?"

The wine cushioned embarrassment. Without it, she might never have said it out loud. "I sometimes thought it would be nice when I was little to have brothers and sisters... I don't know, grandparents to visit, family squabbles. Of course, I had stepsiblings from time to time. Things were usually finished before we'd gotten used to each other."

"Come here." He shifted over so he could put an arm around her. "Feel any better?"

"A lot." She sighed and rested her head. "I appreciate it."

Her hair smelled like the air outside the windows. Clean, quiet. The urge to turn his face into it was natural, and he did it without thinking. "I wish you hadn't had so much wine."

"Why?"

"Then it wouldn't be against the rules for me to seduce you."

She surprised herself by turning her face to his. She didn't like the word "seduce." It implied a lack of will. But just now it sounded liberating, and more than tempting. "You live by the rules?"

"Not many of them." He brought his hand to her hair. "I want to make love with you, Johanna, but when I do I want you to have your wits about you. So for now I'll settle for a little less."

He nipped at her lower lip, testing its softness, experimenting with tastes. Here was warmth, just edging toward heat, and acceptance, only a step away from surrender.

Of all the visions and fantasies he'd already had of being with her, the one that was the strongest was of him just holding her like this, with the stars overhead and the night breezes blowing cool and clean.

She could have pulled away. His touch was so gentle she knew he would never have pushed. Not this time. There would be others. She already accepted that. On another night when the breeze was just ruffling the leaves he'd hold her like this, and his mood wouldn't be as patient. Nor, she was afraid, would hers. Something had taken root, no matter how hard she'd tried to pull it free. With a little sigh, she brought a hand to his face.

It was torture, but he ran his hand along her bare shoulders. He wanted to take the feel of her with him when he drew away. Just as he would take the taste of her, the scent of her skin, with him on the long, lonely trip home.

"I wish I knew what I was feeling," she murmured when she could speak again. It wasn't the wine. It would have been a lie to blame it on anything so ordinary. Her eyes were heavy, a bit dazed. Her mouth was soft. Just by looking at her Sam knew he could have her. One more easy nudge and they would be lovers.

He reminded himself about rules and fragile women.

"We're going to have to talk about it." He kissed her again, briefly. "Then we're going to have to do something about it. But right now I'm going to take you home."

Six

Johanna considered Saturdays the day the work force had been given to catch up on everything their jobs had forced them to ignore during the week. Rather than a day off, she thought of it as an alternate. Saturdays weren't for sleeping late—even if you were slightly hung over and punchy. They were for weeding the garden, marketing, dealing with personal correspondence and bookkeeping. Her Saturdays, like the rest of her days, had a routine she rarely varied. Johanna depended on organization because a well-ordered life was a safe one.

She dealt with the cleaning first. Though she'd never thought of herself as particularly domestic, Johanna had never considered hiring someone to do the housekeeping. The house was her personal life, and as in all areas of that life, she preferred to handle it herself.

The vacuuming and dusting, the scrubbing down and polishing up, were never mundane chores. There was a certain basic pleasure in them, but more compelling was the feeling that her house, her things, deserved her attention. It was as simple as that. She could haul a bucket and dust rags from room to room with the same dedication and enjoyment she put into reading contracts or balancing budgets.

She preferred the radio loud so that she could hear it in whatever corner of the house she decided to tackle first. This was a day for both production and solitude. Over the years, Johanna had developed a dependency on both.

She did think about the car, and thinking of that naturally turned her thoughts to Sam. She hoped he didn't forget his promise to have someone drop it off, but if he did she'd simply forgo her Saturday marketing and have Bethany pick her up on Monday morning.

Johanna never depended on promises or other people's memories.

But she did think of him, and if her thoughts weren't completely comfortable she couldn't forget that he'd been kind, and gentler than she'd expected. She remembered, a little too well, how she'd felt when she'd kissed him. Full, edgy, tempted. Just a little more tempted each time she was with him to throw away the pact she'd made with herself so many years ago. The pact said no relationships that couldn't be controlled, by her, from the outset—no dependencies, no promises, long- or short-term.

It was a sensible pact, unwritten but binding. The fact that Sam had nearly lured her into forgetting it worried her. But it made her wonder more.

Just what was it about him that made her lose a bit of ground every time they were together? She could discount his looks, however delightful they were. She might appreciate a great physique, but she wouldn't swoon over one.

Not that she was swooning over Sam Weaver, Johanna reminded herself as she poured hot water into her bucket. She thought very little of women who built fantasies or relationships around cleft chins and bulging biceps.

Nor was it his reputation. That, in fact, worked against him. Johanna dunked her mop in hot, soapy water, then began to wash her kitchen floor. The fact that he was an actor was a strike against him. The fact that he was an actor with a reputation with women was a bigger one.

Of course, she knew that such reports were usually exaggerated and often outright lies. But there were times... There were times, Johanna thought as she swiped the mop back and forth, that the press didn't even come close to making rumor as outrageous as the truth.

The press had never known her truth. Her mother's truth. With the care and firmness of experience, she locked that thought away.

So it wasn't his looks or his reputed way with women. It certainly wasn't his fame. Growing up as she had, Johanna had had to tolerate vicarious fame all her life. It wasn't his talent, either, though she certainly respected that. She knew people were often drawn to talent and power. Her father, and the stream of women in his life, were proof of that. They were also drawn to wealth and position. Johanna was too ambitious and had spent too much time trying to perfect her own skills to be swayed by anyone else's.

So if it wasn't one of the attributes he was so obviously endowed with, just what was it that was making her think about him when she shouldn't?

It hadn't started with that first kiss. It would have been easy to blame it on basic sexual attraction, but Johanna preferred honest self-analysis. The seed of something had been there from that first meeting. If not, she wouldn't have gone out of her way to give him a hard time.

Defense mechanism, Johanna thought, recognizing and acknowledging it.

There was his charm, of course. She wrung out the mop and began to rinse. It wasn't stylized or deliberate. That she would have been immune to. It was natural, easy, even friendly. The roses had managed to turn the key in an old, well-guarded lock. The kiss had managed to blow it open briefly, just long enough to give her cause for alarm.

Alarm. Yes, that was what she'd felt overlaying every other emotion he'd drawn out of her. Now that she'd admitted it, she had to decide what to do about it.

She could ignore him. But she didn't believe that would do much good. She could—cautiously—go along with his suggestion that they get to know each other better. Slowly. And she could stick to her guns and not get involved beyond a wary friendship.

The solution had to be in there somewhere, she thought. She'd come up with it, and the next time she had to deal with him she'd be prepared.

She was incredible. Sam stood in the kitchen doorway and watched her mop the kitchen floor. He'd knocked, but the music she had blaring in the other room had drowned out the sound. Since the door hadn't been locked, he'd simply walked in and wandered through until he'd found her.

Johanna Patterson. She was just a bit different every time he saw her. Sophisticated one minute, wonderfully simple the next.

Alluring, then cool. Nervous, then tough. A man could take years getting to know all of her. Sam figured he had time.

Right now she was dressed in faded cotton pants rolled up at the ankles and a big man-styled shirt pushed to her elbows. Her feet were bare, and her hair was pinned up untidily. She handled the mop with smooth, easy strokes, not skimming over the job and not swearing over it. He imagined she took to such things as housekeeping with the same steady drive she took to everything else. He liked that, and he liked her for it.

He knew exactly why he was attracted to Johanna. She was beautiful, but that wouldn't have been enough. She was smart, but though he respected a sharp mind that wouldn't have kept him coming back. She was vulnerable. Normally that would have made him take a cautious step back instead of these continued steps forward. She had an edge to her that in another few years might become hard. But now, just now, Johanna was a cautious woman with a few bruises who wasn't easily impressed by status. The combination was more than enough to keep pulling him toward her.

And she'd rather he didn't, Sam thought. On the surface, at least, she'd have preferred that he step out of her life and stay out. But deep down, he believed, she was looking for someone, for something, just as he was.

He wasn't naive enough to believe it was so just because that was what he wanted, but he was determined to find out.

He stood where he was as the strokes of the mop brought her closer. When she rammed into him, he took her arm to keep her from overbalancing.

Johanna whirled around, automatically gripping the mop like a weapon. The relief when she saw him turned quickly to anger.

"How the hell did you get in here?"

"The door," he told her easily. "It wasn't locked. I did knock. I guess you didn't hear me."

"No, I didn't." She was shouting to be heard over the music. "Apparently you took that as an invitation."

"I took it to mean you didn't hear me." He held up the keys she'd given him the night before. "I thought you'd want your car back."

"Thanks." She stuffed them in her pocket. It wasn't anger nearly as much as it was embarrassment. She didn't care to be sneaked up on unaware.

"You're welcome." He handed her a bouquet of painted daisies and snapdragons. As he'd suspected they would, her eyes softened. "I stole them from Mae's garden. I figured she wouldn't notice."

"They're pretty." With a sigh that was only partially one of resignation, she took them. "I do appreciate you bringing my car back." She knew she was weakening, and she struggled not to. "You've caught me at a bad time. I can't even offer you a drink because the floor's wet, and I'm really busy."

"I'll take you out for one. Better, let's go have some lunch."

"I can't. I've only half finished here, and I'm not dressed to go out. Besides, I—"

"Look fine," he finished for her. "You'd better put those in water. They're starting to droop."

She could have been rude. Johanna knew she was capable of it, but she found she hadn't the heart. Instead, she said nothing. She plucked an old square bottle from a shelf and went into the bathroom to fill it. As she did, she heard the volume of the music go down several notches. He was in the living room studying her collection of antique glass when she came back.

"My mother used to have some plates like this green stuff here. Depression glass, right?"

"Yes."

"I thought that meant it made her sad. I could never figure out why she kept it."

She wouldn't be amused, Johanna told herself. At least not very. "Sam, you really shouldn't keep whoever followed you up waiting outside."

"No one followed me up." He hooked his thumbs in his pockets and smiled. Some might have thought the look sheepish, but Johanna wasn't fooled.

"Now I suppose you want me to drive you back."

"Sooner or later."

"I'll call you a cab," she said, turning to the phone. "I'll even pay for it."

He put his hand over hers on the receiver. "Johanna, you're being unfriendly again."

"You're being pushy."

"Yeah, but subtleties don't work with you." He reached over to stick a loose pin back in her hair. He'd have preferred to have pulled it out, and the rest of them besides, but bided his time. "So how about lunch?"

"I'm not hungry."

"So, we'll take a drive first." He skimmed his hand from her hair to her cheek. "I really think we should, because if we stay in here too much longer I'm going to want to make love with you, and since I figure you're not ready, a drive's a better idea."

Johanna cleared her throat and took another stab at persuasion. "I appreciate your logic, but I don't have time for a drive, either."

"You've got an appointment?"

"No," she said, then wished she could bite off her tongue. "That is, I—"

"You already said no." He watched her eyes narrow and thought she was almost as pretty annoyed as she was amused. You're already sunk waist-deep, Sam, he told himself. Another few steps and you're over your head. But what the hell. "It's too nice a day to stay indoors cleaning a house that's already clean enough."

"That's my business."

"Okay, then I'll wait for you to finish before we go out."

"Sam—"

"I'm persistent, Johanna. You told me so yourself."

"I'll drive you home," she said, giving up.

"Not good enough." He caught her again, this time by the shoulders. There was something about the way he spread his fingers over her, about the way his palm fit so truly over her. His expression had changed just enough to make her uneasy. The amusement was gone, but it hadn't been replaced by anger. She wouldn't have been uneasy about anger. This was determination, solid and unshakable. "I want to spend the day with you. You know damn well I want to spend the night with you, as well, but I'll settle for the day. Give me five reasons why not and I'll walk down to the freeway and hitch a ride."

"Because I don't want to."

"That's a statement, not a reason. And I don't buy it, anyway."

"Your ego won't buy it."

"Suit yourself." Refusing to be annoyed, he sat on the arm of her couch, absently picked up one of her pillows and began to toss it. "Look, I've got all day. I don't mind sitting around until you've stopped fussing with your imaginary dust. Hell, I'll even give you a hand, but then we're going to have to get out of here, because being alone with you for long periods of time isn't easy." She opened her mouth, but he continued before she could make a suggestion. "I keep wanting to touch you, Johanna, in all kinds of interesting places."

"We'll go out," she said quickly, before she could admit she wanted it, too.

"Good idea. Listen, why don't I drive?"

She started to protest even that—on principle—then decided he'd be less likely to give her trouble if he had his eyes on the road. "Fine." After switching off the radio, she dumped the keys back in his hands. "It'll take me a few minutes to change."

"You look fine," he said again, and took her hand. "I happen to like this Johanna every bit as much as the others I've met over the last couple of weeks."

She decided not to ask him what he was talking about. "We'll have to make it a very informal lunch, then."

"It will be." He opened the door of the car for her. "I promise."

He was as good as his word.

The hot dog dripped mustard, and the noise level was intense. Johanna sat almost in the shade and watched pink elephants circle overhead. It wasn't a dream, or the last remnants of a hangover. It was Disneyland.

"I don't believe this." She took another bite of the hot dog as a boy in mouse ears dashed by, yelling for his parents to hurry up.

"Pretty great, isn't it?" Sam wore sunglasses and a low-brimmed cowboy hat that Johanna was forced to admit suited him. So did the chinos and the simple T-shirt. The disguise wasn't very imaginative, and it would have been transparent as glass if anyone had looked closely enough. Sam had told her that the best place to be anonymous was a crowd. They certainly had one.

"You come here for lunch often?"

"Great hot dogs in Fantasyland." He took an enormous bite to prove his point. "Besides, I'm hooked on the Haunted Mansion. It's terrific, don't you think?"

"I don't know. I've never been in it."

"Never?" His tone of quick astonishment wasn't feigned. Wanting a better look, he tipped down his tinted glasses and studied her. "You grew up here, didn't you?"

She only shrugged. Yes, she'd grown up a short drive from Anaheim, but neither her father nor her succession of stepmothers or "aunts," as she'd been taught to call the other women in her father's life, had been inclined to take a day trip to an amusement park.

"You're not telling me you've never been to Disneyland at all?"

"It's not a requirement."

He pushed his glasses back on his nose as she wiped her hands on a napkin. He remembered the impersonal non-kiss her father had given her the night before. His family was always, had always been, demonstrative, both physically and vocally. No, Disneyland, like other small pleasures, wasn't a requirement. But it should be.

"Come on, your education's lacking."

"Where are we going?"

"To take Mr. Toad's Wild Ride. You're going to love it."

Oddly enough, she did.

It was fast and foolish and certainly designed for the younger set, but Johanna found herself gasping and giggling as the car swerved and twisted through the tunnels. She'd barely put her foot on the ground again before Sam was dragging her off to the next line.

They rode down a mountain in a raft, and the final waterfall drop surprised a scream out of her. Wet and breathless, she didn't even protest when he pulled her along again. By the time they'd done Fantasyland to his satisfaction, she'd been spun, twirled, flown and floated. The Mad Hatter's Tea Party had left her giddy and weak-kneed and without the least notion that she was being educated.

He bought her mouse ears with her name stitched across the front, using her own hairpins to secure it even when she grumbled.

"Looks cute," he decided, then kissed her. She might not have known it, Sam thought, but she was more relaxed than he'd ever seen her. "I think you're ready for the Haunted Mansion."

"Does it spin?"

"No, it strikes terror into your heart. That's why you're going to hang on to me and make me feel brave." He swung an arm around her shoulders and began to walk. Johanna had already discovered he knew the park very well.

"You really do come here a lot, don't you?"

"When I first came to California I had two priorities. Get a job—an acting job—and go to Disneyland. Whenever my family comes out we always spend at least one day here."

Johanna looked around as they walked. There were families, so many families. Infants and toddlers pushed in strollers, children with sticky faces riding piggyback and pointing toward the next adventure.

"I guess it is an amazing place. Everything seems real while it's going on."

"It is real when it's going on." He stepped to the back of the line, undaunted by its length. After a moment's hesitation, he took a chance. "I was Pluto for six weeks."

"Pluto?"

"The dog, not the planet."

"I know who Pluto is," she murmured. Absently adjusting her hat, she frowned at him. "You actually worked here?"

"In a dog suit. A very hot dog suit—no pun intended. It paid my first month's rent."

"What exactly did you do?" The line shifted up.

"Marched in the parade, posed for pictures, waved and sweated a lot. I really wanted to be Captain Hook, because he gets to have sword fights and look evil, but Pluto was all that was open."

Johanna tried to imagine it, and nearly could. "I always thought he was cute."

"I was a terrific Pluto. Very lovable and loyal. I did cut it from my résumé after a while, but that was on Marv's suggestion."

"Marv? Oh, your agent?"

"He thought playing a six-foot dog was the wrong image to project."

While Johanna thought that one through, they were ushered inside. The spiel was camp and full of bad puns, but she couldn't help being pulled in. The pictures on the walls changed, the room shrank, the lights went out. There was no turning back.

By the time they were in their tram and starting on the tour she was, so to speak, entering into the spirit of things.

The producer in her couldn't fail to be impressed by the show. Holograms, music and elaborate props were blended to entertain, to raise goose pimples and nervous chuckles. Not so scary that the toddlers in the group would go home with nightmares, but not so tame that the adults felt cheated out of the price of a ticket, Johanna decided as she watched ghosts and spirits whirl around in a dilapidated, cobweb-draped dining room.

Sam had been right about one thing. It was real while it was going on. Not everything in life could be trusted to be the same.

She didn't have to be prodded any further, not to visit a pirate's den and dodge cannon fire, nor to take a cruise up the Amazon or a train ride through Indian territory. She watched mechanical bears perform, ate dripping ice cream and forgot she was a grown woman who had been to Paris and dined in an English manor but had never been to Disneyland.

By the time they started back to the car she was exhausted, but in the most pleasant way she could remember.

"I did not scream," she insisted, holding the small stuffed Pluto he'd bought her in a headlock.

"You never stopped screaming," Sam corrected. "From the minute that car started moving through Space Mountain until it stopped again. You've got excellent lungs."

"Everyone else was screaming." In truth, she hadn't a clue whether she'd screamed or not. The car had taken its first dive, and planets had raced toward her. Johanna had simply squeezed her eyes shut and held on.

"Want to go back and do it again?"

"No," she said definitely. "Once was quite enough."

Sam opened the car door but turned before she could climb in. "Don't you like thrills, Johanna?"

"Now and again."

"How about now?" He cupped her face in his hands. "And again later."

He kissed her as he'd wanted to do since he'd seen her studiously mopping her floor that morning. Her lips were warm, as he'd known they would be, but softer, incredibly softer, than he'd remembered. They hesitated. There was a sweetness in that, a sweetness that was its own allure.

So he lingered, longer than he'd intended. He wanted, more than was wise. When she started to back away, he gathered her closer and took, more than either of them had expected.

It wasn't supposed to be like this, Johanna told herself even as she stopped resisting both of them. She was supposed to be strong, in charge, reachable only when and if she chose to be. With him, he only had to touch... No, he only had to look and she began losing ground.

All her careful analysis that morning was blown to dust the minute his mouth was on hers.

I don't want this. Her mind tried to cling to that thought while her heart beat out steadily: But you do, yes, you do. She could almost feel herself separating into two parts, one aloof, one almost pitifully vulnerable. The most frightening thing was that this time she was more than afraid that vulnerability would be the stronger.

"I want to be alone with you, Johanna." He said it against her lips, then again against her cheek as he trailed kisses there. "Anywhere, anywhere at all as long as it's only you and me. I haven't been able to get you out of my system."

"I don't think you've been trying."

"You're wrong." He kissed her again, feeling her renewed resistance swerve toward passion. That was the most exciting, the most irresistible thing about her, the way she wanted, held back and wanted again. "I've actually given it a hell of a shot. I kept telling myself you're too complicated, too uptight, too driven." He felt her lips move into a frown and was seduced into nibbling on them. "Then I find ways to see you again."

"I'm not uptight."

He sensed her change of mood but could only be amused by it. Johanna, outraged, was fascinating. "Lady, half the time you're like a spring that's wound to the limit and just waiting to bust out. And I damn well intend to be there when you do."

"That's ridiculous. And don't call me lady." She snatched the keys from him, decided she'd do the driving this time.

"We'll see about that." He climbed into the car and nearly managed to stretch out his legs and get comfortable. "Going to give me a lift home?"

She was tempted, more than tempted, to order him out and strand him in the parking lot, right under Donald Duck's cheerful beak. Instead, she decided to give him the ride of his life. "Sure." Johanna put the car in gear.

She drove cautiously enough through the lot. It was, after all, full of pedestrians, many of them children. Things changed when she hit the freeway. She whipped around three cars, settled in the fast lane and rammed down on the gas pedal.

Drives like she's ready to bust, too, Sam thought, but said nothing. Her speedometer might have been hovering around ninety, but her hands were competent on the wheel. And she might, he thought, burn off that temper that had fired up when he'd called her uptight.

She hated it that he was right. That was the worst of it. She knew very well that she was full of nerves and hang-ups and insecurities. Didn't she spend most of her time fighting them off or blanketing them over? It didn't do her any good to hear Sam pinpoint it so casually.

When she'd made the conscious and very calculated decision to make love with a fellow college student, he, too, had called her uptight. Sexually. "Loosen up" had been his sage advice. She hadn't been able to, not with him, who she'd been fond of, nor with any of the men she'd developed careful relationships with. So she'd stopped trying.

She wasn't a man-hater. That would be absurd. She simply didn't want to be tied to one, emotionally or sexually. Her eyes had been opened young, and she'd never forgotten how those two tools could be used. So perhaps she was uptight, though she detested the word. Better that than loose enough to tumble for a pair of wonderful blue eyes or a lazy drawl.

Mad as hell, Sam thought. That was fine. He preferred strong emotion. As a matter of fact, he preferred any emotion at all when it came from Johanna. He didn't mind her being angry with him, because if she was angry she was thinking. About him. He wanted her to do a lot of that.

God knew he'd been thinking about her. Constantly. He'd been telling her no less than the truth when he'd said he'd tried to get her out of his system. When it hadn't worked, he'd decided to stop beating his head against the wall and see where the road would lead.

It was a bumpy ride, but he was enjoying every minute of it.

He was going to have her, sooner or later. Sooner, he hoped for the sake of his sanity. But for now he'd let her drive awhile.

When he saw she was going to miss the exit, he gestured. "You want to get off here."

Johanna switched lanes, aggressively challenging traffic, and breezed onto the ramp.

"How about dinner next week?" He said it casually, as though the interlude in the parking lot had been as make-believe as the rest of the day. When she said nothing, he fought back a grin and tossed his arm over the seat. "Wednesday's good for me. I can pick you up at your office."

"I'm busy next week."

"You've got to eat. Let's make it six."

She downshifted for a turn. "You're going to have to learn to take no for an answer."

"I don't think so. Take the left fork."

"I remember," she said between her teeth, though she didn't.

She drove in silence, slowing down only slightly when she passed through the gate of his ranch. Sam leaned over casually and tooted her horn. When she stopped in front of his house he sat there a moment, as though gathering his thoughts.

"Want to come in?"

"No."

"Want to fight?"

She would not be amused or charmed or soothed. "No."

"All right, we can fight some other time. Want to hear a theory of mine? Never mind," he said before she could answer. "Listen anyway. The way I figure it, there are three stages to a relationship. First you like somebody. Then, if things work out, you start to care for them. When the big guns hit, you fall in love with them."

She kept her hands on the wheel because they'd gone damp all at once. "That's very interesting. If only life worked that neatly."

"I've always thought it does—if you let it. Anyway, Johanna, I went past liking you last night and went straight into the second stage. A woman like you wants reasons for that kind of thing, but I haven't got a handle on them yet."

Her hands had stopped sweating and were now as cold as ice, though the heat was baking right through the windshield. "Sam, I said before I don't think this is a good idea. I still believe that."

"No, you still want to believe that." He waited patiently until she looked at him. "There's a difference, Johanna. A big one. I care for you, and I figured we'd do better if I let you know." He leaned over to kiss her. A very gentle threat. "You've got until Wednesday to think about it."

He got out of the car, then leaned in through the window. "Drive carefully, will you? You can always kick something when you get home if you're still mad."

Seven

It had been a long day. In fact, it had been several long days. Johanna didn't mind. The pressure to solve problems and work through a few minor crises had kept her mind off her personal life.

Her lighting director had chosen Monday, taping day, to have an appendectomy. She sent flowers and wished him—not for totally altruistic reasons—a speedy recovery. John Jay, in the middle of contract negotiations, had decided to have laryngitis. Johanna had been forced to pamper and cajole—and make a few veiled threats—to work an instant and miraculous cure. Her assistant lighting man had proven to be competent and unruffled, even after three technical hitches. Still, the day had been lengthened by two hours.

Tuesday had stretched even further with meetings to discuss the photo sessions for the ads and the final preparations for the following week's contest. Security had been strengthened to guard that set of questions. A special safe had been purchased, and only she had the combination. Only she and Bethany knew which five questions had been sealed inside. Johanna began to feel like the head of the CIA.

A meeting with her father had been draining and difficult. They'd both been professional, executive producer to producer, as they'd discussed the show's status and plans for expansion. He'd absently mentioned an engagement party and told her his secretary would be in touch.

And, of course, because she considered it part of her job, Johanna watched *Trivia* every morning. It was just a nasty trick of fate that Sam's appearance ran this week. It was difficult enough not to think of him, and impossible when she was forced to watch him every day—long shots, close-ups. By Wednesday they had already received a stack of mail from delighted viewers.

Wednesday.

He'd given her until Wednesday to think about it. To think about him. Them. She just hadn't had the time, Johanna told herself as she turned up the volume and prepared to watch the day's segment. If she'd allowed herself to think about it she would have come up with a way, a polite and reasonable way, to get out of a dinner she hadn't even accepted.

The bright, bouncy opening theme came on, the lights flashed. The two celebrity panelists walked through the arch, then paused for applause before they took their seats. Johanna struggled to look at the big picture, but she kept focusing on him.

Relaxed. He always looked so relaxed, so confident about who he was. That was something she couldn't help but admire about him. He was at ease and put his partner at ease while still maintaining that larger-than-life quality people expected from stars.

So he was good at his job, Johanna told herself as she paced back and forth during the commercial break. That didn't mean she was infatuated with him.

When the show came back on, she took her chair again, wishing she didn't need to have that very small and indirect contact with him.

It's my job, Johanna reminded herself. But she lost track of the game as she watched him. And she remembered, a bit too clearly, that after this segment had been taped she had had her first real conversation with him. She'd taken a dare, and had lost. Since that one miscalculation, nothing had been the same.

She wanted it to be the same. The quick panic surprised her, but she fought it back and tried to think logically. She did want it to be the same as it had been before, when her life had been focused on career and nudged by ambition, both heated and cooled by pride. There hadn't been any sleepless nights then. Tension and self-doubt, perhaps, but no sleepless nights.

And there hadn't been any rides down a mountain on a raft, either, her mind echoed.

She didn't need them. Sam could keep his thrills. All she required was peace of mind.

He was in the winner's circle, surrounded by lights and the audience's total support. Johanna remembered that the quick, cocky grin had been for her benefit. The minute the congratulatory applause began, she snapped off the set.

On impulse, she went to the phone. Rather than going through her secretary, Johanna dialed direct. Such minor precautions were a bit late, since her picture—with Sam—had already been in the paper, and the speculation about them as a couple had already begun. Johanna had decided there was no use adding to the gossip that was already buzzing around the office.

She was calm, she told herself even as she wound the phone cord around her fingers. She wasn't being stubborn or spiteful, but sensible.

A woman's voice answered. Hearing it gave Johanna all the justification she needed. A man like Sam would always have women around. And a man like that was precisely what she wanted to avoid.

"I'd like to speak with Mr. Weaver. This is Johanna Patterson calling."

"Sam's not in. I'd be happy to take a message." On the other end of the line, Mae was digging for the notepad she always carried in her apron pocket. "Patterson?" she repeated, then shifted the phone and grinned. "Sam's spoken about you. You're the one who does *Trivia Alert*."

Johanna frowned for a moment at the idea of Sam talking about her to one of his women. "Yes, I am. Would you mind—"

"I never miss it," Mae continued conversationally. "I always keep it on when I'm cleaning. Then I see if Joe can answer any of the questions that night at dinner. Joe's my husband. I'm Mae Block."

So this was Mae, the one who shoveled out the dust and grew the snapdragons. Johanna's vision of a pretty morning visitor faded and left her more than a little ashamed. "I'm glad you like the show."

"Crazy about it," Mae assured her. "As a matter of fact, I just had it on. Got a real kick out of seeing our Sam on it. Thought he did real good, too. I even put it on the VCR so Joe could see it later. We're all just crazy about Sam. He speaks real kindly of you, too. Did you like your flowers?''

Having at last found a space in Mae's rapid-fire conversation for a word, Johanna managed to insert one. "Flowers?''

"Sam doesn't think I saw him snitch them.''

"They were lovely.'' Despite all her resolutions, Johanna felt herself soften. "I hope you didn't mind.''

"Plenty more where they came from. I figure flowers should be enjoyed, don't you?''

"Yes. Yes, I do. Mrs. Block—''

"Mae. Just Mae, honey.''

"Mae, if you could tell Sam I called.'' Coward, her mind said all too clearly. Johanna closed herself off from it and continued. "And that—''

"Well, you can tell him yourself, honey, 'cause he just this minute walked in. Hold on now.''

Before Johanna could babble an excuse, she heard Mae yelling. "Sam, that lady you've been mooning about's on the phone. And I'd like to know what you're thinking of wearing a white shirt when you're wrestling with horses. How you expect me to get out those stains is more than I can understand. Did you wipe your feet? I just washed that kitchen floor.''

"Yes, ma'am. It's an old shirt,'' he added in a half apology Johanna recognized even over the wire.

"Old or not, it's a dust rag now. A boy your age oughta know better. Don't keep your lady waiting all day. I'll make you a sandwich.''

"Thanks. Hello, Johanna.''

Mae hadn't mentioned her name. *The lady you've been mooning about.* That was something Johanna would have to think about later. "I'm sorry to bother you in the middle of the day. You must be busy.''

"Having my wrist slapped.'' He pulled out a bandanna and wiped the line of sweat from his temple. "I'm glad you called. I've been thinking about you.''

"Yes, well…'' Where were all the neat excuses she'd thought up? "About tonight.''

"Yes?''

Very carefully she unwrapped the cord from around her fingers. "We'd left things a bit unstructured, and as it turns out, I have a late meeting. I can't be sure what time I'll wrap things up, so—"

"So why don't you drive out here when you're finished?" He recognized a lie when he heard one. "You should know the way by now."

"Yes, but it might run late. I don't want to mess up your evening."

"The only way you'd mess it up is not to come."

She hadn't a clue as to how to respond to that. "I never actually agreed to come." Her conscience insisted on reminding her she hadn't stuck by a refusal, either. "Why don't we make it some other time?"

"Johanna," he said, very patiently, "you don't want me to camp on your doorstep, do you?"

"I just think it would be better—"

"Safer."

Yes. "Better," she insisted.

"Whatever. If you don't show up by eight I'm coming after you. Take your choice."

Bristling wasn't nearly as effective over the phone. "I don't like ultimatums."

"That's a pity. I'll see you when you get here. Don't work too hard."

Johanna scowled at the dial tone, then dropped the phone on the hook. She wouldn't go. She would be damned if she did.

Of course, she went.

Only to prove that she wasn't a coward, Johanna assured herself. In any case, avoiding a situation didn't solve anything, it only postponed things. Loose ends were something she invariably tied up.

It was true that she enjoyed his company, so there was no reason to be out of sorts. Except for the fact that she'd been maneuvered again. No, he hadn't done the maneuvering, she corrected. She'd done that all by herself, thank you very much. If she hadn't wanted to go, she would never have called him to say she wasn't going to. Deep down she'd wanted to keep the engagement because she'd always had a need to face up to whatever could be faced.

She could certainly face Sam Weaver.

A simple dinner, she decided. Between friends. They could, cautiously, be called friends by this time. A little conversation never hurt, particularly between two people who were in the same business. Game shows or movies, it all came down to entertainment. She picked up speed a bit, and the plastic bags over this week's dry cleaning snapped and rustled on their hangers behind her.

At least this time she had her own transportation. She would leave when she was ready to leave. There was some security in that.

When she passed through the gates leading to the ranch, she promised herself that she would enjoy the evening for what it was. A simple dinner with a friend. She stopped her car in front of his house and stepped out, refusing to glance in the visor mirror. She wouldn't fuss with or freshen her makeup any more than she had fussed with her outfit. Her gray suit was stylish but certainly businesslike, as were the three hanging in the car. Her low-heeled pumps were comfortable, purchased as much for that as for fashion.

She glanced at her watch and was pleased with the time. Seventhirty. Not so early that it would appear that she'd been cowed, nor so late that it made her look spiteful.

She looked as she had on that first day, Sam thought. Composed, coolheaded, subtly sexy. His reaction to her now was exactly the same as it had been then. Instant fascination. Stepping out on the porch, he smiled at her.

"Hi."

"Hello." She didn't want to be unnerved, not again, not the way she seemed to be every time she saw him. She answered his smile, though cautiously, and started up the steps. His next move was so unexpected that she had no chance to block it.

He cupped a hand around the base of her neck and kissed her, not passionately, not urgently, but with a casual intimacy that shot straight through her. Welcome home, it seemed to say, and left her speechless.

"I love the way you wear a suit, Johanna."

"I didn't have time to change."

"I'm glad." He glanced beyond her at the sound of a truck. With a half smile, he shaded his eyes. "You forgot to blow your horn," he told her.

"Everything all right here, Sam?" In the cab of a pickup was a man of about fifty with shoulders like cinder blocks.

"Everything's fine." Sam slipped an arm around Johanna's waist.

The man in the truck chuckled, then spun the wheel and made a U-turn. "I can see that. Night."

"That was Joe," Sam explained as they watched the truck cruise down the hard-packed road. "He and Mae keep an eye on the place. And me."

"So I see." It was entirely too easy, standing on the porch, his arm around her, as the sun lowered. Johanna didn't deliberately step away. The move was automatic. "Your housekeeper told me she watches *Trivia*."

She also said you were mooning over me. Johanna kept the fact that she'd overheard that little piece of information to herself. It was ridiculous, of course. Men like Sam Weaver didn't moon over anyone.

"Religiously," he murmured, studying her. She was nervous. He'd thought they'd passed that point, and he wasn't sure whether to be pleased or frustrated to discover otherwise. "In fact, Mae considers my, ah...performance so far this week the height of my career."

The smile came quickly. Her fingers relaxed their grip on the railing. "Emmy material, I'm sure."

"Is that a smirk?"

"I never smirk, and especially not about my show. I suppose I'll have to risk inflating your ego, but we've already gotten a tremendous amount of mail. 'Sam Weaver is the cutest thing on two legs,'" Johanna quoted, and was amused when he grimaced. "That was from a seventy-five-year-old woman in Tucson."

"Yeah." He took her hand and drew her inside. "When you've finished smirking—"

"I told you, I never smirk."

"Right, and when you're finished we'll see about dinner. I figured we'd barbecue, since I wasn't sure when you'd wind up that meeting."

"Meeting?" The lie had slipped away from her. Remembering, Johanna did something else she couldn't remember having done before. She blushed. Just a little, but enough. "Oh, well, it moved along faster than I'd expected."

"Lucky for both of us." He could have pinned her on it, Sam mused, but decided to let her escape. If he understood Johanna as well as he believed he was coming to understand her, she was already berating herself for the excuse, and for botching it. "I've got some swordfish. Why don't you pour yourself some wine and I'll heat up the grill?"

"All right." The bottle was already open. Johanna filled the two glasses he'd set on the kitchen counter as he breezed through the back door.

He'd known the meeting was nothing more than a weak excuse. She couldn't remember ever having been quite so transparent. Johanna sighed, sipped, then sighed again. He was letting it go so that she wouldn't be embarrassed. That only made it worse. The least she could do, she thought as she picked up his glass, was to be pleasant company for the rest of the evening.

The pool looked cool and delightfully inviting. Swimming had been a daily habit when she'd lived in her father's house. Now she couldn't seem to find time for the health club she'd conscientiously joined. She skirted around the pool to where Sam stood by the stone barbecue pit with two fish steaks on a platter, but she did glance at the water rather wistfully.

"You want to take a quick swim before dinner?" he asked.

It was tempting. Johanna found herself tempted too often when around him. "No, thanks."

"There's always after." He set the steaks on the grill, where they sizzled. Taking his glass from her, he clinked it lightly against hers, then drank. "Go ahead and sit down. These won't take long."

Instead, she wandered a short distance away, looking at his land, the tidy outbuildings, the isolation. He seemed so comfortable here, she thought, so much at home. He could be anybody, an ordinary person. But she remembered that she'd read about him just that morning.

"There's a very hot write-up in this week's *TV Guide* about *No Roses for Sarah*."

"I saw it." He saw, too, how the sun bounced off the water of the pool and onto her skin, making her seem like an illusion. The trim gray suit didn't make him think of offices or board meetings, but of quiet evenings after the day was over.

"*Variety* was equally enthusiastic. 'Gripping, not to be missed,' and so on." She smiled a little as she turned to him again. "What was the adjective used to describe you...'' She trailed off as if she couldn't quite remember, though the exact quote had engraved itself on her brain. "'Weaver executes a'— Was it 'sterling performance'?''

Sam flipped the steaks, and they hissed. Smoke rose up, hot and sultry. "'Sizzling,''' he corrected, knowing when he was being strung along.

"Yes, sizzling." She paused to touch her tongue to her upper lip. "'A sizzling performance as a down-on-his-luck drifter who seduces Sarah and the audience with equal panache.' Panache," she repeated. "That one rolls around on the tongue, doesn't it?''

"I didn't realize you were such a smart aleck, Johanna."

She laughed and crossed over to him. "I'm also human. Nothing could drag me away from my set on Sunday night when the first part's aired."

"And Monday?"

"That'll depend, won't it?" She sipped her drink and sniffed appreciatively at the mesquite smoke. "On how *sizzling* you were on Sunday."

The grin was fast and crooked, as if he had no doubt where she would be at nine o'clock Monday night. "Keep an eye on these, will you? I'll be right back."

She'd keep an eye on them, but she hoped the steaks didn't do anything they weren't supposed to do until he got back. Alone, she stretched her arms and worked the muscles in her back. The late meeting had been a lie, but the long day hadn't. Wistfully she glanced at the pool again. It really was tempting.

If she were just anyone—if he were just anyone—she could

share this meal with him, laugh a little over something that had happened during the day. Afterward, while the wine was still cool and the air still hot, they could slide into the water and relax together. Just two people who enjoyed each other and a quiet evening.

Later, when the moon came out, they might stay in the water, talking quietly, touching, easing gently into a more intimate form of relaxation. He would have music on again, and the candles on the table would burn down and drown in their own melted wax.

When something brushed against her legs, she jolted, sloshing wine over her hand. The fantasy had come through a bit too clearly, too compellingly, and that wasn't like her. Johanna turned away from the pool and the ideas it had had stirring inside her. With a hand to her heart, she looked down at a fat gray cat. He rubbed up against her calf again, sent her a long, shrewd look, then settled down to wash.

"Where did you come from?" Johanna wondered as she bent to scratch his ears.

"The barn," Sam told her, coming up from behind her. "Silas is one of the barn cats, and I'd guess he got a whiff of the fish and came down to see if he could charm any out of us."

She didn't look at Sam right away, concentrating on the cat instead. The daydream was still a bit too real. "I thought barn cats were fast and skinny."

Not when someone was always taking them down scraps, Sam thought ruefully as he set the bowl of pasta salad on the table and flipped the fish onto a platter. "Silas can be pretty charming," he said, and pulled out a chair for Johanna.

"Silas is pretty huge."

"You don't like cats?"

"No, actually, I do. I've even thought of getting one myself. Why Silas?"

"Marner," Sam explained easily as he served her. "You know how he hoarded gold. Well, this Silas hoards mice."

"Oh."

He laughed at her expression and topped off her wine. "You wanted to know. I've been meaning to ask you," he said, thinking she deserved a change of subject, "when you go on nighttime."

"Two weeks." Johanna told herself she wasn't nervous, not nervous at all. "We tape in two weeks, actually, and go on in four."

"Adding more crew?"

"Some. For the most part it just means that we'll be taping two days a week instead of one. Interested in making another appearance?"

"I'm going to be a bit tied up for a while."

"The new movie." She relaxed a few more degrees. This was how her practical mind had imagined the evening. Shoptalk, nothing more. "When do you start?"

"Any day, theoretically. Realistically, in a week or two. After some preproduction and studio work here, we'll head east. They figure about three weeks on location in Maryland, in and around Baltimore."

"You must be anxious to begin."

"I always get lazy between pictures. Nothing like a few six a.m. calls to get you back in gear. How's your fish?"

"It's wonderful." And once again, she'd all but cleared her plate without realizing it. "I bought a grill a few months ago, but I burned everything I put on it."

"A low flame," he said, and something in his voice made her skin tingle. "A careful eye." He took her hand, linking their fingers. "And patience."

"I—" He brought her hand to his lips, watching her over it as he kissed her fingers. "I'll have to give it another try."

"Your skin always smells as though you've walked through the rain. Even when you're not here I can't help thinking about that."

"We should—" Stop pretending, she thought. Acquiesce. Take what we want. "Go for a walk," she managed. "I'd like to see your pond again."

"All right." Patience, Sam reminded himself. But the flame wasn't as low as it had been. "Hold on a minute." He tossed a few scraps onto the grass before gathering up the dishes. She knew she should have offered her help, but she wanted, needed—badly needed—a moment alone.

She watched the cat saunter over to the fish with an arrogance that told her he'd been certain all along he'd get what he'd come for. Sam walked like that, Johanna thought, and suddenly cold, she rubbed her hands over her arms.

She wasn't afraid of him. She reminded herself of that to boost her confidence. But it was no less than the truth. She wasn't afraid of Sam: fear of herself, however, was another matter.

She was here because she wanted to be here. Wasn't it time to face that one fact? She'd already admitted that she hadn't come because he'd maneuvered her. She'd maneuvered herself, or that part of herself that was still determined to stand apart.

There was another part of herself, a part that was slowly taking charge, that knew exactly what she wanted. Who she wanted. That was a part that had already made an enormous mistake by falling in love with Sam.

Before she had a chance to deal with the enormity of that realization, he was back, carrying a plastic bag filled with crackers.

"They'll expect to be— Are you all right?"

She was pale, and her eyes were huge. If Sam hadn't known better he would have sworn someone had come along and given her a fast, unexpected backhand.

"I'm fine." Thank God her voice was steady. She still had that much under control. "Your pets keep you under their thumb, don't they?"

Her smile didn't quite reach her eyes, but he nodded. "It looks that way." He touched her face. She didn't flinch, but he felt the muscles of her jaw tense. "You look a little dazed, Johanna."

Terrified was the word. In love with him, her mind repeated. Good Lord, when, how and, most of all, *why?* "It's probably the wine. I'll walk it off."

It had nothing to do with the wine, but he let it go. Taking her hand firmly in his, he started toward the path. "Next time you come, you're going to have to dress for this. As sensible as those shoes are, boots or sneakers are better for the hike."

Sensible. Frowning, Johanna looked down at her trim, low-heeled Italian pumps. Damn it, they were sensible. She managed to bite off the sigh. Sensible. Like her. "I told you I didn't have time to change."

"That's okay, I can always carry you."

"That won't be necessary."

There it was again, that low, cool tone. He didn't bother to fight back the smile as he steered her along.

The sun was nearly down, so the light was soft and pearly. There were wildflowers along the path that hadn't yet bloomed the last time they'd taken this walk. He imagined Johanna could name them for him if he asked, but he preferred to let them pop out of the ground anonymously.

He could smell the water now, and could just hear its faint lap against the high grass. Every time he'd walked there in the last few weeks he'd thought of her. The birds were quiet now, settling down for the night. Those that called the night their own had yet to stir. He liked the quiet of dusk, the aloneness of it, and wondered if she felt the same. He remembered how she'd knelt in front of a bank of flowers at sundown and figured that she did.

The water of the pond was darkening, like the sky. The shadows of the trees were long and dim across it. It still made her smile to see the ducks gliding over it, preening a bit in anticipation of an audience.

"I take it Silas and his companions don't bother them."

"Too much effort to come all the way out here and get wet when they've got the barn. Here." He handed her the bag. As she had before, Johanna laughed at the ducks' antics as she tossed the crackers to them.

"I guess no one spoils them like this when you're away."

"Mae does. She wouldn't admit it, though."

"Oh, I didn't see the drake close up before." She skimmed a cracker to him. "He's beautiful. And look how the babies have grown." She scattered crumbs on the water until the bag was empty. Without thinking, she tucked it into her pocket. "It's so nice here," she murmured. "Just the water, and the grass." And you, she thought. But she didn't look at him, not until his hand was on her cheek, gently urging her to.

It was just as it had been the first time. And yet it was nothing like it. This time she knew exactly how she would feel, how she would want, when he kissed her. She knew he would touch her hair before he drew her close. She knew her mind would cloud and her pulse would quicken.

She knew, but it still stunned her.

He felt as though he'd waited forever. It hadn't been merely weeks since he'd first seen her. She'd been under his skin, inside his heart, for as long as he could remember. A dream, a half-formed wish that had only taken one look at her to click solidly into place. It was so right. Somehow it was exactly right when his mouth found hers.

She still wasn't sure. He could feel the hesitation even as he felt the passion that drummed beneath it. But he was sure enough for both of them.

It was meant to be here, here where those first shock waves had passed through both of them. It was meant to be now, before night fell.

She tightened her grip on his shirt, holding on, holding back. In a moment, she knew, she wouldn't be able to think clearly. It would be wise to withdraw now, to leave things as they had been. But his lips coaxed her to stay. To trust.

She murmured, tensing up when she felt him slip the jacket from her shoulders. A step was being taken. Then he was soothing her, giving her time, plenty of time, but no choice at all. The buttons that ran down her back were loosened one by one in an agony of sweetness and promise. When she felt his fingers brush her skin, she shuddered at the contact and searched for the will to end it.

But his lips skimmed her throat as he peeled the blouse from her. She was helpless, but the sensation was no longer frightening.

Is this what it felt like to give in, at last, fully, completely give in to something not quite known but only sensed? Hadn't she waited for it, anticipated it, even while she'd struggled against it? Now the struggle was almost over.

He had to use every ounce of self-control not to rush her. He knew she needed time and care, even as his own needs balled like fists inside him. He'd already imagined what it would be like to touch her like this, to feel her tremble when he did. Her skirt slid down her hips. His hands followed it.

The sun had dropped away, but he could see her, her hair haloed around her face, her eyes wide and uncertain. He kissed her again, slowly, trailing his lips over her jaw as he shrugged out of his shirt. He saw her start to reach for him, then hesitate just short of contact. Taking her hand, he brought it, palm up, to his lips and felt her go limp.

He lowered her to the grass.

It was cool, soft and damp with early dew—a sensation Johanna knew she would remember always. He was over her, so she could only see his face, then only his eyes. She heard the first owl call before he bent to her. Then there was only him.

He touched. She shuddered, no longer from fear or from doubt, but from a pleasure so pure she could never have described it. He tasted. She floated, no longer helpless, but a willing partner. And when she reached for him, drew him closer, the world was shut off for both of them.

She was so soft, so generous. He wondered that he could still be surprised by how many facets there were to her. She'd opened to him now, as completely as he could have hoped.

If her touch was still shy, it was only more endearing. He wanted it to be sweet for her, memorable, and as special as he already knew it would be for him. Somewhere along the line she had stopped being a woman, however desirable, however fascinating, and had become his woman.

He took her, gently, higher.

When she moaned, desire thrummed in him, hard, demanding. He fought it back, wanting her to ride the wave as long as they could both stand it. Slowly, drawing out the process, he slipped her teddy down to her waist, then to her hips, letting the hunger build inside him.

Her fingers dug into the grass as he brushed his lips over her. She could feel her skin tremble wherever he chose to linger. Then, abruptly, the pleasure rocketed up, beyond anything she'd dreamed possible. She cried out his name, her body arching up. Pleasure doubled back, and he was with her again. Now her fingers dug into his shoulders desperately.

Stars began to wink to life above them.

The breath was dragging in and out of his lungs when he filled her. Now he was helpless, his face buried in her hair, his body more her prisoner than she had ever been his. Need expanded and became the focus of his world, and then even that shattered, leaving only her.

Eight

He couldn't speak. At the moment Sam wasn't sure his mind would ever be able to direct that basic function again. He knew he should shift his weight from her but couldn't bear to break the bond.

Whatever else it had been—passion, desire, chemistry—it had forged a bond.

Overhead, the stars were still coming out. Johanna could see them now, but all she could think of was the way Sam's heart still raced against hers. She hadn't known she was capable of giving or receiving that kind of pleasure. Though the heat had eased, his body was still warm, a continuing contrast to the cool grass that waved around them. The water, pushed by the night breezes, lapped only a few feet away.

It had been a shock to realize she was capable of feeling anything this intensely, but more, she had seen his eyes, felt his body shudder, and had known for the first time in her life that she could give.

Hardly realizing she was doing so, she lifted a hand to stroke his hair. Sam was aware, even if she wasn't, that it was the first time she'd touched him without being backed into a corner. He closed his eyes and held on to that thought. What would once have been a small thing to him was now an enormous one. He'd slipped into the third phase, into love, almost painlessly.

"Johanna." When he could speak, her name was the first thing that formed. Because he wanted to see her, he found the strength to raise himself onto his elbows. Her hair was spread out on the grass that had bent under them. Her eyes were half-closed, but what he could see was still dazed with pleasure. "You're so lovely."

Her lips curved a bit, and she touched him again, her fingers on his face. "I didn't think this would happen. I didn't think it could."

"I imagined it, here, just like this." He lowered his head, just to brush his lips against hers. "But my fantasy didn't even come close to the real thing. Nothing ever has." He felt her withdraw at that, just a fraction, but enough that he felt compelled to take her face in his hand. "Nothing and no one, Johanna."

His eyes insisted that she believe him, and she wanted to, but there was still too much of a block within her to make that possible. "I've wanted you." At least she could be honest with both of them. "I can't think about what happens next."

"We're both going to have to. I've no intention of letting you go." She opened her mouth to protest, to make some excuse, and only managed to moan as she felt him harden inside her. "Not a chance," he murmured, before desire clouded his mind completely.

When she could think again, she tried to draw away. She was going to need time to put this in perspective, to work out the steps. The first was to be an adult, and not to expect.

They had shared something. Perhaps it hadn't been casual for her, but she'd always understood that every relationship had its limitations. Better to remember that now and face it from the outset. She cared, too much for her own good, but she still knew better than to cuddle up at his side and start thinking about tomorrows.

"It's late." She pulled her hands through her hair as she sat up. "I have to go."

He'd have been surprised if he could have moved again for eight hours. "Go where?"

"I have to go home." She reached for her teddy but missed by an inch when his hand braceleted her wrist.

"If you expect me to let you go anywhere tonight, you're crazy."

"I don't know what you're talking about." Her voice was amused as she tugged on her hand. "In the first place, it's not a matter of you *letting* me go anywhere." After picking up her teddy, she shook it out. "And I can hardly sleep in the grass all night."

"You're absolutely right." If she hadn't been so relaxed, she would have realized he'd given in too easily. "Here, put on my shirt. It'll be easier for you to dress inside."

Because it made sense, Johanna allowed him to bundle her into it. It carried his scent. Unconsciously she rubbed her cheek against the collar as Sam pulled on his jeans.

"Let me give you a hand with those." Sam took her now-folded clothes and draped them over his arm. "Better let me go first. There isn't much light tonight."

Johanna followed him down the path, hoping she seemed as casual and at ease as he. What had happened by the pond, weeks ago and now tonight, had been beautiful. She didn't want to lose the importance of it. But she didn't want to exaggerate its importance, either.

Nothing and no one else.

No, she'd be a fool to believe it—to hope for it. He might have meant it at the moment he'd said it. She could believe that because she'd come to understand that Sam wasn't a man for lies, even pretty ones. She could believe, too, that he cared for her—again, for the moment.

Intense feelings rarely lasted, and all the hopes and promises built on those feelings eventually crumbled. So she didn't allow herself to hope and refused to make promises.

They still had a long way to go, Sam mused. She wasn't ready to take what he'd discovered he was ready to give. The trouble was, now that he was in love with her he wouldn't be able to be so patient. Johanna was just going to have to keep pace.

As they stepped onto the terrace, he set her clothes neatly on the table. A frown formed between her brows as he casually stripped off his jeans.

"What are you doing?"

He stood before her, undeniably magnificent in the light of the moon. With a smile that warned her an instant too late, he hauled her into his arms.

"It's what *we're* doing," he said simply, and jumped into the pool.

The water was several degrees warmer than the night air, but it was still a shock. Before it closed over her head, she had time for one surprised shriek. Her legs tangled with his as the plunge separated them and the shirt billowed up around her head. Then her feet touched bottom, and instinctively she pushed upward. Gasping, she surfaced, blinking water from her eyes.

"Damn it!" She drew her arm through the water, hand fisted, and shot a spray into his grinning face.

"Nothing like a midnight swim, is there, Jo-Jo?"

"Don't call me that. You must be out of your mind."

"Only about you," he told her, then sent an unloverly splash in her direction.

Johanna dodged it, barely, telling herself she wasn't amused. "What the hell would you have done if I couldn't swim?"

"Saved you." He treaded water with little effort. "I was born to be a hero."

"Jerk," she corrected. She turned, and in two strokes had reached the side. Before she could haul herself out, Sam caught her by the waist.

"When you stop being mad, you'll admit you like it." He nuzzled the back of her neck. "Want to race?"

"What I want to do is—" She turned—another miscalculation. His hands slid up her wet skin to her breasts as he bent his lips to her throat.

"Me too," he murmured.

She lifted a hand to his shoulder where it skimmed over cool skin just beginning to heat. "Sam, I can't."

"That's okay. I can." He slid into her.

Johanna woke with a faint grumble and tried to roll over. It took her several confusing seconds to realize that Sam's arm had her pinned. Lying still, she turned her head cautiously to look at him.

He slept more on her pillow than on his own. No, they were both his pillows, Johanna reminded herself. His bed, his house. Would he think her a fool or a freak if she told him this was the first time she'd ever woken up in a man's bed? It didn't matter; she wouldn't tell him. How could she tell him he was the first man she'd cared for enough, trusted enough, to share that private vulnerability called sleep?

She still wasn't quite sure how he'd managed to nudge her into it. One minute she'd been standing, naked and dripping, by the side of the pool, and the next... They hadn't even made love there, but had simply fallen into bed much like two exhausted children.

He'd made her laugh, too, and he'd given her, all unknowing, the sweet daydream of her own making.

Now it was morning and she had to remind herself again that she was an adult. They had wanted each other, enjoyed each other. It was important not to add complications to that simple formula. There wouldn't be regret. Regret usually meant blame, and she didn't want that, either. Wisely or not, she'd made a decision. The decision had taken her into intimacy with Sam. She wouldn't use the word *affair*.

Now that it was done, she had to be realistic. This intensity, this flash of feeling, would fade, and when that happened, she'd be hurt. It couldn't be prevented, only prepared for.

Her emotions had already deepened beyond her control, but she still had her strength and her sense. No strings. He'd said it. She'd meant it.

Despite that, she lifted a fingertip to brush the hair from his forehead.

Oh, God, I'm in love with him, I'm so ridiculously in love with him, and I'm bound to make a fool of myself.

When he opened his eyes, those dark, heavy-lidded eyes, she didn't give a damn.

"Hi."

She lowered her hand, flustered because he'd caught her petting him. "Good morning."

It was there, even after their incredible night together. The trace of shyness he found so appealing. So exciting. Because he didn't want to give her time to layer it over with composure, he rolled on top of her.

"Sam—"

"It occurs to me," he began as he drew longer, lazier kisses from her, "that we never made love in bed." He ran his hand down her side, from shoulder to hip, from hip to thigh. "I'm feeling traditional this morning."

She didn't have time to analyze what she was feeling. Even as she tried to say his name again, her breath caught. This morning he wasn't so patient—or perhaps she, knowing what could be, was more sensitive.

She curled around him and let herself go.

Time had gotten away from her. Everything had gotten away from her, Johanna corrected as she stepped out of the shower and began to towel off quickly. If she threw on her clothes, let her hair air-dry on the way to work and pushed the speed limit, she might just make it.

She grabbed a few basic cosmetics out of her purse. The effort would be sketchy, but it was all she could afford. In the bedroom she ripped the plastic off the first suit Sam had brought up from her car. Yesterday's blouse would have to work with it. Cursing herself for not having planned properly, she zipped the skirt and ran down the hall carrying her shoes.

"Where's the fire?" Sam asked her as she rested a hand against the wall and struggled into her shoes.

"I'm running late."

He lifted a brow. "Do you get demerits for being tardy?"

"I'm never late."

"Good, then you can afford to be. Have some coffee."

She took the cup he offered, grateful. "Thanks. I really have to run."

"You haven't eaten anything."

"I never eat breakfast."

"Today you do." He had her arm. To prevent the contents of the cup sloshing all over her freshly laundered suit, she kept up with him. "Five minutes, Johanna. Catch your breath, drink your coffee. If you argue, it'll take ten."

She swore, but downed more coffee as he pulled her into the kitchen. "Sam, you're the one who's on vacation, not me. I've got a full day scheduled that might, if I'm lucky, end before six."

"All the more reason you should have a decent breakfast." He couldn't remember ever having felt better in the morning, more alive or full of energy. Briefly he wished he was in the middle of filming so that he could pour some of that energy into a part. "Sit. I'll fix you some eggs."

Because her temper was beginning to fray, she drank more coffee. "I appreciate it, really I do, but I don't have time. We're shooting ads today for the home viewers' contest, and I'm the only one who can handle John Jay."

"A dubious talent." The English muffin he'd dropped in the toaster popped up. "You can at least eat this."

Annoyed, she snatched it from him, ignored the butter and jam on the table and bit into it. "There," she said, and swallowed. "Satisfied?"

Her hair was still dripping around her face, and she'd forgotten her lipstick. Eyes still shadowed from the long night glared at him. He grinned and flicked a crumb off her chin. "I love you, Johanna."

If he'd drawn back and planted his fist on her chin she would have been no less shocked. She stared at him as the muffin slipped out of her boneless fingers onto the table. Her step back was instinctive, defensive. Sam lifted his brow at it, but that was all.

"Don't say that to me," she managed at length. "I don't need to hear that. I don't want to hear it."

She needed to hear it all right, he thought. She might not have wanted to, but she needed to. He was going to see that she did, at regular intervals, but right now she'd gone pale again. "All right," he said slowly. "It doesn't change the facts one way or the other."

"I—I have to go." She ransacked her purse almost desperately for her keys. "I'm really running late." What was she supposed to say? What was supposed to be said on the morning after the night? With her keys clutched in her hand, she looked up. "Goodbye."

"I'll walk you out." His arm went around her shoulders. She tried not to tense. She tried not to lean against him. She could feel the tug-of-war as they walked. "There's something I'd like to tell you, Johanna."

"Please, it isn't necessary. We agreed even before—before last night—that there wouldn't be any promises."

"Did we?" Damned if he remembered that, but if he had agreed, that was one agreement that would have to be broken. He pushed the front door open and stepped onto the porch before turning her to him. "We'll have to talk about that."

"All right." She would have agreed to almost anything if it had meant he'd let her go. Because she wanted to stay. More than she'd ever wanted anything, she wanted to toss her keys over her shoulder, throw herself into his arms and stay as long as he'd have her.

"In the meantime, I want you to know that I've never had another woman in that bed." He saw the flash of doubt in her eyes before she was able to mask it. And before he could stop himself, he'd hauled her up by the lapels. "Damn it, a man gets tired of having everything he says dissected in that brain of yours. I didn't say there haven't been other women, Johanna, but there's never been another woman here. Because here's special to me. It's important. And so are you." He let her go. "Chew on that for a while."

Johanna thumbed another antacid tablet from the roll. She'd told Sam no less than the truth when she'd said she was the only one who could handle John Jay. It just so happened that today she wasn't doing a good job of it. The two-hour photo session had stretched into three, and tempers were fraying. If she didn't have the crew, equipment and two cars out of the studio in another forty-five minutes she was going to have the producer of *Noon with Nina* on her back.

Resigned, Johanna chewed the antacid and prayed it did its job better than she was doing hers. She signaled for a halt and hoped the five-minute break would keep the photographer from strangling her host.

"John Jay." She knew the game. Johanna pasted a smile on her face as she crossed to him. "Can I have a minute?" Her voice was calm, her touch light and friendly, as she took his arm to guide him to a corner. "Sessions like this are so annoying, aren't they?"

He literally pounced on the sympathy. "You have no idea, Johanna. You know I want what's best for the show, darling, but that man..." He glanced over at the photographer with loathing. "He has no conception of mood or image."

"That man" was one of the tops in his business and was being paid by the incredibly expensive hour. Johanna bit off an oath in time to have it slip out as a sigh. "I know, but unfortunately we have to work with him. We're running behind schedule, and the last thing I want is to have him take shots of the cars only." She let the threat hang until she was certain it had sunk in. "After all, there are three stars here. The cars, the show itself and, of course, you. The teasers went beautifully, by the way."

"I was fresh." He fussed with the knot of his tie.

"I understand perfectly. But I have to ask you to keep the energy up for just a few more minutes. That suit's very becoming, John Jay."

"It is, isn't it?" He held out an arm, turning it over to study the sleeve.

"These shots are going to make quite a statement." If she didn't strangle him herself first. "All I want you to do is stand between those two cars and flash the smile America loves."

"For you, darling." He squeezed her hand, ready to sacrifice himself to the masses. "You know, you're looking a little dragged-out."

Her smile didn't fade, only froze. "It's lucky I'm not having my picture taken."

"It certainly is," he agreed, patting Johanna's head. He already knew his producer could grow fangs if he patted her elsewhere. "You have to try to relax more, Johanna, and take those vitamins I told you about. God knows I couldn't get through the day without them." He watched the photographer come back on the set. With a sniff, John Jay signaled for make up. "Johanna, there's a rumor running rampant that you're seeing Sam Weaver."

"Is there?" Johanna ground her teeth as John Jay got a dusting of powder. "It's amazing how these things get started."

"What a town." Satisfied that he was perfect, John Jay strode over to do his duty.

It took only twenty minutes more. The moment she'd sent her host on his way, Johanna apologized to the photographer, offered him and his assistant lunch on her and handed out tickets to Monday night's taping.

By the time she drove from the studio in Burbank back to her offices in Century City, she was two hours behind schedule and had consumed almost half the roll of antacids in her pocket.

"You've got a half-dozen messages," Bethany told her the moment she walked in. "Only two of which require answers yesterday. I contacted Tom Bradley's agent. He's interested in doing the pilot."

"Good. Let's set it up." In her office, Johanna dropped her briefcase, accepted the cup of coffee Beth was already offering and sat on the edge of her desk. "I've thought of twenty-seven ways to successfully murder John Jay Johnson."

"Would you like me to type them up?"

"Not yet. I want to wait until I have an even thirty." Johanna sipped her coffee and wished for five minutes, five full minutes to be completely alone, so that she could take her shoes off, put her feet up and close her eyes. "Bradley has a reputation as being very professional."

"A veteran. Did his first show in '72, when he was still wet behind the ears. It ran for five years, and he slid right into the old classic *Word Bingo*. That was on the air from '77 to '85. Pretty amazing. He retired as sort of the guru of game shows, but his face is still recognizable from occasional appearances on other daytime shows and grand-marshaling parades. Luring him back to the fold would be no small accomplishment."

She stopped because Johanna was drinking coffee and staring out the window. There were shadows under her eyes, Bethany noted, and a definite look of melancholy in them. "Johanna, you look terrible."

Taken aback, Johanna set her coffee aside. "So I've been told."

"Is everything all right?"

"Everything's fine." Except that Sam said he was in love with her and she was so terrified she wanted to get in her car and keep driving. She drew out her roll of tablets.

Frowning, Beth eyed it. "Was that a new roll this morning?"

"It was, before I spent most of it with John Jay."

"Have any lunch?"

"Don't ask."

"Johanna, why don't you take the rest of the day off, go home, take a nap, watch the soaps?"

With a small smile, Johanna rose to move behind her desk. "I've got to answer those questions yesterday. Beth, let's see if we can set that pilot up for the week after next. Be sure to notify Patterson Productions."

Bethany shrugged and stood. "You're the boss," she said, and set the stack of messages on Johanna's desk.

Absolutely true, Johanna thought as Bethany closed the door behind her. She was the boss. Johanna rubbed at the headache behind her temple and wondered why she felt as though someone else were pulling the strings.

He didn't know what he was doing there, sitting on her front steps like a lovesick teenager. Because he was lovesick, Sam told himself as he crossed his booted ankles.

He hadn't felt this stupid about a woman since he'd fallen like a ton of bricks for Mary Alice Reeder. She'd been an older woman, sophisticated, wise and like most sixteen-year-old girls, not very interested in a fourteen-year-old pest. But he'd loved pretty little Mary Alice with a kind of worshipful devotion that had lasted nearly nine months.

Calf love, his mother had called it, not unkindly.

Since then he'd fallen into the second stage, the care-for stage, with a number of women. But he hadn't loved anyone else since Mary Alice Reeder. Until Johanna.

He almost wished he could go back to that calf love. However painful it was, it passed, and it left a man with sweet and rather filmy memories. Hearts and initials carved surreptitiously in a tree trunk, daydreams that always ended with him saving his girl from some horrendous disaster that opened her eyes to his charm and bravery.

Sam laughed at himself and looked at a spiky blue flower that was just beginning to bloom in Johanna's garden. Times changed. Mary Alice had slipped through his shaky fingers. But he wasn't fourteen anymore, and Johanna, like it or not, was going nowhere.

He wanted her. Just sitting there in front of her quiet, empty house, with a basket beside him and her flowers sleeping in the evening sun, he wanted her. For good. It wasn't a decision he'd made with a snap of his fingers, though she might think so. It was something that had happened to him, and not entirely in a way he liked. The only plans he'd counted on, the only pressure he'd expected, had been career-oriented.

If he'd had his choice, he would have cruised along for another few months, a year. Ten years. Time didn't have a damn thing to do with it. He'd looked at her, he'd touched her, and the decision had been made for him.

Hadn't he sat right here not so long before and told her they should get to know each other better? Companions, with no strings. He'd meant it, every bit as honestly as he'd meant it when he'd told her he loved her.

She'd accepted the first—warily, but she had accepted it. The second had been met with pure panic.

What was it that made Johanna so skittish? Another man? She'd never mentioned one, never even hinted at one. Unless he was completely obtuse, the woman he'd made love with the night before had been almost frighteningly innocent. If she'd been hurt, he felt it must be buried deep in the past, and it was time for her to let it go.

Time. He didn't have much of that, he thought as he lifted the lid of the basket to check on his gift. Any day he could get the call that would send him three thousand miles away. It would be weeks before he could be with her again. He could handle that. He thought he could handle that, but only if she gave him something to take with him.

When he heard the car he set the lid carefully back in place. Lovesick, he thought as his stomach knotted and his nerves began to jangle. It was a very apt phrase.

Johanna pulled in behind his car and wondered what the hell she was going to do. She'd been so sure she would be able to come home, close herself in, maybe dive into bed and sleep for hours without thinking at all. But he was here, invading her privacy, stealing away her quiet hours. The worst of it was, she was glad, so glad to see him.

"You put in a long day." He rose but didn't cross to her.

"A lot of things are coming to a head at once."

He waited until she stood in front of him. "I know what you

mean.'' He touched her then, just a light stroke down her cheek. ''You look tired.''

''So I've been informed, with annoying regularity.''

''Are you going to let me come in?''

''All right.'' He hadn't kissed her. Johanna had expected it this time, had been prepared for it. As she turned toward the house she suspected that was exactly why he hadn't done it. She spotted the wicker basket and paused as he scooped it up. ''What did you do, bring sandwiches in case I was late?''

''Not exactly.'' He followed her inside. It was precisely as it had been the last time, neat, homey, smelling faintly of potpourri and fresh flowers. They were peonies this time, fat red blooms in a dark blue jar.

Johanna started to slip out of her shoes, caught herself and set down her briefcase.

''Can I get you a drink?''

''Why don't you sit down and I'll fix you one?'' He set the basket down next to the jar of flowers. ''I'm the one on vacation, remember?''

''I usually just get some coffee, but—''

''Fine. I'll get it.''

''But—''

''Relax, Johanna. It'll just take a minute.''

He strode off as she stood where she was. As far as she could remember, no one had ever cut her off in the middle of so many sentences. Well, he'd invited himself, she decided. He could heat up the coffee as well as she. And she did want to sit down, for just a minute.

She chose the corner of the sofa and thought she might rest her eyes until she heard Sam coming back. Johanna stifled a yawn, shut her eyes and was asleep in seconds.

She awoke the same way, instantly. Somehow she'd snuggled down and had pulled an afghan up to her chin. Sitting up, Johanna dragged her hands through her hair just before she spotted Sam sitting across from her drinking coffee.

''I'm sorry.'' She cleared the huskiness out of her voice. ''I must have dozed off.''

She'd slept like a rock for half an hour. He'd tucked her up himself. "How do you feel?"

"Embarrassed."

He smiled and rose to go to the coffeepot he'd set on a warmer. "Want this now?"

"Yes, thanks."

"You didn't get much sleep last night."

"No." She took the coffee, studying the little painted cup as though it fascinated her. "Neither did you."

"I didn't put in a ten-hour day." He sat beside her. She was up like a spring.

"I'm starving," she said quickly. "There isn't much out in the kitchen, but I can put together a couple of sandwiches."

"I'll give you a hand."

Even as he rose, she was shrugging out of her jacket. "That's all right, it's no trouble." Nervous, she turned the jacket over, spilling out the contents of the pockets. Sam bent over and picked up loose change, a hairpin and what was left of the roll of antacids.

"What do you need these for?"

"Survival." Taking everything from him, she set them on the table.

"You put yourself under too much pressure. How many of these do you take?"

"For heaven's sake, Sam, they're more candy than medicine."

Her defensive tone had his eyes narrowing. Too many, he decided. "I'm entitled to worry about you." When she started to shake her head, he cupped her chin in his hand. "Yes, I am. I love you, Johanna, whether you can deal with it yet or not."

"You're pushing me too fast."

"I haven't even started to push yet."

With her face still caught in his hand, he kissed her. His lips demanded response, nothing timid, nothing cool. She could taste the trace of anger on them, the hint of frustration. Desire, kicked into high gear by other emotions, held sway. If it had been possible, she would have pulled back, ended it then and there. But it wasn't possible.

She touched a hand to his cheek, not even aware that she sought to soothe. As the kiss deepened, she slid her hand up into his hair.

His name was like a sigh from her lips to his. Then she was locked close.

It was the whirlwind again, fast and furious. This time it was she who tugged at his shirt, wanting that contact, that intimate, secret feel of flesh against flesh. Her need was a springboard for his. Tangled, groping at buttons, they tumbled onto the couch.

Even last night, in that first burgeoning passion, she hadn't been like this. She trembled as she had trembled before, but now it was anticipation, even impatience, that shivered through her. To be swept away wasn't what she looked for now; to be taken wasn't enough. It had only taken one night for her to realize her own power. Now she was driven to test it again.

He struggled to keep his hands gentle as the insistence of hers had desire clawing at him. Her mouth, open and hungry, sought the taste of him, chest, shoulders, throat, while she tugged at the snap of his jeans and sent his stomach muscles dancing.

"Johanna." As much for her preservation as his own, he tried to slow the pace. Then her mouth was back on his, silencing him, ripping the last shreds of control.

The last light of day streamed through the windows of a room scented by flowers in a house tucked almost secretly in the hills. As long as he lived he would think of her that way—in soft light, in fresh scents, alone.

She hadn't known she could be like this, so full of need, so desperate to be filled. Heedless, daring, reckless. She felt the teddy he'd slipped so carefully from her the night before tear as he yanked aside the barrier.

Then she captured him, drawing him in, arching high as pleasure arrowed into her. Fast, then faster still, she drove them both in a race for that final dazzling release.

He held on to her, even after her body went lax, after his own emptied. Her shyness had delighted him, lured him, but this Johanna, the one who could flash with white heat, could make him a slave. He wasn't certain what he'd done, he only remembered the grasping, titanic lunge into delirium.

"Did I hurt you?" he murmured.

"No." She was too stunned by her own behavior to notice any bruises. "Did I hurt you?"

He grinned against her throat. "I didn't feel a thing." He tried
to shift her to a more comfortable position and spotted the remains
of her teddy on the floor. "I owe you some lingerie," he murmured as he lifted it up.

Johanna studied the torn strap and rent seam. Abruptly she began to laugh. She felt like that, torn open, and God only knew
what would pour through the holes. "I've never attacked a man
before," she managed.

"You can practice on me anytime. Here." He picked up his
shirt and slipped it over her shoulders. "I always seem to be
lending you a shirt. Johanna, I want you to tell me how you feel.
I need you to."

Slowly, hoping to gather up some of her scattered senses, she
buttoned the shirt. "There are reasons... I can't talk about them,
Sam, but there are reasons why I don't want things to get serious."

"Things already are serious."

He was right. She knew he was right even before she looked
into his eyes and felt it. "How serious?"

"I think you know. But I'm willing to spell it out for you
again."

She wasn't being fair. It was so important, and sometimes so
impossible, to be fair. There was too much she couldn't tell him,
she thought. Too much he'd never be able to understand even if
she could. "I need time."

"I've got a couple of hours."

"Please."

"All right." It wasn't easy, but he promised himself he'd give
her time, even though he felt it slipping away. He tugged on his
jeans, then remembered the basket. "I almost forgot. I brought
you a present." He plucked up the basket and set it in her lap.

He wasn't going to push. She shot him a quick look of gratitude,
then added a smile. "What, a picnic?" She flipped back the lid,
but instead of cold chicken she saw a small dozing kitten. Johanna
drew him out and was instantly in love. "Oh, Sam! He's ador-
able." The kitten mewed sleepily as she rubbed its rust-colored
fur against her cheek.

"Blanche had a litter last month." He tickled the kitten's ears.

"Blanche? As in Dubois?"

"Now you're catching on. She's sort of a faded Southern belle who likes to pit the toms against each other. This one's weaned, and there's enough cat food in the basket to get you through about a week."

The kitten climbed down the front of her skirt and began to fight with one of the buttons. "Thank you." Johanna turned to him as he stroked the kitten's head. For the first time, she threw her arms around Sam's neck and hugged him.

Nine

He knew he shouldn't be nervous. It was an excellent production, with a quality script, top-notch casting and a talented director. He'd already seen the rushes, as well as a preview of the press screening. He knew he'd done a good job. But still he paced and watched the clock and wished like hell it was nine.

No, he wished it was eleven and the damn thing was over.

It was worse because Johanna was engrossed in the script Max Heddison had sent him. So Sam was left to worry, nurse the brandy he had no desire for and pace her living room. Even the redheaded kitten, which Johanna had christened Lucy, was too busy to bother with him. She was involved with wrestling a ball of yarn under Johanna's feet.

Sam made himself sit, poked at the Sunday paper, then was up again.

"You could take a walk outside for a change of scenery," Johanna suggested from across the room.

"She speaks! Johanna, why don't we go for a ride?"

"I have to finish this. Sam, Michael's a wonderful part for you, a really wonderful part."

He'd already decided that, but it was Luke, the character who would be exposed to millions of eyes in a matter of thirty minutes, who worried him. If he took on Michael, that would be another worry at another time. "Yeah. Johanna, it's lousy for your eyes to hold papers that close."

She moved them back automatically. In less than a minute she had her nose against them again. "This is wonderful, really wonderful. You're going to take it, aren't you?"

"For a chance to work with Max Heddison, I'd take it if it was garbage."

"Then you're lucky it shines. God, this scene here, the one on Christmas Eve, just leaves you limp."

He stopped pacing long enough to glance at her again. She was rereading it as avidly as she'd read it the first time. And the papers were an inch from her face.

"You keep that up, you're going to need glasses." He saw the frown come and go and was distracted enough to smile. "Unless you already do."

Without bothering to glance up, she turned a page. "Shut up, Sam, you're breaking my concentration."

Instead, he pulled the script away and held it at a reasonable distance. "Read me some dialogue."

"You already know what it says." She made a grab for the script, but he inched it away.

"You can't, can you? Where are your glasses, Johanna?"

"I don't need glasses."

"Then read me some dialogue."

She squinted, but the words ran together. "My eyes are just tired."

"Like hell." He set the script down to take her hands. "Don't tell me my sensible Johanna's too vain to wear reading glasses."

"I'm not vain, and I don't need glasses."

"You'd look cute in them." When she pulled her hands away, he made two circles out of his index fingers and thumbs and held them over her eyes. "Studiously sexy. Dark frames—yes, that would be best. Very conservative. I'd love to take you to bed while you were wearing them."

"I never wear them."

"Ah, but you do have them. Where?"

She made a grab for the script, but he blocked her. "You're just trying to distract yourself."

"You're right. Johanna, I'm dying in here."

She softened enough to touch his face. It was something she still did rarely. Automatically he lifted his hand to her wrist and held it there. "The reviews couldn't have been better, Sam. America waits for nine o'clock with bated breath."

"And America might be snoring by nine-fifteen."

"Not a chance." Reaching over, she picked up the remote to

turn on the set. "Sit down. We'll watch something else until it starts."

He eased into the chair with her, shifting her until she stretched across his lap. "I'd rather nibble on your ear until it starts."

"Then we'll miss the first scene." Content, she rested her head against his shoulder.

It had been an odd weekend, she thought. He'd stayed with her. After her first unease, they'd fallen into a simple routine that was no routine at all. Lovemaking, sleep, walks, the little chores a house required, even a trip to the market to fuss over fresh vegetables.

She hadn't felt like a producer for forty-eight hours, nor had she thought of Sam as an actor. Or a celebrity. He'd been her lover—or, as he had once put it, her companion. How lovely life would be if it could be that simple. It had been difficult, even for these short two days, to pretend it could be. It had been much less difficult to wish.

She'd changed his life. He didn't know how to explain it, or how to put it into words she might understand, but change it she had. He'd known that for certain when he'd gotten the script.

Max Heddison had been as good as his word. Sam had felt like a first-year drama student being offered the lead in a summer-stock production. It had come through Marv, of course, along with Marv's opinion about potential, the old school and the new, a million five plus percentages. Sam had taken it all in. It was never wise to forget that show business remained a business. Then he had devoured the script.

There was a part of him, a part he hoped would always be there, that could break out in a sweat at the chance to take on a new role. The character of Michael was complex, confused, desperately trying to unravel the mystery of his much-loved, much-detested father. He could already see Max Heddison in that role. Slowly, trying to see the script as a whole, as well as a vehicle, he'd read it again.

And he'd known he wanted to do it. Had to do it.

If Marv could get a million five, fine and dandy. If he could get peanuts and a keg of beer, that was all right, too. But rather than picking up the phone and calling his agent with a go-ahead, he'd bundled up the script and taken it to Johanna.

He'd needed her to read it. He'd needed her opinion, though throughout his career he'd always gone on his own gut instinct. Agent or not, the final decision had always been his. Now that had changed.

In a matter of weeks she'd become entwined with his life, his thoughts, his motives. Though he'd never thought of himself as a solitary person, he'd stopped being alone. She was there now, to share with—the big things, like the script, and the small things, like a new litter of kittens. It might have been true that she still held back from him, but in the last two days he'd seen her relax. Degree by degree, certainly, but he'd been able to see the change. That morning she'd seemed almost used to waking beside him.

He was giving her time, Sam thought as he brushed his lips over her hair. But he was also making his moves.

"Here come the teasers," Johanna murmured, and he was jerked back to the present. His stomach clenched. He swore at himself, but it tightened anyway, as it did whenever he prepared to watch himself on-screen. He flashed on, wearing only faded jeans, a battered panama and a grin, while the voice-over promised the sultry and the shocking.

"It is a nice chest." She smiled and kissed him on the cheek.

"They spent half the time spraying it so it'd have that nice jungle-fatigue shine. Do women really pant over a sweaty chest?"

"You bet," she told him, and settled down to watch the opening credits.

She was drawn in before the first five minutes were over. Luke drifted into town with two dollars in his pocket, a reputation on his back and an eye for the ladies. She knew it was Sam, pulling bits and pieces of his art together to meld with the writer's, but it rang true. You could almost smell the sweat and boredom of the sleepy little town in Georgia.

During the first commercial he slid down to the floor to give her the chair. He didn't want to ask her now, didn't want to break the rhythm. But he rested a hand on her calf.

For two hours they said nothing. She rose once and came back with cold drinks, but they didn't exchange words. On screen she watched the man she'd slept with, the man she'd loved, seduce another woman. She watched him talk himself out of one fight and raise his fists for another. He got drunk. He bled. He lied.

But she'd stopped thinking of him as Sam. The man she watched was Luke. She felt the slight pressure of Sam's fingers against her leg and kept her eyes on Luke.

He was irresistible. He was unforgivable.

When the segment ended, it left her hanging and Sarah's roses dying in the bowl.

Sam still said nothing. His instincts told him it was good. It was better than good. It was the best he'd ever done. Everything had fallen into place—the performances, the atmosphere, those lazy two-edged words that had first caught his imagination and his ambition. But he wanted to hear it from her.

Rising, he shifted to sit on the arm of her chair. Johanna, his Johanna, was still frowning at the screen. "How could he do that to her?" she demanded. "How could he use her that way?"

Sam waited a moment, still careful. "He's a user. It's all he knows."

"But she trusts him. She knows he's lied and cheated, but she still trusts him. And he's—"

"What?"

"He's a bastard, but— Damn, there's something compelling about him, something likable. You want to believe he could change, that she could change him." Unsettled, moved, she looked up at him. "What are you grinning at?"

"It worked." He hauled her up and kissed her. "It worked, Johanna."

She backed up enough to breathe. "I didn't tell you how good I thought you were."

"You just did." He kissed her again, then began tugging up her shirt.

"Sam—"

"I suddenly find myself with all this energy—incredible energy. Let me show you." He slid back into the chair, taking her with him.

"Wait a minute." She laughed, then moaned when his hands began to wander. "Sam, give me a minute."

"I've got hours for you. Hours and hours."

"Sam." With one laughing shove, she held him off. "I want to talk to you."

"Is it going to take long?" He tugged at the waistband of her slacks.

"No." To stop him, she framed his face with her hands. "I want to tell you how really exceptional you were. I pretended once that I didn't pay attention to your films, but I have. And you were never better than tonight."

"Thanks. It means a lot coming from you."

She took a deep breath, managing to push herself out of the chair. "You put a lot into that part."

She was leading somewhere. Though he wasn't sure he'd like the destination, he let her take the lead. "A part's not worth anything unless you do. Nothing is."

No, nothing was. "I, ah…I almost forget, when we're like this, who you are. These past few weeks, here, at the ranch, it hasn't been like being with Sam Weaver in capital letters."

Puzzled, he rose with her. "Johanna, you're not going to try to tell me you're intimidated by actors? You've been around the business all your life."

"All my life," she murmured. She didn't want to love him. She didn't want to love anyone, but most particularly not an actor, a movie star, a household name. The trouble was, she already did. "It's not a matter of being intimidated, it's just that it's been easy to forget you're not just an ordinary man who I ran into and grew fond of."

"Fond of," he repeated, drawing out the phrase. "Well, we're improving." He had her by the shoulders. That lazy drawl of a voice could fool you into forgetting how quick he was. "I don't know what the hell this is about, but we'll get to it in a minute. Right now, I want you to look at me. Really look at me, Johanna," he repeated, adding a little shake. "And tell me if you're in love with me."

"I never said—"

"No one knows better than I what you've never said." He drew her a little closer, insisting that her eyes stay on his. "I want to hear it now, and it has nothing to do with how I make my living, what the critics say or how much I'm worth at the box office. Do you love me?''

She started to shake her head but simply couldn't force it to move. How could she lie when he was looking at her, when he was touching her? She drew a deep breath to be certain her voice was calm. ''Yes.''

He wanted to take her then, just gather her close and hold on. But he knew that not only did he have to hear the words, she had to say them. ''Yes, what?''

''Yes, I love you.''

He looked at her for a long time. She was trembling a little, so he lowered his head and pressed his lips to her forehead. He didn't know why it was so difficult for her to say.

Not yet. But he was determined to find out.

''That should make things easier.''

''But it doesn't,'' she murmured. ''It doesn't change anything.''

''We'll talk about it. Let's sit down.''

She nodded. She didn't know what there was to say, but there had to be something. Trying to make it seem normal, she started to the front door to lock up for the night. Then she heard the quick report on the evening news.

''Sources report that Carl W. Patterson, respected producer, has suffered a heart attack this evening. Paramedics were summoned to his Beverly Hills estate, which he shares with his fiancée, Toni DuMonde. His condition at this hour remains critical.''

''Johanna.'' Sam laid a hand on her arm. She hadn't gasped or cried out. There were no tears in her eyes. She had simply stopped in her tracks as though she'd run into a wall. ''Get your purse. I'll take you to the hospital.''

''What?''

''I'll drive you.'' He switched off the set and went to get her bag himself. ''Come on.''

She only nodded and let him lead her out.

No one had called her. The oddness of it struck Sam as they rode the elevator up to Cardiac Care. Her father had had a heart attack, and she hadn't been notified.

The year before, when his mother had broken her ankle in a

nasty fall on the ice, he'd received three calls in a matter of hours. One from his sister, another from his father and the last from his mother, telling him that his sister and father were fussbudgets.

Nonetheless the ankle had worried him enough to have him do some quick scheduling adjustments so that he could make the trip back east. He'd only had thirty-six hours to spare, but it had been time enough to see his mother for himself, sign her cast and put his mind at rest.

And a broken ankle was a far cry from a heart attack.

Johanna was Patterson's only child, yet she'd had to hear about her father's illness on the eleven-o'clock news. Even if they weren't close, as he'd already deduced, they were family. In Sam's experience, families stuck together in times of crisis.

She'd barely said a word since they'd left the house. He'd tried to comfort her, to offer both hope and support, but she hadn't responded. It seemed to him that she was just going through the motions, pale, a little dazed, but with the automatic control that had slipped effortlessly back into place. He watched her approach the nurse's station. Her hands were steady, her voice was calm and unwavering when she spoke.

"Carl Patterson was admitted this evening. They told me downstairs he's in CCU."

The nurse—sturdy, mid-forties and used to the night shift—barely glanced up. "I'm sorry, we're not permitted to give out patient information."

"He's my father," Johanna said flatly.

The nurse looked up. Reporters and the curious used all kinds of ploys to glean information on the famous. She'd already discouraged a few of them that evening. The woman on the other side of the counter didn't look like a reporter—the nurse prided herself on having a nose for them—but she hadn't been told to expect family, either. Recognizing doubt, Johanna drew out her wallet and identification.

"I'd like to see him, if that's possible, and speak with his doctor."

The nurse felt a stirring of sympathy. Her gaze shifted and locked on Sam. She recognized him, and though seeing him face-to-face would give her something to tell her husband when they passed over the breakfast table, she wasn't overly impressed. After twenty years of nursing in Beverly Hills she was accustomed to seeing celebrities, often naked, sick and vulnerable. But she did remember reading that Sam Weaver was having a fling with Carl Patterson's daughter.

"I'll be happy to page the doctor for you, Miss Patterson. There's a waiting room down the hall and to the left. Miss Dumonde is already there."

"Thank you." She turned and started down, refusing to think past the moment, refusing to think past the action required to get beyond that moment. She heard a bell ding quietly, almost secretively, then the soft slap of crepe-soled shoes.

The panic was gone, that first thunder of panic that had filled her head when she'd heard the news report. Replacing it was the knowledge that she had to put one foot in front of the other and do whatever needed to be done. She was used to doing such things alone.

"Sam, I have no idea how long this might take. Why don't you go home? I can take a cab back when I'm ready."

"Don't be ridiculous," was all he said.

It was enough, more than enough to cause her breath to hitch. She wanted to turn to him, to press her face against his chest. She wanted to be held, to be passive, to let him handle whatever had to be done. Instead, she turned into the waiting room.

"Sam!" Toni's eyes, already damp, spilled over. She sprang out of her chair and launched herself into his arms. "Oh, Sam, I'm so glad you're here. I've been so frightened. It's a nightmare. I'm just sick with worry, Sam. I don't know what I'll do if Carl dies."

"Pull yourself together." Sam led her back to a chair, then lit one of the cigarettes she'd spilled from a pack onto the table. He stuck it between her fingers. "What did the doctor say?"

"I don't know. He was so technical and grim faced." She held out a hand to a blond man in a dinner jacket. "I never would have survived this without Jack. He's been a wall, an absolute wall. Hello, Johanna." She sniffled into a lacy handkerchief.

"Sam." Jack Vandear nodded as he patted Toni's hand. He'd directed two of Patterson's productions and had run into Sam at least a half-dozen times on the party circuit. "It's been a rough night."

"So we heard. This is Patterson's daughter."

"Oh." Jack rose and offered a hand.

"I'd like to know what happened."

"It was horrible." Toni looked up at Johanna through an attractive veil of tears. "Just horrible."

Jack sent her a look that was three parts impatient, one part sympathetic. He hadn't minded comforting her, but the truth was, he'd come for Carl. It went through his mind that with Sam here, the soggy-eyed Toni could be passed along.

"We were having a small dinner party. Carl looked a bit tired, but I took it to mean he'd been working too hard, as usual. Then it seemed he couldn't get his breath. He collapsed into a chair. He complained of pain in his chest and his arm. We called the paramedics." He started to skim over the rest, then decided Johanna looked strong enough to handle it. "They had to bring him back once." At that Toni put up a low, heartbreaking sob and was ignored. "The doctor said it was a massive coronary. They've been working to stabilize him."

Her legs were shaking. She could keep her hands steady and her face impassive, but she couldn't stop her legs from trembling. Massive coronary. Darlene, her father's wry and witty third wife, would have said that Carl W. Patterson never did anything halfway.

"Did they tell you his chances?"

"They haven't told us much of anything."

"We've been waiting forever." Toni dabbed at her eyes again, then drew on her cigarette. In her own way, she was fond of Carl. She wanted to marry him even though she knew that divorce would be at the end of the rainbow. Divorce was easy. Death was another matter. "The press was here five minutes after we were. I knew how much Carl would hate having them report this."

Johanna sat and for the first time looked, really looked, at her father's fiancée. Whatever she was, the woman obviously knew Carl. The heart attack was a weakness, and he would detest having it made public knowledge. "I'll handle the press," she said tonelessly. "It might be best if you, both of you," she said, including Jack, "told them as little as possible. Have you seen him?"

"Not since they took him in." Toni took another drag as she looked out into the corridor. "I hate hospitals." After crushing out the cigarette, she began to pleat the handkerchief. The silver sequins on her evening dress sparkled opulently in the dim waiting room. "We were supposed to go to Monaco next week. Carl had some business there, but for the most part it was to be a kind of prehoneymoon. He seemed so...well, so virile." The tears started again when the doctor came into the waiting room.

"Miss DuMonde."

She was up and clutching at both his hands, the picture of the distressed lover barely holding back hysteria. It surprised her to discover it was only half an act. "He's all right. Tell me Carl's all right."

"His condition's stabilized. We're running tests to determine the extent of the damage. He's a strong man, Miss DuMonde, and overall his health seems excellent."

He looked tired, Johanna thought as she studied the doctor. Unbearably tired, but she recognized the truth. She rose as he glanced her way.

"You're Mr. Patterson's daughter?"

"I'm Johanna Patterson. How serious is his condition?"

"I have to tell you it's very serious. However, he's getting the best care possible."

"I'd like to see him."

"For a few moments. Miss DuMonde?"

"He wouldn't want me to see him this way. He'd hate it."

Because Johanna could only agree, she ignored the little stab of resentment and followed the doctor out. "He's sedated," she was told. "And he's being monitored very closely. The next twenty-four hours will tell the tale, but your father's relatively young, Miss Patterson. An incident like this is often a warning, to slow down, to take a hard look at your own mortality."

It had to be said, just once out loud, though she knew she would get no absolutes. "Is he going to die?"

"Not if we can help it." The doctor pushed open a glass door. There was her father. She'd lived in his house, eaten his food, obeyed his rules. And she barely knew him. The machines that eased his breathing and monitored his vital signs hummed. His eyes were shut, his face pasty under his tan. He looked old. It occurred to her that she'd never thought of him as old, even when she'd been a child. He'd always been handsome, ageless, virile.

She remembered Toni using that word. Virile. That was so important to Carl. He'd often been described as a man's man—salty tongued, strong shouldered, reckless with women. He'd always been impatient with weaknesses, excuses, illnesses. Perhaps that was why, when he'd reached the middle of his life, the women he'd brought into it had become younger and younger.

He was a hard man, even a cold one, but he'd always been full of life. There was a genius in him, a genius she'd admired as much as she'd feared it. He was an honest man, a man of his word, but never one to give an inch more than he chose.

She touched him once, just a hand over his. It was a gesture she would never have considered making had he been awake.

"Will it happen again?"

"He has an excellent chance of full recovery, if he throws away the cigars, watches his alcohol intake and cuts back on his schedule. There's his diet, of course," the doctor went on, but Johanna was already shaking her head.

"I can't imagine him doing any of those things."

"People often do what others can't imagine after they end up in CCU. It'll be his choice, of course, but he's not a stupid man."

"No, he's not." She removed her hand. "We'll need a press release. I can take care of that. When will he be awake?"

"You should be able to talk to him in the morning."

"I'd appreciate a call if there's any change before then. I'll leave my number at the nurse's station."

"I should be able to tell you more in the morning." The doctor pushed open the door again. "You'd do well to get some rest yourself. A recovering cardiac patient can be wearing."

"Thank you." Alone, she started back down the hall. In self-defense, she blocked out the image of her father in the hospital bed. The moment she walked back in, Toni was up and grabbing both her hands.

"How is he, Johanna? Tell me the truth, tell me everything."

"He's resting. The doctor's very optimistic."

"Thank God."

"Carl will have to make some adjustments—diet, work load, that sort of thing. You'll be able to see him tomorrow."

"Oh, I must look a wreck." The need to check was so ingrained that Toni was already reaching for her compact. "I'll have to take care of that by tomorrow. I wouldn't want him to see me with my eyes all red and my hair a fright."

Again, because it was true, Johanna held back her sarcasm. "He won't wake up until tomorrow, according to the doctor. I'm going to handle the press—through a hospital spokesman, I think—and make certain his publicist has time to work up a statement. It might be a day or two before he's able to make those decisions for himself."

She wavered there a moment, trying to imagine her father unable to make any decision. "The important thing for you to do is to keep him calm. Go home and get some rest. They'll call if there's any change before morning."

"How about you?" Sam asked her when Jack had taken Toni down the corridor. "Are you all right?"

"Yes, I'm fine."

Wanting to judge for himself, he took her chin in his hand. There was something about the eyes, he thought. More than shock, certainly different than grief. Big secrets, he decided. Big fears. "Talk to me, Johanna."

"I've told you everything."

"About your father's condition." Though she tried to draw away, he held on. "I want to know about yours."

"I'm a little tired. I'd like to go home."

"Okay." Better, he thought, that they hash this, whatever it was, out at home. "We'll go back. But I'm staying with you."

"Sam, there's no need."

"There's every need. Let's go home."

Ten

It was after one a.m. when they arrived at Johanna's house, but she went straight to the phone. With a pen in one hand, she began to flip through her address book. "It shouldn't take long for me to set this up," she told Sam, "but you don't have to wait up."

"I'll wait." There were things that had to be said, and he wanted them said before she had a chance to build the barricades again. Though she looked steady, perhaps too steady, he was coming to understand her. Still, he left her alone as she began to dial.

There was little enough she could do. She was certain her father would tolerate only the slightest interference from her, but he would want his people informed. Johanna fed information to his publicist, then hashed out a simple, straightforward press release.

While she was calming her father's assistant and making sure that the daily business of Patterson Productions would run as smoothly as possible, Sam handed her a mug. Grateful, Johanna sipped, expecting coffee. Instead she tasted the soothing herbal tea she'd bought on impulse and brewed occasionally after a particularly long day.

"I'll be able to tell you more tomorrow, Whitfield. No, whatever can't be handled by you or another member of the staff will have to be canceled. That would appear to be your problem, wouldn't it?"

Across the room, Sam had no choice but to smile at her tone. As producers went, he'd never heard better.

"Where's Loman? Well, call him back." She made a quick notation on a pad. "Yes, that's right, but I'm sure he'll be giving you instructions himself in a couple of days. You'll have to check with the doctor on that, but I don't think you'll be able to discuss that or anything else with Carl for at least forty-eight hours." Her voice changed, went frigid. "That's not really the issue here,

Whitfield. You'll have to consider Carl unavailable until further notice. No, I won't take the responsibility, you will. That's what you're paid for.''

She hung up, incensed by the man's insensitivity. "Idiot," she muttered as she picked up her tea again. "His main concern is that Carl insisted on supervising the editing of *Fields of Fire*, and the heart attack is going to put the project behind schedule.''

"Are you finished?"

Still frowning, she skimmed down her notes. "I don't think there's any more I can do.''

"Come and sit down.'' He waited until she'd joined him on the sofa, then poured more tea into her cup from the pot he'd brewed. Sensing tension even before he touched her, Sam began to massage her shoulders. "It's hard, only being able to wait.''

"Yes.''

"You handle yourself well, Johanna.''

She sipped tea and stared straight ahead. "I had a good teacher.''

"Tell me about your father.''

"I told you everything the doctor told me.''

"I don't mean that.'' She was tensing up again, even as he massaged the muscles. "Tell me about him, about you and him.''

"There's really nothing to tell. We've never been particularly close.''

"Because of your mother?''

She went stiff at that. "What does my mother have to do with it?''

"I don't know. You tell me.'' He'd been shooting in the dark, but he wasn't surprised that he'd hit the target. "Johanna, you don't have to be a gossip buff to know that your parents divorced when you were, what—four?''

"I'd just turned five.'' It still hurt. No matter how often she told herself it was foolish, even unhealthy, the child's pain and confusion leaked into the woman. "That's history, Sam.''

He didn't think so. Instinct told him it was as much a part of the present as he was. "She went back to England,'' he prompted. "And your father retained custody of you.''

"He didn't have much choice." The bitterness leaked out. She made a conscientious and difficult effort to bury it again. "It really isn't relevant."

"I'm not Whitfield, Johanna," he murmured. "Humor me."

She was silent for so long he decided to try another tactic. Then she sighed and began. "My mother went back to England to try to pick up the stage career she felt she'd sacrificed when she'd married. I didn't have a place there."

"You must have missed her."

"I got over it."

He didn't think so. "I don't suppose divorce is ever easy on a kid, but it's got to be worse when one of the parents ends up several thousand miles away."

"It was better that way, for everyone. They always fought terribly. Neither of them were happy with their marriage or..." She trailed off before she could say what was in her mind. *Me. Neither of them wanted me.* "With the situation," she finished.

"You'd have been pretty young to have known that." He'd begun to get a picture of five-year-old Johanna, dealing with the inexplicable ups and downs of a rocky marriage.

"You don't have to be very old to recognize turmoil. In any case, my mother explained it to me. She sent me a telegram from the airport." Her tea had gone cold, but she sipped automatically.

A telegram's just like a letter, the pretty young maid had told Johanna. If the maid hadn't been new, the telegram would have been handed over to Carl and disposed of. But the maid had been avid to know the contents, and more than willing to help Johanna struggle over the words.

My darling girl. I'm devastated to leave you like this, but I have no choice. My situation, my life, has become desperate. Believe me, I have tried, but I've come to understand that divorce and a complete separation from what was, is the only way I can survive. I despise myself for leaving you in your father's hands, but for now mine are too frail to hold on to you. One day you'll understand and forgive. Love. Mother.

She remembered it still, word for word, though at the time all she had understood was that her mother was leaving her because she wasn't happy.

Sam was staring at her, amazed that she could be so matter-of-fact. "She sent you a telegram?"

"Yes. I wasn't old enough to fully understand, but I caught the drift. She was miserably unhappy and desperate to find a way out."

Bitch. The word rose up in his throat, hotly, and he had to swallow it. He couldn't imagine anyone being so self-absorbed and selfish as to say goodbye to her only child by telegram. He tried to remember that Johanna had told him how her mother had taken her to feed the ducks, but he couldn't equate the two acts with the same woman.

"It must have been rough on you." He put his arm around her, as if he could find a way to protect her from what had already happened.

"Children are resilient." She rose, knowing that if he offered comfort she would break. She hadn't broken in over twenty years. "She did what she had to do, but I don't think she was ever happy. She died about ten years ago."

Suicide. He swore at himself for not remembering it before. Glenna Howard, Johanna's unhappy mother, had never quite achieved the sparkling comeback she'd sought. Disappointment had been eased by pills and alcohol until she'd taken a deliberate overdose of both.

"I'm sorry, Johanna. Losing her twice. It must have been hell for you."

"I never knew her that well." She reached for her tea again, for something to keep her hands busy. "And it was a long time ago."

He went to her, though she turned away. Patient but determined, he drew her back. "I don't think things like that ever stop hurting. Don't back off from me, Johanna."

"There's no use dredging all this up."

"I think there is." He took her shoulders, firmly enough to let her know he wasn't easing off. "I've wondered all along why you held off. I thought at first it was because you'd had a bad experience with another man. But it goes back farther than that, and deeper.''

She looked at him then, her face set but her eyes desperate. She'd said too much, more than she'd ever said before. In saying it, the memories became all too clear. ''I'm not my mother.''

''No.'' He lifted a hand to brush at her hair. ''No, you're not. And you're not your father either.''

''I don't even know if he *is* my father.''

The moment it was said, she went white. The hands she had fisted unballed and went limp. Not once in all of her life had she said it out loud. The knowledge had been there, locked tight but never completely silent. Now she heard her words echo back to her and was afraid, terribly afraid, she'd be ill.

''Johanna, what are you talking about?''

His voice was calm and quiet, but it shot like a bullet through her shock. ''Nothing, nothing. I'm upset. I'm tired. Tomorrow's going to be a difficult day, Sam. I need to sleep.''

''We both know you're too wired to sleep.'' He could feel the violent shudders begin as he held her there. ''And you will be until you get the rest of it out. Tell me about your father, Johanna. About Carl.''

''Will you leave me alone?'' There were tears in her voice that only frightened her more. She could feel the walls cracking, the foundation giving way, but didn't have the strength to shore it up again. ''For God's sake, can't you see I've had all I can manage? I don't want to talk about my mother. I don't want to talk about him. He could be dying.'' The tears spilled out, and she knew she'd lost. ''He could be dying, and I should feel something. But I don't. I don't even know who he is. I don't know who I am.''

She fought him, pushing away as he gathered her to him, swearing at him as he held her there. Then she collapsed in a storm of weeping.

He didn't offer comforting words. He hadn't a clue which ones to choose. Instead, he lifted her into his arms. With her sobs muffled against his throat, he sat down, cradling her to him. Sam stroked her hair and let her purge herself. He hadn't known it was possible to hold that many tears inside.

She felt ill. Her throat and eyes burned, her stomach heaved.

Even when the tears were over, the raw, sick feeling remained. Her strength had been sapped, as if someone had pulled a plug and let it drain away. She didn't object when Sam shifted her, nor when he rose. He was going away. It was something she accepted even as her own battered heart suffered another crack.

Then he was sitting beside her again, placing a snifter in her hands. "It might help some," he murmured. "Take it slow."

If there'd been any left, more tears would have fallen. She nodded, took a sip of brandy and let it coat the raw wounds.

"I was always in awe of him," Johanna began without looking up. "I don't know even now if I loved him as a child, but he was always the largest and most important figure in my life. After my mother left—" she paused to sip again "—after my mother left I was terrified that he'd leave, too, or send me away. I didn't understand then how important it was to him to keep his private affairs private. The public could accept and be entertained by his romances and marriages, but if he'd shipped off his only child without a blink, they'd have taken a different view. No one forgot that he'd been married to Glenna Howard and that she'd had his child. No one except him."

How could she explain how lost she had been? How confusing it had been to see her father entertain other women as though her mother had never existed.

"When he married again it was horrible. There was a big, splashy wedding, lots of photographers, microphones, strangers. They dressed me up and told me to smile. I hated it—the stares and innuendos about my mother. The whispers about her. He could ignore it. He'd always had that kind of presence, but all I could think was that my mother was being replaced with someone I didn't even know. And I had to smile."

Insensitive, selfish idiots. Even as he thought it, he tightened his arms around her. "Wasn't there anyone else...any family?"

"His parents had died years before. I remember hearing or being told somewhere along the line that he'd been raised by his grandmother. By that time she was gone, too. I'd never met her. I had what you'd call a governess, who would have literally died for my father. Women react that way to him," she said wearily. "Nothing could have stopped it—my being in the wedding was important. Impressions, photo opportunities, that kind of thing. After it was over, I didn't see him again for three months. He was spending a lot of time in Italy.''

''You stayed behind.''

''I was in school.'' She pulled a hand through her hair, then clasped them in her lap. ''It was perfectly legitimate for him to leave me behind with my tutors and instructors. In any case, his second wife had little tolerance for children. Few of his liaisons did.''

Because she could feel his sympathy reaching out to her, she shook her head. ''I was happier here. I spent a lot of time with the Heddisons. They were wonderful to me.''

''I'm glad for that.'' He drew her hand into his. ''Go on.''

''It was after his second divorce, when he was involved with…it doesn't matter who. Anyway, I was out of school and feeling sorry for myself. I went up to his room. I don't even know why, except to be there, to see if I could solve the mystery of my father. I solved it.

''I'd always felt inadequate, awkward around him. There seemed to be something lacking in me that kept him from loving me the way that he should. He had this wonderful old desk in his room, one with all these fascinating cubbyholes and compartments. He was away again, so I didn't have to worry about him catching me poking around. I found letters. Some of them were from his women, and I was old enough to be embarrassed, so I put them away again. Then I found one from my mother. An old one, one she'd written right after she'd gone back to England. Holding it was like seeing her again. Sometimes I hadn't been able to bring the picture of her into my head, but the minute I had that letter, I saw her exactly as she'd been. God, she was beautiful, so fragile and haunted. I could even hear her voice, that trained, extraordinary voice. I'd loved her so much.''

He took the snifter from her and set it on the table. ''You read the letter?''

''I wish to God I hadn't.'' She squeezed her eyes shut for a moment, but it was now, as it had been then, too late to turn back. ''I was so hungry for anything she'd touched, any part of her, that I didn't even realize at first when I was reading. She must have been furious when she wrote it. It came across, the anger, the bitterness, the need to punish. I'd known, even as a child, that their marriage hadn't been smooth. But until I'd read the letter I'd had no idea how much hate had been built up between them.''

"People say things they don't mean, or at least things that shouldn't be said under those kind of circumstances.''

"Well, she's gone, has been gone, and there's no way of knowing if she meant what she'd said. No way for me to know, no way for my father—for Carl to know.''

Her mouth was dry, but she no longer wanted the brandy. Johanna pressed her lips together and continued. "She brought up every hurt, every broken promise, every real or imagined infidelity. Then she brought out the big guns. Leaving me with him was the biggest payback she could think of. She was saddling him with a child who wasn't even his own. Not that he could ever prove it, or that she would ever tell him who had fathered the child he'd given a name to. There was, of course, the possibility that the child was his, but... She wished him a lifetime of hell wondering. And because I read the letter, she gave me the same.''

Sam stared out the darkened window for a long time. The rage was so keen, so close to the surface, he was afraid to speak. She'd been a child, innocent, helpless. And no one had given a damn.

"Did you ever speak to him about it?''

"No, there was no reason to. He didn't change toward me. I was well tended, well educated and allowed to pursue my own interests as long as I didn't embarrass him.''

"They didn't deserve you. Either of them.''

"It doesn't matter,'' she said wearily. "I'm not a child anymore.'' Nor had she been from the moment she'd read the letter.

"It matters to me.'' He cupped her face in his hands. "You matter to me, Johanna.''

"I never meant to tell you, or anyone. But now that I have, you must understand why I can't let what's between us go too far.''

"No.''

"Sam—''

"What I understand is that you had a lousy childhood, and that things went on around you that no kid should ever be a part of. And I understand that there're bound to be scars.''

"Scars?" She gave a quick, brittle laugh as she rose. "Don't you see, my mother was ill. Oh, it was kept quiet, out of the press, but I managed to dig it up. She was in and out of sanitariums the last few years of her life. Manic depression, instability, alcohol addiction. And the drugs..." Johanna pressed her fingers to her eyes and struggled to get a grip on herself. "She didn't raise me, and I can't be sure who my father is, but she was my mother. I can't forget that, or what I may have inherited from her."

He rose slowly. His first instinct was to tread carefully, but then he realized it was the wrong one. She needed to be brought up short, and quickly. "It's not like you to be melodramatic, Johanna."

His words had exactly the effect he'd hoped for. Anger flashed into her eyes and whipped color back into her cheeks. "How dare you say that to me?"

"How dare you stand there and make up insufficient excuses why you can't commit to me?"

"They're not excuses, they're facts."

"I don't give a damn who your mother was, or your father. I'm in love with you, Johanna. Sooner or later you're going to have to swallow it and take the next step."

"I've told you all along that it couldn't lead anywhere. Now I'm telling you why. And that's only half of it. My half."

"There's more?" He hooked his thumbs in his pockets and rocked back on his heels. "Okay, give me the rest."

"You're an actor."

"Right the first time, but you're not going to set any bells ringing with that answer."

"I've been around actors all of my life," she continued, searching for patience. "I understand the strain and demands of the job, the impossibility, especially for a talented actor, of maintaining a private life that keeps anything truly private. And I know that even with the best of intentions and effort relationships suffer. If I believed in marriage—which I don't—I still wouldn't believe in marriage to an actor."

"I see." It was difficult enough not to be angry with her, and it was impossible not to be furious with the people who had had the major hand in forming her beliefs. "Then you're saying that because I'm an actor—worse yet, a good one—I'm too big a risk.''

''I'm saying that what there is between us can't go any farther.'' She stopped, wanting to be strong. ''And that if you don't want to see me again, I'll understand.''

''Will you?'' For a moment he studied her, as though he were considering it. A few steps away, Johanna prepared herself. She'd known it would hurt when it ended, but even her worst fears hadn't come close to this. When he crossed to her, she made herself look in his eyes. She could read nothing in them.

''You're an idiot, Johanna.'' He yanked her against him so hard that her breath whistled out in surprise. ''Do you think I can turn my feelings for you on and off? Damn it, you do, don't you? I can see it in your face. Well, I'm not going to step neatly out of your life, and if you think you can push me out, you're going to be disappointed.''

''I don't want you to go.'' Tears clouded her eyes, though she'd thought she was through with them. ''I just don't think—''

''Then don't think.'' He swept her up into his arms. ''You do too much thinking.''

She didn't protest when he carried her upstairs. She was through with arguing, with excuses, with reasons. Perhaps it was a weakness to want to be taken care of, but she couldn't find the strength to stand on her own tonight. She didn't want to think. He was right about that. She didn't want to think at all for whatever hours of the night were left. For once, feelings took no effort and she could let them dominate.

She needed him. If she hadn't been so drained it would have frightened her to realize it.

The bedroom was dark, but he didn't turn on the light. The fragrances from her garden were carried up and through the windows on the night air. In silence he lay her on the bed and sat beside her.

There was too much to say to speak at all just yet. He'd once thought her cool, tough and self-sufficient. That woman had attracted and intrigued him. Intrigued him enough, Sam thought, to have caused him to dig deeper. The more he knew about her, the more layers he'd discovered.

She was tough, in the best sense of the word. She'd taken the blows, the disappointments, and had worked her way through them. Some people, he knew, would have buckled under, found a crutch or given up. But Johanna, his Johanna, had carved a place for herself and had made it work.

Underneath the toughness he'd found passion. He'd sensed and now was certain that it had gone untapped. Whether it was fate, blind luck or timing, he'd found the key that had released it. He wouldn't allow it to be locked again, or to be opened by anyone but himself.

Beneath the passion was a touching shyness. A sweetness that was a miracle in itself, considering her childhood and the disillusionments she'd faced so early in life.

Now, beneath all the rest, he'd found a core of fragility. He was determined to protect that vulnerability. And it was to the fragile Johanna that he would make love tonight.

In kindness as much as love. In compassion, as well as desire.

Softly, his touch barely a whisper, he brushed her hair away from her face. There were tears still drying on her cheeks. With his fingertips, he wiped them away. He wouldn't be able to prevent more from being shed, but he would do whatever he could to see that she didn't shed them alone.

He kissed her once, then twice, where the tears had lain. Then he kissed her again, tenderly. Night shadows shifted across her face, but he could see her eyes, half closed with fatigue but very aware, as she watched him.

"Do you want to sleep?" he asked her.

"No." She put her hand over his. "No, I don't want to sleep. And I don't want you to go."

"Then relax." He brought her hand to his lips. His eyes, so dark and intense, seemed to absorb everything she was. "And let me love you."

It was just that easy.

She hadn't known love could be soothing. He hadn't shown her that before. Tonight, when her emotions were raw and her self-esteem at its lowest ebb, he showed her another side of desire. A desire to please, and one to nurture. A desire to have, and one to heal. He touched her as though she alone mattered.

He drew off her shirt so that the material trailed over her skin before it was discarded, but he didn't take what she would have given. With his eyes on hers, he removed his own. When she reached for him, he took her hands, pressing them both to his lips.

He undressed her slowly, carefully, as though she were asleep and he didn't want to disturb her. The tenderness of it brought its own strange ache. Though she was naked and totally open to him, he contented himself with long, lazy kisses and the feel of her hair under his hands.

Her skin looked so white against the dark spread. He ran his hand down her arm, watching the movement. The moon had waned to a thin crescent, shedding little light, but he already knew her so well. Still, he traced her face with his fingertip, outlining her features for his own pleasure.

He'd never treated her like this before. Johanna closed her eyes as she began to drift into contentment. Even through passion and hunger, he'd always shown her an unexpected sweetness. But this...this was what it meant to be cherished. This was the way promises were given when they were meant to be kept. It made her eyes swim and her heart break, just a little, at the beauty of it.

He felt stronger somehow, being gentle. He'd never wanted her more than he did at this moment, and yet he had never felt less need to rush. The passion was there, and growing, but it was filled with a need to comfort.

Time passed unnoticed, unheeded. In the darkest hours of the morning, he led her gently higher.

The rhythm of her heart beat under his lips, fast, unsteady, but not yet desperate. Her arms were around him, holding him close, but there was no urgent press of fingers. She moved with him, willing to let him set the pace, grateful that he had understood, even if she hadn't, that she needed care.

Had she ever noticed how strong he was? How the muscles of his back and shoulders flexed and rippled with his movements? She'd touched him before, held him just like this, but each time she had she'd been driven close to the edge. Now the ride was quiet and unhurried, like floating on a raft on a still lake.

Inspired by love, she sought to give him the same gentleness he showed her. Her touch was easy, her demands few. She heard in the murmur of her name that he felt as she did. They might never come together so perfectly, so unselfishly, again.

Her sigh was quiet as she opened for him. They merged without heat but with much warmth.

Later, much later, she lay beside him, sleepless as the sky began to lighten.

Eleven

He could have strangled her. When Sam woke, he found himself alone in bed and the house empty. In the bath, her still-damp towel hung tidily over the rail. The room carried, very faintly, the scent of her. The clothes he'd removed from her the night before had been put away. Downstairs, he saw that her briefcase was gone and the flowers freshened. Her phone machine had been cleared of messages and reset.

In crisis or in control, Johanna was always organized.

He was sure he would strangle her.

In the kitchen he found the glasses they'd used the night before conscientiously rinsed and draining. Propped against the coffeepot was a note in Johanna's neat handwriting. *I didn't want to wake you. I needed to get to the hospital early, then to the studio. The coffee's fresh.*

She'd written something else, crossed it out, then signed the note simply *Johanna.*

His mother could have written it, Sam thought as he skimmed it a second time. Only she might have added, *Leave the kitchen the way you found it.* Damn it, Johanna.

He stood in the kitchen dressed only in jeans and tossed her note onto the counter. No one would ever accuse Johanna of not having her feet firmly on the ground. But there were times when it was better, even necessary, to keep them planted beside someone else's. She still needed to accept that he was that someone else. He'd been sure he'd gotten through, but he'd forgotten how incredibly stubborn she could be.

Absently he bent down and picked up the kitten, who was doing figure eights between his legs. She wasn't hungry. Johanna had left Lucy well taken care of, with a full dish in the corner. She only wanted some affection. Most creatures did, Sam mused as he stroked her fur. Apparently that wasn't enough to make Johanna purr and settle trustingly in his arms.

It looked as if he still had a fight on his hands. Sam gave the kitten's ears a last scratch before he set her down again. He could be hardheaded, as well.

She was thinking of him. Sam would have been amazed if he had known how hard and long she'd struggled over those few brief lines she'd left him. She'd wanted to thank him for being with her and to tell him how much it had meant to her that he'd been kind and understanding when she'd been down for the count. She'd wanted to tell him that she loved him in a way she had never before and would never again love. But the words had seemed so empty and inadequate on paper.

It was hard to need someone, really need him, when you'd spent your entire life making certain you could handle anything and everything on your own. How would he have felt if he'd known how close she'd come to waking him and asking him to come with her because she'd been dreading the thought of facing this day alone? She couldn't ask, any more than she could forget that she now had no secrets from him, physically or emotionally. Dealing with this day alone was imperative if she was ever to face another without him.

The nurse on duty this morning was younger and more approachable than the one the night before. She told Johanna that her father was resting comfortably, then asked her to have a seat until Dr. Merritt could be located.

Johanna chose the waiting room because the corridors seemed so public. She'd managed to evade the reporters outside but didn't want to take any chances on having to deal with any who'd been clever enough to sneak in.

Inside, an elderly woman and a boy of about twenty sat half dozing on a sofa, hands linked. On the wall-mounted television a morning show flashed cheerfully, showing a demonstration of gourmet cooking. Johanna moved to a table where twin pots of coffee and hot water sat on warmers. She bypassed the tea bags, ignored the little bags of powdered cream and sugar and poured a cup black. As she took the first sip, she heard the break for local news.

Carl W. Patterson was the top story. Dispassionately she listened to the newscaster recite the press release she and the publicist had written over the phone the night before. It gave a great deal more information on Carl's career than it did on his illness, and she knew Carl would have given it his nod of approval. The report ended by saying that Toni DuMonde, Patterson's housemate and fiancée, could not be reached for comment.

At least the woman wasn't a fool, Johanna thought as she chose a seat. There were some, she knew, who would have spilled their guts to the press and enjoyed the melodrama. And if Toni had, Johanna imagined, Carl would have cut whatever strings tied them together as soon as he was able.

"Miss Patterson?"

Johanna rose automatically. The moment she saw the doctor, her calm fled. The nurse had said Carl was resting comfortably, but that was hospital talk. She fought back the touch of fear and offered her hand.

"Dr. Merritt, I hope I'm not too early." Or too late.

"No, as a matter of fact your father's awake and stable. As a matter of precaution we'll keep him in CCU for another twenty-four hours. If he continues to progress, he can be moved to a private room."

"The prognosis?"

"The prognosis is good, if he cooperates. A lighter work load is essential. How much influence do you have over him?"

Her smile was almost amused. "None at all."

"Well, then, he might find himself confined to the hospital a day or two longer than he's counting on." Merritt took off his glasses to polish the lenses on the hem of his coat. "As I explained to you last night, certain adjustments will have to be made. Mr. Patterson will have to realize that, like the rest of us, he has certain limitations."

"I understand. And I wish you the best of luck explaining the same to him."

"I've already spoken to him briefly." Merritt slid the glasses back on his nose. He gave Johanna a smile that was gone almost before it formed. "At the moment, it's more important to reassure him. We'll speak about future care soon enough. He's asked to see Miss DuMonde and someone named Whitfield. It may be good for him to see his fiancée, but—"

"Don't worry about Whitfield. I'll handle it."

Merritt only nodded. He'd already decided Patterson's daughter had a good head on her shoulders. "Your father's a fortunate man. If he's sensible, there isn't any reason why he shouldn't lead a full and productive life."

"Can I see him?"

"Fifteen minutes only. He needs calm and quiet."

She was both as she walked into the small curtained-off room in CCU. Her father was as he'd been the night before, eyes closed, wired to machines. But his color was better. She stood by the bed, studying him, until his eyes flickered open.

It took him a moment to focus. It occurred to Johanna that this was certainly the longest their eyes had ever held. When she saw recognition in his, she bent to brush his cheek with hers.

"Good morning," she said, keeping her voice carefully neutral. "You gave us a scare."

"Johanna." He took her hand, surprising her. He'd never been quite so alone or quite so weak. "What have they told you?"

Why, he's frightened, she thought, and felt a stirring of sympathy. It had never occurred to her that he could be frightened. "That you're a fortunate man," she said briskly. "And that if you're sensible the world will still see quite a number of Carl W. Patterson productions."

It was exactly the right thing to say. She hadn't realized she'd known him so well. "Damned inconvenient time for my body to set booby traps for me." He glanced around the room, and the moment of closeness vanished.

"The hospital's contacting Toni," Johanna told him. "I'm sure she'll be here soon."

Satisfied, Carl looked back at his daughter. "They say they intend to keep me strapped down here another day."

"Yes. More if you make a fuss."

"I've work to do that can't be done from a hospital bed."

"Fine. I'll tell them to release you. You might be able to edit *Fields of Fire* before you keel over again."

His expression changed from impatience to astonishment, then to something she'd rarely seen directed at her—amusement. "I suppose I could spare a few days. But I don't want that ham-handed Whitfield to get his hands on it."

"I've sent for Loman." His expression tightened immediately, and he became the cool, disapproving man she'd lived with most of her life. "I'm sorry if I overstepped my bounds, but when I contacted Whitfield last night and saw how things were, I thought you'd prefer Loman."

"All right, all right." He waved away her apology. "I do prefer Loman. Whitfield has his place, but God knows it's not in an editing room. What about the press?"

He'd forgotten to be frightened. Johanna thought, and bit back a sigh. It was business as usual. "Under control. Your publicist issued a release this morning and will update it as becomes necessary."

"Good, good. I'll meet with Loman this afternoon. Set that up for me, Johanna."

"No."

The effort of making plans had already sapped his strength, and that only made him more furious. "No? What the hell do you mean, no?"

"It's out of the question." Her voice was calm, which pleased her. There had been a time he could have used that tone and made her quake. "It should be all right in a day or two, once you're in a private room and stronger."

"I run my own life."

"No one's more aware of that than I."

"If you've got some idea about taking over while I'm down—"

The fury leaped into her eyes and stopped him cold. He'd never seen that look before, or the power behind it. Or, if it had been there, he'd never bothered to look. "I don't want anything from you. I did once, but I learned to live without it. Now, if you'll excuse me, I've got a show of my own to produce."

"Johanna." She started to whip the curtain aside. It was the tremor in his voice that stopped her.

"Yes?"

"I apologize."

Another first, she thought, and made herself turn back. "All right. The doctor told me not to stay long, and I've probably already overtired you."

"I almost died."

He said it like an old man, an old, frightened man. "You're going to be fine."

"I almost died," he repeated. "And though I can't say my life flashed in front of my eyes, I did screen a few clips." He closed his eyes. It infuriated him that he had to stop just to gather the strength to speak. "I remember getting in the back of the limo— on my way to the airport, I think. You were standing on the steps with that dog Max forced on me. You looked as though you wanted to call me back."

Johanna didn't remember that particular incident because there'd been so many of them. "If I had, would you have stayed?"

"No." He sighed, not with regret but with acknowledgement. "Work has always come first. I've never been able to put a marriage together the way I could a film. Your mother—"

"I don't want to talk about my mother."

Carl opened his eyes again. "She could have loved you more if she'd hated me less."

It hurt. Even having known it all these years, it hurt to hear it said aloud. "And you?"

"Work has always come first," he repeated. He was tired, much too tired for regrets or apologies. "Will you come back?"

"Yes. I'll come back after the taping."

He was asleep before she drew the curtain aside.

Max Heddison's estate was as distinguished and well-tended as the man. Sam was ushered through the thirty-room house the actor had purchased a quarter of a century before. On the terrace were thickly padded chaises and half a dozen wicker chairs that invited company to spread out and be comfortable. An aging golden retriever was curled up in one, snoring.

In the sparkling L-shaped pool beyond the terrace, Max Heddison was doing laps. Across the sloping lawn, partially hidden by squared-off hedges, were tennis courts. To the east, identifiable only by a distant flag, was a putting green.

A houseboy in a spotless white jacket offered Sam his choice of chairs. Sun or shade. Sam chose the sun. As he watched, Sam counted ten laps, cleanly stroked and paced, and wondered idly how many Max had done before he'd arrived. The official bio said Max was seventy. It could have taken off fifteen years and still have been believable.

He accepted coffee and waited while Max hauled himself out of the pool.

"Good to see you again." Max dragged a towel over his hair before he shrugged into a robe.

"I appreciate you letting me drop by this way." Sam had risen automatically.

"Sit down, boy, you make me feel like a king about to be deposed. Had breakfast?"

"Yes, thanks."

The moment Max sat, the houseboy was back with a tray of fresh fruit and dry toast. "Thank you, Jose. Bring Mr. Weaver some juice. Straight from our own oranges," he told Sam. "I figure it only costs me about three dollars a glass." With a grin, he dug into his breakfast. "My wife's the health nut. No additives, no preservatives. Enough to drive a man to drink. She's at her morning class, which means I'll have time to sneak a cigarette before she gets back."

Sam's juice was served in cut crystal. He sipped, letting Max fall into a conversation about pruning and organic sprays.

"Well, I don't suppose you came here to discuss fertilizers." Max pushed his tray aside and reached in his pocket for a pack of unfiltered cigarettes. "What did you think of the script?"

"Who do I have to kill to get the part?"

Max chuckled and drew in smoke with great pleasure. "I'll hold that in reserve. You know, I don't care too much for today's moviemakers—money-makers, I should say. In the old days, men like Mayer might have been despots, but they knew how to make films. Today they're a bunch of damn accountants running around with ledgers and red pencils—more interested in profit than entertainment. But my gut tells me we might be able to give them both with this one.''

"It made my palms sweat," Sam said simply.

"I know the feeling." Max settled back, regretting only that his cigarette was nearly done. "I've been making movies since before you were born. Over eighty of them, and only a handful ever made me feel that way."

"I want to thank you for thinking of me."

"No need for that. Ten pages into the script and your name popped into my head. It was still there when I finished." He crushed out his cigarette, sighing. "And, of course, I went straight to my consultant with it—my wife." He grinned, drank more coffee and thought it a pity his wife had ordered decaf. "I've relied on her opinion for over forty years."

It made Sam remember how important it had been for him to hear Johanna's.

"She finished it, handed it back to me and said if I didn't do it I was crazy. Then she told me to get young Sam Weaver to play Michael. By the way, she admires your...build," Max said. "My sainted wife's an earthy woman."

The grin came quickly and lingered. "I'd love to meet her."

"We'll arrange it. Did I mention that Kincaid's been signed to direct?"

"No." Sam's interest was piqued again. "You don't get much better."

"Thought the same myself." Max watched Sam thoughtfully from under his bushy white brows. "Patterson's producing." He saw Sam's eyes sharpen and reached casually for more coffee. "Problem?"

"There might be." He wanted the part, more than he could remember wanting any other. But not at the cost of his still-too-tenuous relationship with Johanna.

"If you're concerned about Jo-Jo, I don't think it's necessary. The complete professional, our Jo-Jo. And she respects her father's work." He saw the dull anger in Sam's eyes and nodded. "So, it's gotten that far, has it? I wasn't sure Johanna would ever let anyone get that close."

"It wasn't so much a matter of choice as circumstance." He

hadn't come just to talk about the script. When Sam had called to make the appointment, he'd already decided to dig for whatever Max might have buried. "I take it you haven't heard that Patterson had a heart attack last night."

"No." The concern came automatically. The friendship went back a quarter of a century. "I haven't so much as flicked the news on today. I go for days at a time without it. How bad?"

"Bad enough. As far as I know, he's stable. Johanna went back to the hospital this morning."

"He lives hard," Max mused. "Carl never seemed to be able to settle down long enough to enjoy what he was working for. I hope he still gets the chance." Max tipped back in his chair and looked out over the pool, the grounds. "You know, I have three children of my own. Five grandchildren now, and the first great-grandchild on the way. There were times I wasn't there for them, and I'll always regret it. Holding a family and a career together in this business is like juggling eggs. There's always some break-age."

"Some people juggle better than others."

"True enough. It takes a lot of effort and more than a few concessions to make it work."

"It seems to me that in Johanna's case she made all the con-cessions."

Max said nothing for a moment. He considered having another cigarette but decided his wife's sensitive nose would find him out. "I hate old men who poke into young people's business. Ought to be out playing checkers or feeding pigeons. But...just how serious are you about Jo-Jo?"

"We're going to get married," Sam heard himself say, to his own astonishment. "As soon as I talk her into it."

"Good luck. And that comes from the heart. I've always had a soft spot for that girl." Max poured another cup of coffee and knew he was a long way from ready to feed pigeons. "How much did she tell you?"

"Enough to make me understand I've got an uphill battle."

"And how much do you love her?"

"Enough to keep climbing."

Max decided to risk a second cigarette. If his wife came sniffing around, he could always blame it on Sam. He lit it slowly, savoring the taste. "I'm going to tell you things she wouldn't appreciate me saying. Whether it'll give you an edge or not I can't say. I can tell you I hope it does."

"I appreciate it."

With the smoke trailing lazily from between his fingers, Max looked back. A long way. "I knew her mother well. A beautiful woman. A glorious face. Bone structure always makes the difference. Johanna favors her physically, but it ends there. I can say I've never known anyone more completely her own woman than Johanna."

"Neither have I," Sam murmured. "It doesn't always make it easy."

"You're too young to want things easy," Max told him from the comfortable perspective of seven decades. "When something comes easy, you usually let it go the same way. That's my philosophy for the day. Now, Glenna was selfish, driven by her own demons. She married Carl after a brief and very torrid affair. Affairs were just as torrid thirty years ago, only a bit more discreet."

He drew in smoke and remembered a few of his own. Though he'd let them go without regret upon his marriage, he could still be grateful for the experience.

"They were a golden couple, the photographers' darlings. Carl was dark, ruggedly handsome, broad shouldered. Glenna was almost waiflike, pale, fragile. They threw incredible parties and incredible tantrums. To be honest, I quite enjoyed both. You may have heard I was a hellion in my youth."

"I heard you were a hellion," Sam agreed. "But I didn't hear it was something in the past."

"We'll work well together," Max declared. He took one last drag before crushing the second cigarette out. "When Glenna was pregnant, she spent thousands decorating the nursery. Then she started to lose her figure and went on a rampage. She could sit for a photographer like a Madonna, then toss back a Scotch and curse like a sailor. Glenna had no middle ground."

"Johanna told me she was ill, a manic-depressive."

"Perhaps. I don't pretend to understand psychiatry. I will say she was weak—not weak-minded, but weak-spirited—and tormented by the fact that she was never as successful as she needed to be. There was talent in her, real talent, but she didn't have the drive or the grit to stay on top. It became easy for her to blame Carl for that, and the marriage. Then it became easier to blame the child. After Johanna was born, Glenna went through phases of being a devoted, loving mother. Then she'd be almost obscenely neglectful. The marriage was crumbling. Carl had affairs, she had affairs, and neither of them ever considered putting the child first. Not in their nature, Sam,'' he added when he saw the fury flare. ''That's not an excuse, of course, but it is a reason. Carl wouldn't have cared if Glenna had had one child or thirty. He'd had no more than a passing interest. When the break finally came, Glenna used the child as a weapon. I don't mean to make Carl a hero, but at least he never used Johanna. Unfortunately, she was never that important to him.''

''How could two people like that ever have someone like Johanna?''

''Another question for the ages.''

''Is Patterson her father?''

Max lifted both brows. ''Why do you ask?''

It was a confidence he felt he had to break. Not for himself. Sam had already decided her parentage meant less than nothing to him, but the truth would be important to Johanna.

''Because when she was still a child, Johanna found a letter her mother had written to Patterson right after she'd gone back to England. She told him she'd never been sure if he was Johanna's father.''

''Good God.'' Max ran a hand over his face. ''I had no idea about that. It's a wonder it didn't destroy Johanna.''

''No, she wasn't destroyed, but it did plenty of damage.''

''Poor little Jo-Jo,'' Max murmured. ''She was always such a lonely little girl. Spent more time with the gardener than anyone else. It might not have mattered if Carl had been different. I wish she'd come to me with this.''

''I don't think she's told anyone about it until last night.''

''You'd better not let her down.''

''I don't intend to.''

Max fell silent for a time, thinking. Johanna's parents had been his friends. He'd been able to accept them for what they were and for what they weren't, all the while regretting it for the child's sake.

"For what it's worth, I'd say the letter was pure spite and total nonsense. If another man had fathered Johanna, Glenna would have blurted it out long before the separation. She could never keep a secret for more than two hours. Make that two minutes if you added a drink. Carl knew that." His face clouded as he hunched over the table. "I'm sorry to say that if Carl had suspected Johanna wasn't his flesh and blood he never would have kept her under his roof. He'd have put her on a plane to her mother without a backward glance."

"That doesn't make him a saint."

"No, but it does make him Johanna's father."

"We have something special for our home audience," John Jay began, giving the camera a brilliant smile. "If you've been listening this week, you know that our Drive American contest is already underway. We at *Trivia Alert* are very excited about having the chance to show all of you at home how much we appreciate you. To win, all you have to do is watch and answer. Every day this week, sometime during the show, I'll be asking questions. Today it's time to tell you at home what you have a chance to win."

He paused, giving the announcer the time to describe the cars and eligibility requirements. As requested, the studio audience applauded and cheered.

"The week of Fourth of July," John Jay continued on cue, "one of you at home will win not one but both luxury cars. All you have to do is answer five questions in order. Send your answers to Trivia Alert, Drive American, Post Office Box 1776, Burbank, California 91501. Now for today's question."

There was a dramatic pause as he drew the sealed envelope from the slot. "Question number three. What is the name of Captain America's alter ego? Write down your answer and be sure to tune in tomorrow for the fourth question. All complete sets of correct answers will be part of a random drawing. Now, back to our game."

Johanna checked her watch and wondered how she could get through two more segments. They were already behind schedule due to a delay caused by an overenthusiastic member of the studio audience who had called out answers during the speed round. They'd had to stop, reset, calm the contestant and begin again with a new batch of questions. Usually she took that sort of thing in stride, but somewhere along the way her stride had broken. For the past few hours, Johanna had been struggling to find her pace again.

When the segment ended, she nearly groaned with relief. She had fifteen minutes before they would begin again. "Beth, I have to make a call. I'll be in the office if a crisis comes up."

Without waiting for a response, she hurried off the set. At the end of the corridor a small room was set up with the essentials. A phone, a desk and a chair. Making use of all three, Johanna called the hospital. She still had ten minutes left when she learned that Carl had been downgraded from critical to serious condition. She was rubbing her eyes and thinking about another cup of coffee when the door opened.

"Beth, if it isn't a matter of life and death, put it on hold."

"It might be."

She straightened immediately at the sound of Sam's voice. "Oh, hello. I didn't expect you."

"You don't expect me nearly often enough." He closed the door behind him. "How are you doing?"

"Not bad."

"Your father?"

"Better. They think he can be moved out of CCU tomorrow."

"That's good." He came over to the desk and sat on the edge before giving her a long, critical study. "You're dead on your feet, Johanna. Let me take you home."

"We haven't finished, and I promised to stop by the hospital after the taping."

"Okay, I'll go with you."

"No, please. It's not necessary, and I'd be lousy company tonight."

He looked down at her hands. They were linked together tightly.

Deliberately he took them in his own and separated them. "Are you trying to pull back, Johanna?"

"No. I don't know." She took a long breath, and her hands relaxed in his. "Sam, I appreciate what you did for me last night more than I can ever tell you—the way you listened and didn't judge. You were there when I needed you, and I'll never forget it."

"Sounds like a kiss-off," he murmured.

"No, of course it isn't. But you should understand now why I feel so strongly about being involved with you. Why it won't work."

"I must be pretty stupid, because I don't. I do understand why you're scared. Johanna, we have to talk."

"I have to get back. There's only a few more minutes."

"Sit down," he told her as she started to rise. She might have ignored the order, but the look in his eyes had her sitting again. "I'll try to make it quick. Time's either a blessing or a curse now, anyway. I've got to fly East the day after tomorrow to start filming."

"Oh." She dug deep for a smile. "Well, that's good. I know you've been anxious to start."

"I'll be gone three weeks, probably more. It isn't possible for me to put this off."

"Of course not. I hope—well, I hope you let me know how it's going."

"Johanna, I want you to come with me."

"What?"

"I said I want you to come with me."

"I—I can't. How could I? I have my job, and—"

"I'm not asking you to make a choice between your job and us. Any more than I'd expect you to ask me to make one between mine and the way I feel about you."

"No, of course I wouldn't."

"I'd like to think you meant that." He paused a moment, searching her face. "The script that Max sent me—I want to do it."

"You should do it. It's perfect for you."

"Maybe, but I want to know if it's perfect for you. Your father's producing it, Johanna."

"Oh." She looked down at her hands a moment, hands that were still caught in his. "Well, then, you've got the best."

"I want to know how you feel about it, Johanna. How you really feel."

"It's more a matter of how you feel."

"Not this time. Don't make me use pliers."

"Sam, your professional choices have to be yours, but I'd say you'd be a fool not to grab a chance to work with Max and Patterson Productions. That script might have been written for you, and I'd be disappointed if I didn't see you in it."

"Always sensible."

"I hope so."

"Then be sensible about this. Take a few days off and come east with me." Before she could protest again, he was continuing. "You've got a tight crew, Johanna. I've seen them work firsthand. You know they could run things for a couple of weeks."

"I suppose, but not without any notice. Then there's my father..." She let her words trail off. There must have been dozens of reasons, but they seemed to slide away before she could get a grip on them.

"All right. Take a week to make sure your crew is on top of things and that your father's recovering. Then fly out and meet me."

"Why?"

"I wondered when you'd ask." He reached in his pocket to pull out a box. Through his life he'd done a great many things on impulse. This wasn't one of them. He'd thought it through carefully, and had kept coming up with one answer. He needed her. "Things like this usually speak for themselves." After opening the lid, he took her hand and set the box in her palm. "I want you to marry me."

She stared at the single flawless diamond. It was square-cut, very classic and simple. The kind of ring, Johanna thought, girls dreamed about when they thought of white chargers and castles in the sky.

"I can't."

"Can't what?"

"I can't marry you. You know I can't. I had no idea you'd started thinking like this."

"Neither had I, until today. When Marv called I knew I had two choices. I could go East and stew about it or I could take the step and let you stew about it." He touched her hair, just the tips. "I'm sure, Johanna."

"I'm sorry." She offered the box back to him. When he didn't take it, she set it on the desk. "I don't want to hurt you, you know I don't. That's why I can't."

"It's about time you unloaded some of the baggage you've been carrying around, Johanna." Rising, he drew her up with him. "We both know what we've got doesn't come along every day. You might think you're doing me a favor by turning me down, but you're wrong. Dead wrong."

His fingers tangled in her hair as he kissed her. Unable to deny him—or herself—she curled her arms up his back until she gripped his shoulders. She held on to him even while her mind whirled with dozens of questions.

"Do you believe me when I tell you I love you?" he demanded.

"Yes." She held him tighter, burying her face against his shoulder to absorb his scent. "Sam, I don't want you to go. I know you have to, and I know how much I'll miss you, but I can't give you what you want. If I could...if I could you're the only one I'd give it to."

He hadn't expected to hear even that much. Another man might have been discouraged, but he'd run into too many walls in his life to be put off by one more. Particularly since he had every intention of tearing this one down, brick by brick.

He pressed a kiss to her temple. "I already know what I need and what I want." He drew her away until their eyes met. "You'd better start thinking about yourself, Johanna. About what you want, what you need. Just you. I figure you're smart enough to come up with an answer before too long." He kissed her again until she was breathless. "Keep in touch."

She didn't have the strength to do anything but sink into the chair when he left her. The show was starting, but she continued to sit, staring at the ring he'd left behind.

Twelve

The man was playing games. Johanna knew it, and though she tried not to nibble at the bait, she was already being reeled in. He'd been gone two weeks, and she hadn't gotten a single phone call.

But there had been flowers.

They'd arrived every evening. Black-eyed Susans one day, white orchids another. She couldn't walk into any room of her house without thinking of him. After the first week they'd begun to arrive at her office—a small clutch of violets, a huge bouquet of tea roses. She couldn't even escape from him there.

The man was definitely playing, and he wasn't playing fair.

Of course, she wasn't going to marry him. That was absurd. She didn't believe people could love, honor and cherish for a lifetime. She'd told him so, and she'd been sorry, but she had no intention of changing her mind.

She might carry the ring with her—for safekeeping, that is— but she hadn't taken it out of its box. At least not more than two or three times.

She was grateful that her work load had intensified so that she was unceasingly busy. It didn't leave much time to mope around missing him. Unless you counted the long, solitary nights when she kept listening for the phone.

He'd told her to keep in touch, but he hadn't told her where he'd be staying. If she'd wanted to, she could have found out easily enough. It did happen that a few discreet inquiries had put the name and address of his hotel in her hands, but that didn't mean she would call him. If she called, he'd know she'd gone to some trouble—damn it, a great deal of trouble—to find out where he was.

Then he would know she'd not only nibbled at the bait but swallowed it whole.

By the end of the second week, she was furious with him. He'd pushed her into a corner where she didn't want to be, wedged her in and then strolled off, leaving her trapped. A man didn't ask a woman to marry him, drop a ring in her hand, then waltz off.

Once she'd considered putting the ring in the mail and shipping it off to him. That had been at three o'clock in the morning on the fifteenth day. Johanna had rolled over, slammed the pillow a few satisfactory times and vowed to do just that the minute the post office opened in the morning.

She would have, too, if she hadn't been running a few minutes late. Then she'd been tied up at lunchtime and unable to get five free minutes until after six. She decided against mailing it, thinking it would be more civil and courteous to throw it in his face when he got back into town.

It was just her bad luck he'd chosen to send forget-me-nots that day. They happened to be one of her particular favorites.

As the third week approached, she was a wreck. Johanna knew she deserved the wary glances of her staff. She pushed through Monday's taping, growling at every interruption. Her excuse was that she'd agreed to take duplicates to her father that evening.

He wasn't particularly interested in the show, she knew, but his recuperation wasn't sitting well with him. He wanted to live badly enough to follow his doctor's orders, but that didn't mean he couldn't review everything Patterson Productions had a part in. Johanna waited impatiently for the copies, pacing the set and toying with the ring box in her pocket.

"Here you go." Bethany put on an exaggerated smile. "Try not to gnaw on them on the way home."

Johanna dumped them in her bag. "I'll need you here by nine. We can work until it's time to set up for taping."

"Whatever you say."

Johanna narrowed her eyes at the overbright tone. "Have you got a problem?"

"Me?" All innocence, Bethany opened her eyes wide. "No, not me. Well, there is my back."

"Your back? What's wrong with it?"

"It's nothing really. It always aches a bit when I've been flogged."

Johanna opened her mouth, then shut it again on a puff of air. "I'm sorry. I guess I've been a little edgy."

"Just a tad. Funny, if someone had been sending me flowers every day for weeks I'd be a bit more cheerful."

"He thinks that's all it takes to twist me around his finger."

"There are worse positions to be in. Forget I said it," Bethany said immediately, holding up a hand. "There's nothing more diabolical than sending a basket of tiger lilies. The man's obviously slime."

For the first time in days, Johanna smiled. "He's wonderful."

The smile confirmed what Johanna's scowls had already told her. "You miss him?"

"Yes, I miss him. Just like he knew I would."

Bethany looked at romance in the most straightforward of terms. If you cared, you showed it, then put all your energy into making it work. Her solution for Johanna was just as simple. "You know, Johanna, it's the same distance from the West to the East Coast as it is from East to West."

She'd already thought of going. Not that she'd *considered* it, but she had thought of it. "No, I can't." She fingered the box in her pocket. "It wouldn't be fair to him."

"Because?"

"Because I won't...can't..." On impulse she pulled the box out and opened it. "Because of this."

"Oh, my." Bethany couldn't help the long-drawn-out sigh. "My, oh, my," she managed, already smelling orange blossoms. "Congratulations, best wishes and bon voyage. Where's a bottle of champagne when you need it?"

"No, I didn't accept it. I'm not going to. I told him no."

"Then why do you still have it?"

Because the question was so reasonable, Johanna could only frown and stare at the diamond while it winked at her. "He just dropped it in my hand and walked off."

"Romantic devil, isn't he?"

"Well, it wasn't exactly— That's close enough," she decided.

"It was more of an ultimatum than a proposal, but either way, I told him no."

It sounded wonderfully romantic to Bethany. She stuck her tongue in her cheek. "So you just decided to walk around with it in your pocket for a few days."

"No, I..." There had to be a reasonable excuse. "I wanted to have it handy so I could give it back to him."

Bethany thought that over, then tilted her head. "I think that's the first lie I've ever heard you tell."

"I don't know why I've still got it." Johanna closed the box with a snap, then pushed it into her pocket. "It's not important."

"No, I've never thought proposals of marriage or gorgeous engagement rings were anything to get excited about." She put a hand on Johanna's shoulder. "What you need is some fresh air."

"I don't believe in marriage."

"That's like not believing in Santa Claus." At Johanna's lifted brow, Bethany shook her head. "Johanna, don't tell me you don't believe in him, either? He might be something of a fantasy, but he's been around a while, and he's going to stay around."

It was hard to argue with that kind of logic. Johanna decided she was too tired to try. "We'll talk about the logic of that some other time. I have to drop off these tapes." With Bethany beside her, she started out. "I'd like you to keep this to yourself."

"It goes with me to the grave."

"You're good for me," Johanna said with a laugh. "I'm going to be sorry to lose you."

"Am I fired?"

"Sooner or later you're going to fire me. You won't be content to be anyone's assistant for long." Outside, Johanna took a deep breath. So much had changed since she'd walked with Bethany from the studio weeks before. "Leaving Santa Claus out of it, do you believe in marriage, Beth?"

"I'm just an old-fashioned girl with strong feminist underpinnings. Yeah, I believe in marriage as long as two people are willing to give it their best shot."

"You know what the odds are of a marriage making it in this town?"

"Lousy. But strikeout or home run, you've got to step up to bat. See you tomorrow."

"Good night, Beth."

She did a great deal of thinking as she drove to Beverly Hills. Not all of it was clear, but every thought circled back to Sam. Johanna was coming to realize that her thoughts would, whether she was with or without him.

The gates were locked, as they always were. Reaching out, she pressed the button on the intercom and waited for her father's housekeeper to ask her name. In moments the gates opened soundlessly.

The drive toward the house didn't stir any childish memories. She saw the estate as an adult. Perhaps she always had. It was stunning—the white columns, the terraces and balconies. The exterior had changed little from her earliest recollections.

Inside, it had gone through major overhauls, depending on its mistress. Her mother had preferred the feminine and delicate look of *Louis Quinze.* Darlene had chosen art nouveau, right down to the light fixtures. Its last mistress had gone for the opulently elegant. Johanna didn't think it would take Toni long to put her stamp on it.

The door was opened for her by the gray-uniformed maid before she'd reached the top of the wide, curved steps.

"Good evening, Miss Patterson."

"Good evening. Is Mr. Patterson expecting me?"

"He and Miss DuMonde are in the sitting room."

"Thank you."

Johanna crossed the glossy tiles, skirting the fish pond her father's last wife had installed. She found her father looking well, and impatient, in a dark blue smoking jacket. Toni sprawled lazily on the sofa across from him, sipping wine and flipping through a magazine. Johanna nearly smiled when she saw that it was one on home fashion and decoration.

"I expected you an hour ago," Carl said without preamble.

"We ran late." She took the tapes from her bag to set them on the table beside him. "You're looking well."

"There's nothing wrong with me."

"Carl's a bit bored." Toni stretched herself into a sitting position. She wore silk lounging pajamas the color of ripe peaches. The pout she wore went with them beautifully. "Perhaps you can entertain him better than I." Rising, she stalked gracefully out of the room.

Johanna lifted a brow. "Have I come at a bad time?"

"No." Carl pushed himself up and headed for the bar. Johanna bit back a protest and was relieved when he poured club soda. "Do you want anything?"

"No, thank you. I can't stay."

Carl halfheartedly added a twist of lime. "I assumed you'd stay until I'd previewed the tapes."

"You don't need me for that." He wanted company, she realized. Because she remembered how old and alone he'd looked in the hospital, she relented. "I could put them in for you, answer whatever questions you might have about the first segment or two."

"I've seen the show before, Johanna. I doubt I'd have any questions about my own show."

"No." She picked up the bag she'd just set down. "Then I'll leave you to it."

"Johanna." He cleared his throat and he turned back, then took his seat again. "You've done a good job with it."

This time both brows rose. "Thank you." She set her bag down again and checked her watch.

"If you've got some damn appointment, go on, then."

"No, actually, I was just marking the time. Since it's the first time in my life you've ever complimented me on anything, I want to remember when it happened."

"There's no need to be sarcastic."

"Maybe not." She crossed the room to sit but stayed on the edge of her chair. She'd never been comfortable in this house. "I'm glad you're doing so well. If you're interested, I can see that you get dupes of tomorrow's taping for the evening shows. We're giving away a trip for two to Puerto Vallarta during the speed round."

He only grunted at that. Johanna folded her hands and continued. "If a contestant reaches the winner's circle and can answer all of the questions himself, without deferring to his partner, he'll win a car. We're using a sedan this week. Four-door.''

"I'm not interested in the prizes.''

"I thought not, but you might prefer a different angle or see a flaw when you preview. I'm sure you know that you can accomplish as much here as most men can in an office.''

"I won't be sitting here forever.''

"There's no question of that.'' No, he would be back, full steam, very soon. Maybe this was the time, the only time. "Before I go, I'd like to ask you something.''

"If it has to do with the new pilot, I've already seen it and approved it.''

"No, it's personal.''

He sat, cradling his glass. He didn't mind giving up liquor half so much as doing without his cigars. Rather than answer, he simply nodded for her to go on.

"Why do you want to marry Toni DuMonde?''

As far as Carl was concerned, the question had come out of left field. No one questioned his motives or his reasons. "I'd say that was between Toni and myself. If you're uncomfortable with the age difference—''

"It would hardly matter to me if there was twice as much difference as there already is,'' Johanna said. "I'm just curious.''

"I'm marrying her because I want to.''

Johanna sat for a minute, studying him. Maybe it was just that simple with Carl. I want, I do. I covet, I take. "Do you plan to stay married to her?''

"As long as it suits both of us.''

She smiled a little and nodded. That, at least, was the unvarnished truth. "Why did you marry my mother?''

If her first question had surprised him, this one left him speechless. Staring at Johanna, he saw the resemblance he'd always ignored. But there was more character in this face. More courage. "Why are you bringing this up now? You never asked about her before.''

"Maybe I should have. We began to talk about her when you were in the hospital, but I suppose I wasn't ready. Now I have a decision of my own to make, and I can't do it until I understand a little better. Did you love her?''

"Of course. She was beautiful, fascinating. We were both building our careers. There wasn't a man who met Glenna in those days who didn't love her.''

She didn't find reasons for love and fidelity in those answers. "But you're the only one who married her. And the only one who divorced her.''

"The marriage was a mistake,'' he said, abruptly uncomfortable. "We both realized it before the first year was out. Not that we weren't attracted to each other. As I said, she was beautiful, very delicate. You favor her.'' His glass paused halfway to his lips when he saw her expression. Perhaps he'd never been a loving father, but he'd always been an astute man. "If you're concerned about her health, don't be. Glenna was always erratic. Drinking made her more so, but I've never seen any part of that in you. Believe me, I've watched for it.''

"Have you?'' Johanna murmured.

"You've never been one for extremes,'' he went on. "Apparently you inherited enough from me to offset the rest.''

"Did I?'' This time her voice was firm and her eyes level. "I've always wondered what, if anything, I inherited from you.''

His look was so blank that she couldn't believe he feigned it. "You're a producer, aren't you? And a good one. That should say something. The Pattersons have always been strong, practical people. Ambitious. I'd say, now that I think of it, that you take after my grandmother. She was strong minded, never one to sit around and let the world go by. Got the hair from her, too,'' he decided, looking thoroughly at his daughter for the first time in years.

A little dazed, Johanna reached up to touch her hair. "*Your* grandmother?''

"Didn't get it from your mother,'' he said with a sour laugh. "Got hers from her hairdresser. That was one of her most prized secrets. Hers was brown, mousy brown. God knows you didn't get your drive from her. That's the Patterson in you.'' He didn't say it with pride, just stated it as fact.

So this was her father after all. Johanna sat, waiting for a flood of feeling. When none came, she sighed. Nothing had really changed. Then her lips curved. Then again, maybe everything had.

"I'd like to hear about her sometime. Your grandmother." She rose, taking a look at her watch in earnest. "I really have to go. I'm going to be out of town. Everything should run smoothly enough without me for a few days."

"Out of town? When?"

"Tonight."

Johanna caught the last plane out. She'd had just enough time before final boarding to call Bethany and give her quick and not completely coherent instructions about the next day's business and the care and feeding of her cat. Bethany had been awakened out of a sound sleep, but she could be depended on.

Strapped in, Johanna watched L.A., and the resolutions she'd lived with all of her life, slip away. She'd taken a step, the largest one of her life, without even being sure she would land on solid ground.

Somewhere over Nevada she dozed, then woke over New Mexico in a kind of blind panic. What in God's name was she doing, traveling thousands of miles without so much as a toothbrush? It wasn't like her not to plan or make lists. They were taping the next day. Who would handle the details, check the staff? Who would deal with John Jay?

Someone else, she told herself. For once it would just have to be someone else.

She traveled from one coast to the other, sleeping in fits and starts and wondering if she'd lost her mind. In Houston she nearly lost her nerve, as well. But she changed planes and strapped in a second time, determined to see it through.

Perhaps she wasn't being smart or responsible, but everyone was entitled to do something on impulse once. Even if they lived to regret it.

Almost certain she would, she arrived in Baltimore just after dawn. The terminal was deserted except for a few napping passengers waiting for connections. The air was cool in Maryland, and she was grateful for her suit jacket. The same jacket, Johanna remembered, that she'd put on that morning when she'd still been sane. The sky, full of pewter clouds, promised rain as she climbed into a cab and gave the driver the name of Sam's hotel.

This was it, she told herself. It helped a little to close her eyes and ignore the unfamiliar landscape. If she didn't watch it, she wouldn't think too much about being on the other side of the country. In L.A. people were rolling over in bed, snuggling into pillows with morning still hours away. Here they were waking up, preparing to face the day.

So was she.

She paid off the driver and tried not to think. The rain began as she walked into the lobby.

Suite 621. At least she knew the number, so she'd be spared the embarrassment of going to the desk and convincing the clerk she wasn't a fan. Clutching the strap of her bag, she rode to the sixth floor. It was easy enough to step from the elevator. She even managed to walk down the hall to his door.

Then she stared at it.

What if he didn't want her there? What if he wasn't alone? After all, she had no claim on him, had made no promises. She'd refused to accept, even to listen to, his promises. He was free to…to do whatever he wanted, with whomever he wanted.

Certain she couldn't go through with it, she turned away and took two steps back from the door.

It was absurd, she told herself. She'd just spent hours in a plane, traveled thousands of miles, and now she couldn't even get up the nerve to knock on a door.

With her shoulders straight and her chin up, she knocked. When her stomach rolled, she reached in her pocket automatically for her antacids. Her fingers closed over the small velvet box. She drummed up her courage and knocked again.

He woke swearing. They'd worked until after two, and he'd barely had the energy to strip before tumbling into bed. Now the damn assistant director was banging on the door. Any idiot knew they couldn't film any of the scheduled outside shots in the rain.

Groggy and full of the desire for vengeance, Sam dragged the top sheet from the bed and wrapped it around him. He tripped over the hem, cursed again, then yanked open the door.

"Goddamn it—" His mouth dried up. He had to be dreaming.

Johanna was a continent away, snuggled under the covers. Then he saw her lips curve before she began to stumble out an apology.

"I'm sorry I woke you. I should have...waited. Called." *Stayed away,* she thought desperately.

Then she didn't think at all, because he was dragging her inside. The door slammed and she was pressed back against it, her mouth captive.

"Don't say a word," he ordered when she sucked in her breath. "Not a word. Not yet."

It would have been impossible to speak. Even as he pulled her through the sitting room, he was peeling off her jacket, fighting the buttons on her blouse. With a throaty laugh, she tugged at the sheet. It was left behind in a stream of white as they worked their way to the bedroom.

Her skirt slid down to her hips, and he lifted her out of it. While his hands played over her, she stepped out of one shoe. They were nearly at the bedroom door before she managed to rid herself of the other.

He wasn't even awake. Sam clung to the drowsy fingers of sleep as they fell onto the bed.

She was here. Dream or reality, she was here. Her skin was just as soft under his hands, just as fragrant. Her lips as they parted for his had the same unique flavor he'd craved since he'd tasted them last. At her sigh, as her arms locked around him, he heard everything he needed to hear.

Delighted with each other, they rolled over the already rumpled bed as the rain grew heavy and streaked the windows.

She'd been right to come. Whatever had happened before, whatever happened after, she'd been right to take this moment. And to give this time to him. There would be no questions, no need for explanations or excuses, just gladness that was racing harder and faster toward dazzling pleasure.

In tune, body and mind, they came together, taking that pleasure to its pinnacle.

The thunder started as he gathered her against him again. Or perhaps it had been there all along but they hadn't heard it. Now, as the storm rattled over the city, they were together and alone and in love. Sometimes that really was all that mattered.

She kept her hand on his heart and her head on his shoulder as they floated down to solid ground. The gloom kept the room dim, but for Johanna there had never been a more beautiful morning.

"Were you just passing through?" Sam murmured.

She spread her fingers over his chest, watching the movement. "I had urgent and unexpected business on the East Coast."

"I see." He hoped he did, but he could afford to wait. "You on a contestant search?"

"Not exactly." The nerves began leaking back. "I take it you don't have an early call today."

"If the rain keeps up, please God, I won't have one at all." Slowly, like a man who had all the time in the world, he stretched. "We were scheduled to shoot down at the Inner Harbor. Terrific place. Best crab I've ever eaten." He was already imagining showing it to her himself. "Once that's wrapped, we'll be finished here."

A pout, something she never allowed herself, formed on her lips. "You've run a little over your three weeks."

He certainly hoped it was annoyance he detected in her voice. "A little."

"I guess you've been too busy to call and let me know how things were going."

"No."

"No?" She propped herself on her elbow to frown at him.

"No, I haven't been too busy to call. I didn't call."

"Oh, I see." She started to push herself up and found herself flat on her back again with Sam leaning over her.

"I hope you don't think you're getting out of this room."

"I told you I have business."

"So you did. Is it a coincidence that you have business in Baltimore and just happen to be staying at the same hotel—apparently in my room?"

"I'm not staying."

"Guess again." He nipped her gently on the jaw. "Why did you come, Johanna?"

"I'd rather not discuss it. I'd like my clothes," she said stiffly.

"Sure. Let me get them for you." He strolled out, leaving Johanna with the dubious cover of a pillow. She started to rise when he came back in with her suit bundled in his arms. Then she could only gape, openmouthed, as he opened the window and tossed them out.

"What in the hell are you doing?" She forgot the pillow as she leaped up and ran to the window. "You threw out my clothes." Dumbfounded, she could only stare at him. "You threw them out the window."

"Sure looks that way."

"Are you out of your mind? I flew out here with the shirt on my back, and now it's six floors down and soaked. I don't have anything to wear out of here but my shoes."

"I was counting on that. Seemed like the best way to guarantee your staying put."

"You *are* out of your mind." She started to crane out of the window, remembered she was naked, then dropped on the bed. "What am I supposed to do now?"

"Borrow another of my shirts, I guess. Help yourself." He gestured toward the closet. "You might toss me a pair of jeans while you're at it. It's hard for me to talk to you reasonably when we're not wearing anything but smiles."

"I'm not smiling," she told him between her teeth as she heaved jeans in his direction. "That was one of my best suits, and I—" Her fingers froze on the buttons of the shirt she'd pulled on. "Oh, God. Oh, my God, in the jacket. I had it in the jacket." With the shirt still half buttoned she jumped for the door. Sam was just quick enough to slam it closed before she ran out.

"I don't think you're dressed for a stroll, Johanna. Not that you don't look terrific. In fact, you look so terrific I think I'd like you to give me my shirt back."

"Will you stop being an idiot?" She tried to shove him aside but met with solid resistance. "You threw it out the window. I can't believe what a complete fool you are. You threw my ring out the window."

"Whose ring?"

"My ring, the one you gave me. Oh, for God's sake." She ducked under his arm to run to the window again. "Someone's going to take it."

"Your suit?"

"No, I don't care about the suit. The hell with the suit. I want my ring."

"All right. Here." Sam drew it off his pinky and offered it. "The box must have dropped out of your pocket when—when I said hello." Johanna had given a cry of relief and grabbed for it before she realized she'd been taken.

"Damn it, Sam, you had it all the time and you let me think it was gone."

"It was nice to know it was important to you." He held it between them. "Are you going to let me put it on you?"

"You can take it and—"

"I'm open to suggestions." Then he smiled at her in a way she found completely unfair. Even her temper failed her.

"I'd like to sit down a minute." She did, sinking into the bed. The relief was gone, and the anger. She'd come for a purpose. and it was time to see it through. "I came to see you."

"No? Really?"

"Don't make fun of me."

"All right." He sat beside her, draping an arm over her shoulders. "Then I guess I can tell you that if you hadn't come, or called within the next twenty-four hours, I was heading back, movie or no movie."

"You didn't call me."

"No, I didn't, because I think we both knew you had to make the next move. And I hope you suffered as much as I did." He pressed his lips to her hair. "So what's it going to be?"

"I want to tell you that I spoke with my father last night." She tilted her head so that she could look at him. "He is my father."

Gently he brushed her hair back from her face. "Is everything all right?"

"It's not like a story where everything turns out beautifully at the end, but it's all right. I don't suppose we'll ever be close, and I can accept that now. I'm not like him, nor like my mother, either. It's taken me all this time to figure out that that's okay. I'm okay."

He kissed her hair again, enjoying the fragrance as much as the familiarity. "I could have told you that, if you'd listened."

"I can listen now, now that I've told myself." With a long

breath, she took his hands in hers. "I need to ask you something, Sam. You could almost say it was the championship question."

"I work best under pressure."

But her eyes didn't smile. "Why do you want to marry me?"

"That's it?" His brows rose, and then he was laughing and holding her close. "I thought you were going to ask me a tough one. I want to marry you because I love you and I need you in my life. It changed when you walked into it."

"And tomorrow?"

"A two-part question," he murmured. "I could promise you anything." He drew her away to kiss her cheek, then her brow, then her lips. "I wish there were guarantees, but there aren't. I can only tell you that when I think about tomorrow, when I think about ten years from tomorrow, I think about you. I think about us."

He couldn't have said it better, she thought as she touched his face. No, there weren't any guarantees, but they had a chance. A good one.

"Can I ask you one more thing?"

"As long as I'm going to get an answer eventually."

"Do you believe in Santa Claus?"

What made it perfect, even more than perfect, was that he didn't even hesitate. "Sure. Doesn't everyone?"

Now she smiled, completely. "I love you, Sam."

"That's the answer I wanted."

"Looks like you win." She held out her hand so that he could slip the ring on her finger. It felt as though it belonged, and so did she. "Looks like we both do."

*   *   *   *   *

For my sons—
Life's a circus.
Go for it!

NORA ROBERTS

Untamed

Harlequin
Mills & Boon

First Published 1983
First Australian Paperback Edition 2005
ISBN 0 733 56241 8

Published by
Harlequin Mills & Boon
3 Gibbes Street
CHATSWOOD NSW 2067
AUSTRALIA

HARLEQUIN MILLS & BOON and the Rose Device are trademarks used
under license and registered in Australia, New Zealand, Philippines, United
States Patent & Trademark Office and in other countries.

Printed and bound in Australia by
McPherson's Printing Group

One

At the crack of the whip, twelve lions stood on their haunches and pawed the air. On command, they began to leap from pedestal to pedestal in a quick, close-formation, figure-eight pattern. This required split-second timing. With voice and hand commands the trainer kept the tawny, springing bodies moving.

"Well done, Pandora."

At her name and the signal, the muscular lioness leaped to the ground and lay down on her side. One by one the others followed suit, until, snarling and baring their teeth, they stretched across the tanbark. A male was positioned beside each female; at a sharp reproof from the trainer, Merlin ceased nibbling on Ophelia's ear.

"Heads up!" They obeyed as the trainer walked briskly in front of them. The whip was tossed aside with a flourish, then, with apparent nonchalance, the trainer reclined lengthwise across the warm bodies. The center cat, a full-maned African, let out a great, echoing bellow. As a reward for his response to the cue, his ear was given a good scratching. The trainer rose from the feline couch, clapped hands and brought the lions to their feet. Then, with a hand signal, each was called by name and sent through the chute and into their cages. One stayed behind, a huge, black-maned cat who, like an ordinary tabby, circled and rubbed up against his trainer's legs.

Deftly, a rope was attached to a chain that was hidden under his mane. Then, with swift agility, the trainer mounted the lion's back. As the door of the big cage opened, lion and rider passed through for a tour of the practice ring. When they reached the back door of the ring barn, Merlin, the obliging lion, was transferred to a wheel cage.

"Well, Duffy." Jo turned after the cage was secured. "Are we ready for the road?"

Duffy was a small, round man with a monk's fringe of chestnut hair and a face that exploded with ginger freckles. His open smile and Irish blue eyes gave him the look of an aging choirboy. His mind was sharp, shrewd and scrappy. He was the best manager Prescott's Circus Colossus could have had.

"Since we open in Ocala tomorrow," he replied in a raspy voice, "you'd better be ready." He shifted his fat cigar stump from the right side of his mouth to the left.

Jo merely smiled, then stretched to loosen muscles grown taut during the thirty minutes in the cage. "My cats are ready, Duffy. It's been a long winter. They need to get back on the road as much as the rest of us."

Duffy frowned. As circumstances had it, he stood only inches higher than his animal trainer. Widely spaced, almond-shaped eyes stared back at him. They were as sharp and green as emeralds, surrounded by thick, inky lashes. At the moment they were fearless and amused, but Duffy had seen them frightened, vulnerable and lost. He shifted his cigar again and took two quick puffs as Jo gave a cage hand instructions.

He remembered Steve Wilder, Jo's father. He had been one of the best cat men in the business. Jo was as good with the cats as Wilder had been. In some ways, Duffy acknowledged, even better. But she had the traits of her mother: delicate build; dark, passionate looks. Jolivette Wilder was as slender as her aerialist mother had been, with bold green eyes and straight, raven black hair that fell to just below her waist. Her brows were delicately arched, her nose small and straight, her cheekbones high and elegant, while her mouth was full and soft. Her skin was tawny from the Florida sun; it added to her gypsy-like appearance. Confidence added spark to the beauty.

Finishing her instructions, Jo tucked her arm through Duffy's. She had seen that frown before. "Somebody quit?" she asked as they began to walk toward Duffy's office.

"Nope."

His monosyllabic reply caused Jo to lift a brow. It was not often Duffy answered any question briefly. Years of experience told her to hold her tongue as they moved across the compound.

Rehearsals were going on everywhere. Vito the wire walker informally sharpened his act on a cable stretched between two trees. The Mendalsons called out to each other as they tossed their juggling pins high in the air, while the equestrian act led their horses into the ring barn. She saw one of the Stevenson girls walking on stilts. She'd be six now, Jo mused, tossing the hair from her eyes as she watched the young girl's wavering progress. Jo remembered the year she had been born. It had been that same year that she had been allowed to work the big cage alone. She had been sixteen, and it had been another full year before she had been permitted to work an audience.

For Jo, there had never been any home but the circus. She had been born during the winter break, had been tucked into her parents' trailer the following spring to spend her first year and each subsequent one of her life thereafter on the road. She had inherited both her fascination and her flair with animals from her father, her style and grace of movement from her mother. Though she had lost both parents fifteen years before, they continued to influence her. Their legacy to her had been a world of restlessness, a world of fantasies. She had grown up playing with lion cubs, riding elephants, wearing spangles and traveling like a gypsy.

Jo glanced down at a cluster of daffodils growing by the side of Prescott's winter office and smiled. She remembered planting them when she had been thirteen and in love with a tumbler. She remembered, too, the man who had stooped beside her, offering advice on bulb planting and broken hearts. As Jo thought of Frank Prescott, her smile grew sad.

"I still can't believe he's gone," she murmured as she and Duffy moved inside.

Duffy's office was sparsely furnished with a wooden desk, metal filing cabinets and two spindly chairs. A collage of posters adorned the walls. They promised the amazing, the astounding, the incredible: elephants that danced, men who flew through the air, beautiful girls who spun by their teeth, raging tigers that rode horseback. Tumblers, clowns, lions, strong men, fat ladies, boys who could balance on their forefingers; they brought the magic of the circus into the drab little room.

As Jo glanced over at a narrow pine door, Duffy followed her gaze. "I keep expecting him to come busting through there with some crazy new idea,'' he mumbled as he began to fiddle with his prize possession, an automatic coffee maker.

"Do you?" With a sigh Jo straddled a chair, then rested her chin on its back. "We all miss him. It's not going to seem the same without him this year." She looked up suddenly, and her eyes were angry. "He wasn't an old man, Duffy. Heart attacks should be for old men." She brooded into space, touched again with the injustice of Frank Prescott's death.

He had been barely into his fifties and full of laughter and simple kindness. Jo had loved him and trusted him without reservation. At his death she had grieved for him more acutely than she had for her own parents. In her longest memory he had been the core of her life.

"It's been nearly six months," Duffy said gruffly as he studied her face. When Jo glanced up, he stuck out a mug of coffee.

"I know." She took the mug, letting it warm her hands in the chilly March morning. Resolutely, she shook off the mood. Frank would not have wanted to leave sadness behind. Jo studied the coffee, then sipped. It was predictably dreadful. "Rumor has it we're following last year's route to the letter. Thirteen states." Jo smiled, watching Duffy wince over his coffee before he downed it. "Not superstitious, are you?" She grinned, knowing he kept a four-leaf clover in his billfold.

"*Pah!*" he said indignantly, coloring under his freckles. He set down his empty cup, then moved around his desk and sat behind it. When he folded his hands on the yellow blotter, Jo knew he was getting down to business. Through the open window she could hear the band rehearsing. "We should be in Ocala by six tomorrow," he began. Dutifully, Jo nodded. "Should have the tents up before nine."

"The parade should be over by ten, and the matinee will start at two," Jo finished with a smile. "Duffy, you're not going to ask me to work the menagerie in the side show again, are you?"

"Should be a good crowd," he replied, adroitly skirting her question. "Bonzo predicts clear skies."

"Bonzo should stick with pratfalls and unicycles." She watched as Duffy chewed on the stub of a now dead cigar. "Okay," she said firmly, "let's have it."

"Someone's going to be joining us in Ocala, at least temporarily.'' He pursed his lips as his eyes met Jo's. His were blue, faded with age. ''I don't know if he'll finish out the season with us.''

''Oh, Duffy, not some first of mayer we have to break in this late?'' Jo demanded, using the circus term for novice. ''What is he, some energetic writer who wants an epic on the vanishing tent circus? He'll spend a few weeks as a roustabout and swear he knows all there is to know about it.''

''I don't think he'll be working as a roustabout,'' Duffy muttered. Striking a match, he coaxed the cigar back to life. Jo frowned, watching the smoke struggle toward the ceiling.

''It's a bit late to work in a new act now, isn't it?''

''He's not a performer.'' Duffy swore lightly under his breath, then met Jo's eyes again. ''He owns us.''

For a moment Jo said nothing. She sat unmoving, as Duffy had seen her from time to time when she trained a young cat. ''No!'' She rose suddenly, shaking her head. ''Not him. Not now. Why does he have to come? What does he want here?''

''It's his circus,'' Duffy reminded her. His voice was both rough and sympathetic.

''It'll never be his circus,'' Jo retorted passionately. Her eyes lit and glowed with a temper she rarely let have sway. ''It's Frank's circus.''

''Frank's dead,'' Duffy stated in a quiet, final tone. ''Now the circus belongs to his son.''

''Son?'' Jo countered. She lifted her fingers to press them against her temple. Slowly, she moved to the window. Outside, the sun was pouring over the heads of troupers. She watched the members of the trapeze act, in thick robes worn over their tights, head toward the ring barn. The chatter of mixed languages was so familiar she failed to notice it. She placed her palms on the window sill and with a little sigh, steadied her temper. ''What sort of son is it who never bothers to visit his father? In thirty years he never came to see Frank. He never wrote. He didn't even come to the funeral.'' Jo swallowed the tears of anger that rose to her throat and thickened her voice. ''Why should he come now?''

''You've got to learn that life's a two-sided coin, kiddo,'' Duffy said briskly. ''You weren't even alive thirty years ago.

You don't know why Frank's wife up and left him or why the boy never visited.''

"He's not a boy, Duffy, he's a man." Jo turned back, and he saw that she again had herself under control. "He's thirty-one, thirty-two years old now, a very successful attorney with a fancy Chicago office. He's very wealthy, did you know?" A small smile played on her lips but failed to reach her eyes. "And not just from court cases and legal fees; there's quite a lot of money on his mother's side. Nice, quiet, old money. I can't understand what a rich city lawyer would want with a tent circus."

Duffy shrugged his broad, round shoulders. "Could be he wants a tax shelter. Could be he wants to ride an elephant. Could be anything. He might want to take inventory and sell us off, piece by piece."

"Oh, Duffy, no!" Emotion flew back into Jo's face. "He couldn't do that."

"The heck he couldn't," Duffy muttered as he stubbed out his cigar. "He can do as he pleases. If he wants to liquidate, he liquidates."

"But we have contracts through October...."

"You're too smart for that, Jo." Duffy frowned, scratching his rim of hair. "He can buy them off or let them play through. He's a lawyer. He can figure the way out of a contract if he wants to. He can wait till August when we start to negotiate again and let them all lapse." Seeing Jo's distress, he backpedaled. "Listen, kiddo, I didn't say he was going to sell, I said he *could.*"

Jo ran a hand through her hair. "There must be something we can do."

"We can show a profit by the end of the season," Duffy said wryly. "We can show the new owner what we have to offer. I think it's important that he sees we're not just a mud show but a profitable three-ring circus with class acts. He should see what Frank built, how he lived, what he wanted to do. I think," Duffy added, watching Jo's face, "that you should be in charge of his education."

"Me?" Jo was too incredulous to be angry. "Why? You're better qualified in the public relations department than I am. I train lions, not lawyers.'' She could not keep the hint of scorn from her voice.

''You were closer to Frank than anyone. And there isn't anyone here who knows this circus better than you.'' Again he frowned. ''And you've got brains. Never thought much use would come of all those fancy books you read, but maybe I was wrong.''

''Duffy.'' Her lips curved into a smile. ''Just because I like to read Shakespeare doesn't mean I can deal with Keane Prescott. Even thinking about him makes me furious. How will I act when I meet him face to face?''

''Well.'' Duffy shrugged before he pursed his lips. ''If you don't think you can handle it...''

''I didn't say I *couldn't* handle it,'' Jo muttered.

''Of course, if you're afraid...''

''I'm not afraid of anything, and I'm certainly not afraid of some Chicago lawyer who doesn't know sawdust from tanbark.'' Sticking her hands in her pockets, she paced the length of the small room. ''If Keane Prescott, attorney-at-law, wants to spend his summer with the circus, I'll do my best to make it a memorable one.''

''Nicely,'' Duffy cautioned as Jo moved to the door.

''Duffy,'' she paused and gave him an innocent smile. ''You know what a gentle touch I have.'' To prove it, Jo slammed the door behind her.

Dawn was hovering over the horizon as the circus caravan drew up in a large, grassy field. Colors were just a promise in a pale gray sky. In the distance was grove upon grove of orange trees. As Jo stepped from the cab of her truck, the fragrance met her. It's a perfect day, she decided, then took a long, greedy breath. To her, there was no more beautiful sight than dawn struggling to life.

The air was vaguely chilly. She zipped up her gray sweat jacket as she watched the rest of the circus troupe pouring out of their trucks and cars and trailers. The morning quiet was soon shattered by voices. Work began immediately. As the Big Top canvas was being unrolled out of the spool truck, Jo went to see how her lions had fared the fifty-mile journey.

Three handlers unloaded the traveling cages. Buck had been with Jo the longest. He had worked for her father, and during the interim between his death and Jo's professional debut, he had worked up a small act with four male lions. His shyness had made his retirement from performing a relief. To Buck, two people were a crowd. He stood six-feet-four, and his build was powerful enough for him to pad the sideshow from time to time as Hercules the Strong Man. He had an impressive head of wild blond hair and a full, curling beard. His hands were wide, with thick, strong fingers, but Jo remembered their gentleness when the two of them had delivered a lioness of a pair of cubs.

Pete's small frame seemed puny beside Buck's. He was of indeterminable age. Jo guessed between forty and fifty, but she was never certain. He was a quiet man with skin like polished mahogany and a rich, low-pitched voice. He had come to Jo five years before, asking for a job. She had never asked where he had come from, and he had never told her. He wore a fielder's cap and was never seen without a wad of gum moving gently in his teeth. He read Jo's books and was the undisputed king of the poker table.

Gerry was nineteen and eager. He was nearly six feet and still carried the lankiness of his youth. His mother sewed, and his father was a souvenir salesman, or a candy butcher, as circus jargon had it. Working the big cage was Gerry's dream, and because it had been hers, Jo had finally agreed to tutor him.

"How are my babies?" she demanded as she approached. At each cage she paused and soothed a nervous cat, calling each by name until they had settled. "They've traveled well. Hamlet's still edgy, but it's his first year on the road."

"He's a mean one," Buck muttered, watching Jo move from cage to cage.

"Yes, I know," she replied absently. "He's smart, too." She had twisted her hair into one thick braid and now tossed it to her back. "Look, here come some towners." A few cars and a smattering of bikes drew into the field.

These were the people from the outlying towns who wanted to see a Big Top raised, who wanted to see the circus, if only for a moment, from the other side. Some would watch while others would lend a hand with tent poles, stretching canvas and rigging. They would earn a show pass and an unforgettable experience.

"Keep them clear of the cages," Jo ordered, nodding to Pete before she moved toward the still flaccid canvas. Buck lumbered beside her.

The field was alive with ropes and wire and people. Six elephants were harnessed but idle, with their handlers standing by the stake line. As workers pulled on guy ropes, the dusky brown canvas billowed up like a giant mushroom.

The poles were positioned—side, quarter, center—while the canvas muffled the sounds of scrambling workers. In the east the sun was rising fast, streaking the sky with pink. There were shouted instructions from the head canvas man, laughter from adventuresome boys and an occasional oath. As the quarter poles were driven into the sag of canvas, Jo signaled Maggie, the large African elephant. Obligingly, Maggie lowered her trunk. Jo stepped nimbly into the *u*, then scrambled onto the wide, gray back.

The sun grew higher by the second, shooting the first streams of light onto the field. The scent of orange blossoms mingled with the odor of leather harnesses. Jo had watched the canvas rise under a lightening sky countless times. Each time it was special, and the first raising each season was the most special of all. Maggie lifted her head and trumpeted as if pleased to be around for another season. With a laugh Jo reached back and swatted her rough, wrinkled rump. She felt free and fresh and incredibly alive. If there were a moment, she thought suddenly, that I could capture and bottle, it would be this one. Then, when I'm very old, I could take it out and feel young again. Smiling, she glanced down at the people swarming below her.

Her attention was caught by a man who stood by a coil of cable. Typically, she noted his build first. A well-proportioned body was essential to a performer. He was lean and stood straight. She noted he had good shoulders but doubted if there was much muscle in his arms. Though he was dressed casually in jeans, *city* stood out all over him. His hair was a dark, rich blond, and the early breeze had disturbed it so that it teased his forehead. He was clean-shaven, with a narrow, firm-jawed face. It was an attractive face. It was not, Jo mused, smoothly handsome like Vito the wire walker's but more aware, more demanding. Jo liked the face, liked the shape of the long, unsmiling mouth, liked the hint of bone beneath his tawny skin. Most of all she liked the directness of the amber eyes that stared back at her. They're like Ari's, she observed, thinking of her favorite lion. She was certain that he had been watching her long before she had looked down. Knowing this, Jo was impressed with his unselfconsciousness. He continued to stare, making no effort to camouflage his interest. She laughed, unperturbed, and tossed her braid from her shoulder.

"Want a ride?" she called out. Too many strangers had walked in and out of her world for her to be aloof. She watched his brow lift in acknowledgment of her offer. She would see if it was only his eyes that were like Ari's. "Maggie won't hurt you. She's gentle as a lamb, just bigger." Instantly, she saw he had understood the challenge. He walked across the grass until he stood beside her. He moved well, she noted. Jo tapped Maggie's side with the bull hook she carried. Wearily, the elephant knelt down on her trunklike front legs. Jo held out her hand. With an agility that surprised her, the man mounted the elephant and slid into place behind her.

For a moment she said nothing, a bit stunned by the trembling that had coursed up her arm as her palm had met his. The contact had been brief. Jo decided she had imagined it. "Up, Maggie," she said, giving her mount another tap. With an elephantine sigh, Maggie obeyed, rocking her passengers gently from side to side.

"Do you always pick up strange men?" the voice behind her inquired. It was a smooth, well-keyed voice, a good pitchman's voice.

Jo grinned over her shoulder. "Maggie's doing the picking up."

"So she is. Are you aware that she's remarkably uncomfortable?"

Jo laughed with genuine enjoyment. "You should try riding her a few miles in a street parade while keeping a smile on your face."

"I'll pass. Are you in charge of her?"

"Maggie? No, but I know how to handle her. You have eyes

like one of my cats," she told him. "I like them. And since you seemed to be interested in Maggie and me, I asked you up."

This time it was he who laughed. Jo twisted her head, wanting to see his face. There was humor in his eyes now, and his teeth were white and straight. Liking his smile, she answered with one of her own. "Fascinating. You asked me to take a ride on an elephant because I have eyes like your cat's. And no offense to the lady beneath me, but I was looking at you."

"Oh?" Jo pursed her lips in thought. "Why?"

For several seconds he studied her in silence. "Strange, I believe you really don't know."

"I wouldn't ask if I did," she returned, shifting her weight slightly. "It would be a waste of time to ask a question if I knew the answer." She shifted again and turned away from him. "Hold on now. Maggie's got to earn her bale of hay."

The poles hung between the canvas and the ground at forty-five degree angles. Quickly the elephant's chains were hooked to the metal rings at the base of the quarter poles. Jo urged Maggie forward in unison with her coworkers. Poles skidded along the ground, then up into place, pushing the canvas with it. The Big Top billowed to life under the early morning sky.

Her job done, Maggie moved through the flaps and into the light. "Beautiful, isn't it?" Jo murmured. "It's born fresh every day."

Vito walked by, calling out to Jo in Italian. Sending him a wave, she called back in his own language, then signaled to Maggie to kneel again. Jo waited until her passenger had dismounted before she slid off. It surprised her, when they stood face to face, that he was so tall. Tilting back her head, she judged him to be only two inches shy of Buck.

"You looked shorter when I was up on Maggie," she told him with her usual candor.

"You looked taller."

Jo chuckled, patting Maggie behind the ear. "Will you see the show?" She knew that she wanted him to, knew as well that she wanted to see him again. She found this both strange and intriguing. Men had always taken a second place to her cats, and towners had never interested her.

"Yes, I'm going to see the show." There was a slight smile

on his face, but he was studying her thoughtfully. "Do you perform?"

"I have an act with my cats."

"I see. Somehow I pictured you in an aerial act, flying from the trapeze."

She sent him an easy smile. "My mother was an aerialist." Someone called her name, and looking, Jo saw Maggie was needed for raising the sideshow tent. "I have to go. I hope you like the show."

He took her hand before she could lead Maggie away. Jo stood still, again surprised by a trembling up her arm. "I'd like to see you tonight."

Glancing up, she met his eyes. They were direct and unself-conscious. "Why?" The question was sincere. Jo knew she wanted to see him as well but was unsure why.

This time he did not laugh. Gently, he ran a finger down the length of her braid. "Because you're beautiful, and you intrigue me."

"Oh." Jo considered. She had never thought of herself as beautiful. Striking, perhaps, in her costume, surrounded by her cats, but in jeans, without makeup, she doubted it. Still, it was an interesting thought. "All right, if there's no trouble with the cats. Ari hasn't been well."

A smile played at the corners of his mouth. "I'm sorry to hear that."

There was another loud summons for Jo, and both looked toward it. "I see you're needed," he said with a nod. "Perhaps you could point out Bill Duffy for me before you go."

"Duffy?" Jo repeated, surprised. "You can't be looking for a job?" There was incredulity in her voice, and he grinned.

"Why can't I?"

"Because you don't fit any of the types."

"Are there types?" he asked, both interested and amused. Jo shook her head in annoyance.

"Yes, of course, and you don't fit into any of them."

"Actually, I'm not looking for a job, so to speak," he told her, still smiling. "But I am looking for Bill Duffy."

It was against Jo's nature to probe. Privacy was both guarded and respected in the circus. Shielding her eyes with her hand, Jo looked around until she spotted Duffy supervising the raising of the cookhouse tent. "There," she said, pointing. "Duffy's the one with the red checked jacket. He still dresses like an outside talker."

"A what?"

"You'd call it a barker, I imagine." With easy grace she mounted the patient Maggie. "That's a towner's term, not a circus one." She smiled at him, then urged Maggie into a walk. "Tell Duffy Jo said to give you a pass," she called over her shoulder, then waved and turned away.

Dawn was over, and it was morning.

Two

Jo stood at the back door of the Big Top waiting for her cue. Beside her was Jamie Carter, alias Topo. He was a third generation clown and wore his bright face and orange wig naturally. He was young and limber and used these traits as well as his makeup to bring enthusiasm to his craft. To Jo, Jamie was more brother than friend. He was tall and thin, and under his grease-paint his face was mobile and pleasant. He and Jo had grown up together.

"Did she say anything?" Jamie demanded for the third time. With a sigh, Jo tossed closed the flap of the tent. Inside, clowns were performing around the hippodrome track while hands set up the big cage.

"Carmen said nothing. I don't know why you waste your time." Her voice was sharp, and Jamie bristled.

"I don't expect you to understand," he said with great dignity. His thin shoulders drew straight under his red polka dot shirt. "After all, Ari's the closest you've come to being involved with the opposite sex."

"That's very cute," Jo replied, unoffended by the jibe. Her annoyance stemmed from seeing Jamie make a fool of himself over Carmen Gribalti, the middle sister of the flying Gribaltis. She was darkly beautiful, graceful, talented, selfish and sublimely indifferent to Jamie. Looking into his happy, painted face and moody eyes, Jo's irritation dissipated. "She probably hasn't had a chance to answer the note you sent her," she soothed. "The first day of a new season's always wild."

"I suppose," Jamie muttered with a grudging shrug. "I don't know what she sees in Vito."

Jo thought of the wire walker's dark, cocky looks and rippling muscles. Wisely, she refrained from mentioning them. "Who can account for taste?'' She gave him a smacking kiss on his round, red nose. ''Personally, I get all wobbly when I see a man with thick, orange hair.''

Jamie grinned. ''Proves you know what to look for in a man.''

Turning, Jo lifted the flap again, noting Jamie's cue was nearly upon them. ''Did you happen to notice a towner hanging around today?''

''Only a couple dozen of them,'' Jamie answered dryly as he lifted the pail of confetti he used to finish the gag now being performed inside.

Jo shot him a half-hearted glare. ''Not the usual type. About thirty, I think,'' she continued. ''Wearing jeans and a T-shirt. He was tall, six-one, six-two,'' she went on as laughter poured out of the open flap to drown out her words. ''He had dark blond straight hair.''

''Yeah, I saw him.'' Jamie nudged her out of his way and prepared to make his entrance. ''He was going into the red wagon with Duffy.'' With a wild, high-pitched scream, Topo the clown bounded into the Big Top in size fifteen tennis shoes, brandishing his bucket of confetti.

Thoughtfully, Jo watched Jamie chase three other clowns around the track. It was odd, she thought, for Duffy to take a towner into the administration trailer. He had said he wasn't looking for a job. He wasn't a drifter; there was an unmistakable air of stability about him. He wasn't a circus hand from another show, either. His palm had been too smooth. And, her mind added as she vaulted onto Babette, a pure white mare, there had been an undeniable aura of urbanity about him. Success, as well, she thought. And authority. No, he had not been looking for a job.

Jo shrugged, annoyed that a stranger was crowding into her thoughts. It irritated her further that she had scanned the crowds for him during the parade and that even now she wondered if he sat somewhere in the circular arena. He hadn't been at the matinee. Jo patted the mare's neck absently, then straightened as she heard the ringmaster's whistle.

''Ladies and gentlemen,'' he called in deep, musical tones. ''Presenting the most spectacular exhibition of animal subjugation under the Big Top. Jovilette, Queen of the Jungle Cats!''

Jo nudged Babette with her heels and raced into the arena. The applause rose to meet her as the audience appreciated the dashing figure she cut. Swathed in a black cape, raven hair flying free under a glittering tiara, she galloped bareback on the snow white mare. In each hand she held a long, thin whip, which she cracked alternately overhead. At the entrance to the big cage she leaped from the still racing horse. While Babette galloped out of the back door and into the care of a handler, Jo shifted both whips into one hand, then removed the cape with a flourish. Her costume was a close-fitting, one-piece jumpsuit, dazzling in white and spangled with gold sequins. In dramatic contrast, her hair hung straight and severe down her back.

Make an entrance, Frank had always said. And Jovilette made an entrance.

The twelve cats were already in the cage, banding its inside edge as they perched on blue and white pedestals. Entering the main cage appeared routine to the audience, but Jo knew it was one of the most dangerous moments of the act. To enter, she had to pass directly between two cats as she moved from the safety cage to the main arena. She always stationed her best behaved cats there, but if one was irritated, or even playful, he could easily strike out with a powerful paw. Even with sharp claws retracted, the damage could be deadly.

She entered swiftly and was surrounded by cats on all sides. Her spangles and tiara caught the lights and played with them as she began to move around the cage, cracking the whip for showmanship while using her voice to command the cats to rise on their haunches. She moved them through their routine, adjusting the timing to compensate for any feline reluctance, letting one trick begin where the last ended.

Jo disliked overdone propping, preferring action and movement. The contrast of the big, tawny cats and the small white and gold woman were the best props available to her. She used them well. Hers was a *picture act,* relying on style and flash, rather than a *fighting act,* which emphasized the ferocity of the big cats by employing blank-bulleted guns and rehearsed charges, or *bounces.* Her confidence transmitted itself to the audience, making her handling of the cats appear effortless. In truth, her body was coiled for any danger, and her mind was focused so intently on her cats, there might have been no audience at all.

She stood between two high pedestals as the cats leaped over her head from both directions. They set up a light breeze, which stirred her hair. They roared when she cued them, setting up an echoing din. Now and then one reached out to paw at the stock of her whip, and she stopped him with a quick command. She sent her best leaper through a hoop of flame and coaxed her best balancer to walk on a glistening silver ball. She ended to waves of applause by trotting Merlin around the hippodrome track.

At the back door Merlin jumped into a wheel cage and was turned over to Pete. "Nice show," he said as he handed her a long chenille robe. "Smooth as silk."

"Thanks." Cold, she bundled into the robe. The spring night was frigid in contrast to the hot lights and heat in the big cage. "Listen, Pete, tell Gerry he can feed the cats tonight. They're behaving themselves."

Pete snapped his gum and chuckled. "Won't he be riding high tonight." As he moved to the truck that would pull the cage to the cat area, Jo called after him.

"Pete." She bit her lip, then shrugged when he twisted his head. "You'll keep an eye on him, won't you?"

Pete grinned and climbed into the cab of the truck. "Who you worried about, Jo? Those big cats or that skinny boy?"

"Both," she answered. The rhinestones in her tiara sparkled as she tossed her head and laughed. Knowing she had nearly an hour before the finale parade, Jo walked away from the Big Top. She thought of wandering to the cookhouse for some coffee. Mentally, she began replaying every segment of her act. It had gone well, she thought, pleased with the timing and the flow. If Pete had said it had been smooth, Jo knew it had. She had heard his criticisms more than once over the past five years. True, Hamlet had tested her once or twice, but no one knew that but Jo and the cat. She doubted if anyone but Buck would have seen that he had given her trouble. Closing her eyes a moment, Jo rolled her shoulders, loosening tight, tensed muscles.

"That's quite an act you have."

Jo whirled around at the sound of the voice. She could feel her heart rate accelerate. Though she wondered at her interest in

a man she barely knew, Jo was aware that she had been waiting
for him. There was a quick surge of pleasure as she watched him
approach, and she allowed it to show on her face.

"Hello." She saw that he smoked a cigar, but unlike Duffy's,
his was long and slim. Again she admired the elegance of his
hands. "Did you like the show?"

He stopped in front of her, then studied her face with a thor-
oughness that made her wonder if her makeup had smeared. Then
he gave a small, surprised laugh and shook his head. "Do you
know," he began, "when you told me this morning that you did
an act with cats, I had Siamese in mind rather than African."

"Siamese?" Jo repeated blankly, then laughed. "House
cats?" He brushed her hair behind her back while Jo giggled at
the thought of coaxing a Siamese to jump through a flaming
hoop.

"From my point of view," he told her as he let a strand of
her hair linger between his fingers, "it made more sense than a
little thing like you walking into a cage with a dozen lions."

"I'm not little," Jo corrected good-naturedly. "Besides, size
hardly matters to twelve lions."

"No, I suppose it doesn't." He lifted his eyes from her hair
and met hers. Jo continued to smile, enjoying looking at him.
"Why do you do it?" he asked suddenly.

Jo gave him a curious look. "Why? Because it's my job."

By the way he studied her, Jo could see that he was not satisfied with the simplicity of her answer. "Perhaps I should ask
how you became a lion tamer."

"Trainer," Jo corrected automatically. To her left, she could
hear the audience's muffled applause. "The Beirots are starting,"
she said with a glance toward the sound. "You shouldn't miss
their act. They're first-rate acrobats."

"Don't you want to tell me?" His voice was soft.

She lifted a brow, seeing that he truly wanted to know. "Why,
it's not a secret. My father was a trainer, and I have a knack for
working with cats. It just followed." Jo had never thought about
her career past this point, and she shrugged it aside. "You
shouldn't waste your ticket standing out here. You can stand by
the back door and watch the rest of the act." Jo turned to lead

the way to the performer's entrance but stopped when his hand took hers.

He stepped forward until their bodies were nearly touching. Jo could feel the heat from his as she watched his face. Her heart was thudding in a quick, steady rhythm. She could hear it vibrate through her the same way it did when she approached a new cat for the first time. Here was something new, something untested. She tingled with the excitement of the unknown when he lifted his hand to touch her cheek. She did not move but let the warmth spread while she watched him carefully, gauging him. Her eyes were wide, curious and unafraid.

"Are you going to kiss me?" she asked in a tone that expressed more interest than desire.

His eyes lit with humor and glittered in the dim light. "I had given it some thought," he answered. "Do you have any objections?"

Jo considered a moment, dropping her eyes to his mouth. She liked its shape and wondered how it would feel against hers. He brought her no closer. One hand still held hers while the other slid around to cradle her neck. Jo shifted her gaze until their eyes met again. "No," she decided. "I haven't any objections."

The corners of his mouth twitched as he tightened his hold slightly on the base of her neck. Slowly, he lowered his head toward hers. Curious and a bit wary, Jo kept her eyes open, watching his. She knew from experience that you could tell more about people and about cats from the eyes. To her surprise, his remained open as well, even as their lips met.

It was a gentle kiss, without pressure, only a whisper of a touch. Amazed, Jo thought she felt the ground tremble under her feet. Dimly, she wondered if the elephants were being led by. But it can't be time, she thought in confusion. His lips moved lightly over hers, and his eyes remained steady. Jo's pulse drummed under her skin. They stood, barely touching, as the Big Top throbbed with noise behind them. Lazily, he traced her lips with the tip of his tongue, teasing them open. Still there was no demand in the kiss, only testing. Unhurried, confident, he explored her mouth while Jo felt her breath accelerating. A soft moan escaped her as her lids fluttered down.

For an instant she surrendered utterly to him, to the new sensations swimming through her. She leaned against him, straining toward pleasure, sighing with it as the kiss lingered.

He drew her away, but their faces remained close. Dizzily, Jo realized that she had risen to her toes to compensate for their difference in height. His hand was still light on the back of her neck. His eyes were gold in the darkening night.

"What an incredible female you are, Jovilette," he murmured. "One surprise after another."

Jo felt stunningly alive. Her skin seemed to tingle with new feelings. She smiled. "I don't know your name."

He laughed, releasing her neck to take her other hand in his. Before he could speak, Duffy called out from the direction of the Big Top. Jo turned to watch as he moved toward them in his quick, rolling walk.

"Well, well, well," he said in his jolly, rough voice. "I didn't know you two had met. Has Jo been showing you around already?" Reaching them, he squeezed Jo's shoulder. "Knew I could count on you, kiddo." Jo glanced at him in puzzlement, but he continued before she could form a question. "Yes, sir, this little girl puts on quite a show, doesn't she? Always a grabber. And she knows this circus like the back of her hand. Born and raised to it," he continued. Jo relaxed. She recognized that Duffy was into one of his spiels, and there was no stopping him. "Yessiree, any questions you got, you just ask our Jo, and she'll tell you. 'Course, I'm always at your disposal, too. Anything I can tell you about the books or accounts or contracts and the like, you just let me know." Duffy puffed twice on his cigar as Jo felt her first hint of unease.

Why was Duffy rambling about books and contracts? Jo glanced at the man who still held her hands in his. He was watching Duffy with an easy, amused smile.

"Are you a bookkeeper?" Jo asked, perplexed. Duffy laughed and patted her head.

"You know Mr. Prescott's a lawyer, Jo. Don't miss your cue." He gave them both a friendly nod and toddled off.

Jo had stiffened almost imperceptibly at Duffy's offhand information, but Keane had felt it. His brows lowered as he studied her. "Now you know my name."

"Yes." All warmth fled from Jo. Her voice was as cool as her blood. "Would you let go of my hands, Mr. Prescott?"

After a brief hesitation Keane inclined his head and obliged. Jo stuffed her hands quickly into the pockets of her robe. "Don't you think we've progressed to the first name stage of our relationship, Jo?"

"I assure you, Mr. Prescott, if I had known who you were, we wouldn't have progressed at all." Jo's words were stiff with dignity. Inside, though she tried to ignore it, she felt betrayal, anger, humiliation. All pleasure had died from the evening. Now the kiss that had left her feeling clean and alive seemed cheap and shabby. No, she would not use his first name, she vowed. She would never use it. "If you'll excuse me, I have some things to do before my cue."

"Why the turnaround?" he asked, halting her with a hand on her arm. "Don't you like lawyers?"

Coldly, Jo studied him. She wondered how it was possible that she had completely misjudged the man she had met that morning. "I don't categorize people, Mr. Prescott."

"I see." Keane's tone became detached, his eyes assessing. "Then it would appear that you have an aversion to my name. Should I assume you hold a grudge against my father?"

Jo's eyes glittered with quick fury. She jerked her arm from his hold. "Frank Prescott was the most generous, the kindest, most unselfish man I've ever known. I don't even associate you with Frank, Mr. Prescott. You have no right to him." Though it was nearly impossible, Jo forced herself to speak in a normal tone of voice. She would not shout and draw anyone's attention. This would be kept strictly between Keane Prescott and herself. "It would have been much better if you had told me who you were right away, then there would have been no mix-up."

"Is that what we've had?" he countered mildly. "A mix-up?"

His cool tone was nearly Jo's undoing. He watched her with a dispassionate curiosity that tempted her to slap him. She fought to keep her fury from spilling over into her voice. "You have no right to Frank's circus, Mr. Prescott," she managed quietly. "Leaving it to you is the only thing I've ever faulted him for." Knowing her control was slipping, Jo whirled, running across the grass until she merged with the darkness.

Three

The morning was surprisingly warm. There were no trees to block the sun, and the smell of the earth was strong. The circus had moved north in the early hours. All the usual scents merged into the aroma of circus: canvas, leather, sweating horses, greasepaint and powder, coffee and oilcloth. The trailers and trucks sat in the accustomed spots, forming the "back yard" that would always take the same formation each time the circus made a stop along the thousands of miles it traveled. The flag over the cookhouse tent signaled that lunch was being served. The Big Top stood waiting for the matinee.

Rose hurried along the midway toward the animal cages. Her dark hair was pinned neatly in a bun at the back of her neck. Her big brown eyes darted about searchingly, while her mouth sat softly in a pout. She was wrapped in a terry cloth robe and wore tennis shoes over her tights. When she saw Jo standing in front of Ari's cage, she waved and broke into a half-run. Watching her, Jo shifted her attention from Ari. Rose was always a diversion, and Jo felt in need of one.

"Jo!" She waved again as if Jo had not seen her the first time, then came to a breathless halt. "Jo, I only have a few minutes. Hello, Ari," she added out of politeness. "I was looking for Jamie."

"Yes, I gathered." Jo smiled, knowing Rose had set her heart on capturing Topo's alter ego. And if he had any sense, she thought, he'd let himself be caught instead of pining over Carmen. Silly, she decided, dismissing all affairs of the heart. Lions were easier to understand. "I haven't seen him all morning, Rose. Maybe he's rehearsing."

"Drooling over Carmen, more likely," Rose muttered, sending a sulky glare in the direction of the Gribalti trailer. "He makes a fool of himself."

"That's what he's paid for," Jo reminded her, but Rose did not respond to the humor. Jo sighed. She had a true affection for Rose. She was bright and fun and without pretentions. "Rose," she said, keeping her voice both light and kind. "Don't give up on him. He's a little slow, you know," she explained. "He's just a bit dazzled by Carmen right now. It'll pass."

"I don't know why I bother," she grumbled, but Jo saw the dark mood was already passing. Rose was a creature of quick passions that flared and soon died. "He's not so very handsome, you know."

"No," Jo agreed. "But he has a cute nose."

"Lucky for him I like red," Rose returned and grinned. "Ah, now we're speaking of handsome," she murmured as her eyes drifted from Jo. "Who is this?"

At the question, Jo glanced over her shoulder. The humor fled from her eyes. "That's the owner," she said colorlessly.

"Keane Prescott? No one told me he was so handsome. Or so tall," she added, admiring him openly as he crossed the back yard. Jo noted that Rose always became more Mexican around men. "Such shoulders. Lucky for Jamie I'm a one-man woman."

"Lucky for you your mama can't hear you," Jo muttered, earning an elbow in the ribs.

"But he comes here, *amiga,* and he looks at you. La, la, my papa would have Jamie to the altar *pronto* if he looked at me that way."

"You're an idiot," Jo snapped, annoyed.

"Ah, Jo," Rose said with mock despair. "I am a romantic."

Jo was helpless against the smile that tugged at her lips. Her eyes were laughing when she glanced up and met Keane's. Hastily, she struggled to dampen their brilliance, turning her mouth into a sober line.

"Good morning, Jovilette." He spoke her name too easily, she thought, as if he had been saying it for years.

"Good morning, Mr. Prescott," she returned. Rose gave a loud, none-too-subtle cough. "This is Rose Sanches."

"It's a pleasure, Mr. Prescott." Rose extended a hand, trying out a smile she had been saving for Jamie. "I heard you were traveling with us."

Keane accepted the hand and smiled in return. Jo noticed with annoyance that it was the same easy, disarming smile of the stranger she had met the morning before. "Hello, Rose, it's nice to meet you."

Seeing her friend's Mexican blood heat her cheeks, Jo intervened. She would not permit Keane Prescott to make a conquest here. "Rose, you only have ten minutes to get back and into makeup."

"Holy cow!" she said, forgetting her attempt at sophistication. "I've got to run." She began to do so, then called over her shoulder, "Don't tell Jamie I was looking for him, the pig!" She ran a little further, then turned and ran backwards. "I'll look for him later," she said with a laugh, then turned back and streaked toward the midway.

Keane watched her dart across the compound while holding up the long skirts of her robe in one hand. "Charming."

"She's only eighteen," Jo offered before she could stop herself.

When Keane turned to her, his look was one of amusement. "I see," he said. "I'll take that information under advisement. And what does the eighteen-year-old Rose do?" he asked, slipping his thumbs into the front pockets of his jeans. "Wrestle alligators?"

"No." Jo returned without batting an eye. "Rose is Serpentina, your premier sideshow attraction. The snake charmer." She was pleased with the incredulous look that passed over his face. It was replaced quickly, however, with one of genuine humor.

"Perfect." He brushed Jo's hair from her cheek before she could protest by word or action. "Cobras?" he asked, ignoring the flash in her eyes.

"And boa constrictors," she returned sweetly. Jo brushed the dust from the knees of her faded jeans. "Now, if you'll excuse me..."

"No, I don't think so." Keane's voice was cool, but she recognized the underlying authority. She did her best not to struggle against it. He *was* the owner, she reminded herself.

"Mr. Prescott," she began, banking down hard on the urge to

mutiny. "I'm very busy. I have to get ready for the afternoon show."

"You've got an hour and a half until you're on," he countered smoothly. "I think you might spare me a portion of that time. You've been assigned to show me around. Why don't we start now?" The tone of the question left room for only one answer. Jo's mind fidgeted in search of a way out.

Tilting her head back, she met his eyes. He won't be easy to beat, she concluded, studying his steady, measuring gaze. I'd better study his moves more carefully before I start a battle. "Where would you like to begin?" she asked aloud.

"With you."

Keane's easy answer brought a deep frown to Jo's brows. "I don't understand what you mean."

For a moment Keane watched her. There was no coyness or guile in her eyes as they looked into his. "No, I can see you don't," he agreed with a nod. "Let's start with your cats."

"Oh." Jo's frown cleared instantly. "All right." She watched as he pulled out a thin cigar, waiting until the flame of his lighter licked the tip before speaking. "I have thirteen—seven males, six females. They're all African lions between four-and-a-half and twenty-two years."

"I thought you worked with twelve," Keane commented as he dropped his lighter into his pocket.

"That's right, but Ari's retired." Turning, Jo indicated the large male lion dozing in a cage. "He travels with me because he always has, but I don't work him anymore. He's twenty-two, the oldest. My father kept him, even though he was born in captivity, because he was born the same day I was." Jo sighed, and her voice became softer. "He's the last of my father's stock. I couldn't sell him to a zoo. It seemed like shoving an old relative into a home and abandoning him. He's been with this circus every day of his life, just as I have. His name is Hebrew for *lion*." Jo laughed, forgetting the man beside her as she sifted through memories. "My father always gave his cats names that meant lion somehow or other. Leo, Leonard, Leonara. Ari was a first-class leaper in his prime. He could climb, too; some cats won't. I could teach Ari anything. Smart cat, aren't you, Ari?" The altered tone of her voice caused the big cat to stir. Opening his eyes, he stared back at Jo. The sound he made was more grumble than roar before he dozed again. "He's tired," Jo murmured, fighting a shaft of gloom. "Twenty-two's old for a lion."

"What is it?" Keane demanded, touching her shoulder before she could turn away. Her eyes were drenched with sadness.

"He's dying," she said unsteadily. "And I can't stop it." Stuffing her hands in her pockets, Jo moved away to the main group of cages. To steady herself, she took two deep breaths while waiting for Keane to join her. Regaining her composure, she began again. "I work with these twelve," she told him, making a sweeping gesture. "They're fed once a day, raw meat six days a week and eggs and milk on the seventh. They were all imported directly from Africa and were cage broken when I got them."

The faint sound of a calliope reached them, signaling the opening of the midway. "This is Merlin, the one I ride out on at the finish. He's ten, and the most even-tempered cat I've ever worked with. Heathcliff," she continued as she moved down the line of cages, "he's six, my best leaper. And this is Faust, the baby at four and a half." The lions paced their cages as Jo walked Keane down the line. Unable to prevent herself, Jo gave Faust a signal by raising her hand. Obediently, he sent out a huge, deafening roar. To Jo's disappointment, Keane did not scramble for cover.

"Very impressive," he said mildly. "You put him in the center when you lie down on them, don't you?"

"Yes." She frowned, then spoke her thoughts candidly. "You're very observant—and you've got steady nerves."

"My profession requires them, too, to an extent," he returned.

Jo considered this a moment, then turned back to the lions. "Lazareth, he's twelve and a natural ham. Bolingbroke, he's ten, from the same lioness as Merlin. Hamlet," she said stopping again, "he's five. I bought him to replace Ari in the act." Jo stared into the tawny eyes. "He has potential, but he's arrogant. Patient, too. He's just waiting for me to make a mistake."

"Why?" Keane glanced over at Jo. Her eyes were cool and steady on Hamlet's.

"So he can get a good clean swipe at me," she told him without altering her expression. "It's his first season in the big cage. Pandora,'' Jo continued, pointing out the females. "A very classy lady. She's six. Hester, at seven, my best all-around. And Portia; it's her first year, too. She's mostly a seat-warmer."

"Seat-warmer?"

"Just what it sounds like," Jo explained. "She hasn't mastered any complicated tricks yet. She evens out the act, does a few basics and warms the seat." Jo moved on. "Dulcinea, the prettiest of the ladies. Ophelia, who had a litter last year; and Abra, eight, a bit bad-tempered but a good balancer."

Hearing her name, the cat rose, stretched her long, golden body, then began to rub it against the bars of the cage. A deep sound rumbled in her throat. Jo scowled and jammed her hands into her pockets. "She likes you," she muttered.

"Oh?" Lifting a brow, Keane studied the three-hundred-pound Abra more carefully. "How do you know?"

"When a lion likes you, it does exactly what a house cat does. It rubs against you. Abra's rubbing against the bars because she can't get any closer."

"I see." Humor touched his mouth. "I must admit, I'm at a loss on how to return the compliment." He drew on his cigar, then regarded Jo through a haze of smoke. "Your choice of names is fascinating."

"I like to read," she stated, leaving it at that. "Is there anything else you'd like to know about the cats?" Jo was determined to keep their conversation on a professional level. His smile had reminded her all too clearly of their encounter the night before.

"Do you drug them before a performance?"

Fury sparked Jo's eyes. "Certainly not."

"Was that an unreasonable question?" Keane countered. He dropped his cigar to the ground, then crushed it out with his heel.

"Not for a first of mayer," Jo decided with a sigh. She tossed her hair carelessly behind her back. "Drugging is not only cruel, it's stupid. A drugged animal won't perform."

"You don't touch the lions with that whip," Keane commented. He watched the light breeze tease a few strands of her hair. "Why do you use it?"

"To get their attention and to keep the audience awake." She smiled reluctantly.

Keane took her arm. Instantly, Jo stiffened. "Let's walk," he suggested. He began to lead her away from the cages. Spotting several people roaming the back yard, Jo refrained from pulling away. The last thing she wanted was the story spreading that she was having a tiff with the owner. "How do you tame them?" he asked her.

"I don't. They're not tame, they're trained." A tall blond woman walked by carrying a tiny white poodle. "Merlin's hungry today," Jo called out with a grin.

The woman bundled the dog closer to her breast in mock alarm and began a rapid scolding in French. Jo laughed, telling her in the same language that Fifi was too tough a mouthful for Merlin.

"Fifi can do a double somersault on the back of a moving horse," Jo explained as they began to walk again. "She's trained just as my cats are trained, but she's also domesticated. The cats are wild." Jo turned her face up to Keane's. The sun cast a sheen over her hair and threw gold flecks into her eyes. "A wild thing can never be tamed, and anyone who tries is foolish. If you take something wild and turn it into a pet, you've stolen its character, blanked out its spark. And still, there's always an essence of the wild that can come back to life. When a dog turns on his master, it's ugly. When a lion turns, it's lethal." She was beginning to become accustomed to his hand on her arm, finding it easy to talk to him because he listened. "A full-grown male stands three feet at the shoulder and weighs over five hundred pounds. One well-directed swipe can break a man's neck, not to mention what teeth and claws can do." Jo gave a smile and a shrug. "Those aren't the virtues of a pet."

"Yet you go into a cage with twelve of them, armed with a whip?"

"The whip's window dressing." Jo discounted it with a gesture of her hand. "It would hardly be a defense against even one cat at full charge. A lion is a very tenacious enemy. A tiger is more bloodthirsty, but it normally strikes only once. If it misses, it takes it philosophically. A lion charges again and again. Do you know the line Byron wrote about a tiger's spring? 'Deadly, quick and crushing.'" Jo had completely forgotten her animosity and began to enjoy her walk and conversation with this handsome stranger. "It's a true description, but a lion is totally fearless when he charges, and stubborn. He's not the razzle-dazzle fighter the tiger is, just accurate. I'd bet on a lion against a tiger any day. And a man simply hasn't a prayer against one.''

''Then how do you manage to stay in one piece?''

The calliope music was just a hint in the air now. Jo turned, noting with surprise that they had walked a good distance from camp. She could see the trailers and tents, hear occasional shouts and laughter, but she felt oddly separated from it all. She sat down cross-legged on the grass and plucked a blade. ''I'm smarter than they are. At least I make them think so. And I dominate them, partly by a force of will. In training, you have to develop a rapport, a mutual respect, and if you're lucky, a certain affection. But you can't trust them to the point where you grow careless. And above all,'' she added, glancing over as he sat down beside her, ''you have to remember the basic rule of poker. Bluff.'' Jo grinned, leaning back on her elbows. ''Do you play poker?''

''I've been known to.'' Her hair trailed out along the grass, and he lifted a strand. ''Do you?''

''Sometimes. My assistant handler, Pete...'' Jo scanned the back yard, then smiled and pointed. ''There he is, by the second trailer, sitting with Mac Stevenson, the one with the fielder's cap. Pete organizes a game now and then.''

''Who's the little girl on stilts?''

''That's Mac's youngest, Katie. She wants to walk on them in the street parade. She's getting pretty good. There's Jamie,'' she said, then laughed as he did a pratfall and landed at Katie's wooden stilts.

''Rose's Jamie?'' Keane asked, watching the impromptu show in the back yard.

''If she has her way. He's currently dazzled by Carmen Gribalti. Carmen won't give Jamie the time of day. She bats her lashes at Vito, the wire walker. He bats his at everyone.''

''A complicated state of affairs,'' Keane commented. He twisted Jo's hair around his fingers. ''Romance seems to be very popular in circus life.''

''From what I read,'' she countered, ''it's popular everywhere.''

''Who dazzles you, Jovilette?'' He gave her hair a tug to bring her face around to his.

Jo hadn't realized he was so close. She need do no more than sway for her mouth to touch his. Her eyes measured his while she waited for her pulse to calm. It was odd, she thought, that he had such an effect on her. With sudden clarity, she could smell the grass, a clean, sweet scent, and feel the sun. The sounds of the circus were muted in the background. She could hear birds call out with an occasional high-pitched trill. She remembered the taste of his mouth and wondered if it would be the same.

"I've been too busy to be dazzled," she replied. Her voice was steady, but her eyes were curious.

For the first time, Jo truly *wanted* to be kissed by a man. She wanted to feel again what she had felt the night before. She wanted to be held, not lightly as he had held her before, but close, with his arms tight around her. She wanted to renew the feeling of weightlessness. She had never experienced a strong physical desire, and for a moment she explored the sensation. There was a quiver in her stomach which was both pleasant and disturbing. Throughout her silent contemplations Keane watched her, intrigued by the intensity of her eyes.

"What are you thinking of?"

"I'm wondering why you make me feel so odd," she told him with simple frankness. He smiled, and she noticed that it grew in his eyes seconds before it grew on his mouth.

"Do I?" He appeared to enjoy the information. "Did you know your hair catches the sunlight?" Keane took a handful, letting it spill from between his fingers. "I've never seen another woman with hair like this. It's a temptation all in itself. In what way do I make you feel odd, Jovilette?" he asked as his eyes trailed back up to hers.

"I'm not sure yet." Jo found her voice husky. Abruptly, she decided it would not do to go on feeling odd or to go on wanting to be kissed by Keane Prescott. She scrambled up and brushed off the seat of her pants.

"Running away?" As Keane rose, Jo's head snapped up.

"I never run away from anything, Mr. Prescott." Ice sharpened her voice. She was annoyed that she had allowed herself to fall under his charm again. "I certainly won't run from a city-bred lawyer." Her words were laced with scorn. "Why don't you go back to Chicago and get someone thrown in jail?"

"I'm a defense attorney," Keane countered easily. "I get people out of jail."

"Fine. Go put a criminal back on the streets, then."

Keane laughed, bringing Jo's temper even closer to the surface. "That covers both sides of the issue, doesn't it? You dazzle me, Jovilette."

"Well, it's strictly unintentional." She took a step back from the amusement in his eyes. She would not tolerate him making fun of her. "You don't belong here," she blurted out. "You have no business here."

"On the contrary," he disagreed in a cool, untroubled voice. "I have every business here. I own this circus."

"Why?" she demanded, throwing out her hands as if to push his words aside. "Because it says so on a piece of paper? That's all lawyers understand, I imagine—pieces of paper with strange little words. Why did you come? To look us over and calculate the profit and loss? What's the liquidation value of a dream, Mr. Prescott? What price do you put on the human spirit? Look at it!" she demanded, swinging her arm to encompass the lot behind them. "You only see tents and a huddle of trailers. You can't possibly understand what it all means. But Frank understood. He loved it."

"I'm aware of that." Keane's voice was still calm but had taken on a thin edge of steel. Jo saw that his eyes had grown dark and guarded. "He also left it to me."

"I don't understand why." In frustration, Jo stuffed her hands in her pockets and turned away.

"Neither do I, I assure you, but the fact remains that he did."

"Not once in thirty years did you visit him." Jo whirled back around. Her hair followed in a passionate arch. "Not once."

"Quite true," Keane agreed. He stood with his weight even on both legs and watched her. "Of course, some might look at it differently. Not once in thirty years did he visit me."

"Your mother left him and took you to Chicago—"

"I won't discuss my mother," Keane interrupted in a tone of clipped finality.

Jo bit off a retort, spinning away from him again. Still she could not find the reins to her control. "What are you going to do with it?" she demanded.

"That's my business."

"Oh!" Jo spun back, then shut her eyes and muttered in a language he failed to understand. "Can you be so arrogant? Can you be so dispassionate?" Her lashes fluttered up, revealing eyes dark with anger. "Do the lives of all those people mean nothing to you? Does Frank's dream mean nothing? Haven't you enough money already without hurting people to get more? Greed isn't something you inherited from Frank."

"I'll only be pushed so far," Keane warned.

"I'd push you all the way back to Chicago if I could manage it," she snapped.

"I wondered how much of a temper there was behind those sharp green eyes," Keane commented, watching her passion pour color into her cheeks. "It appears it's a full-grown one." Jo started to retort, but Keane cut her off. "Just hold on a minute," he ordered. "With or without your approval, I own this circus. It might be easier for you if you adjusted to that. Be quiet," he added when her mouth opened again. "Legally, I can do with my—" He hesitated a moment, then continued in a mordant tone. "—inheritance as I choose. I have no obligation or intention of justifying my decision to you."

Jo dug her nails into her palms to help keep her voice from shaking. "I never knew I could grow to dislike someone so quickly."

"Jovilette." Keane dipped his hands into his pockets, then rocked back on his heels. "You disliked me before you ever saw me."

"That's true," she replied evenly. "But I've learned to dislike you in person in less than twenty-four hours. I have a show to do," she said, turning back toward the lot. Though he did not follow, she felt his eyes on her until she reached her trailer and closed the door behind her.

Thirty minutes later Jamie sprang through the back door of the Big Top. He was breathless after a lengthy routine and hooked one hand through his purple suspenders as he took in gulps of air. He spotted Jo standing beside the white mare. Her eyes were dark and stormy, her shoulders set and rigid. Jamie recognized the signs. Something or someone had put Jo in a temper, and she had barely ten minutes to work her way out of it before her cue.

He crossed to her and gave a tug on her hair. "Hey."

"Hello, Jamie." Jo struggled to keep her voice pleasant, but he heard the traces of emotion.

"Hello, Jo," he replied in precisely the same tone.

"Cut it out," she ordered before taking a few steps away. The mare followed docilely. Jo had been trying for some time to put her emotions back into some semblance of order. She was not succeeding.

"What happened?" Jamie asked from directly behind her.

"Nothing," Jo snapped, then hated herself for the short nastiness of the word.

Jamie persisted, knowing her too well to be offended. "Nothing is one of my favorite topics of conversation." He put his hands on her shoulders, ignoring her quick, bad-tempered jerk. "Let's talk about it."

"There's nothing to talk about."

"Exactly." He began massaging the tension in her shoulders with his white gloved hands.

"Oh, Jamie." His good-heartedness was irresistible. Sighing, she allowed herself to be soothed. "You're an idiot."

"I'm not here to be flattered."

"I had an argument with the owner." Jo let out a long breath and shut her eyes.

"What're you doing having arguments with the owner?"

"He infuriates me." Jo whirled around. Her cape whipped and snapped with the movement. "He shouldn't be here. If he were back in Chicago..."

"Hold it." With a slight shake of her shoulders, Jamie halted Jo's outburst. "You know better than to get yourself worked up like this right before a show. You can't afford to have your mind on anything but what you're doing when you're in that cage."

"I'll be all right," she mumbled.

"Jo." There was censure in his voice mixed with affection and exasperation.

Reluctantly, Jo brought her gaze up to his. It was impossible to resist the grave eyes in the brightly painted face. With something between a sigh and a moan, she dropped her forehead to

his chest. "Jamie, he makes me so mad! He could ruin everything."

"Let's worry about it when the time comes," Jamie suggested,
patting her hair.

"But he doesn't understand us. He doesn't understand anything."

"Well, then it's up to us to make him understand, isn't it?"

Jo looked up and wrinkled her nose. "You're so logical."

"Of course I am," he agreed and struck a pose. As he wiggled
his orange eyebrows, Jo laughed. "Okay?" he asked, then picked
up his prop bucket.

"Okay," she agreed and smiled.

"Good, 'cause there's my cue."

When he disappeared behind the flap, Jo leaned her cheek
against the mare and nuzzled a moment. "I don't think I'm the
one to make him understand, though."

I wish he'd never come, she added silently as she vaulted onto
the mare's back. I wish I'd never noticed how his eyes are like
Ari's and how nice his mouth is when he smiles, she thought. Jo
ran the tip of her tongue gingerly over her lips. I wish he'd never
kissed me. *Liar.* Her conscience spoke softly in her ear: *Admit
it, you're glad he kissed you. You've never felt anything like that
before, and no matter what, you're glad he kissed you last night.
You even wanted him to kiss you again today.*

She forced her mind clear, taking deep, even breaths until she
heard the ringmaster announce her. With a flick of her heels, she
sent the mare sprinting into the tent.

It did not go well. The audience cheered her, oblivious to any
problem, but Jo was aware that the routine was far from smooth.
And the cats sensed her preoccupation. Again and again they
tested her, and again and again Jo was forced to alter her timing
to compensate. When the act was over, her head throbbed from
the strain of concentration. Her hands were clammy as she turned
Merlin over to Buck.

The big man came back to her after securing the cage.
"What's the matter with you?" he demanded without preamble.
By the underlying and very rare anger in his voice, Jo knew he
had observed at least a portion of her act. Unlike the audience,

Buck would note any deviation. "You go in the cage like that again, one of those cats is going to find out what you taste like."

"My timing was a little off, that's all." Jo fought against the trembling in her stomach and tried to sound casual.

"A little?" Buck glowered, looking formidable behind the mass of blond beard. "Who do you think you're fooling? I've been around these ugly cats since before you were born. When you go in the cage, you've got to take your brain in with you."

Only too aware that he was right, Jo conceded. "I know, Buck. You're right." With a weary hand she pushed back her hair. "It won't happen again. I guess I was tired and a little off-balance." She sent him an apologetic smile.

Buck frowned and shuffled. Never in his forty-five years had he managed to resist feminine smiles. "All right," he muttered, then sniffed and made his voice firm. "But you go take a nap right after the finale. No coffee. I don't want to see you around again until dinner time."

"Okay, Buck." Jo kept her voice humble, though she was tempted to grin. The weakness was going out of her legs, and the dull buzz of fear was fading from between her temples. Still she felt exhausted and agreeable to Buck's uncharacteristic tone of command. A nap, she decided as Buck drove Merlin away, was just what she needed, not to mention that it was as good a way as any to avoid Keane Prescott for the rest of the day. Shooing this thought aside, Jo decided to while away the time until the finale in casual conversation with Vito the wire walker.

Four

It rained for three days. It was a solid downpour, not heavy but insistent. As the circus wound its way north, the rain followed. Nevertheless, canvas men pitched the tents in soggy fields and muddy lots while straw was laid on the hippodrome track and performers scurried from trailers to tents under dripping umbrellas.

The lot near Waycross, Georgia, was scattered with puddles under a thick, gray sky. Jo could only be grateful that no evening show had been scheduled. By six, it was nearly dark, with a chill teasing the damp air. She hustled from the cookhouse after an early supper. She would check on the cats, she decided, then closet herself in her trailer, draw the curtains against the rain and curl up with a book. Shivering, she concluded that the idea was inspired.

She carried no umbrella but sought questionable shelter under a gray rolled-brimmed hat and thin windbreaker. Keeping her head lowered, she jogged across the mud, skimming around or hopping over puddles. She hummed lightly, anticipating the simple pleasures of an idle evening. Her humming ended in a muffled gasp as she ran into a solid object. Fingers wrapped around her upper arms. Even before she lifted her head, Jo knew it was Keane who held her. She recognized his touch. Through some clever maneuvering, she had managed to avoid being alone with him since they had walked together and looked back on the circus.

"Excuse me, Mr. Prescott. I'm afraid I wasn't looking where I was going."

"Perhaps the weather's dampened your radar, Jovilette." He made no move to release her. Annoyed, Jo was forced to hold her hat steady with one hand as she tilted her head to meet his eyes. Rain fell cool on her face.

"I don't know what you mean."

"Oh, I think you do," Keane countered. "There's not another soul around. You've been careful to keep yourself in a crowd for days."

Jo blinked rain from her lashes. She admitted ruefully that it had been foolish to suppose he wouldn't notice her ploy. She saw he carried no umbrella either, nor did he bother with a hat. His hair was darkened with rain, much the same color that one of her cats would be if caught in an unexpected shower. It was difficult, in the murky light, to clearly make out his features, but the rain could not disguise his mockery.

"That's an interesting observation, Mr. Prescott," Jo said coolly. "Now, if you don't mind, I'm getting wet." She was surprised when she remained in his hold after a strong attempt on her part to pull away. Frowning, she put both hands against his chest and pushed. She discovered that she had been wrong; under the lean frame was an amazing amount of strength. Infuriated that she had misjudged him and that she was outmatched, Jo raised her eyes again. "Let me go," she demanded between clenched teeth.

"No," Keane returned mildly. "I don't believe I will."

Jo glared at him. "Mr. Prescott, I'm cold and wet and I'd like to go to my trailer. Now, what do you want?"

"First, I want you to stop calling me Mr. Prescott." Jo pouted but she kept silent. "Second, I'd like an hour of your time for going over a list of personnel." He paused. Through her windbreaker Jo could feel his fingers unyielding on her arms.

"Is there anything else?" she demanded, trying to sound bored.

For a moment there was only the sound of rain drumming on the ground and splashing into puddles. "Yes," Keane said quietly. "I think I'll just get this out of my system."

Jo's instincts were swift but they were standing too close for her to evade him. And he was quick. Her protest was muffled against his mouth. Her arms were pinioned to her sides as his locked around her. Jo had felt a man's body against her own before—working out with the tumblers, practicing with the equestrians—but never with such clarity as this. She was aware of Keane in every fiber of her being. His body was whipcord lean and hard, his arms holding the strength she had discounted the first time she had seen him. But more, it was his mouth that mystified her. Now it was not gentle or testing; it took and plundered and demanded more before she could withhold a response.

Jo forgot the rain, though it continued to fall against her face. She forgot the cold. The warmth spread from inside, where her blood flowed fast, as her body was molded to Keane's. She forgot herself, or the woman she had thought herself to be, and discovered another. When he lifted his mouth, Jo kept her eyes closed, savoring the lingering pleasures, inviting fresh ones.

"More?" he murmured as his hand trailed up, then down her spine. Heat raced after it. "Kissing can be a dangerous pastime, Jo." He lowered his mouth again, then nipped at her soft bottom lip. "But you know all about danger, don't you?" He kissed her hard, leaving her breathless. "How courageous are you without your cats?"

Suddenly her heart raced to her throat. Her legs became rubbery, and a tingle sprinted up her spine. Jo recognized the feeling. It was the way she felt when she experienced a close call with the cats. Reaction would set in after the door of the safety cage locked behind her and the crisis had passed. It was then that fear found her. She studied Keane's bold, amber eyes, and her mouth went dry. She shuddered.

"You're cold." His voice was abruptly brisk. "Small wonder. We'll go to my trailer and get you some coffee."

"No!" Jo's protest was sharp and instantaneous. She knew she was vulnerable and she knew as well that she did not yet possess the experience to fight him. To be alone with him now was too great a risk.

Keane drew her away, but his grip remained firm. She could not read his expression as he searched her face. "What happened just now was personal," he told her. "Strictly man to woman. I'm of the opinion that love making should be personal. You're an appealing armful, Jovilette, and I'm accustomed to taking what I want, one way or another."

His words were like a shot of adrenaline. Jo's chin thrust forward, and her eyes flamed. "No one *takes* me, one way or another." She spoke with the deadly calm of fury. "If I make love with anyone, it's only because I want to."

"Of course," Keane agreed with an easy nod. "We're both aware you'll be willing when the time comes. We could make love quite successfully tonight, but I think it best if we know each other better first."

Jo's mouth trembled open and closed twice before she could speak. "Of all the arrogant, outrageous..."

"Truthful," Keane supplied, tossing her into incoherency again. "But for now, we have business, and while I don't mind kissing in the rain, I prefer to conduct business in a drier climate." He held up a hand as Jo started to protest. "I told you, the kiss was between a man and a woman. The business we have now is between the owner of this circus and a performer under contract. Understood?"

Jo took a long, deep breath to bring her voice to a normal level. "Understood," she agreed. Without another word she let him lead her across the slippery lot.

When they reached Keane's trailer, he hustled Jo inside without preliminaries. She blinked against the change in light when he hit the wall switch. "Take off your coat," he said briskly, pulling down her zipper before she could perform the task for herself. Instinctively, her hand reached for it as she took a step backward. Keane merely lifted a brow, then stripped off his own jacket. "I'll get the coffee." He moved down the length of the narrow trailer and disappeared around the corner where the tiny kitchen was set.

Slowly, Jo pulled off her dripping hat, letting her hair tumble free from where it had been piled under its confinement. With automatic movements she hung both her hat and coat on the hooks by the trailer door. It had been almost six months since she had stood in Frank's trailer, and like a woman visiting an old friend, she searched for changes.

The same faded lampshade adorned the maple table lamp that Frank had used for reading. The shade sat straight now, however, not at its usual slightly askew angle. The pillow that Lillie from wardrobe had sewn for him on some long-ago Christmas still sat over the small burn hole in the seat cushion of the couch. Jo doubted that Keane knew of the hole's existence. Frank's pipe stand sat, as always, on the counter by the side window. Unable to resist, Jo crossed over to run her finger over the worn bowl of his favorite pipe.

"Never could pack it right," she murmured to his well-loved ghost. Abruptly, her senses quivered. She twisted her head to see Keane watching her. Jo dropped her hand. A rare blush mantled her cheeks as she found herself caught unguarded.

"How do you take your coffee, Jo?"

She swallowed. "Black," she told him, aware that he was granting her the privacy of her thoughts. "Just black. Thank you."

Keane nodded, then turned to pick up two steaming mugs. "Come, sit down." He moved toward the Formica table that sat directly across from the kitchen. "You'd better take off your shoes. They're wet."

After squeaking her way down the length of the trailer, Jo sat down and pulled at the damp laces. Keane set both mugs on the table before disappearing into the back of the trailer. When he returned, Jo was already sipping at the coffee.

"Here." He offered her a pair of socks.

Surprised, Jo shook her head. "No, that's all right. I don't need..."

Her polite refusal trailed off as he knelt at her feet. "Your feet are like ice," he commented after cupping them in his palms. Briskly, he rubbed them while Jo sat mute, oddly disarmed by the gesture. The warmth was spreading dangerously past her ankles. "Since I'm responsible for keeping you out in the rain," he went on as he slipped a sock over her foot, "I'd best see to it you don't cough and sneeze your way through tomorrow's show. Such small feet," he murmured, running his thumb over the curve of her ankle as she stared wordlessly at the top of his head.

Raindrops still clung to and glistened in his hair. Jo found herself longing to brush them away and feel the texture of his hair beneath her fingers. She was sharply aware of him and wondered if it would always be this way when she was near him. Keane pulled on the second sock. His fingers lingered on her calf as he lifted his eyes. Hers were darkened with confusion as they met his. The body over which she had always held supreme control was journeying into frontiers her mind had not yet explored.

"Still cold?" Keane asked softly.

Jo moistened her lips and shook her head. "No. No, I'm fine."

He smiled a lazy, masculine smile that said as clearly as words that he was aware of his effect on her. His eyes told her he enjoyed it. Unsmiling, Jo watched him rise to his feet.

"It doesn't mean you'll win," she said aloud in response to their silent communication.

"No, it doesn't." Keane's smile remained as his gaze roamed possessively over her face. "That only makes it more interesting. Open and shut cases are invariably boring, hardly worth the trouble of going on if you've won before you've finished your opening statement."

Jo lifted her coffee and sipped, taking a moment to settle her nerves. "Are we here to discuss the law or circus business, counselor?" she asked, letting her eyes drift to his again as she set the mug back on the table. "If it's law, I'm afraid I'm going to disappoint you. I don't know much about it."

"What do you know about, Jovilette?" Keane slid into the chair beside hers.

"Cats," she said. "And Prescott's Circus Colossus. I'll be glad to let you know whatever I can about either."

"Tell me about you," he countered, and leaning back, pulled a cigar from his pocket.

"Mr. Prescott—" Jo began.

"Keane," he interrupted, flicking on his lighter. He glanced at the tip of his cigar, then back up at her through the thin haze of smoke.

"I was under the impression you wanted to be briefed on the personnel."

"You are a member of this circus, are you not?" Casually, Keane blew smoke at the ceiling. "I have every intention of being briefed on the entire troupe and see no reason why you shouldn't start with yourself." His eyes traveled back to hers. "Humor me."

Jo decided to take the line of least resistance. "It's a short enough story," she said with a shrug. "I've been with the circus all my life. When I was old enough, I started work as a generally useful.''

"A what?" Keane paused in the action of reaching for the coffeepot.

"Generally useful," Jo repeated, letting him freshen her cup. "It's a circus term that means exactly what it says. Rose's parents, for instance, are generally usefuls. We get a lot of drifters who work that way, too. It's also written into every performer's contract, after the specific terms, that they make themselves generally useful. There isn't room in most circuses, and certainly not in a tent circus, for performers with star complexes. You do what's necessary, what's needed. Buck, my handler, fills in during a slump at the sideshow, and he's one of the best canvas men around. Pete is the best mechanic in the troupe. Jamie knows as much about lighting as most shandies—electricians,'' she supplied as Keane lifted a brow. "He's also a better-than-average tumbler."

"What about you?" Keane interrupted the flow of Jo's words. For a moment she faltered, and the hands that had been gesturing became still. "Besides riding a galloping horse without reins or saddle, giving orders to elephants and facing lions?" He lifted his cup, watching her as he sipped. A smile lurked in his eyes. Jo frowned, studying him.

"Are you making fun of me?"

His smile sobered instantly. "No, Jo, I'm not making fun of you."

She continued. "In a pinch, I run the menagerie in the sideshow or I fill in the aerial act. Not the trap," she explained, relaxing again. "They have to practice together constantly to keep the timing. But sometimes I fill in on the Spanish Web, the big costume number where the girls hang from ropes and do identical moves. They're using butterfly costumes this year."

"Yes, I know the one." Keane continued to watch her as he drew on his cigar.

"But mostly Duffy likes to use girls who are more curvy. They double as showgirls in the finale."

"I see." A smile tugged at the corners of Keane's mouth. "Tell me, were your parents European?"

"No." Diverted, Jo shook her head. "Why do you ask?"

"Your name. And the ease with which I've heard you speak both French and Italian."

"It's easy to pick up languages in the circus," Jo said.

"Your accent was perfect in both cases."

"What? Oh." She shrugged and absently shifted in her chair, bringing her feet up to sit cross-legged. "We have a wide variety of nationalities here. Frank used to say that the world could take a lesson from the circus. We have French, Italian, Spanish, German, Russian, Mexican, Americans from all parts of the country and more."

"I know. It's like a traveling United Nations." He tipped his cigar ash in a glass tray. "So you picked up some French and Italian along the way. But if you've traveled with the circus all your life, what about the rest of your schooling?"

The hint of censure in his voice brought up her chin. "I went to school during the winter break and had a tutor on the road. I learned my ABC's, counselor, and a bit more, besides. I probably know more about geography and world history than you, and from more interesting sources than textbooks. I imagine I know more about animals than a third-year veterinary student and have more practical experience healing them. I can speak seven languages and—"

"Seven?" Keane interrupted. "Seven languages?"

"Well, five fluently," she corrected grudgingly. "I still have a bit of trouble with Greek and German, unless I can really take my time, and I can't read Greek yet at all."

"What else besides French, Italian and English?"

"Spanish and Russian." Jo scowled into her coffee. "The Russian's handy. I use it for swearing at the cats during the act. Not too many people understand Russian cursing, so it's safe."

Keane's laughter brought Jo's attention from her coffee. He was leaning back in his chair, his eyes gold with their mirth. Jo's scowl deepened. "What's so funny?"

"You are, Jovilette." Stung, she started to scramble up, but his hands on her shoulders stopped her. "No, don't be offended. I can't help but find it amusing that you toss out so offhandedly an accomplishment that any language major would brag about." Carelessly, he ran a finger over her sulky mouth. "You continually amaze me." He brushed a hand through her hair. "You

mumbled something at me the other day. Were you swearing at
me in Russian?''

''Probably.''

Grinning, Keane dropped his hand and settled into his chair
again. ''When did you start working with the cats?''

''In front of an audience? When I was seventeen. Frank
wouldn't let me start any earlier. He was my legal guardian as
well as the owner, so he had me both ways. I was ready when I
was fifteen.''

''How did you lose your parents?''

The question caught her off guard. ''In a fire,'' she said lev-
elly. ''When I was seven.''

''Here?''

She knew Keane was not referring to their locale but to the
circus. Jo sipped her cooling coffee. ''Yes.''

''Didn't you have any other family?''

''The circus is a family,'' she countered. ''I was never given
the chance to be an orphan. And I always had Frank.''

''Did you?'' Keane's smile was faintly sarcastic. ''How was
he as a father figure?''

Jo studied him for a moment. Was he bitter? she wondered.
Or amused? Or simply curious? ''He never took my father's
place,'' she replied quietly. ''He never tried to, because neither
of us wanted it. We were friends, as close as I think it's possible
for friends to be, but I'd already had a father, and he'd already
had a child. We weren't looking for substitutes. You look nothing
like him, you know.''

''No,'' Keane replied with a shrug. ''I know.''

''He had a comfortable face, all creases and folds.'' Jo smiled,
thinking of it while she ran a finger absently around the rim of
her mug. ''He was dark, too, just beginning to gray when...''
She trailed off, then brought herself back with a quick shake of
her head. ''Your voice is rather like his, though; he had a truly
beautiful voice. I'll ask you a question now.''

Keane's expression became attentive, then he gestured with
the back of his hand. ''Go ahead.''

''Why are you here? I lost my temper when I asked you before,
but I do want to know.'' It was against her nature to probe, and
some of her discomfort found its way into her voice. ''It must

have caused you some difficulty to leave your practice, even for a few weeks.''

Keane frowned at the end of his cigar before he slowly crushed it out. ''Let's say I wanted to see firsthand what had fascinated my father all these years.''

''You never came when he was alive.'' Jo gripped her hands together under the table. ''You didn't even bother to come to his funeral.''

''I would've been the worst kind of hypocrite to attend his funeral, don't you think?''

''He was your father.'' Jo's eyes grew dark and her tone sharp in reproof.

''You're smarter than that, Jo,'' Keane countered calmly. ''It takes more than an accident of birth to make a father. Frank Prescott was a complete stranger to me.''

''You resent him.'' Jo felt suddenly torn between loyalty for Frank and understanding for the man who sat beside her.

''No.'' Keane shook his head thoughtfully. ''No, I believe I actively resented him when I was growing up, but...'' He shrugged the thought aside. ''I grew rather ambivalent over the years.''

''He was a good man,'' Jo stated, leaning forward as she willed him to understand. ''He only wanted to give people pleasure, to show them a little magic. Maybe he wasn't made to be a father—some men aren't—but he was kind and gentle. And he was proud of you.''

''Of me?'' Keane seemed amused. ''How?''

''Oh, you're hateful,'' Jo whispered, hurt by his careless attitude. She slipped from her chair, but before she could step away, Keane took her arm.

''No, tell me. I'm interested.'' His hold on her arm was light, but she knew it would tighten if she resisted.

''All right.'' Jo tossed her head to send her hair behind her back. ''He had the Chicago paper delivered to his Florida office. He always looked for any mention of you, any article on a court case you were involved in or a dinner party you attended. Anything. You have to understand that to us a write-up is very important. Frank wasn't a performer, but he was one of us. Sometimes he'd read me an article before he put it away. He kept a scrapbook.''

Jo pulled her arm away and strode past Keane into the bedroom. The oversize wooden chest was where it had always been, at the foot of Frank's bed. Kneeling down, Jo tossed up the lid. "This is where he kept all the things that mattered to him." Jo began to shift through papers and mementos quickly; she had not been able to bring herself to sort through the chest before. Keane stood in the doorway and watched her. "He called it his memory box." She pushed at her hair with an annoyed hand, then continued to search. "He said memories were the rewards for growing old. Here it is." Jo pulled out a dark green scrapbook, then sat back on her heels. Silently, she held it out to Keane. After a moment he crossed the room and took it from her. Jo could hear the rain hissing on the ground outside as their eyes held. His expression was unfathomable as he opened the book. The pages rustled to join the quiet sound of the rain.

"What an odd man he must have been," Keane murmured, "to keep a scrapbook on a son he never knew." There was no rancor in his voice. "What was he?" he asked suddenly, shifting his eyes back to Jo.

"A dreamer," she answered. "His watch was always five minutes slow. If he hung a picture on the wall, it was always crooked. He'd never straighten it because he'd never notice. He was always thinking about tomorrow. I guess that's why he kept yesterday in this box." Glancing down, she began to straighten the chaos she had caused while looking for the book. A snatch of red caught her eye. Reaching for it, her fingers found a familiar shape. Jo hesitated, then drew the old doll out of the chest.

It was a sad piece of plastic and faded silk with its face nearly washed away. One arm was broken off, leaving an empty sleeve. The golden hair was straggled but brave under its red cap. Ballet shoes were painted on the dainty feet. Tears backed up behind Jo's eyes as she made a soft sound of joy and despair.

"What is it?" Keane demanded, glancing down to see her clutching the battered ballerina.

"Nothing." Her voice was unsteady as she scrambled quickly to her feet. "I have to go." Though she tried, Jo could not bring herself to drop the doll back into the box. She swallowed. She did not wish to reveal her emotions before his intelligent, gold eyes. Perhaps he would be cynical, or worse, amused. "May I have this, please?" She was careful with the tone of the request.

Slowly, Keane crossed the distance between them, then cradled her chin in his hand. "It appears to be yours already."

"It was." Her fingers tightened on the doll's waist. "I didn't know Frank had kept it. Please," she whispered. Her emotions were already dangerously heightened. She could feel a need to rest her head against his shoulder. The evening had been a roller coaster for her feelings, climaxing now with the discovery of her most prized childhood possession. She knew that if she did not escape, she would seek comfort in his arms. Her own weakness frightened her. "Let me by."

For a moment, Jo read refusal in his eyes. Then he stepped aside. Jo let out a quiet, shaky breath. "I'll walk you back to your trailer."

"No," she said quickly, too quickly. "It isn't necessary," she amended, moving by him and into the kitchen. Sitting down, she pulled on her shoes, too distraught to remember she still wore his socks. "There's no reason for us both to get wet again." She rambled on, knowing he was watching her hurried movement, but unable to stop. "And I'm going to check on my cats before I go in, and..."

She stopped short when he took her shoulders and pulled her to her feet. "And you don't want to take the chance of being alone in your trailer with me in case I change my mind."

A sharp denial trembled on her lips, but the knowledge in his eyes crushed it. "All right," she admitted. "That, too."

Keane brushed her hair from her neck and shook his head. He kissed her nose and moved down to pluck her hat and coat from their hooks. Cautiously, Jo followed him. When he held out her coat, she turned and slipped her arms into the sleeves. Before she could murmur her thanks, he turned her back and pulled up the zipper. For a moment his fingers lingered at her neck, his eyes on hers. Taking her hair into his hand, he piled it atop her head, then dropped on her hat. The gestures were innocent, but Jo was rocked by a feeling of intimacy she had never experienced.

"I'll see you tomorrow," he said, pulling the brim of her hat down further over her eyes.

Jo nodded. Holding the doll against her side, she pushed open the door. The sound of rain was amplified through the trailer. "Good night," she murmured, then moved quickly into the night.

Five

The morning scent was clean. In the new lot rainbows glistened in puddles. At last the sky was blue with only harmless white puffs of clouds floating over its surface. In the cookhouse a loud, crowded breakfast was being served. Finding herself without appetite, Jo skipped going to the cookhouse altogether. She was restless and tense. No matter how she disciplined her mind, her thoughts wandered back to Keane Prescott and to the evening they had spent together. Jo remembered it all, from the quick passion of the kiss in the rain to the calmness of his voice when he had said good-night. It was odd, she mused, that whenever she began to talk to him, she forgot he was the owner, forgot he was Frank's son. Always she was forced to remind herself of their positions.

Deep in thought, Jo slipped into tights and a leotard. It was true, she admitted, that she had failed to keep their relationship from becoming personal. She found it difficult to corral her urge to laugh with him, to share a joke, to open for him the doorway to the magic of the circus. If he could feel it, she thought, he would understand. Though she could admit her interest in him privately, she could not find a clear reason for his apparent interest in her.

Why me? she wondered with a shake of her head. Turning, she opened her wardrobe closet and studied herself in the full-length glass on the back of the door. There she saw a woman of slightly less-than-average height with a body lacking the generous curves of Duffy's showgirls. The legs, she decided, were not bad. They were long and well-shaped with slim thighs. The hips were narrow, more, she thought with a pout, like a boy's than a woman's; and the bust line was sadly inadequate. She knew many women

in the troupe with more appeal and a dozen with more experience.

Jo could see nothing in the mirror that would attract a sophisticated Chicago attorney. She did not note the honesty that shone
from the exotically shaped green eyes or the strength in her chin
or the full promise of her mouth. She saw the touch of gypsy in
the tawny complexion and raven hair but remained unaware of
the appeal that came from the hint of something wild and untamed just under the surface. The plain black leotard showed her
firm, lithe body to perfection, but Jo thought nothing of the
smooth satiny sheen of her skin. She was frowning as she pulled
her hair back and began to braid it.

He must know dozens of women, she thought as her hands
worked to confine her thick mane of hair. He probably takes a
different one to dinner every night. They wear beautiful clothes
and expensive perfume, she mused, torturing herself with the
thought. They have names like Laura and Patricia, and they have
low, sophisticated laughs. Jo lifted a brow at the reflection in the
mirror and gave a light, low laugh. She wrinkled her brow at the
hollowness of the sound. They discuss mutual friends, the Wal-
laces or the Jamesons, over candlelight and Beaujolais. And
when he takes the most beautiful one home, they listen to Chopin
and drink brandy in front of the fire. Then they make love. Jo
felt an odd tightening in her stomach but pursued the fantasy to
the finish. The lovely lady is experienced, passionate and
worldly. Her skin is soft and white. When he leaves, she is not
devastated but mature. She doesn't even care if he loves her or
not.

Jo stared at the woman in the glass and saw her cheeks were
wet. On a cry of frustration, she slammed the door shut. *What's
wrong with me?* she demanded, brushing all traces of tears from
her face. I haven't been myself for days! I need to shake myself
out of this—this...whatever it is that I'm in. Slipping on gym-
nastic shoes and tossing a robe over her arm, Jo hustled from the
trailer.

She moved carefully, avoiding puddles and any further speculation on Keane Prescott's romantic life. Before she was halfway across the lot, she saw Rose. From the expression on her
face, Jo could see she was in a temper.

"Hello, Rose," she said, strategically stepping aside as the snake charmer splashed through a puddle.

"He's hopeless," Rose tossed back. "I tell you," she continued, stopping and wagging a finger at Jo, "I'm through this time. Why should I waste my time?"

"You've certainly been patient," Jo agreed, deciding that sympathy was the wisest course. "It's more than he deserves."

"Patient?" Rose raised a dramatic hand to her breast. "I have the patience of a saint. Yet even a saint has her limits!" Rose tossed her hair behind her shoulders. She sighed heavily. "*Adios.* I think I hear Mama calling me."

Jo continued her walk toward the Big Top. Jamie walked by, his hands in his pockets. "She's crazy," he muttered. He stopped and spread his arms wide. His look was that of a man ill-used and innocent. Jo shrugged. Shaking his head, Jamie moved away. "She's crazy," he said again.

Jo watched him until he was out of sight, then darted to the Big Top.

Inside, Carmen watched adoringly while Vito practiced a new routine on the incline wire. The tent echoed with the sounds of rehearsals: voices and thumps, the rattle of rigging, the yapping of clown dogs. In the first ring Jo spotted the Six Beirots, an acrobatic act that was just beginning its warm-ups. Pleased with her timing, Jo walked the length of the arena. A raucous whistle sounded over her head, and she glanced up to shake a friendly fist at Vito. He called from fifteen feet above her as he balanced on a slender wire set at a forty-five-degree angle.

"Hey, chickie, you have a nice rear view. You're almost as cute as me."

"No one's as cute as you, Vito," she called back.

"Ah, I know." With a weighty sigh, he executed a neat pivot. "But I have learned to live with it." He sent down a lewd wink. "When you going into town with me, chickie?" he asked as he always did.

"When you teach my cats to walk the wire," Jo answered as she always did. Vito laughed and began a light-footed cha-cha. Carmen fired Jo a glare. She must have it bad, Jo decided, if she takes Vito's harmless flirting seriously. Stopping beside her, Jo leaned close and spoke in a conspirator's whisper. "He'd fall off his wire if I said I'd go."

"I'd go," Carmen said with a lovely pout, "if he'd just ask me."

Jo shook her head, wondering why romances were invariably complicated. She was lucky not to have the problem. Giving Carmen an encouraging pat on the shoulder, Jo set off toward the first ring.

The Six Beirots were brothers. They were all small-statured, dark men who had immigrated from Belgium. Jo worked out with them often to keep herself limber and to keep her reflexes sharp. She liked them all, knew their wives and children, and understood their unique blending of French and English. Raoul was the oldest, and the stockiest of the six brothers. Because of his build and strength, he was the under-stander in their human pyramid. It was he who spotted Jo and first lifted a hand in greeting.

"Halo." He grinned and ran his palm over his receding hairline. "You gonna tumble?"

Jo laughed and did a quick handspring into the ring. She stuck out her tongue when the unanimous critique was "sloppy." "I just need to warm up," she said, assuming an air of injured dignity. "My muscles need tuning."

For the next thirty minutes Jo worked with them, doing muscle stretches and limbering exercises, rib stretches and lung expanders. Her muscles warmed and loosened, her heart pumped steadily. She was filled with energy. Her mind was clear. Because of her lightened mood, Jo was easily cajoled into a few impromptu acrobatics. Leaving the more complicated feats to the experts, she did simple back flips, handsprings or twists at Raoul's command. She did a brief, semi-successful thirty seconds atop the rolling globe and earned catcalls from her comrades at her dismount.

She stood back as they began the leaps. One after another they lined up to take turns running along a ramp, bounding upon a springboard and flying up to do flips or twists before landing on the mat. There was a constant stream of French as they called out to each other.

"Hokay, Jo." Raoul gestured with his hand. "Your turn."

"Oh, no." She shook her head and reached for her robe. "Uh-uh." There was a chorus of coaxing, teasing French. "I've got to give my cats their vitamins," she told them, still shaking her head.

"Come on, Jo. It's fun." Raoul grinned and wiggled his eyebrows. "Don't you like to fly?" As she glanced at the ramp, Raoul knew she was tempted. "You take a good spring," he told her."Do one forward somersault, then land on my shoulders." He patted them to show their ability to handle the job.

Jo smiled and nibbled pensively on her lower lip. It had been a long while since she had taken the time to go up on the trapeze and really fly. It did look like fun. She gave Raoul a stern look. "You'll catch me?"

"Raoul never misses," he said proudly, then turned to his brothers. *"Ne c'est pas?"* His brothers shrugged and rolled their eyes to the ceiling with indistinguishable mutters. "Ah." He waved them away with the back of his hand.

Knowing Raoul was indeed a top flight under-stander, Jo approached the ramp. Still she gave him one last narrow-eyed look. "You catch me," she ordered, shaking her finger at him.

"Cherie." He took his position with a stylish movement of his hand. "It's a piece of pie."

"Cake," Jo corrected, took a deep breath, held it and ran. When she came off the springboard, she tucked into the somersault and watched the Big Top turn upside down. She felt good. As the tent began to right itself, she straightened for her landing, keeping herself loose. Her feet connected with Raoul's powerful shoulders, and she tilted only briefly before he took her ankles in a firm grip. Straightening her poor posture, Jo styled elaborately with both arms while she received exaggerated applause and whistles. She leaped down nimbly as Raoul took her waist to give her landing bounce.

"When do you want to join the act?" he asked her, giving her a friendly pat on the bottom. "We'll put you up on the sway pole."

"That's okay." Grinning, Jo again reached for her robe. "I'll stick with the cats." After a cheerful wave, she slipped one arm into a sleeve and started back down the hippodrome track. She pulled up short when she spotted Keane leaning up against the front seat rail.

"Amazing," he said, then straightened to move to her. "But then, the circus is supposed to be amazing, isn't it?" He lifted the forgotten sleeve to her robe, then slipped her other arm into it. "Is there anything here you can't do?"

"Hundreds of things," Jo answered, taking him seriously. "I'm only really proficient with animals. The rest is just show and play."

"You looked amazingly proficient to me for the last half hour or so," he countered as he pulled out her braid from where it was trapped by her robe.

"Have you been here that long?"

"I walked in as Vito was commenting on your rear view."

"Oh." Jo laughed, glancing back to where Vito now stood flirting with Carmen. "He's crazy."

"Perhaps," Keane agreed, taking her arm. "But his eyesight's good enough. Would you like some coffee?"

Jo was reminded instantly of the evening before. Leery of being drawn to his charms again, she shook her head. "I've got to change," she told him, belting her robe. "We've got a show at two. I want to rehearse the cats."

"It's incredible how much time you people devote to your art. Rehearsals seem to run into the beginning of a show, and a show seems to run into more rehearsals."

Jo softened when he referred to circus skills as art. "Performers always look for just a bit more in themselves. It's a constant struggle for perfection. Even when a performance goes beautifully and you know it, you start thinking about the next time. How can I do it better or bigger or higher or faster?"

"Never satisfied?" Keane asked as they stepped out into the sunlight.

"If we were, we wouldn't have much of a reason to come back and do it all over again."

He nodded, but there was something absent in the gesture, as if his mind was elsewhere. "I have to leave this afternoon," he said almost to himself.

"Leave?" Jo's heart skidded to a stop. Her distress was overwhelming and so unexpected that she was forced to take an extra moment to steady herself. "Back to Chicago?"

"*Hmm?*" Keane stopped, turning to face her. "Oh, yes."

"And the circus?" Jo asked, thoroughly ashamed that it had not been her first concern. She didn't want him to leave, she suddenly realized.

Keane frowned a moment, then continued to walk. "I see no purpose in disrupting this year's schedule." His voice was brisk now and businesslike.

"This year's?" Jo repeated cautiously.

Keane turned and looked at her. "I haven't decided its ultimate fate, but I won't do anything until the end of the summer."

"I see." She let out a long breath. "So we have a reprieve."

"In a manner of speaking," Keane agreed.

Jo was silent for a moment but could not prevent herself from asking, "Then you won't—I mean, you'll be staying in Chicago now; you won't be traveling with us?"

They negotiated their way around a puddle before Keane answered. "I don't feel I can make a judicious decision about the circus after so brief an exposure. There's a complication in one of my cases that needs my personal attention, but I should be back in a week or two."

Relief flooded through her. He would be back, a voice shouted in her ear. It shouldn't matter to you, another whispered. "We'll be in South Carolina in a couple of weeks," Jo said casually. They had reached her trailer, and she took the handle of her door before she turned to face him. *It's just that I want him to understand what this circus means,* she told herself as she looked up into his eyes. *That's the only reason I want him to come back.* Knowing she was lying to herself made it difficult to keep her gaze steady.

Keane smiled, letting his eyes travel over her face. "Yes, Duffy's given me a route list. I'll find you. Aren't you going to ask me in?"

"In?" Jo repeated. "Oh, no, I told you, I have to change, and..." He stepped forward as she talked. Something in his eyes told her a firm stand was necessary. She had seen a similar look in a lion's eyes while he contemplated taking a dangerous liberty. "I simply don't have time right now. If I don't see you before you go, have a good trip.'' She turned and opened the door. Aware of a movement, she turned back, but not before he had nudged her through the door and followed. As it closed at his back, Jo bristled with fury. She did not enjoy being outmaneuvered. ''Tell me, counselor, do you know anything about a law concerning breaking and entering?''

''Doesn't apply,'' he returned smoothly. ''There was no lock involved.'' He glanced around at the attractive simplicity of Jo's trailer. The colors were restful earth tones without frills. The beige- and brown-flecked linoleum floor was spotlessly clean. It was the same basic floorplan as Frank's trailer, but here there were softer touches. There were curtains rather than shades at the windows; large, comfortable pillows tossed onto a forest green sofa; a spray of fresh wildflowers tucked into a thin, glass vase. Without comment Keane wandered to a black lacquer trunk that sat directly opposite the door. On it was a book that he picked up while Jo fumed. *''The Count of Monte Cristo,''* he read aloud and flipped it open. ''In French,'' he stated, lifting a brow.

''It was written in French,'' Jo muttered, pulling it from his hand. ''So I read it in French.'' Annoyed, she lifted the lid on the trunk, preparing to drop the book inside and out of his reach.

''Good heavens, are those all yours?'' Keane stopped the lid on its downswing, then pushed books around with his other hand. ''Tolstoy, Cervantes, Voltaire, Steinbeck. When do you have time in this crazy, twenty-four-hour world you live in to read this stuff?''

''I make time,'' Jo snapped as her eyes sparked. ''My *own* time. Just because you're the owner doesn't mean you can barge in here and poke through my things and demand an account of my time. This is my trailer. I own everything in it.''

''Hold on.'' Keane halted her rushing stream of words. ''I wasn't demanding an account of your time, I was simply astonished that you could find enough of it to do this type of reading. Since I can't claim to be an expert on your work, it would be remarkably foolish of me to criticize the amount of time you spend on it. Secondly,'' he said, taking a step toward her—and though Jo stiffened in anticipation, he did not touch her—''I apologize for 'poking through your things,' as you put it. I was

interested for several reasons. One being I have quite an extensive library myself. It seems we have a common interest, whether
we like it or not. As for barging into your trailer, I can only
plead guilty. If you choose to prosecute, I can recommend a
couple of lousy attorneys who overcharge.''

His last comment forced a smile onto Jo's reluctant lips. "I'll
give it some thought." With more care than she had originally
intended, Jo lowered the lid of the trunk. She was reminded that
she had not been gracious. "I'm sorry," she said as she turned
back to him.

His eyes reflected curiosity. "What for?"

"For snapping at you." She lifted her shoulders, then let them
fall. "I thought you were criticizing me. I suppose I'm too sensitive."

Several seconds passed before he spoke. "Unnecessary apology accepted if you answer one question."

Mystified, Jo frowned at him. "What question?"

"Is the Tolstoy in Russian?"

Jo laughed, pushing loose strands of hair from her face. "Yes,
it is."

Keane smiled, enjoying the two tiny dimples that flickered in
her cheeks when she laughed. "Did you know that though you're
lovely in any case, you grow even more so when you smile?"

Jo's laughter stilled. She was unaccustomed to this sort of
compliment and studied him without any idea of how to respond.
It occurred to her that any of the sophisticated women she had
imagined that morning would have known precisely what to say.
She would have been able to smile or laugh as she tossed back
the appropriate comment. That woman, Jo admitted, was not Jovilette Wilder. Gravely, she kept her eyes on his. "I don't know
how to flirt," she said simply.

Keane tilted his head, and an expression came and went in his
eyes before she could analyze it. He stepped toward her. "I
wasn't flirting with you, Jo, I was making an observation. Hasn't
anyone ever told you that you're beautiful?"

He was much too close now, but in the narrow confines of the
trailer, Jo had little room to maneuver. She was forced to tilt
back her head to keep her eyes level with his. "Not precisely
the way you did." Quickly, she put her hand to his chest to keep

the slight but important distance between them. She knew she was trapped, but that did not mean she was defeated.

Gently, Keane lifted her protesting hand, turning it palm up as he brought it to his lips. An involuntary breath rushed in and out of Jo's lungs. "Your hands are exquisite," he murmured, tracing the fine line of blue up the back. "Narrow-boned, long-fingered. And the palms show hard work. That makes them more interesting." He lifted his eyes from her hand to her face. "Like you."

Jo's voice had grown husky, but she could do nothing to alter it. "I don't know what I'm supposed to say when you tell me things like that." Beneath her robe her breasts rose and fell with her quickening heart. "I'd rather you didn't."

"Do you really?" Keane ran the back of his hand along her jaw line. "That's a pity, because the more I look at you, the more I find to say. You're a bewitching creature, Jovilette."

"I have to change," she said in the firmest voice she could muster. "You'll have to go."

"That's unfortunately true," he murmured, then cupped her chin. "Come, then, kiss me goodbye."

Jo stiffened. "I hardly think that's necessary...."

"You couldn't be more wrong," he told her as he lowered his mouth. "It's extremely necessary." In a light, teasing whisper, his lips met hers. His arms encircled her, bringing her closer with only the slightest pressure. "Kiss me back, Jo," he ordered softly. "Put your arms around me and kiss me back."

For a moment longer she resisted, but the lure of his mouth nibbling at hers was too strong. Letting instinct rule her will, Jo lifted her arms and circled his neck. Her mouth grew mobile under his, parting and offering. Her surrender seemed to lick the flames of his passion. The kiss grew urgent. His arms locked, crushing her against him. Her quiet moan was not of protest but of wonder. Her fingers found their way into his hair, tangling in its thickness as they urged him closer. She felt her robe loosen, then his hands trail up her rib cage. At his touch, she shivered, feeling her skin grow hot, then cold, then hot again in rapid succession.

When his hand took her breast, she shied, drawing in her breath quickly. "Steady," he murmured against her mouth. His hands stroked gently, coaxing her to relax again. He kissed the corners of her mouth, waiting until she quieted before he took her deep again. The thin leotard molded her body. It created no barrier against the warmth of his searching fingers. They moved slowly, lingering over the peak of her breast, exploring its softness, wandering to her waist, then tracing her hip and thigh.

No man had ever touched her so freely. Jo was helpless to stop him, helpless against her own growing need for him to touch her again. Was this the passion she had read of so often? The passion that drove men to war, to struggle against all reason, to risk everything? She felt she could understand it now. She clung to him as he taught her—as she learned—the demands of her own body. Her mouth grew hungrier for the taste of him. She was certain she remained in his arms while seasons flew by, while decades passed, while worlds were destroyed and built again.

But when he drew away, Jo saw the same sun spilling through her windows. Eternity had only been moments.

Unable to speak, she merely stared up at him. Her eyes were dark and aware, her cheeks flushed with desire. But somehow, though it still tingled from his, her mouth maintained a youthful innocence. Keane's eyes dropped to it as his hands loitered at the small of her back.

"It's difficult to believe I'm the first man to touch you," he murmured. His eyes roamed to hers. "And quite desperately arousing. Particularly when I find you've passion to match your looks. I think I'd like to make love with you in the daylight first so that I can watch that marvelous control of yours slip away layer by layer. We'll have to discuss it when I get back."

Jo forced strength back into her limbs, knowing she was on the brink of losing her will to him. "Just because I let you kiss me and touch me doesn't mean I'll let you make love to me." She lifted her chin, feeling her confidence surging back. "If I do, it'll be because it's what I want, not because you tell me to."

The expression in Keane's eyes altered. "Fair enough," he agreed and nodded. "It'll simply be my job to make it what you want." He took her chin in his hand and lowered his mouth to hers for a brief kiss. As she had the first time, Jo kept her eyes open and watched him. She felt him grin against her mouth before he raised his head. "You are the most fascinating woman

I've ever met.'' Turning, he crossed to the door. ''I'll be back,'' he said with a careless wave before it closed behind him. Dumbly, Jo stared into empty space.

Fascinating? she repeated, tracing her still warm lips with her fingertips. Quickly, she ran to the window, and kneeling on the sofa below it, watched Keane stride away.

She realized with a sudden jolt that she missed him already.

Six

Jo learned that weeks could drag like years. During the second week of Keane's absence she had searched each new lot for a sign of him. She had scanned the crowds of towers who came to watch the raising of the Big Top, and as the days stretched on and on, she balanced between anger and despair at his continued absence. Only in the cage did she manage to isolate her concentration, knowing she could not afford to do otherwise. But after each performance Jo found it more and more difficult to relax. Each morning she felt certain he would be back. Each night she lay restless, waiting for the sun to rise.

Spring was in full bloom. The high grass lots smelled of it. Often there were wildflowers crushed underfoot, leaving their heavy fragrances in the air. Even as the circus caravan traveled north, the days grew warm, sunlight lingering further into evening. While other troupers enjoyed the balmy air and providentially sunny skies, Jo lived on nerves.

It occurred to her that after returning to his life in Chicago, Keane had decided against coming back. In Chicago he had comfort and wealth and elegant women. Why should he come back? Jo closed her mind against the ultimate fate of the circus, unwilling to face the possibility that Keane might close the show at the end of the season. She told herself the only reason she wanted him to come back was to convince him to keep the circus open. But the memory of being in his arms intruded too often into her thoughts. Gradually, she grew resigned, filling the strange void she felt with her work.

Several times each week she found time to give the eager Gerry more training. At first she had only permitted him to work with the two menagerie cubs, allowing him, with the protection of leather gloves, to play with them and to feed them. She en-

couraged him to teach them simple tricks with the aid of small
pieces of raw meat. Jo was as pleased as he when the cats responded to his patience and obeyed.

Jo saw potential in Gerry, in his genuine affection for animals
and in his determination. Her primary concern was that he had
not yet developed a healthy fear. He was still too casual, and
with casualness, Jo knew, came carelessness. When she thought
he had progressed far enough, Jo decided to take him to the next
step of his training.

There was no matinee that day, and the Big Top was scattered
with rehearsing troupers. Jo was dressed in boots and khakis with
a long-sleeved blouse tucked into the waist. She studied Gerry
as she ran the stock of her whip through her hand. They stood
together in the safety cage while she issued instructions.

"All right, Buck's going to let Merlin through the chute. He's
the most tractable of the cats, except for Ari." She paused a
moment while her eyes grew sad. "Ari isn't up to even a short
practice session." She pushed away the depression that threat-
ened and continued. "Merlin knows you, he's familiar with your
voice and your scent." Gerry nodded and swallowed. "When we
go in, you're to be my shadow. You move when I move, and
don't speak until I tell you. If you get frightened, don't run." Jo
took his arm for emphasis. "That's *important,* understand? Don't
run. Tell me if you want out, and I'll get you to the safety cage."

"I won't run, Jo," he promised and wiped hands, damp with
excitement, on his jeans.

"Are you ready?"

Gerry grinned and nodded. "Yeah."

Jo opened the door leading to the big cage and let Gerry
through behind her before securing it. She walked to the center
of the arena in easy, confident strides. "Let him in, Buck," she
called and heard the immediate rattle of bars. Merlin entered
without hurry, then leaped onto his pedestal. He yawned hugely
before looking at Jo. "A solo today, Merlin," she said as she
advanced toward him. "And you're the star. Stay with me," she
ordered as Gerry merely stood still and stared at the big cat.
Merlin gave Gerry a disinterested glance and waited.

With an upward move of her arm, she sent Merlin into a sit-up. "You know," she told the boy behind her, "that teaching a cat to take his seat is the first trick. The audience won't even consider it one. The sit-up," she continued while signaling Merlin to bring his front paws back down, "is usually next and takes quite a bit of time. It's necessary to strengthen the cat's back muscles first." Again she signaled Merlin to sit up, then, with a quick command, she had him pawing the air and roaring. "Marvelous old ham," she said with a grin and brought him back down. "The primary move of each cue is always given from the same position with the same tone of voice. It takes patience and repetition. I'm going to bring him down off the pedestal now."

Jo flicked the whip against the tanbark, and Merlin leaped down. "Now I maneuver him to the spot in the arena where I want him to lie down." As she moved, Jo made certain her student moved with her. "The cage is a circle, forty feet in diameter. You have to know every inch of it inside your head. You have to know precisely how far you are from the bars at all times. If you back up into the bars, you've got no room to maneuver if there's trouble. It's one of the biggest mistakes a trainer can make." At her signal Merlin laid down, then shifted to his side. "Over, Merlin," she said briskly, sending him into a series of rolls. "Use their names often; it keeps them in tune with you. You have to know each cat and their individual tendencies."

Jo moved with Merlin, then signaled him to stop. When he roared, she rubbed the top of his head with the stock of her whip. "They like to be petted just like house cats, but they are not tabbies. It's essential that you never give them your complete trust and that you remember always to maintain your dominance. You subjugate not by poking them or beating or shouting, which is not only cruel but makes for a mean, undependable cat, but with patience, respect and will. Never humiliate them; they have a right to their pride. You bluff them, Gerry," she said as she raised both arms and brought Merlin up on his hind legs. "Man is the unknown factor. That's why we use jungle-bred rather than captivity-bred cats. Ari is the exception. A cat born and raised in captivity is too familiar with man, so you lose your edge." She moved forward, keeping her arms raised. Merlin followed, walking on his hind legs. He spread seven feet into the air and towered over his trainer. "They might have a sense of affection for you, but there's no fear and little respect. Unfortunately, this often happens if a cat's been with a trainer a long time. They don't become more docile the longer they're in an act, but they become more dangerous. They test you constantly. The trick is to make them believe you're indestructible.''

She brought Merlin down, and he gave another yawn before she sent him back to his seat. "If one swipes at you, you have to stop it then and there, because they try again and again, getting closer each time. Usually, if a trainer's hurt in the cage, it's because he's made a mistake. The cats are quick to spot them; sometimes they let them pass, sometimes they don't. This one's given me a good smack on the shoulder now and again. He's kept his claws retracted, but there's always the possibility that one time he'll forget he's just playing. Any questions?''

"Hundreds," Gerry answered, wiping his mouth with the back of his hand. "I just can't focus on one right now.''

Jo chuckled and again scratched Merlin's head when he roared. "They'll come to you later. It's hard to absorb anything the first time, but it'll come back to you when you're relaxed again. All right, you know the cue. Make him sit up.''

"Me?''

Jo stepped to the side, giving Merlin a clear view of her student. "You can be as scared as you like," she said easily. "Just don't let it show in your voice. Watch his eyes.''

Gerry rubbed his palm on the thighs of his jeans, then lifted it as he had seen Jo do hundreds of times. "Up," he told the cat in a passably firm voice.

Merlin studied him a moment, then looked at Jo. This, his eyes told her clearly, was an amateur and beneath his notice. Carefully, Jo kept her face expressionless. "He's testing you," she told Gerry. "He's an old hand and a bit harder to bluff. Be firm and use his name this time.''

Gerry took a deep breath and repeated the hand signal. "Up, Merlin.''

Merlin glanced back at him, then stared with measuring, amber eyes. "Again," Jo instructed and heard Gerry swallow audibly. "Put some authority into your voice. He thinks you're a pushover.''

"Up, Merlin!" Gerry repeated, annoyed enough by Jo's description to put some dominance into his voice. Though his reluctance was obvious, Merlin obeyed. "He did it," Gerry whispered on a long, shaky breath. "He really did it."

"Very good," Jo said, pleased with both the lion and her student. "Now bring him down." When this was accomplished, Jo had him bring Merlin from the seat. "Here." She handed Gerry the whip. "Use the stock to scratch his head. He likes it best just behind the ear." She felt the faint tremble in his hand as he took the whip, but he held it steady, even as Merlin closed his eyes and roared.

Because he had performed well, Jo afforded Merlin the liberty of rubbing against her legs before she called for Buck to let him out. The rattle of the bars was the cat's cue to exit, and like a trouper, he took it with his head held high. "You did very well," she told Gerry when they were alone in the cage.

"It was great." He handed her back the whip, the stock damp from his sweaty palms. "It was just great. When can I do it again?"

Jo smiled and patted his shoulder. "Soon," she promised. "Just remember the things I've told you and come to me when you remember all those questions."

"Okay, thanks, Jo." He stepped through the safety cage. "Thanks a lot. I want to go tell the guys."

"Go ahead." Jo watched him scramble away, leaping over the ring and darting through the back door. With a grin, she leaned against the bars. "Was I like that?" she asked Buck, who stood at the opposite end of the cage.

"The first time you got a cat to sit up on your own, we heard about it for a week. Twelve years old and you thought you were ready for the big show."

Jo laughed, and wiping the damp stock of her whip against her pants, turned. It was then she saw him standing behind her. "Keane!" she used the name she had sworn not to use as pleasure flooded through her. It shone on her face. Just as she had given up hope of seeing him again, he was there. She took two steps toward him before she could check herself. "I didn't know you were back." Jo gripped the stock of the whip with both hands to prevent herself from reaching out to touch him.

"I believe you missed me." His voice was as she remembered, low and smooth.

Jo cursed herself for being so naïve and transparent. "Perhaps I did, a little," she admitted cautiously. "I suppose I'd gotten used to you, and you were gone longer than you said you'd be." He looks the same, she thought rapidly, exactly the same. She reminded herself that it had only been a month. It had seemed like years.

"*Mmm,* yes. I had more to see to than I had expected. You look a bit pale," he observed and touched her cheek with his fingertip.

"I suppose I haven't been getting much sun," she said with quick prevarication. "How was Chicago?" Jo needed to turn the conversation away from personal lines until she had an opportunity to gauge her emotions; seeing him suddenly had tossed them into confusion.

"Cool," he told her, making a long, thorough survey of her face. "Have you ever been there?"

"No. We play near there toward the end of the season, but I've never had time to go all the way into the city."

Nodding absently, Keane glanced into the empty cage behind her. "I see you're training Gerry."

"Yes." Relieved that they had lapsed into a professional discussion, Jo let the muscles of her shoulders ease. "This was the first time with an adult cat and no bars between. He did very well."

Keane looked back at her. His eyes were serious and probing. "He was trembling. I could see it from where I stood watching you."

"It was his first time—" she began in Gerry's defense.

"I wasn't criticizing him," Keane interrupted with a tinge of impatience. "It's just that he stood beside you, shaking from head to foot, and you were totally cool and in complete control."

"It's my job to be in control," Jo reminded him.

"That lion must have stood seven feet tall when he went up on his hind legs, and you walked under him without any protection, not even the traditional chair."

"I do a picture act," she explained, "not a fighting act."

. "Jo," he said so sharply she blinked. "Aren't you ever frightened in there?"

"Frightened?" she repeated, lifting a brow. "Of course I'm frightened. More frightened than Gerry was—or than you would be."

"What are you talking about?" Keane demanded. Jo noted with some curiosity that he was angry. "I could see that boy sweat in there."

"That was mostly excitement," Jo told him patiently. "He hasn't the experience to be truly frightened yet." She tossed back her hair and let out a long breath. Jo did not like to talk of her fears with anyone and found it especially difficult with Keane. Only because she felt it necessary that he understand this to understand the circus did she continue. "Real fear comes from knowing them, working with them, understanding them. You can only speculate on what they can do to a man. I *know*. I know exactly what they're capable of. They have an incredible courage, but more, they have an incredible guile. I've seen what they can do." Her eyes were calm and clear as they looked into his. "My father almost lost a leg once. I was about five, but I remember it perfectly. He made a mistake, and a five-hundred-pound Nubian sunk into his thigh and dragged him around the arena. Luckily, the cat was diverted by a female in season. Cats are unpredictable when they have sex on their minds, which is probably one of the reasons he attacked my father in the first place. They're fiercely jealous once they've set their minds on a mate. My father was able to get into the safety cage before any of the other cats took an interest in him. I can't remember how many stitches he had or how long it was before he could walk properly again, but I do remember the look in that cat's eyes. You learn quickly about fear when you're in the cage, but you control it, you channel it or you find another line of work."

"Then why?" Keane demanded. He took her shoulders before she could turn away. "Why do you do it? And don't tell me because it's your job. That's not good enough."

It puzzled Jo why he seemed angry. His eyes were darkened with temper, and his fingers dug into her shoulders. As if wanting to draw out her answer, he gave her one quick shake. "All right," Jo said slowly, ignoring the ache in her flesh. "That is part of it, but not all. It's all I've ever known, that's part of it, too. It's what I'm good at.'' While she spoke, she searched his face for a clue to his mood. She wondered if perhaps he had felt it wrong of her to take Gerry into the cage. ''Gerry's going to be good at it, too,'' she told him. ''I imagine everyone needs to be good—really good—at something. And I enjoy giving the people who come to see me the best show I can. But over all, I suppose it's because I love them. It's difficult for a layman to understand a trainer's feeling for his animals. I love their intelligence, their really awesome beauty, their strength, the unquenchable streak of wildness that separates them from well-trained horses. They're exciting, challenging and terrifying.''

Keane was silent for a moment. She saw that his eyes were still angry, but his fingers relaxed on her shoulders. Jo felt a light throbbing where bruises would certainly show in the morning. ''I suppose excitement becomes addicting—difficult to live without once it's become a habit.''

''I don't know,'' Jo replied, grateful that his temper was apparently cooling. ''I've never thought about it.''

''No, I suppose you'd have little reason to.'' With a nod, he turned to walk away.

Jo took a step after him. ''Keane.'' His name raced through her lips before she could prevent it. When he turned back to her, she realized she could not ask any of the dozens of questions that flew through her mind. There was only one she felt she had any right to ask. ''Have you thought any more about what you're going to do with us...with the circus?''

For an instant she saw temper flare again into his eyes. ''No.'' The word was curt and final. As he turned his back on her again, she felt a spurt of anger and reached for his arm.

''How can you be so callous, so unfeeling?'' she demanded. ''How is it possible to be so casual when you hold the lives of over a hundred people in your hands?''

Carefully, he removed her hand from his arm. ''Don't push me, Jo.'' There was warning in his eyes and in his voice.

''I'm not trying to,'' she returned, then ran a frustrated hand through her hair. ''I'm only asking you to be fair, to be...kind,'' she finished lamely.

''Don't ask me anything,'' he ordered in a brisk, authoritative tone. Jo's chin rose in response. "I'm here," he reminded her. "You'll have to be satisfied with that for now."

Jo battled with her temper. She could not deny that in coming back he had proved himself true to his word. She had the rest of the season if nothing else. "I don't suppose I have any choice," she said quietly.

"No," he agreed with a faint nod. "You don't."

Frowning, Jo watched him stride away in a smooth, fluid gait she was forced to admire. She noticed for the first time that her palms were as damp as Gerry's had been. Annoyed, she rubbed them over her hips.

"Want to talk about it?"

Jo turned quickly to find Jamie behind her in full clown gear. She knew her preoccupation had been deep for her to be caught so completely unaware. "Oh, Jamie, I didn't see you."

"You haven't seen anything but Prescott since you stepped out of the cage," Jamie pointed out.

"What are you doing in makeup?" she asked, skirting his comment.

He gestured toward the dog at her feet. "This mutt won't respond to me unless I'm in my face. Do you want to talk about it?"

"Talk about what?"

"About Prescott, about the way you feel about him."

The dog sat patiently at Jamie's heels and thumped his tail. Casually, Jo stopped and ruffled his gray fur.

"I don't know what you're talking about."

"Look, I'm not saying it can't work out, but I don't want to see you get hurt. I know how it is to be nuts about somebody."

"What in the world makes you think I'm nuts about Keane Prescott?" Jo gave the dog her full attention.

"Hey, it's me, remember?" Jamie took her arm and pulled her to her feet. "Not everybody would've noticed, maybe, but not everybody knows you the way I do. You've been miserable since he went back to Chicago, looking for him in every car that drove on the lot. And just now, when you saw him, you lit up like the midway on Saturday night. I'm not saying there's anything wrong with you being in love with him, but—"

"In love with him?" Jo repeated, incredulous.

"Yeah." Jamie spoke patiently. "In love with him."

Jo stared at Jamie as the realization slid over her. "In love with him," she murmured, trying out the words. "Oh, no." She sighed, closing her eyes. "Oh, no."

"Didn't you have enough sense to figure it out for yourself?" Jamie said gently. Seeing Jo's distress, he ran a hand gently up her arm.

"No, I guess I'm pretty stupid about this sort of thing." Jo opened her eyes and looked around, wondering if the world should look any different. "What am I going to do?"

"Heck, I don't know." Jamie kicked sawdust with an over-sized shoe. "I'm not exactly getting rave notices myself in that department." He gave Jo a reassuring pat. "I just wanted you to know that you always have a sympathetic ear here." He grinned engagingly before he turned to walk away, leaving Jo distracted and confused.

Jo spent the rest of the afternoon absorbed with the idea of being in love with Keane Prescott. For a short time she allowed herself to enjoy the sensation, the novel experience of loving someone not as a friend but as a lover. She could feel the light and the power spread through her, as if she had caught the sun in her hand. She daydreamed.

Keane was in love with her. He'd told her hundreds of times as he'd held her under a moonlit sky. He wanted to marry her, he couldn't bear to live without her. She was suddenly sophisticated and worldly enough to deal with the country club set on their own ground. She could exchange droll stories with the wives of other attorneys. There would be children and a house in the country. How would it feel to wake up in the same town every morning? She would learn to cook and give dinner parties. There would be long, quiet evenings when they would be alone together. There would be candlelight and music. When they slept together, his arms would stay around her until morning.

Idiot. Jo dragged herself back sternly. As she and Pete fed the cats, she tried to remember that fairy tales were for children. None of those things are ever going to happen, she reminded herself. I have to figure out how to handle this before I get in any deeper.

"Pete," she began, keeping her voice conversational as she put Abra's quota of raw meat on a long stick. "Have you ever been in love?"

Pete chewed his gum gently, watching Jo hoist the meat through the bars. "Well, now, let's see." Thrusting out his lower lip, he considered. "Only 'bout eight or ten times, I guess. Maybe twelve."

Jo laughed, moving down to the next cage. "I'm serious," she told him. "I mean *really* in love."

"I fall in love easy," Pete confessed gravely. "I'm a pushover for a pretty face. Matter of fact, I'm a pushover for an ugly face." He grinned. "Yes sir, the only thing like being in love is drawing an ace-high flush when the pot's ripe."

Jo shook her head and continued down the line. "Okay, since you're such an expert, tell me what you do when you're in love with a person and the person doesn't love you back and you don't want that person to know that you're in love because you don't want to make a fool of yourself."

"Just a minute." Pete squeezed his eyes tight. "I got to think this one through first." For a moment he was silent as his lips moved with his thoughts. "Okay, let's see if I've got this straight." Opening his eyes, he frowned in concentration. "You're in love—"

"I didn't say *I* was in love," Jo interrupted hastily.

Pete lifted his brows and pursed his lips. "Let's just use *you* in the general sense to avoid confusion," he suggested. Jo nodded, pretending to absorb herself with the feeding of the cats. "So, you're in love, but the guy doesn't love you. First off, you've got to be sure he doesn't."

"He doesn't," Jo murmured, then added quickly, "let's say he doesn't."

Pete shot her a look out of the corner of his eye, then shifted his gum to the other side of his mouth. "Okay, then the first thing you should do is change his mind."

"Change his mind?" Jo repeated, frowning at him.

"Sure." Pete gestured with his hand to show the simplicity of the procedure. "You fall in love with him, then he falls in love with you. You play hard to get, or you play easy to get. Or you play flutter and smile." He demonstrated by coyly batting his lashes and giving a winsome smile. Jo giggled and leaned on the feeding pole. Pete in fielder's cap, white T-shirt and faded jeans was the best show she'd seen all day. "You make him jealous," he continued. "Or you flatter his ego. Girl, there're so many ways to get a man, I can't count them, and I've been gotten by them all. Yes, sir, I'm a real pushover." He looked so pleased with his weakness, Jo smiled. How easy it would be, she thought, if I could take love so lightly.

"Suppose I don't want to do any of those things. Suppose I don't really know how and I don't want to humiliate myself by making a mess of it. Suppose the person isn't—well, suppose nothing could ever work between us, anyway. What then?"

"You got too many supposes," Pete concluded, then shook his finger at her. "And I got one for you. Suppose you ain't too smart because you figure you can't win even before you play."

"Sometimes people get hurt when they play," Jo countered quietly. "Especially if they aren't familiar with the game."

"Hurting's nothing," Pete stated with a sweep of his hand. "Winning's the best, but playing's just fine. This whole big life, it's a game, Jo. You know that. And the rules keep changing all the time. You've got nerve," he continued, then laid his rough, brown hand on her shoulder. "More raw nerve than most anybody I've ever known. You've got brains, too, hungry brains. You going to tell me that with all that, you're afraid to take a chance?"

Meeting his eyes, Jo knew hypothetical evasions would not do. "I suppose I only take calculated risks, Pete. I know my turf; I know my moves. And I know exactly what'll happen if I make a mistake. I take a chance that my body might be clawed, not my emotions. I've never rehearsed for anything like this, and I think playing it cold would be suicide."

"I think you've got to believe in Jo Wilder a little more," Pete countered, then gave her cheek a quick pat.

"Hey, Jo." Looking over, Jo saw Rose approaching. She wore straight-leg jeans, a white peasant blouse and a six-foot boa constrictor over her shoulders.

"Hello, Rose." Jo handed Pete the feeding pole. "Taking Baby out for a walk?"

"He needed some air." Rose gave her charge a pat. "I think

he got a little carsick this morning. Does he look peaked to you?''

Jo looked down at the shiny, multicolored skin, then studied the tiny black eyes as Rose held Baby's head up for inspection. ''I don't think so,'' she decided.

''Well, it's a warm day,'' Rose observed, releasing Baby's head. ''I'll give him a bath. That might perk him up.''

Jo noticed Rose's eyes darting around the compound. ''Looking for Jamie?''

''Hmph.'' Rose tossed her black curls. ''I'm not wasting my time on that one.'' She stroked the latter half of Baby's anatomy. ''I'm indifferent.''

''That's another way to do it,'' Pete put in, giving Jo a nudge. ''I forgot about that one. It's a zinger.''

Rose frowned at Pete, then at Jo. ''What's he talking about?''

With a laugh, Jo sat down on a water barrel. ''Catching a man,'' she told her, letting the warm sun play on her face. ''Pete's done a study on it from the male point of view.''

''Oh.'' Rose threw Pete her most disdainful look. ''You think I'm indifferent so he'll get interested?''

''It's a zinger,'' Pete repeated, adjusting his cap. ''You get him confused so he starts thinking about you. You make him crazy wondering why you don't notice him.''

Rose considered the idea. ''Does it usually work?''

''It's got an eighty-seven percent success average,'' Pete assured her, then gave Baby a friendly pat. ''It even works with cats.'' He jerked his thumb behind him and winked at Jo. ''The pretty lady cat, she sits there and stares off into space like she's got important things occupying her mind. The boy in the next cage is doing everything but standing on his head to get her attention. She just gives herself a wash, pretending she doesn't even know he's there. Then, maybe after she's got him banging his head against the bars, she looks over, blinks her big yellow eyes and says, 'Oh, were you talking to me?' '' Pete laughed and stretched his back muscles. ''He's hooked then, brother, just like a fish on a line.''

Rose smiled at the image of Jamie dangling from her own personal line. ''Maybe I won't put Baby in Carmen's trailer after all,'' she murmured. ''Oh, look, here comes Duffy and the owner.'' An inherent flirt, Rose instinctively fluffed her hair. "Really, he is the most handsome man. Don't you think so, Jo?"

Jo's eyes had already locked on Keane's. She seemed helpless to release herself from the gaze. Gripping the edge of the water barrel tightly, she reminded herself not to be a fool. "Yes," she agreed with studied casualness. "He's very attractive."

"Your knuckles are turning white, Jo," Pete muttered next to her ear.

Letting out a frustrated breath, Jo relaxed her hands. Straightening her spine, she determined to show more restraint. Control, she reminded herself, was the basic tool of her trade. If she could train her emotions and outbluff a dozen lions, she could certainly outbluff one man.

"Hello, Duffy." Rose gave the portly man a quick smile, then turned her attention to Keane. "Hello, Mr. Prescott. It's nice to have you back."

"Hello, Rose." He smiled into her upturned face, then lifted a brow as his eyes slid over the reptile around her neck and shoulders. "Who's your friend?"

"Oh, this is Baby." She patted one of the tan-colored saddle marks on Baby's back.

"Of course." Jo noticed how humor enhanced the gold of his eyes. "Hello, Pete." He gave the handler an easy nod before his gaze shifted and then lingered on Jo.

As on the first day they had met, Keane did not bother to camouflage his stare. His look was cool and assessing. He was reaffirming ownership. It shot through Jo that yes, she was in love with him, but she was also afraid of him. She feared his power over her, feared his capacity to hurt her. Still, her face registered none of her thoughts. Fear, she reminded herself as her eyes remained equally cool on his, was something she understood. Love might cause impossible problems, but fear could be dealt with. She would not cower from him, and she would honor the foremost rule of the arena. She would not turn and run.

Silently, they watched each other while the others looked on with varying degrees of curiosity. There was the barest touch of a smile on Keane's lips. The battle of wills continued until Duffy cleared his throat.

"Ah, Jo."

Calmly, without hurry, she shifted her attention. "Yes, Duffy?"

"I just sent one of the web girls into town to see the local dentist. Seems she's got an abscess. I need you to fill in tonight."

"Sure."

"Just for the web and the opening spectacular," he continued. Unable to prevent himself, he cast a quick look at Keane to see if he was still staring at her. He was. Duffy shifted uncomfortably and wondered what the devil was going on. "Take your usual place in the finale. We'll just be one girl shy in the chorus. Wardrobe'll fix you up."

"Okay." Jo smiled at him, though she was very much aware of Keane's eyes on her. "I guess I'd better go practice walking in those three-inch heels. What position do I take?"

"Number four rope."

"Duffy," Rose chimed in and tugged on his sleeve. "When are you going to let me do the web?"

"Rose, how's a pint-sizer like you going to stand up with that heavy costume on?" Duffy shook his head at her, keeping a respectable distance from Baby. After thirty-five years of working carnies, sideshows and circuses, he still was uneasy around snakes.

"I'm pretty strong," Rose claimed, stretching her spine in the hope of looking taller. "And I've been practicing." Anxious to demonstrate her accomplishments, Rose deftly unwound Baby. "Hold him a minute," she requested and dumped several feet of snake into Keane's arms.

"Ah…" Keane shifted the weight in his arms and looked dubiously into Baby's bored eyes. "I hope he's eaten recently."

"He had a nice breakfast," Rose assured him, going into a fluid backbend to show Duffy her flexibility.

"Baby won't eat owners," Jo told Keane. She did not bother to suppress her grin. It was the first time she had seen him disconcerted. "Just a stray towner, occasionally. Rose keeps him on a strict diet."

"I assume," Keane began as Baby slithered into a more comfortable position, "that he's aware I'm the owner."

Grinning at Keane's uncomfortable expression, Jo turned to

Pete. "Gee, I don't know. Did anybody tell Baby about the new owner?"

"Haven't had a chance, myself," Pete drawled, taking out a fresh stick of gum. "Looks a lot like a towner, too. Baby might get confused."

"They're just teasing you, Mr. Prescott," Rose told him as she finished her impromptu audition with a full split. "Baby doesn't eat people at all. He's docile as a lamb. Little kids come up and pet him during a demonstration." She rose and brushed off her jeans. "Now, you take a cobra..."

"No, thank you," Keane declined, unloading the six-foot Baby back into Rose's arms.

Rose slipped the boa back around her neck. "Well, Duffy, I'm off. What do you say?"

"Get one of the girls to teach you the routine," he said with a nod. "Then we'll see." Smiling, he watched Rose saunter away.

"Hey, Duffy!" It was Jamie. "There's a couple of towners looking for you. I sent them over to the red wagon."

"Fine. I'll just go right on along with you." Duffy winked at Jo before turning to catch up with Jamie's long stride.

Keane was standing very close to the barrels. Jo knew getting down from her perch was risky. She knew, too, however, that her pulse was beginning to behave erratically despite her efforts to control it. "I've got to see about my costume." Nimbly, she came down, intending to skirt around him. Even as her boots touched the ground, his hands took her waist. Exercising every atom of willpower, she neither jerked nor struggled but lifted her eyes calmly to his.

His thumbs moved in a lazy arch. She could feel the warmth through the fabric of her blouse. With her entire being she wished he would not hold her. Then, perversely, she wished he would hold her closer. She struggled not to weaken as her lips grew warm under the kiss of his eyes. Her heart began to hammer in her ears.

Keane ran a hand down the length of her long, thick braid. Slowly, his eyes drifted back to hers. Abruptly, he released her and backed up to let her pass. "You'd best go have wardrobe take a few tucks in that costume."

Deciding she was not meant to decipher his changing moods, Jo stepped by him and crossed the compound. If she spent enough time working, she could keep her thoughts from dwelling on Keane Prescott. Maybe.

Seven

The Big Top was packed for the evening show. Jo watched the anticipation in the range of faces as she took her temporary position in the opening spectacular. The band played jumpy, upbeat music, leaning heavily on brass as the theme parade marched around the hippodrome track. As the substitute Bo Peep, Jo wore a demure mopcap and a wide crinoline skirt and led a baby lamb on a leash. Because her act came so swiftly on the tail of the opening, she rarely participated in the spectacular. Now she enjoyed a close-up look at the audience. In the cage, she blocked them out almost completely.

They were, she decided, a well-mixed group: young babies, older children, parents, grandparents, teen-agers. They gave the pageant enthusiastic applause. Jo smiled and waved as she performed the basic choreography with hardly a thought.

After a quick costume change, she took her cue as Queen of the Jungle Cats. After that followed another costume change that transformed her into one of the Twelve Spinning Butterflies.

"Just heard," Jamie whispered in her ear as she took the customary pose by the rope. "You got the job for the next week. Barbara won't be able to handle the teeth grip."

Jo shifted her shoulders to compensate for the weight of her enormous blue wings. "Rose is going to learn the routine," she mumbled back, smiling in the flood of the sunlight. "Duffy's giving her the job if she can stand up under this blasted costume." She made a quick, annoyed sound and smiled brightly. "It weighs a ton."

Slowly, to the beat of the waltz the band played, Jo climbed hand over hand up the rope. "Ah, show biz," she heard Jamie sigh. She vowed to poke him in the ribs when she took her bow.

Then, hooking her foot in the hoop, she began the routine, imitating the other eleven Spinning Butterflies.

She was able to share a cup of coffee with Rose's mother when she returned the butterfly costume to wardrobe and changed into her own white and gold jumpsuit. Her muscles complained a bit due to the unfamiliar weight of the wings, and she gave a passing thought to a long, luxurious bath. That was a dream for September, she reminded herself. Showers were the order of the day on the road.

Jo's last duty in the show was to stand on the head of Maggie, the key elephant in the finale's long mount. Sturdy and dependable, Maggie stood firm while four elephants on each side of her rose on their hind legs, resting their front legs on the back of the one in front. Atop Maggie's broad head, Jo stood glittering under the lights with both arms lifted in the air. It was here, more than any other part of the show, that the applause washed over her. It merged with the music, the ringmaster's whistle, the laughter of children. Where she had been weary, she was now filled with energy. She knew the fatigue would return, so she relished the power of the moment all the more. For those few seconds there was no work, no long hours, no predawn drives. There was only magic. Even when it was over and she slid from Maggie's back, she could still feel it.

Outside the tent, troupers and roustabouts and shandies mingled. There were anecdotes to exchange, performances to dissect, observations to be made. Gradually, they drifted away alone, in pairs or in groups. Some would change and help strike the tents, some would sleep, some would worry over their performances. Too energized to sleep, Jo planned to assist in the striking of the Big Top.

She switched on a low light as she entered her trailer, then absently braided her hair as she moved to the tiny bath. With quick moves she creamed off her stage makeup. The exotic exaggeration of her eyes was whisked away, leaving the thick fringe of her lashes and the dark green of her irises unenhanced. The soft bloom of natural rose tinted her cheeks again, and her mouth, unpainted, appeared oddly vulnerable. Accustomed to the change, Jo did not see the sharp contrast between Jovilette the performer and the small, somewhat fragile woman in the glittering jumpsuit. With her face naked and the simple braid hanging down her back, the look of the wild, of the gypsy, was less apparent. It remained in her movements, but her face rinsed of all artifice and unframed, was both delicate and young, part ingenue, part flare. But Jo saw none of this as she reached for her front zipper. Before she could pull it down, a knock sounded on her door.

"Come in," she called out and flicked her braid behind her back as she started down the aisle. She stopped in her tracks as Keane stepped through the door.

"Didn't anyone ever tell you to ask who it is first?" He shut the door behind him and locked it with a careless flick of his wrist. "You might not have to lock your door against the circus people," he continued blandly as she remained still, "but there are several dozen curious towners still hanging around."

"I can handle a curious towner," Jo replied. The offhand quality of his dominance was infuriating. "I never lock my door."

There was stiffness and annoyance in her voice. Keane ignored them both. "I brought you something from Chicago."

The casual statement succeeded in throwing Jo's temper off the mark. For the first time, she noticed the small package he carried. "What is it?" she asked.

Keane smiled and crossed to her. "It's nothing that bites," he assured her, then held it out.

Still cautious, Jo lifted her eyes to his, then dropped her gaze back to the package. "It's not my birthday," she murmured.

"It's not Christmas, either," Keane pointed out.

The easy patience in the tone caused Jo to lift her eyes again. She wondered how it was he understood her hesitation to accept presents. She kept her gazed locked on his. "Thank you," she said solemnly as she took the gift.

"You're welcome," Keane returned in the same tone.

The amenities done, Jo recklessly ripped the paper. "Oh! It's Dante," she exclaimed, tearing off the remaining paper and tossing it on the table. With reverence she ran her palm over the dark leather binding. The rich scent drifted to her. She knew her quota of books would have been limited to one a year had she bought a volume so handsomely bound. She opened it slowly, as if to prolong the pleasure. The pages were heavy and rich cream in color. The text was Italian, and even as she glanced over the first page, the words ran fluidly through her mind.

"It's beautiful," she murmured, overcome. Lifting her eyes to thank him again, Jo found Keane smiling down at her. Shyness enveloped her suddenly, all the more intense because she had so rarely experienced it. A lifetime in front of crowds had given her a natural confidence in almost any situation. Now color began to surge into her cheeks, and her mind was a jumble of words that would not come to order.

"I'm glad you like it." He ran a finger down her cheek. "Do you always blush when someone gives you a present?"

Because she was at a loss as to how to answer his question, Jo maneuvered around it. "It was nice of you to think of me."

"It seems to come naturally," Keane replied, then watched Jo's lashes flutter down.

"I don't know what to say." She was able to meet his eyes again with her usual directness, but he had again touched her emotions. She felt inadequate to deal with her feelings or with his effect on her.

"You've already said it." He took the book from Jo's hand and paged through it. "Of course, I can't read a word of it. I envy you that." Before Jo could ponder the idea of a man like Keane Prescott envying her anything, he looked back up and smiled. Her thoughts scattered like nervous ants. "Got any coffee?" he asked and set the book back down on the table.

"Coffee?"

"Yes, you know, coffee. They grow it in quantity in Brazil."

Jo gave him a despairing look. "I don't have any made. I'd fix you a cup, but I've got to change before I help strike the tents. The cookhouse will still be serving."

Keane lifted a brow as he let his eyes wander over her face. "Don't you think that between Bo Peep, lions and butterflies, you've done enough work tonight? By the way, you make a very appealing butterfly."

"Thank you, but—"

"Let's put it this way," Keane countered smoothly. He took the tip of her braid in his fingers. "You've got the night off. I'll make the coffee myself if you show me where you keep it."

Though she let out a windy sigh, Jo was more amused than

annoyed. Coffee, she decided, was the least she could do after he had brought her such a lovely present. "I'll make it," she told him, "but you'll probably wish you'd gone to the cookhouse." With this dubious invitation, Jo turned and headed toward the kitchen. He made no sound, but she knew he followed her. For the first time, she felt the smallness of her kitchen.

Setting an undersized copper kettle on one of the two burners, Jo flicked on the power. It was a simple matter to keep her back to him while she plucked cups from the cupboard. She was well aware that if she turned around in the compact kitchen, she would all but be in his arms.

"Did you watch the whole show?" she asked conversationally as she pulled out a jar of instant coffee.

"Duffy had me working props," Keane answered. "He seems to be making me generally useful."

Amused, Jo twisted her head to grin at him. Instantly, she discovered her misstep in strategy. Keane's face was only inches from hers, and in his eyes she read his thoughts. He wanted her, and he intended to have her. Before she could shift her position, Keane took her shoulders and turned her completely around. Jo knew she had backed up against the bars.

Leisurely, he began to loosen her hair, working his fingers through it until it pooled over her shoulders. "I've wanted to do that since the first time I saw you. It's hair to get lost in." His voice was soft as he took a generous handful. The gesture itself seemed to stake his claim. "In the sun it shimmers with red lights, but in the dark it's like night itself." It came to her that each time she was close to him, she was less able to resist him. She became more lost in his eyes, more beguiled by his power. Already her mouth tingled with the memory of his kiss, with the longing for a new one. Behind them the kettle began a feverish whistle.

"The water," she managed and tried to move around him. With one hand in her hair, Keane kept her still as he turned off the burner. The whistle sputtered peevishly, then died. The sound echoed in Jo's head.

"Do you want coffee?" he murmured as his fingers trailed to her throat.

Jo's eyes clung to his. Hers were enormous and direct, his

quiet and searching. ''No,'' she whispered, knowing she wanted nothing more at that moment than to belong to him. He circled her throat with his hand and pressed his fingers against her pulse. It fluttered wildly.

''You're trembling.'' He could feel the light tremor of her body as he brought her closer. ''Is it fear?'' he demanded as his thumbs brushed over her lips. ''Or excitement?''

''Both,'' she answered in a voice thickened with emotion. She made a tiny, confused sound as his palm covered her heart. Its desperate thudding increased. ''Are you...'' She stopped a moment because her voice was breathless and unsteady. ''Are you going to make love to me?'' Did his eyes really darken? she wondered dizzily. Or is it my imagination?

''Beautiful Jovilette,'' he murmured as his mouth lowered to hers. ''No pretentions, no evasions...irresistible.'' The quality of the kiss altered swiftly. His mouth was hungry on hers, and her response leaped past all caution. If loving him was madness, her heart reasoned, could making love take her further beyond sanity? Past wisdom and steeped in sensation, she let her heart rule her will. When her lips parted under his, it was not in surrender but in equal demand.

Keane gentled the kiss. He kept her shimmering on the razor's edge of passion. His mouth teased, promised, then fed her growing need. He found the zipper at the base of her throat and pulled it downward slowly. Her skin was warm, and he sought it, giving a low sound of pleasure as her breast swelled under his hand. He explored without hurry, as if memorizing each curve and plane. Jo no longer trembled but became pliant as her body moved to the rhythm he set. Her sigh was spontaneous, filled with wonder and delight.

With a suddenness that took her breath away, Keane crushed her mouth beneath his in fiery urgency. Jo's instincts responded, thrusting her into a world she had only imagined. His hands grew rougher, more insistent. Jo realized he had relinquished control. They were both riding on the tossing waves of passion. This sea had no horizon and no depth. It was a drowning sea that pulled the unsuspecting under while promising limitless pleasure. Jo did not resist but dove deeper.

At first she thought the knocking was only the sound of her

heart against her ribs. When Keane drew away, she murmured in protest and pulled him back. Instantly, his mouth was avid, but as the knocking continued, he swore and pulled back again.

"Someone's persistent," he muttered. Bewildered, Jo stared up at him. "The door," he explained on a long breath.

"Oh." Flustered, Jo ran a hand through her hair and tried to collect her wits.

"You'd better answer it," Keane suggested as he pulled the zipper to her throat in one quick move. Jo broke the surface into reality abruptly. For a moment Keane watched her, taking in her flushed cheeks and tousled hair before he moved aside. Willing her legs to carry her, Jo walked to the front of the trailer. The door handle resisted, then she remembered that Keane had locked it, and she turned the latch.

"Yes, Buck?" she said calmly enough when she opened the door to her handler.

"Jo." His face was in shadows, but she heard the distress in the single syllable. Her chest tightened. "It's Ari."

He had barely finished the name before Jo was out of the trailer and running across the compound. She found both Pete and Gerry standing near Ari's cage.

"How bad?" she demanded as Pete came to meet her.

He took her shoulders. "Really bad this time, Jo."

For a moment she wanted to shake her head, to deny what she read in Pete's eyes. Instead, she nudged him aside and walked to Ari's cage. The old cat lay on his side as his chest lifted and fell with the effort of breathing. "Open it," she ordered Pete in a voice that revealed nothing. There was the jingle of keys, but she did not turn.

"You're not going in there." Jo heard Keane's voice and felt a restraining grip on her shoulders. Her eyes were opaque as she looked up at him.

"Yes, I am. Ari isn't going to hurt me or anyone else. He's just going to die. Now leave me alone." Her voice was low and toneless. "Open it," she ordered again, then pulled out of Keane's loosened hold. The bars rattled as he slid the door open. Hearing it, Jo turned, then hoisted herself into the cage.

Ari barely stirred. Jo saw, as she knelt beside him, that his eyes were open. They were glazed with weariness and pain.

"Ari," she sighed, seeing there would be no tomorrow for him. His only answer was a hollow wheezing. Putting a hand to his side, she felt the ragged pace of his breathing. He made an effort to respond to her touch, to his name, but managed only to shift his great head on the floor. The gesture tore at Jo's heart. She lowered her face to his mane, remembering him as he had once been: full of strength and a terrifying beauty. She lifted her face again and took one long, steadying breath. "Buck." She heard him approach but kept her eyes on Ari. "Get the medical kit. I want a hypo of pentobarbital." She could feel Buck's brief hesitation before he spoke.

"Okay, Jo."

She sat quietly, stroking Ari's head. In the distance were the sounds of the Big Top going down, the call of men, the rattle of rigging, the clang of wood against metal. An elephant trumpeted, and three cages down, Faust roared half-heartedly in response.

"Jo." She turned her head as Buck called her and pushed her hair from her eyes. "Let me do it."

Jo merely shook her head and held out her hand.

"Jo." Keane stepped up to the bars. His voice was gentle, but his eyes were so like the cat's at her knees, Jo nearly sobbed aloud. "You don't have to do this yourself."

"He's my cat," she responded dully. "I said I'd do it when it was time. It's time." Her eyes shifted to Buck. "Give me the hypo, Buck. Let's get it done." When the syringe was in her hand, Jo stared at it, then closed her fingers around it. Swallowing hard, she turned back to Ari. His eyes were on her face. After more than twenty years in captivity there was still something not quite tamed in the dying cat. But she saw trust in his eyes and wanted to weep. "You were the best," she told him as she passed a hand through his mane. "You were always the best." Jo felt a numbing cold settling over her and prayed it would last until she had finished. "You're tired now. I'm going to help you sleep." She pulled the safety from the point of the hypodermic and waited until she was certain her hands were steady. "This won't hurt, nothing is going to hurt you anymore."

Involuntarily, Jo rubbed the back of her hand over her mouth, then, moving quickly, she plunged the needle into Ari's shoulder. A quiet whimper escaped her as she emptied the syringe. Ari

made no sound but continued to watch her face. Jo offered no
words of comfort but sat with him, methodically stroking his fur
as his eyes grew cloudy. Gradually, the effort of his breathing
lessened, becoming quieter and quieter until it wasn't there at
all. Jo felt him grow still, and her hand balled into a fist inside
the mass of his mane. One quick, convulsive shudder escaped
her. Steeling herself, she moved from the cage, closing the door
behind her. Because her bones felt fragile, she kept them stiff,
as though they might shatter. Even as she stepped back to the
ground, Keane took her arm and began to lead her away.

"Take care of things," he said to Buck as they moved past.

"No." Jo protested, trying and failing to free her arm. "I'll
do it."

"No, you won't." Keane's tone held a quiet finality.
"Enough's enough."

"Don't tell me what to do," she said sharply, letting her grief
take refuge in anger.

"I *am* telling you," he pointed out. His hand was firm on her
arm.

"You *can't* tell me what to do," she insisted as tears rose
treacherously in her throat. "I want you to leave me alone."

Keane stopped, then took her by the shoulders. His eyes caught
the light of a waning moon. "There's no way I'm going to leave
you alone when you're so upset."

"My emotions have nothing to do with you." Even as she
spoke, he took her arm again and pulled her toward her trailer.
Jo wanted desperately to be alone to weep out her grief in private.
The mourning belonged to her, and the tears were personal. As
if her protests were nonexistent, he pulled her into the trailer and
closed the door behind them. "Will you get out of here?" she
demanded, frantically swallowing tears.

"Not until I know you're all right." Keane's answer was calm
as he walked back to the kitchen.

"I'm perfectly all right." Her breath shuddered in and out
quickly. "Or I will be when you leave me alone. You have no
right to poke your nose in my business."

"So you've told me before," Keane answered mildly from the
back of the trailer.

"I just did what had to be done." She held her body rigid and fought against her own quick, uneven breathing. "I put a sick animal out of his misery; it's as simple as that." Her voice broke, and she turned away, hugging her arms. "For heaven's sake, Keane, go away!"

Quietly, he walked back to her carrying a glass of water. "Drink this."

"No." She whirled back to him. Tears spilled out of her eyes and trickled down her cheeks despite her efforts to banish them. Hating herself, she pressed the heel of her hand between her brows and closed her eyes. "I don't want you here." Keane set down the glass, then gathered her into his arms. "No, don't. I don't want you to hold me."

"Too bad." He ran a hand gently up and down her back. "You did a very brave thing, Jo. I know you loved Ari. I know how hard it was to let him go. You're hurting, and I'm not leaving you."

"I don't want to cry in front of you." Her fists were tight balls at his shoulders.

"Why not?" The stroking continued up and down her back as he cradled her head in the curve of his shoulder.

"Why won't you let me be?" she sobbed as her control slipped. Her fingers gripped his shirt convulsively. "Why am I always losing what I love?" She let the grief come. She let his arms soothe her. As desperately as she had protested against it, she clung to his offer of comfort.

She made no objection as he carried her to the couch and cradled her in his arms. He stroked her hair, as she had stroked Ari, to ease the pain of what couldn't be changed. Slowly, her sobbing quieted. Still she lay with her cheek against his chest, with her hair curtaining her face.

"Better?" he asked as the silence grew calmer. Jo nodded, not yet trusting her voice. Keane shifted her as he reached for the glass of water. "Drink this now."

Gratefully, Jo relieved her dry throat, then went without resistance back against his chest. She closed her eyes, thinking it had been a very long time since she had been held in anyone's lap and soothed. "Keane," she murmured. She felt his lips brush over the top of her head.

"Hmm?"

"Nothing." Her voice thickened as she drifted toward sleep. "Just Keane."

Eight

Jo felt the sun on her closed lids. There was the summer morning sound of excited birds. Her mind, levitating slowly toward the surface, told her it must be Monday. Only on Monday would she sleep past sunrise. That was the enroute day, the only day in seven the circus held no show. She thought lazily of getting up. She would set aside two hours for reading. Maybe I'll drive into town and see a movie. What town are we in? With a sleepy sigh she rolled onto her stomach.

I'll give the cats a good going over, maybe hose them down if it gets hot enough. Memory flooded back and snapped her awake. *Ari.* Opening her eyes, Jo rolled onto her back and stared at the ceiling. Now she recalled vividly how the old cat had died with his eyes trusting on her face. She sighed again. The sadness was still there, but not the sharp, desperate grief of the night before. Acceptance was settling in. She realized that Keane's insistence on staying with her during the peak of her mourning had helped her. He had given her someone to rail at, then someone to hold on to. She remembered the incredible comfort of being cradled in his lap, the solid dependability of his chest against her cheek. She had fallen asleep with the sound of his heart in her ear.

Turning her head, Jo looked out the window, then at the patch of white light the sun tossed on the floor. But it isn't Monday, she remembered suddenly. It's Thursday. Jo sat up, pushing at her hair, which seemed to tumble everywhere at once. What was she doing in bed on a Thursday when the sun was up? Without giving herself time to work out the answer, she scrambled out of bed and hurried from the room. She gave a soft gasp as she ran headlong into Keane.

His hand ran down the length of her hair before he took her

shoulder. "I heard you stirring," he said easily, looking down into her stunned face.

"What are you doing here?"

"Making coffee," he answered as he gave her a critical study. "Or I was a moment ago. How are you?"

"I'm all right." Jo lifted her hand to her temple as if to gain her bearings. "I'm a bit disoriented, I suppose. I overslept. It's never happened before."

"I gave you a sleeping pill," Keane told her matter-of-factly. He slipped an arm around her shoulder as he turned back to the kitchen.

"A pill?" Jo's eyes flew to his. "I don't remember taking a pill."

"It was in the water you drank." On the stove the kettle began its piercing whistle. Moving to it, Keane finished making the coffee. "I had my doubts as to whether you'd take it voluntarily."

"No, I wouldn't have," Jo agreed with some annoyance. "I've never taken a sleeping pill in my life."

"Well, you did last night." He held out a mug of coffee. "I sent Gerry for it while you were in the cage with Ari." Again he gave her a quick, intense study. "It didn't seem to do you any harm. You went out like a light. I carried you to bed, changed your clothes—"

"Changed my..." All at once Jo became aware that she wore only a thin white nightshirt. Her hand reached instinctively for the top button that nestled just above her bosom. Thinking hard, she found she could recall nothing beyond falling asleep in his arms.

"I don't think you'd have spent a very comfortable night in your costume," Keane pointed out. Enjoying his coffee, he smiled at the nervous hand she held between her breasts. "I've had a certain amount of experience undressing women in the dark." Jo dropped her hand. It was an unmistakable movement of pride. Keane's eyes softened. "You needed a good night's sleep, Jo. You were worn out."

Without speaking, Jo lifted her coffee to her lips and turned away. Walking to the window, she could see that the back yard was deserted. Her sleep must indeed have been deep to have kept her unaware of camp breaking.

"Everyone's gone but a couple of roustabouts and a generator truck. They'll take off when you don't need power anymore."

The vulnerability Jo felt was overwhelming. Several times in the course of the evening before, she had lost control, which had always been an essential part of her. Each time, it had been Keane who had been there. She wanted to be angry with him for intruding on her privacy but found it impossible. She had needed him, and he had known it.

"You didn't have to stay behind," she said, watching a crow swoop low over the ground outside.

"I wasn't certain you'd be in any shape to drive fifty miles this morning. Pete's driving my trailer."

Her shoulders lifted and fell before she turned around. Sunlight streamed through the window at her back and poured through the thin folds of her nightshirt. Her body was a slender shadow. When she spoke, her voice was low with regret. "I was horribly rude to you last night."

Keane shrugged and lifted his coffee. "You were upset."

"Yes." Her eyes were an open reflection of her sorrow. "Ari was very important to me. I suppose he was an ongoing link with my father, with my childhood. I'd known for some time he wouldn't make it through the season, but I didn't want to face it." She looked down at the mug she held gripped in both hands. A faint wisp of steam rose from it and vanished. "Last night was a relief for him. It was selfish of me to wish it otherwise. And I was wrong to strike out at you the way I did. I'm sorry."

"I don't want your apology, Jo." Because he sounded annoyed, she looked up quickly.

"I'd feel better if you'd take it, Keane. You've been very kind."

To her astonishment, he swore under his breath and turned back to the stove. "I don't care for your gratitude any more than your apology." He set down his mug and poured in more coffee. "Neither of them is necessary."

"They are to me," Jo replied, then took a step toward him. "Keane…" She set down her coffee and touched his arm. When he turned, she let impulse guide her. She rested her head on his shoulder and slipped her arms around his waist. He stiffened, putting his hands to her shoulders as if to draw her away. Then she heard his breath come out in a long sigh as he relaxed. For an instant he brought her closer.

"I never know precisely what to expect from you," he murmured. He lifted her chin with his finger. In automatic response, Jo closed her eyes and offered her mouth. She felt his fingers tighten on her skin before his lips brushed hers lightly. "You'd better go change." His manner was friendly but cool as he stepped away. "We'll stop off in town, and I'll buy you some breakfast."

Puzzled by his attitude but satisfied he was no longer annoyed, Jo nodded. "All right."

Spring became summer as the circus wound its way north. The sun stayed longer, peeking into the Big Top until well after the evening show began. Heavy rain came infrequently, but there were quick summer storms with thunder and lightning. Through June, Prescott's Circus Colossus snaked through North Carolina and into western Tennessee.

During the long weeks while spring tripped over into summer, Jo found Keane's attitude a paradox. His friendliness toward her was offhand. He laughed if she said something amusing, listened if she had a complaint and to her confusion, slipped a thin barrier between them. At times she wondered if the passion that had flared between them the night he had returned from Chicago had truly existed. Had the desire she had tasted on his lips been a fantasy? The closeness she had felt blooming between them had withered and blown away. They were only owner and trouper now.

Keane flew back to Chicago twice more during this period, but he brought no surprise presents back with him. Not once during those long weeks did he come by her trailer. Initially, his altered manner confused her. He was not angry. His mood was neither heated nor icy with temper but fell into an odd middle ground she could not understand. Jo ached with love. As days passed into weeks, she was forced to admit that Keane did not seem to be interested in a close relationship.

* * *

On the eve of the July Fourth show, Jo sat sleepless in her bed. In her hand she held the volume of Dante, but the book was only a reminder of the emptiness she felt. She closed it, then stared at the ceiling. It's time to snap out of it, she lectured herself. It's time to stop pretending he was ever really part of my life. Loving someone only makes him a part of your wishes. He never talked about love, he never promised anything, never offered anything but what he gave to me. He's done nothing to hurt me. Jo squeezed her eyes shut and pressed the book between her fingers. How I wish I could hate him for showing me what life could be like and then turning away, she thought.

But I can't. Jo let out a shaky breath and relaxed her grip on the book. Gently, she ran a finger down its smooth, leather binding. I can't hate him, but I can't love him openly, either. How do I stop? I should be grateful he stopped wanting me. I would have made love with him. Then I'd hurt a hundred times more. Could I hurt a hundred times more? For several moments she lay still, trying to quiet her thoughts.

It's best not to know, she told herself sternly. It's best to remember he was kind to me when I needed him and that I haven't a right to make demands. Summer doesn't last forever. I may never see him again when it's over. At least I can keep the time we have pleasant.

The words sounded hollow in her heart.

Nine

The Fourth of July was a full day with a run to a new lot, the tent raising, a street parade and two shows. But it was a holiday. Elephants wore red, white and blue plumes atop their massive heads. The evening performance would be held an hour earlier to allow for the addition of a fireworks display. Traditionally, Prescott's circus arranged to spend the holiday in the same small town in Tennessee. The license and paperwork for the display were seen to in advance, and the fireworks were shipped ahead to be stored in a warehouse. The procedure had been precisely the same for years. It was one of the circus's most profitable nights. Concessions thrived.

Jo moved through the day with determined cheerfulness. She refused to permit the distance between her and Keane to spoil one of the highlights of the summer. Brooding, she decided, would not change things. The mood of the crowd helped to keep her spirits light.

Between shows came the inevitable lull. Some troupers sat outside their trailers exchanging small talk and enjoying the sun. Others got in a bit more practice or worked out a few kinks. Bull hands washed down the elephants, causing a minor flood in the pen area.

Jo watched the bathing process with amusement. She never ceased to enjoy this particular aspect of circus life, especially if there were one or two inexperienced bull hands involved. Invariably, Maggie or one of the other veteran bulls would spray a trunkful of water over the new hands to initiate them. Though Jo knew the other hands encouraged it, they always displayed remarkable innocence.

Spotting Duffy, Jo moved away from the elephant area and wandered toward him. She could see he was deep in discussion with a towner. He was as short as Duffy but wider, with what she had once heard Frank call a successful frame. His stomach started high and barreled out to below his waist. He had a ruddy complexion and pale eyes that squinted hard against the sun. Jo had seen his type before. She wondered what he was selling and how much he wanted for it. Since Duffy was puffing with annoyance, Jo assumed it was quite a lot.

"I'm telling you, Carlson, we've already paid for storage. I've got a signed receipt. And we pay fifteen bucks delivery, not twenty."

Carlson was smoking a small, unfiltered cigarette and dropped it to the ground. "You paid Myers for storage, not me. I bought the place six weeks ago." He shrugged his wide shoulders. "Not my problem you paid in advance."

Looking over, Jo saw Keane approaching with Pete. Pete was talking rapidly, Keane nodding. As Jo watched, Keane glanced up and gave Carlson a quick study. She had seen that look before and knew the older man had been assessed. Keane caught her eye, smiled and began to move past her. "Hello, Jo."

Unashamedly curious, Jo fell into step beside him. "What's going on?"

"Why don't we find out?" he suggested as they stopped in front of Duffy and Carlson. "Gentlemen," Keane said in an easy tone. "Is there a problem?"

"This character," Duffy spouted, jerking a scornful thumb at Carlson's face, "wants us to pay twice for storage on the fireworks. Then he wants twenty for delivery when we agreed on fifteen."

"Myers agreed on fifteen," Carlson pointed out. He smiled without humor. "I didn't agree on anything. You want your fireworks, you gotta pay for them first—cash," he added, then spared Keane a glance. "Who's this guy?"

Duffy began to wheeze with indignation, but Keane laid a restraining hand on his shoulder. "I'm Prescott," he told him in untroubled tones. "Perhaps you'd like to fill me in."

"Prescott, huh?" Carlson stroked both his chins as he studied Keane. Seeing youth and amiable eyes, he felt closer to success. "Well, now we're getting somewhere," he said jovially and stuck out his hand. Keane accepted it without hesitation. "Jim

Carlson," he continued as he gave Keane's hand a brisk pump. "Nice circus you got here, Prescott. Me and the missus see it every year. Well, now," he said again and hitched up his belt. "Seeing as you're a businessman, too, I'm sure we can straighten all this out. Problem is, your fireworks've been stored in my warehouse. Now, I gotta make a living, they can't just sit there for free. I bought the place off Myers six weeks ago. I can't be held responsible for a deal you made with him, can I?" Carlson gave a stretched-lip smile, pleased that Keane listened so politely. "And as for delivery, well..." He made a helpless gesture and patted Keane's shoulder. "You know about gas prices these days, son. But we can work that out after we settle this other little problem."

Keane nodded agreeably. "That sounds reasonable." He ignored Duffy's huffing and puffing. "You do seem to have a problem, Mr. Carlson."

"I don't have a problem," Carlson countered. His smile suffered a fractional slip. "You've got the problem, unless you don't want the fireworks."

"Oh, we'll have the fireworks, Mr. Carlson," Keane corrected with a smile Jo thought more wolfish than friendly. "According to paragraph three, section five, of the small business code, the lessor is legally bound by all contracts, agreements, liens and mortgages of the previous lessor until such time as all aforesaid contracts, agreements, liens and mortgages are expired or transferred."

"What the..." Carlson began with no smile at all, but Keane continued blandly.

"Of course, we won't pursue the matter in court as long as we get our merchandise. But that doesn't solve your problem."

"My problem?" Carlson sputtered while Jo looked on in frank admiration. "I haven't got a problem. If you think..."

"Oh, but you do, Mr. Carlson, though I'm sure there was no intent to break the law on your part."

"Break the law?" Carlson wiped damp hands on his slacks.

"Storing explosives without a license," Keane pointed out. "Unless, of course, you obtained one after your purchase of the warehouse."

"Well, no, I..."

"I was afraid of that." Keane lifted his brow in pity. "You see, in paragraph six of section five of the small business code it states that all licenses, permits and warrants shall be nontransferable. Authorization for new licenses, permits or warrants must be requested in writing by the current owner. Notarized, naturally." Keane waited a bit to allow Carlson to wrestle with the idea. "If I'm not mistaken," he continued conversationally, "the fine's pretty hefty in this state. Of course, sentencing depends on—"

"Sentencing?" Carlson paled and mopped the back of his neck with a handkerchief.

"Look, tell you what." Keane gave Carlson a sympathetic smile. "You get the fireworks over here and off your property. We don't have to bring the law in on something like this. Just an oversight, after all. We're both businessmen, aren't we?"

Too overwrought to detect sarcasm, Carlson nodded.

"That was fifteen on delivery, right?"

Carlson didn't hesitate but stuck the damp handkerchief back in his pocket and nodded again.

"Good enough. I'll have the cash for you on delivery. Glad to help you out."

Relieved, Carlson turned and headed for his pickup. Jo managed to keep her features grave until he pulled off the lot. Simultaneously, Pete and Duffy began to hoot with laughter.

"Was it true?" Jo demanded and took Keane's arm.

"Was what true?" Keane countered, merely lifting a brow over the hysterics that surrounded him.

"'Paragraph three, section five, of the small business code,'" Jo quoted.

"Never heard of it," Keane answered mildly, nearly sending Pete into orbit.

"You made it up," Jo said in wonder. "You made it all up!"

"Probably," Keane agreed.

"Smoothest con job I've seen in years," Duffy stated and gave Keane a parental slap on the back. "Son, you could go into business."

"I did," Keane told him and grinned.

"I ever need a lawyer," Pete put in, pushing his cap further back on his head, "I know where to go. You come on by the cookhouse tonight, Captain. We're having ourselves a poker game. Come on, Duffy, Buck's gotta hear about this.''

As they moved off, Jo realized that Keane had been officially accepted. Before, he had been the legal owner but an outsider, a towner. Now he was one of them. Turning, she lifted her face to his. ''Welcome aboard.''

''Thank you.'' She saw he understood precisely what had been left unsaid.

''I'll see you at the game,'' she said before her smile became a grin. ''Don't forget your money.''

She turned away, but Keane touched her arm, bringing her back to him. ''Jo,'' he began, puzzling her by the sudden seriousness of his eyes.

''Yes?''

There was a brief hesitation, then he shook his head. ''Nothing, never mind. I'll see you later.'' He rubbed his knuckles over her cheek, then walked away.

Jo studied her hand impassively. On the deal, she had missed a heart flush by one card and now waited for someone to open. Casually, she moved her glance around the table. Duffy was puffing on a cigar, apparently unconcerned with the dwindling chips in front of him. Pete chewed his gum with equal nonchalance. Amy, the wife of the sword swallower, sat beside him, then Jamie, then Raoul. Directly beside Jo was Keane, who, like Pete, was winning consistently.

The pot grew. Chips clinked on the table. Jo discarded and was pleased to exchange a club for the fifth heart. She slipped it into her hand without blinking. Frank had taught her the game. Before the second round of betting Jamie folded in disgust. ''Should never have taken Buck's seat,'' he muttered and frowned when Pete raised the bet.

''You got out cheap, kiddo,'' Duffy told him dolefully as he tossed in chips. ''I'm only staying in so I don't change my standard of living. Money'll do that to you,'' he mumbled obscurely.

''Three kings,'' Pete announced when called, then spread his cards. Amid a flutter of complaints cards were tossed down.

''Heart flush,'' Jo said mildly before Pete could rake in the pot. Duffy leaned back and gave a hoot of laughter.

"Atta, girl, Jo. I hate to see him win all my money."

During the next two hours the cookhouse tent grew hot and ripe with the scents of coffee and tobacco and beer. Jamie's luck proved so consistently poor that he called for Buck to relieve him.

Jo found herself with an indifferent pair of fives. Almost immediately the betting grew heavy as Keane raised Raoul's opening. Curiosity kept Jo in one round, but practicality had her folding after the draw. Divorced from the game, she watched it with interest. Leaning on her elbows, she studied each participant. Keane played a good game, she mused. His eyes gave nothing away. They never did. Casually, he nursed the beer beside him while Duffy, Buck and Amy folded. Studying him closely, Pete chewed his gum. Keane returned the look, keeping the stub of his cigar clamped between his teeth. Raoul muttered in French and scowled at his cards.

"Could be bluffing," Pete considered, seeing Keane's raise. "Let's raise it five more and see what's cooking." Raoul swore in French, then again in English, before he tossed in his hand. Taking his time, Keane counted out the necessary chips and tossed them into the pot. It was a plastic mountain of red, white and blue. Then, he counted out more.

"I'll see your five," he said evenly, "and raise it ten."

There was mumbling around the table. Pete looked into his hand and considered. Shifting his eyes, he took in the generous pile of chips in front of him. He could afford to risk another ten. Glancing up, he studied Keane's face while he fondled his chips. Abruptly, he broke into a grin.

"Nope," he said simply, turning his cards face down. "This one's all yours."

Setting down his cards, Keane raked in a very sweet pot. "Gonna show 'em?" Pete asked. His grin was affable.

Keane pushed a stray chip into the pile and shrugged. With his free hand he turned over the cards. The reaction ranged from oaths to laughter.

"Trash," Pete mumbled with a shake of his head. "Nothing but trash. You've got nerve, Captain." His grin grew wide as he turned over his own cards. "Even I had a pair of sevens."

Raoul gnashed his teeth and swore elegantly in two languages.

Jo grinned at his imaginative choice of words. She rose on a laugh and snatched off the soft felt hat Jamie wore. Deftly, she scooped her chips into it. "Cash me in later," she requested, then gave him a smacking kiss on the mouth. "But don't play with them."

Duffy scowled over at her. "Aren't you cashing in early?"

"You've always told me to leave 'em wanting more," she reminded him. With a grin and a wave, she swung through the door.

"That Jo," said Raoul, chuckling as he shuffled the cards. "She's one smart cracker."

"Cookie," Pete corrected, opening a fresh stick of gum. He noticed that Keane's gaze had drifted to the door she had closed behind her. "Some looker, too," he commented and watched Keane's eyes wander back to his. "Don't you think, Captain?"

Keane slipped his cards into a pile as they were dealt to him. "Jo's lovely."

"Like her mother," Buck put in, frowning at his cards. "She was a beaut, huh, Duffy?" Duffy grunted in agreement and wondered why Lady Luck refused to smile on him. "Always thought it was a crime for her to die that way. Wilder, too," he added with a shake of his head.

"A fire, wasn't it?" Keane asked as he picked up his cards and spread them.

"Electrical fire." Buck nodded and lifted his beer. "A short in their trailer's wiring. What a waste. If they hadn't been in bed asleep, they'd probably still be alive. The trailer was halfway gone before anybody set up an alarm. Just plain couldn't get to the Wilders. Their side of the trailer was like a furnace. Jo's bedroom was on the other side, and we nearly lost her. Frank busted in the window and pulled her out. Poor little tyke. She was holding onto this old doll like it was the last thing she had left. Kept it with her for I don't know how long. Remember, Duffy?" He glanced into his hand and opened for two. "It only had one arm." Duffy grunted again and folded. "Frank sure knew how to handle that little girl."

"She knew how to handle him, more likely," Duffy mumbled. Raoul bumped the pot five, and Keane folded.

"Deal me out the next hand," he said as he rose and moved

to the door. One of the Gribalti brothers took the chair Jo had vacated, and Jamie slipped into Keane's. Curious, he lifted the tip of the cards. He saw a jack-high straight. With a thoughtful frown, he watched the door swing shut.

Outside, Jo moved through the warm night. With a glance at the sky, she thought of the fireworks. They had been wonderful, she mused, stirring up the stars with exploding color. Though it was over and a new day hovered, she felt some magic remained in the night. Far from sleepy, she wandered toward the Big Top.

"Hello, pretty lady."

Jo looked into the shadows and narrowed her eyes. She could just barely make out a form. "Oh, you're Bob, aren't you?" She stopped and gave him a friendly smile. "You're new."

He stepped toward her. "I've been on for nearly three weeks." He was young, Jo guessed about her own age, with a solid build and sharp-featured face. Just that afternoon she had watched Maggie give him a shower.

Jo pushed her hands into the pockets of her cut-offs and continued to smile. It appeared he thought his tenure made him a veteran. "How do you like working with the elephants?"

"It's okay. I like putting up the tent."

Jo understood his feeling. "So do I. There's a game in the cookhouse," she told him with a gesture of her arm. "You might like to sit in."

"I'd rather be with you." As he moved closer, Jo caught the faint whiff of beer. He's been celebrating, she thought and shook her head.

"It's a good thing tomorrow's Monday," she commented. "No one's going to be in any shape to pitch a tent. You should go to bed," she suggested. "Or get some coffee."

"Let's go to your trailer." Bob weaved a little, then took her arm.

"No." Firmly, Jo turned in the opposite direction. "Let's go to the cookhouse." His advances did not trouble her. She was close enough to the cookhouse tent that if she called out, a dozen able-bodied men would come charging. But that was precisely what Jo wanted to avoid.

"I want to go with you," he said, stumbling over the words

as he veered away from the cookhouse again. "You look so pretty in that cage with those lions." He put both arms around her, but Jo felt it was as much for balance as romance. "A fella needs a pretty lady once in a while."

"I'm going to feed you to my lions if you don't let me go," Jo warned.

"Bet you can be a real wildcat," he mumbled and made a fumbling dive for her mouth.

Though her patience was wearing thin, Jo endured the kiss that landed slightly to the left of bull's-eye. His hands, however, had better aim and grabbed the firm roundness of her bottom. Losing her temper, Jo pushed away but found his hold had taken root. In a quick move, she brought up her fist and caught him square on the jaw. With only a faint sound of surprise, Bob sat down hard on the ground.

"Well, so much for rescuing you," Keane commented from behind her.

Turning quickly, Jo pushed at her hair and gave an annoyed sigh. She would have preferred no witnesses. Even in the dim light, she could see he was furious. Instinctively, she stepped between him and the man who sat on the ground fingering his jaw and shaking the buzzing from his ears.

"He—Bob just got a bit overenthusiastic," she said hastily and put a restraining hand on Keane's arm. "He's been celebrating."

"I'm feeling a bit enthusiastic myself," Keane stated. As he made to brush her aside, Jo clung with more fervor.

"No, Keane, please."

Looking down, he fired a glare. "Jo, would you let go so that I can deal with this?"

"Not until you listen." The faint hint of laughter in her eyes only enraged him further, and Jo fought to suppress it. "Keane, please, don't be hard on him. He didn't hurt me."

"He was attacking you," Keane interrupted. He barely resisted the urge to shake her off and drag the still seated Bob by the scruff of the neck.

"No, he was really more just leaning on me. His balance is a trifle impaired. He only tried to kiss me," she pointed out, wisely deleting the wandering hands. "And I hit him much harder than I should have. He's new, Keane, don't fire him."

Exasperated, he stared at her. "Firing was the least of what I had in mind for him."

Jo smiled, unable to keep the gleam from her eyes. "If you were going to avenge my honor, he really didn't do much more than breathe on it. I don't think you should run him through for that. Maybe you could just put him in the stocks for a couple of days."

Keane swore under his breath, but a reluctant smile tugged at his mouth. Seeing it, Jo loosened her hold. "Miss Wilder wants to give you a break," he told the dazed Bob in a tough, no-nonsense voice that Jo decided he used for intimidating witnesses. "She has a softer heart than I do. Therefore, I won't knock you down several more times or kick you off the lot, as I had entertained doing." He paused, allowing Bob time to consider this possibility. "Instead, I'll let you sleep off your—enthusiasm." In one quick jerk, he pulled Bob to his feet. "But if I ever hear of you breathing uninvited on Miss Wilder or any other of my female employees, we'll go back to the first choice. And before I kick you out," he added with low menace, "I'll let it be known that you were decked by one punch from a hundred-pound woman."

"Yes, sir, Mr. Prescott," said Bob as clearly as possible.

"Go to bed," Jo said kindly, seeing him pale. "You'll feel better in the morning."

"Obviously," Keane commented as Bob lurched away, "you haven't done much drinking." He turned to Jo and grinned. "The one thing he's not going to feel in the morning is better." Jo smiled, pleased to have Keane talk to her without the thin shield of politeness. "And where," he asked and took her hand for examination, "did you learn that right jab?"

Jo laughed, allowing Keane's fingers to interlock with hers. "It would hardly have knocked him down if he hadn't already been tilting in that direction." Her face turned up to his and sparkled with starlight. In his eyes an expression she couldn't comprehend came and went. "Is something wrong?"

For a moment he said nothing. In her breast her heart began to hammer as she waited to be kissed. "No, nothing," he said.

The moment was shattered. "Come on, I'll walk you back to your trailer."

"I wasn't going there." Wanting to put him back into an easy mood, she linked her arm with his. "If you come with me, I'll show you some magic." Her smile slanted invitingly. "You like magic, don't you, Keane? Even a sober, dedicated lawyer must like magic."

"Is that how I strike you?" Jo almost laughed at the trace of annoyance in his voice. "As a sober, dedicated lawyer?"

"Oh, not entirely, though that's part of you." She enjoyed feeling that for the moment she had him to herself. "You've also got a streak of adventure and a rather nice sense of humor. And," she added with generous emphasis, "there's your temper."

"You seem to have me all figured out."

"Oh, no." Jo stopped and turned to him. "Not at all. I only know how you are here. I can only speculate on how you are in Chicago."

His brow lifted as she caught his attention. "Would I be different there?"

"I don't know." Jo's forehead wrinkled in thought. "Wouldn't you be? Circumstances would. You probably have a house or a big apartment, and there's a housekeeper who comes in once—no, twice—a week." Caught up in the picture, she gazed off into the distance and built it further. "You have an office with a view of the city, a very efficient secretary and a brilliant law clerk. You go to business lunches at the club. In court you're deadly and very successful. You have your own tailor and work out at the gym three times a week. There's the theater on the weekends, along with something physical. Tennis maybe, not golf. No, handball."

Keane shook his head. "Is this the magic?"

"No." Jo shrugged and began to walk again. "Just guesswork. You don't have to have a great deal of money to know how people who do behave. And I know you take the law seriously. You wouldn't choose a career that wasn't very important to you."

Keane walked in silence. When he spoke, his voice was quiet. "I'm not certain I'm comfortable with your little outline of my life."

"It's very sketchy," Jo told him. "I'd have to understand you better to fill in the gaps."

"Don't you?"

"What?" Jo asked, pausing. "Understand you?" She laughed, tickled at the absurdity of his question. "No, I don't understand you. How could I? You live in a different world." With this, she tossed aside the flap of the Big Top and stepped into its darkness. When she hit the switch, two rows of overhead lights flashed on. Shadows haunted the corners and fell over the arena seats.

"It's wonderful, isn't it?" Her clear voice ran the length of the tent and echoed back. "It's not empty, you know. They're always here—the troupers, the audience, the animals." She walked forward until she stood beside the third ring. "Do you know what this is?" she asked Keane, tossing out her arms and turning a full circle. "It's an ageless wonder in a changing world. No matter what happens on the outside, this is here. We're the most fragile of circuses, at the mercy of the elephants, of emotions, of mechanics, of public whims. But six days a week for twenty-nine weeks we perform miracles. We build a world at dawn, then disappear into the dark. That's part of it—the mystery." She waited until Keane moved forward to join her.

"Tents pop up on an empty lot, elephants and lions walk down Main Street. And we never grow old, because each new generation discovers us all over again." She stood slender and exquisite in a circle of light. "Life here's crazy. And it's hard. Muddy lots, insane hours, sore muscles, but when you've finished your act and you get that feeling that tells you it was special, there's nothing else like it in the world."

"Is that why you do it?" Keane asked.

Jo shook her head and moved out of the circle of light into the dark and into another ring. "It's all part of the same thing. We all have our own reasons, I suppose. You've asked me that before; I'm not certain I can explain. Maybe it's that we all believe in miracles." She turned under the light, and it shimmered around her. "I've been here all my life. I know every trick, every illusion. I know how Jamie's dad gets twenty clowns into a two-seater car. But each time I see it, I laugh and I believe it. It's not just the excitement, Keane, it's the anticipation of the excitement. It's knowing you're going to see the biggest or the smallest or the fastest or the highest.'' Jo ran to the center ring and threw up her arms.

"Ladies and gentlemen," she announced with a toss of her head. "For your amazement and astonishment, for the first time in America, a superabundance of mountainous, mighty pachyderms led in a stupendous exhibition of choreography by the Great Serena.'' Jo laughed and shifted her hair to her back with a quick movement of her hand. "Dancing elephants!'' she said to Keane, pleased that he was smiling. "Or you listen to the talker in the sideshow when he starts his spiel. Step right up. Come a little closer.'' She curled her fingers in invitation. "See the Amazing Serpentina and her monstrous, slithering vipers. Watch the beautiful young girl charm a deadly cobra. Watch her accept the reptilian embrace of the gargantuan boa. Don't miss the chance to see the enchantress of the evil serpent!''

"I suppose Baby might sue for slander.''

Jo laughed and stepped up on the ring. "But when the crowds see little Rose with a boa constrictor wrapped around her shoulders, they've gotten their money's worth. We give them what they come for: color, fantasy, the unique. Thrills. You've seen the audience when Vito does his high wire act without a net.''

"A net seems little enough protection when he's balancing on a wire at two hundred feet.'' Keane stuck his hands in his pockets and frowned. "He risks his life every day.''

"So does a police officer or a fire fighter.'' Jo spoke quietly and rested her hands on his shoulders. It seemed more necessary than ever that she make him understand his father's dream. "I know what you're saying, Keane, but you have to understand us. The element of danger is essential to many of the acts. You can hear the whole audience suck in their breath when Vito does his back somersault on the wire. They'd be impressed if he used a net, but they wouldn't be terrified.''

"Do they need to be?''

Jo's sober expression lightened. "Oh, yes! They need to be terrified and fascinated and mesmerized. It's all included in the price of a ticket. This is a world of superlatives. We test the limit of human daring, and every day it changes. Do you know how long it took before the first man accomplished the triple on the trapeze? Now it's nearly a standard.'' A light of anticipation flared in her eyes. "One day someone will do a quadruple. If a man stands in this ring and juggles three torches today, tomorrow someone will juggle them on horseback and after that there'll be a team tossing them back and forth while swinging on a trap. It's our job to do the incredible, then, when it's done, to do the impossible. It's that simple."

"Simple," Keane murmured, then lifted a hand to caress her hair. "I wonder if you'd think so if you could see it from the outside."

"I don't know." Her fingers tightened on his shoulders as he buried his other hand in her hair. "I never have."

As if his thoughts centered on it, Keane combed his fingers through her hair. Gradually, he pushed it back until only his hands framed her face. They stood in a pool of light that threw their shadows long behind them. "You are so lovely," he murmured.

Jo neither spoke nor moved. There was something different this time in the way he touched her. There was a gentleness and a hesitation she had not felt before. Though they looked directly into hers, she could not read his eyes. Their faces were close, and his breath fluttered against her mouth. Jo slid her arms around his neck and pressed her mouth to his.

Not until that moment had she realized how empty she had felt, how desperately she had needed to hold him. Her lips were hungry for his. She clung while all gentleness fled from his touch. His hands were greedy. The weeks that he had not touched her were forgotten as her skin warmed and hummed with quickening blood. Passion stripped her of inhibitions, and her tongue sought his, taking the kiss into wilder and darker depths. Their lips parted, only to meet again with sharp new demands. She understood that all needs and all desires were ultimately only one—Keane.

His mouth left hers, and for an instant he rested his cheek against her hair. For that moment Jo felt a contentment more complete than she had ever known. Abruptly, he drew away.

Puzzled, she watched as he drew out a cigar. She lifted a hand to run it through the hair he had just disturbed. He flicked on his lighter. "Keane?" She looked at him, knowing her eyes offered everything.

"You've had a long day," he began in an oddly polite tone. Jo winced as if he had struck her. "I'll walk you back to your trailer."

She stepped off the ring and away from him. Pain seared along her skin. "Why are you doing this?" To her humiliation, tears welled in her eyes and lodged in her throat. The tears acted as a prism, refracting the light and clouding her vision. She blinked them back. Keane's brows drew together at the gesture.

"I'll take you back," he said again. The detached tone of his voice accelerated all Jo's fury and grief.

"How dare you!" she demanded. "How dare you make me…" The word *love* nearly slipped through her lips, and she swallowed it. "How dare you make me want you, then turn away! I was right about you from the beginning. I thought I'd been wrong. You're cold and unfeeling." Her breath came quickly and unevenly, but she refused to retreat until she had said it all. Her face was pale with the passion of her emotions. "I don't know why I thought you'd ever understand what Frank had given you. You need a heart to see the intangible. I'll be glad when the season's over and you do whatever it is you're going to do. I'll be glad when I never have to see you again. I won't let you do this to me anymore!" Her voice wavered, but she made no attempt to steady it. "I don't want you to ever touch me again."

Keane studied her for a long moment, then took a careful drag on his cigar. "All right, Jo."

The very calmness of his answer tore a sob from her before she turned and ran from the Big Top.

Ten

In July the troupe circled through Virginia, touched the tip of West Virginia on their way into Kentucky, then moved into Ohio. Audiences fanned themselves as the temperatures in the Big Top rose, but they still came.

Since the evening of the Fourth, Jo had avoided Keane. It was not as difficult as it might have been, as he spent half the month in Chicago dealing with his business. Jo functioned. She ate because eating was necessary in order to maintain her strength. She slept because rest was essential to remaining alert in the cage. She did not find any enjoyment in food nor was her sleep restful. Because so many in the troupe knew her well, Jo struggled to keep on a mask of normalcy. Above all, she needed to avoid any questions, any advice, any sympathy. It was necessary, because of her profession, to put her emotions on hold a great deal of the time. After some struggle and some failure, Jo achieved a reasonable success.

Her training of Gerry continued, as did his progress. The additional duty of working with him helped fill her small snatches of spare time. On afternoons when no matinee was scheduled, Jo took him into the big cage. As he grew more proficient, she brought other cats in to join Merlin. By the first week in August they were working together with her full complement of lions.

The only others who were rehearsing in the Big Top were the equestrian act. They ran through the Thread the Needle routine in the first ring. Hooves echoed dully on tanbark. Jo supervised while Gerry sent the cats into a pyramid. At his urging, Lazarus climbed up the wide, arched ladder that topped the grouping. Twice he balked, and twice Gerry was forced to reissue the command.

"Good," Jo commented when the pyramid was complete.

"He wouldn't go." Gerry began to complain, but she cut him off.

"Don't be in too much of a hurry. Bring them down." Her tone was brisk and professional. "Make certain they dismount and take their seats in the right order. It's important to stick to routine."

Hands resting on hips, Jo watched. In her opinion, Gerry had true potential. His nerves were good, he had a feeling for the animals, and he was slowly developing patience. Still she balked at the next step in his training: leaving him alone in the arena. Even with only Merlin, she felt it too risky. He was still too casual. Not yet did he possess enough respect for the lion's guile.

Jo moved around the arena, and the lions, used to her, were not disturbed. As the cats settled onto their pedestals, she once more moved to stand beside Gerry. "Now we'll walk down the line. You make each do a sit-up before we send them out."

One by one the cats rose on their haunches and pawed the air. Jo and Gerry moved down their ranks. The heat was becoming oppressive, and Jo shifted her shoulders, longing for a cool shower and a change of clothes. When they came to Hamlet, he ignored the command with a rebellious snarl.

Bad-tempered brute, thought Jo absently as she waited for Gerry to reissue the command. He did so but moved forward as if to emphasize the words.

"No, not so close!" Jo warned quickly. Even as she spoke, she saw the change in Hamlet's eyes.

Instinctively, she stepped over, nudging Gerry back and shielding his body with hers. Hamlet struck out, claws extended. There was a moment of blind heat in her shoulder as the skin ripped. Swiftly, she was facing the cat, holding tightly onto Gerry's arm as they stood just out of range.

"Don't run," she ordered, feeling his jerk of panic. Her arm was on fire as the blood began to flow freely. Keeping her movements quick but smooth, she took the whip from Gerry's nerveless hand and cracked it hard, using her left arm. She knew that if Hamlet continued his defiance and attacked, it was hopeless. The other cats were certain to join in a melee. It would be over before anything could be done. Already, Abra shifted restlessly and bared her teeth.

"Open the chute," Jo called out. Her voice was cool as ice. "Back toward the safety cage," she instructed Gerry as she gave the cats their signal to leave the arena. "I've got to get them out one at a time. Move slow, and if I tell you to stop, you stop dead. Understand?"

She heard him swallow as she watched the cats begin to leap off their pedestals and file into the chute. "He got you. Is it bad?" The words were barely a whisper and drenched in terror.

"I said go." Half the cats were gone, and still Hamlet's eyes were locked on hers. There was no time to waste. One part of her brain heard shouting outside the cage, but she blocked it out and focused all her concentration on the cat. "Go now," she repeated to Gerry. "Do as you're told."

He swallowed again and began to back away. Long seconds dragged until she heard the rattle of the safety cage door. When his turn came, Hamlet made no move to leave his seat. Jo was alone with him. She could smell the heat, the scent of the wild and the fragrance of her own blood. Her arm was alive with pain. Slowly, she tested him by backing up. The safety cage seemed hundreds of miles away. The cat tensed immediately, and she stopped. She knew he would not let her cross the arena. Outrunning him was impossible, as the distance between them could be covered in one spring. She had to outbluff him instead.

"Out," she ordered firmly. "Out, Hamlet." As he continued to watch her, Jo felt a trickle of sweat slide down between her shoulder blades. Her skin was clammy with it in contrast to the warmth of the blood that ran down her arm. There was a sudden, vivid picture inside her head of her father being dragged around the cage. Fear tripped inside her throat. There was a lightness fluttering in the top of her head, and she knew that a moment's terror would cause her to faint. She stiffened her spine and pushed it away.

Speed was important. The longer she allowed the cat to remain in the arena after his cue, the more defiant he would become. And the more dangerous. As yet he was unaware that he held her at such a sharp disadvantage. "Out, Hamlet." Jo repeated the command with a crack of the whip. He leaped from the pedestal. Jo's stomach trembled. She locked every muscle, and as the cat hesitated, she repeated the command. He was confused, and she knew this could work as an advantage or a curse. Confused, he might spring or retreat. Her fingers tightened on the stock of the whip and trembled. The cat paced nervously and watched her.

"Hamlet!" She raised her voice and bit off each syllable. "Go out." To the words she added the hand signal she had used before he was fully trained to voice command.

As if rebuffed, Hamlet relaxed his tail and padded into the chute. Before the door slid completely closed, Jo sank to her knees. Her body began to quake fiercely with the aftershock. No more than five minutes had passed since Hamlet had defied Gerry's command, but her muscles bore the strain of hours. For an instant her vision blurred. Even as she shook her head to clear it, Keane was on the ground beside her.

She heard him swear, ripping the tattered sleeve of her blouse from her arm. He fired questions at her, but she could do no more than shake her head and gulp in air. Focusing on him, she noticed his eyes were unusually dark against his face.

"What?" She followed his voice but not the words. He swore again, sharply enough to penetrate the first layer of her shock. He pulled her to her feet, then continuing the motion smoothly, lifted her into his arms. "Don't." Her mind struggled to break through the fog and function. "I'm all right."

"Shut up," he said harshly as he carried her from the cage. "Just shut up."

Because speaking cost her some effort, Jo obeyed. Closing her eyes, she let the mixture of excited voices whirl around her. Her arm screamed with pain, but the throbbing reassured her. Numbness would have terrified her. Still she kept her eyes shut, not yet having the courage to look at the damage. Being alive was enough.

When she opened her eyes again, Keane was carrying her into the administration wagon. At the sound of the chaos that followed them, Duffy strode through from his office. "What the..." he began, then stopped and paled beneath his freckles. He moved quickly forward as Keane set Jo in a chair. "How bad?"

"I don't know yet," Keane muttered. "Get a towel and the first-aid kit."

Buck had come in behind them and, already having secured

the items, handed them to Keane. Then he moved to a cabinet and located a bottle of brandy.

"It's not too bad," Jo managed. Because her voice was tolerably steady, she screwed up her courage and looked down. Keane had fastened a rough bandage from the remains of her sleeve. Though the flow of blood had slowed, there were streaks of it down her arm, and too much spreading from the wound to be certain how extensive the cuts were. Nausea rocked in her stomach.

"How do you know?" Keane demanded between his teeth as he began to clean the wound. He wrung out the towel in the basin Buck set beside him.

"It's not bleeding that badly." Jo swallowed the queasiness. As her mind began to clear, she frowned at the tone of Keane's voice. Feeling her stare, he glanced up. In his eyes was such fury, she pulled away.

"Be still," he ordered roughly and gave his attention back to her arm.

The cat had delivered only a glancing blow, but even so, there were four long slices in her upper arm. Jo set her jaw as pain ripped through her. Keane's brusqueness brought more hurt, and she fought to show no reaction to either. The aftermath of fear was bubbling through her. She longed to be held, to be soothed by the hands that tended to her wound.

"She's going to need stitches," Keane said without looking at her.

"And an antitoxin shot," Buck added, handing Jo a generous glass of brandy. "Drink this, honey. It'll help settle you."

The gentleness in his voice nearly undid her. He laid his big hand against her cheek, and for a moment she pressed against it.

"Drink now," Buck ordered again. Obediently, Jo lifted the glass and swallowed. The room whirled, then snapped into focus. She made a small sound and pressed the glass to her forehead.

"Tell me what happened in there." Buck crouched down beside her as Keane began to apply a temporary bandage.

Jo took a moment to draw air in and out of her lungs. She lowered the glass and spoke steadily. "Hamlet didn't respond, and Gerry repeated a command, but he stepped forward. Too close. I saw Hamlet's eyes, and I knew. I should have moved faster. I should have been watching him more carefully. It was a stupid mistake.'' She stared into the brandy as she berated herself.

''She stepped between the boy and the cat.'' Keane bit off the words as he completed the bandaging. Rising, he moved to the brandy and poured. Not once did he turn to look at Jo. Hurt, she stared at his back before looking back at Buck.

''How's Gerry?''

Buck urged the glass back to her lips. A faint tint of pink was creeping into her cheeks. ''Pete's with him. Got his head between his knees. He'll be fine.''

Jo nodded. ''I guess I'll have to go to town and have this seen to.'' She handed the glass to Buck and wondered if she dare attempt to rise yet. With another deep breath, she glanced at Duffy. ''Make sure he's ready to go in when I get back.''

Keane turned from the window. ''Go in where?'' His face was set in hard lines.

In response, Jo's voice was chilled. ''In the cage.'' She turned her eyes to Buck. ''We should be able to have a short run-through before the evening show.''

''No.'' Jo's head snapped up as Keane spoke. For a long moment they stared at each other with odd, unreasonable antagonism. ''You're not going back in there today.'' His voice held curt authority.

''Of course I am,'' Jo countered, managing to keep the combination of pain and anger from her words. ''And if Gerry wants to be a cat man, he's going in, too.''

''Jo's right,'' Buck put in, trying to soothe what he sensed was an explosive situation. ''It's like falling off a horse. You can't wait too long before you get back up, or you won't ride again.''

Keane never took his eyes from Jo. He continued as if Buck hadn't spoken. ''I won't permit it.''

''You can't stop me.'' Indignation forced her to her feet. The brisk movement caused her arm to protest, and her struggle against it showed momentarily in her eyes.

''Yes, I can.'' Keane took a long swallow of brandy. ''I own this circus.''

Jo's fists tightened at his tone, at his careless use of his authority. Not once since he had knelt beside her in the cage had he given her any sign of comfort or reassurance. She had needed it from him. To masquerade its trembling, she kept her voice low. "But you don't own me, Mr. Prescott. And if you'll check your papers and the legalities, you'll see you don't own the lions or my equipment. I bought them, and I maintain them out of my salary. My contract doesn't give you the right to tell me when I can or can't rehearse my cats."

Keane's face was granite hard. "Neither does it give you the right to set up in the Big Top without my permission."

"Then I'll set up some place else," she tossed back. "But I *will* set up. That cat will be worked again today. I won't take the risk of losing months of training."

"But you will risk being killed," Keane shot back and slammed down his glass.

"What do you care?" Jo shouted. All control deserted her. The cuts were deep on her emotions as well as her flesh. She had passed through a terror more acute than she had known since the night of her parents' death. More than anything else, she wanted to feel Keane's arms around her. She wanted to know the security she had felt when he had let her weep out her grief for Ari in his arms. "I'm nothing to you!" Her head shook quickly, tossing her hair. There was a bubble of hysteria in her voice, and Buck reached out to lay a hand on her shoulder.

"Jo," he warned in his soft, rumbling voice.

"No!" She shook her head and spoke rapidly. "He hasn't the right. You haven't the right to interfere with my life." She flared at Keane again with eyes vivid with emotion. "I know what I have to do. I know what I *will* do. Why should it matter to you? You aren't legally responsible if I get mauled. No one's going to sue you."

"Hold on, Jo." This time Buck spoke firmly. As he took her uninjured arm, he felt the tremors shooting through her. "She's too upset to know what she's saying," he told Keane.

There was a mask over Keane's face which concealed all emotion. "Oh, I think she knows what she's saying," he disagreed quietly. For a moment there was only the sound of Jo shuddering and the splash of brandy being poured into a glass. "You do what you have to do, Jo," he said after drinking again. "You're perfectly correct that I haven't any rights where you're concerned. Take her into town," he told Buck, then turned back to the window.

"Come on, Jo." Buck urged her to the door, slipping a supportive arm around her waist. Even as they stepped outside, Rose came running from the direction of the midway.

"Jo!" Her face was white with concern. "Jo, I just heard." She glanced at the bandage with wide, terrified eyes. "How bad is it?"

"Just scratches, really," Jo assured her. She added the best smile she could muster. "Buck's going to take me into town for a couple of stitches."

"Are you sure?" She looked up at the tall man for reassurance. "Buck?"

"Several stitches," he corrected but patted Rose's hand. "But it's not too bad."

"Do you want me to come with you?" She fell into step beside them as Buck began to lead Jo again.

"No. Thank you, Rose." Jo smiled with more feeling. "I'll be fine."

Because of the smile, Rose was able to relax. "I thought when I heard...well, I imagined all sorts of terrible things. I'm glad you're not badly hurt." They had reached Buck's truck, and Rose leaned over to kiss Jo's cheek. "We all love you so."

"I know." Squeezing her hand, Jo let Buck help her into the cab of his truck. As he maneuvered from the lot, Jo rested her head against the back of the seat and shut her eyes. Never could she remember feeling more spent, more battered.

"Hurt bad?" Buck asked as they switched to an asphalt road.

"Yes," she answered simply, thinking of her heart as much as her arm.

"You'll feel better when you're patched up."

Jo kept her eyes shut, knowing some wounds never heal. Or if they did, they left scars that ached at unexpected times.

"You shouldn't have gone off on him that way, Jo." There was light censure in Buck's voice.

"He shouldn't have interfered," Jo retorted. "It's none of his business. *I'm* none of his business."

"Jo, it's not like you to be so hard."

"Hard?" She opened her eyes and turned to Buck. "What

about him? Couldn't he have been kinder, shown even the barest trace of compassion? Did he have to speak to me as if I were a criminal?''

"Jo, the man was terrified. You're only looking at this from one side.'' He scratched his beard and gave a gusty sigh. "You can't know what it's like to be outside that cage, helpless when someone you care about is facing down death. I had to all but knock him unconscious to keep him out of there until we got it through his head that he'd just get you killed for sure. He was scared, Jo. We were all scared.''

Jo shook her head, certain Buck exaggerated because of his affection for her. Keane's voice had been hard, his eyes angry. "He doesn't care,'' she corrected quietly. "Not like the rest of you. You didn't swear at me. You weren't cold.''

"Jo, people have different ways—'' Buck began, but she interrupted.

"I know he wouldn't want to see me hurt, Buck. He's not heartless or cruel.'' She sighed as all the force of anger and fear washed out of her body and left her empty. "Please, I don't want to talk about him.''

Buck heard the weariness in her voice and patted her hand. "Okay, honey, just relax. We'll have you all fixed up in no time.''

Not all fixed up, Jo thought. Far from all fixed up.

Eleven

As the weeks passed, Jo's arm lost its stiffness. She healed cleanly. The only traces were thin scars that promised to fade but not disappear. She found, however, that some spark had gone out of her life. Constantly, she fought against a vague dissatisfaction. Nothing—not her work, not her friends, not her books—brought about the contentment she had grown up with. She had become a woman, and her needs had shifted. Jo knew the root of her problem was Keane, but the knowledge was not a solution. He had left the circus again on the very night of her accident. Nearly four weeks later he had not returned.

Three times Jo had sat down to write him, needing to assuage her guilt for the harsh things she had said to him. Three times she had torn up the paper in frustration. No matter how she re-arranged the words, they were wrong. Instead, she clung to the hope that he would come back one last time. If, she felt, they could part as friends, without bitterness or hard words, she could accept the separation. Willing this to happen, she was able to return to her routine with some tranquility. She rehearsed, performed, joined in the daily duties of circus life. She waited. The caravan moved closer to Chicago.

Jo stood in the steaming Big Top on a late August afternoon. Dressed in a leotard, she worked on ground exercises with the Beirot Brothers. It was this daily regimentation that had aided in keeping her arm limber. She could now move into a back walk-over without feeling any protest in her injured arm.

"I feel good," Jo told Raoul as they worked out. "I feel really good." She did a quick series of pirouettes.

"You don't keep your shoulder in shape by dancing on your feet," Raoul challenged.

"My shoulder's fine," she tossed back, then proved her point by bending into a handstand. Slowly, she lowered her legs to a forty-five degree angle, bringing one foot to rest on the knee of the opposite leg. "It's perfect." She executed a forward roll and sprang to her feet. "I'm strong as an ox," she claimed and did a quick back handspring followed by a back flip.

She landed at Keane's feet.

The cascade of emotions that raced through her reflected briefly in her eyes before she regained her balance. "I didn't— I didn't know you were back." Instantly, she regretted the inanity of the words but could find no others. The longing was raw in her to hurl herself into his arms. She wondered that he could not feel her need through the pores of her skin.

"I just got in." His eyes continued to search her face after his hands dropped to his sides. "This is my mother," he added. "Rachael Loring, Jovilette Wilder."

At his words, Jo's gaze moved from his face. She saw the woman beside him. If she had seen Rachael Loring in a crowd of two thousand, she would have known her for Keane's mother. The bone structure was the same, though hers was more elegant. Her brows were golden wings, flaring out at the end, as Keane's did. Her hair was smooth, brushed up and away from her face with no gray to mar its tawny perfection. But it was the eyes that sent a jolt through Jo. She had not thought to see them in any-one's face but Keane's. The woman was dressed simply in an unpretentiously tailored suit that bespoke taste and wealth. There was, however, none of the cool, distant polish that Jo had always attributed to the woman who had taken her son and left Frank. There was a charm to the smile that curved in greeting.

"Jovilette, such a lovely name. Keane's told me of you." She extended her hand, and Jo accepted, intending a quick, imper-sonal shake. Rachael Loring, however, laid her other hand atop their joined ones and added warmth. "Keane tells me you were very close to Frank. Perhaps we could talk."

The affection in her voice confused Jo into a stumbling reply. "I—Yes. I—if you'd like."

"I should like very much." She squeezed Jo's hand again before releasing it. "Perhaps you have time to show me around?" She smiled with the question, and Jo found it increas-ingly difficult to remain aloof. "I'm sure there've been some changes since I was here last. You must have some business to attend to,'' she said, looking up at Keane. ''I'm sure Jovilette will take good care of me. Won't you, dear?'' Without waiting for either to respond, Rachael tucked her arm through Jo's and began to walk. ''I knew your parents,'' she said as Keane watched them move away. ''Not terribly well, I'm afraid. They came here the same year I left. But I recall they were both thrilling performers. Keane tells me you've followed your father's profession.''

''Yes, I...'' She hesitated, feeling oddly at a disadvantage. ''I did,'' she finished lamely.

''You're so young.'' Rachael gave her a gentle smile. ''How terribly brave you must be.''

''No...no, not really. It's my job.''

''Yes, of course.'' Rachael laughed at some private memory. ''I've heard that before.''

They were outside now, and she paused to look thoughtfully around her. ''I think perhaps I was wrong. It hasn't really changed, not in thirty years. It's a wonderful place, isn't it?''

''Why did you leave?'' As soon as the words were spoken, Jo regretted them. ''I'm sorry,'' she said quickly. ''I shouldn't have asked.''

''Of course you should.'' Rachael sighed and patted Jo's hand. ''It's only natural. Duffy's still here, Keane tells me.'' At the change in subject, Jo imagined her question had been evaded.

''Yes, I suppose he always will be.''

''Could we have some coffee, or some tea, perhaps?'' Rachael smiled again. ''It's such a long drive from town. Is your trailer nearby?''

''It's just over in the back yard.''

''Oh, yes.'' Rachael laughed and began to walk again. ''The neighborhood that never changes over thousands of miles. Do you know the story of the dog and the bones?'' she asked. Though Jo knew it well, she said nothing. ''One version is that a roustabout gave his dog a bone every night after dinner. The dog would bury the bone under the trailer, then the next day try to dig it back up. Of course, it was fifty miles behind in an empty lot. He never figured it out.'' Quietly, she laughed to herself.

Feeling awkward, Jo opened the door to her trailer. How could this woman be the one she had resented all of her life? How could this be the cold, heartless woman who had left Frank? Oddly, Rachael seemed totally at ease in the narrow confines of the trailer.

"How efficient these are." She looked around with interest and approval. "You must barely realize you're on wheels." Casually, she picked up the volume of Thoreau which lay on Jo's counter. "Keane told me you have an avid interest in literature. In language, too," she added, glancing up from the book. Her eyes were golden and direct like her son's. Jo was tossed back suddenly to the first morning of the season when she had looked down and found Keane's eyes on her.

It made her uncomfortable to learn Keane had discussed her with his mother. "I have some tea," Jo told her as she moved toward the kitchen. "It's a better gamble than my coffee."

"That's fine," Rachael said agreeably and followed her. "I'll just sit here while you fix it." She settled herself with apparent ease at the tiny table across from the kitchen.

"I'm afraid I haven't anything else to offer you." Jo kept her back turned as she routed through her cupboard.

"Tea and conversation," Rachael answered in mild tones, "will be fine."

Jo sighed and turned. "I'm sorry." She shook her head. "I'm being rude. I just don't know what to say to you, Mrs. Loring. I've resented you for as long as I can remember. Now you're here and not at all as I imagined." She managed to smile, albeit ruefully. "You're not cold and hateful, and you look so much like..." She stopped, horrified that she had nearly blurted out Keane's name. For a moment her eyes were utterly naked.

Rachael smoothed over the awkwardness. "I don't wonder you resented me if you were as close to Frank as Keane tells me. Jovilette," she said softly, "did Frank resent me, too?"

Helpless, Jo responded to the hint of sadness. "No. Not while I knew him. I don't think Frank was capable of resentments."

"You understood him well, didn't you?" Rachael watched as Jo poured boiling water into mugs. "I understood him, too," she continued as Jo brought the mugs to the table. "He was a dreamer, a marvelous free spirit." Absently, she stirred her tea.

Consumed with curiosity, Jo sat across from her and waited for the story she sensed was coming.

"I was eighteen when I met him. I had come to the circus with a cousin. The Colossus was a bit smaller in those days," she added with a reminiscent smile, "but it was all the same. Oh, the magic!" She shook her head and sighed. "We tumbled into love so fast, married against all my family's objections and went on the road. It was exciting. I learned the web routine and helped out in wardrobe."

Jo's eyes widened. "You performed?"

"Oh, yes." Rachael's cheeks tinted a bit with pride. "I was quite good. Then I became pregnant. We were both like children waiting for Christmas. I wasn't quite nineteen when I had Keane, and I'd been with the circus for nearly a year. Things became difficult over the next season. I was young and a bit frightened of Keane. I panicked if he sneezed and was constantly dragging Frank into town to see doctors. How patient he was."

Rachael leaned forward and took Jo's hand. "Can you understand how hard this life is for one not meant for it? Can you see that through the magic of it, the excitement and wonder, there are hardships and fears and impossible demands? I was little more than a child myself, with an infant to care for, without the endurance or vocation of a trouper, without the experience or confidence of a mother. I lived on nerves for an entire season." She let out a little rush of breath. "When it was over, I went home to Chicago."

For the first time, Jo imagined the flight from Rachael's point of view. She could see a girl, younger than herself, in a strange, demanding world with a baby to care for. Over the years Jo had seen scores of people try the life she'd led and last only weeks. Still she shook her head in confusion.

"I think I understand how difficult it must have been for you. But if you and Frank loved each other, couldn't you have worked it out somehow?"

"How?" Rachael countered. "Should I have taken a house somewhere and lived with him half a year? I would have hated him. Should he have given up his life here and settled down with me and Keane? It would have destroyed everything I loved about him." Rachael shook her head, giving Jo a soft smile. "We did love each other, Jovilette, but not enough. Compromise isn't always possible, and neither of us were capable of adjusting to the needs of the other. I tried, and Frank would have tried had I asked him. But it was lost before it had really begun. We did the wisest thing under the circumstances.'' Looking into Jo's eyes, she saw youth and confidence. ''It seems cold and hard to you, but it was no use dragging out a painful situation. He gave me Keane and two years I've always treasured. I gave him his freedom without bitterness. Ten years after Frank, I found happiness again.'' She smiled softly with the memory. ''I loved Frank, and that love remains as young and sweet as the day I met him.''

Jo swallowed. She searched for some way to apologize for a grudge held for a lifetime. ''He—Frank kept a scrapbook on Keane. He followed the Chicago papers.''

''Did he?'' Rachael beamed, then leaned back in her chair and lifted her mug. ''How like him. Was he happy, Jovilette? Did he have what he wanted?''

''Yes,'' Jo answered without hesitation. ''Did you?''

Rachael's eyes came back to Jo's. For a moment the look was speculative, then it grew warm. ''What a good heart you have, generous and understanding. Yes, I had what I wanted. And you, Jovilette, what do you want?''

At ease now, Jo shook her head and smiled. ''More than I can have.''

''You're too smart for that,'' Rachael observed, studying her. ''I think you're a fighter, not a dreamer. When the time comes to make your choice, you won't settle for anything less than all.'' She smiled at Jo's intent look, then rose. ''Will you show me your lions? I can't tell you how I'm looking forward to seeing you perform.''

''Yes, of course.'' Jo stood, then hesitated. She held out her hand. ''I'm glad you came.''

Rachael accepted the gesture. ''So am I.''

Throughout the rest of the day Jo looked for Keane without success. After meeting and talking with his mother, it had become even more imperative that she speak with him. Her conscience would have no rest until she made amends. By showtime she had not yet found him.

Each act seemed to run on and on as she fretted for the finish. He would be with his mother in the audience, and undoubtedly she would find him after the show. She strained with impatience as the acts dragged.

After the finale she stood at the back door, unsure whether to wait or to go to his trailer. She was struck with both relief and alarm when she saw him approaching.

"Jovilette." Rachael spoke first, taking Jo's hands in hers. "How marvelous you were, and how stunning. I see why Keane said you had an untamed beauty."

Surprised, Jo glanced up at Keane but met impassive amber eyes. "I'm glad you enjoyed it."

"Oh, I can't tell you how much. The day has brought me some very precious memories. Our talk this afternoon meant a great deal to me." To Jo's surprise, Rachael leaned over and kissed her. "I hope to see you again. I'm going to say goodbye to Duffy before you drive me back, Keane," she continued. "I'll meet you in the car. Goodbye, Jovilette."

"Goodbye, Mrs. Loring." Jo watched her go before she turned to Keane. "She's a wonderful person. She makes me ashamed."

"There's no need for that." He tucked his hands into his pockets and watched her. "We both had our reasons for resentments, and we were both wrong. How's your arm?"

"Oh." Jo's fingers traveled to the wound automatically. "It's fine. There's barely any scarring."

"Good." The word was short and followed by silence. For a moment Jo felt her courage fail her.

"Keane," she began, then forced herself to meet his eyes directly. "I want to apologize for the horrible way I behaved after the accident."

"I told you once before," he said coolly, "I don't care for apologies."

"Please." Jo swallowed her pride and touched his arm. "I've been saving this one for a very long time. I didn't mean those things I said," she added quickly. "I hope you'll forgive me." It wasn't the eloquent apology she had planned, but it was all she could manage. His expression never altered.

"There's nothing to forgive."

"Keane, please." Jo grabbed his arm again as he turned to go.

"Don't leave me feeling as if you don't forgive me. I know I said dreadful things. You have every right to be furious, but couldn't you—can't we be friends again?"

Something flickered over his face. Lifting his hand, he touched the back of it to her cheek. "You have a habit of disconcerting me, Jovilette." He dropped his hand, then thrust it into his pocket. "I've left something for you with Duffy. Be happy." He walked away from her while she dealt with the finality of his tone. He was walking out of her life. She watched him until he disappeared.

Jo had thought she would feel something, but there was nothing; no pain, no tears, no desperation. She had not known a human being could be so empty and still live.

"Jo." Duffy lumbered up to her, then held out a thick envelope. "Keane left this for you." Then he moved past her, anxious to see that all straggling towners were nudged on their way.

Jo felt all emotions had been stripped away. Absently, she glanced at the envelope as she walked to her trailer. Without enthusiasm, she stepped inside, then tore it open. She remained standing as she pulled out the contents. It took her several moments to decipher the legal jargon. She read the group of papers through twice before sitting down.

He's given it to me, she thought. Still she could not comprehend the magnitude of it. *He's given me the circus.*

Twelve

O'Hare Airport was an army of people and a cacophony of sound. Nearly losing herself in the chaos of it, Jo struggled through the masses and competed for a cab. At first she had merely gawked at the snow like a towner seeing his first sword swallower. Then, though she shivered inside the corduroy coat she had bought for the trip, she began to enjoy it. It was beautiful as it lay over the city, and it helped to turn her mind from the purpose of her journey. Never had she been north so late in the year. Chicago in November was a sensational sight.

She had learned, after the initial shock had worn off, that Keane had not only given her the circus but a responsibility as well. Almost immediately there had been contracts to negotiate. She had been tossed into a sea of paperwork, forced to rely heavily on Duffy's experience as she tried to regain her balance. As the season had come to a close, Jo had attempted a dozen times to call Chicago. Each time, she had hung up before Keane's number could be dialed. It would be, she had decided, more appropriate to see him in person. Her trip had been postponed a few weeks due to Jamie and Rose's wedding.

It was there, as she had stood as maid of honor, that Jo had realized what she must do. There was only one thing she truly wanted, and that was to be with Keane. Watching Rose's face as their vows had been exchanged, Jo had recalled her unflagging determination to win the man she loved.

And will I stay here? Jo had demanded of herself thousands of miles away from him. No. Her heart had begun to thud as she had mapped out a plan. She would go to Chicago to see him. She would not be turned away. He had wanted her once; she would make him want her again. She would not live out her life without at least some small portion of it being part of his. He didn't have to love her. It was enough that she loved him.

And so, shivering against the unfamiliar cold, Jo scrambled into a cab and headed across town. She brushed her hair free of snow with chilled fingers, thinking how idiotic she had been to forget to buy a hat and gloves. What if he isn't home? she thought suddenly. What if he's gone to Europe or Japan or California? Panic made her giddy, and she pushed it down. He has to be home. It's Sunday, and he's sitting at home reading or going over a brief—or entertaining a woman, she thought, appalled. I should stop and call. I should tell the driver to take me back to the airport. Closing her eyes, Jo fought to regain her calm. She took long, deep breaths and stared at the buildings and sidewalks. Gradually, she felt the tiny gurgle of hysteria dissipate.

I won't be afraid, she told herself and tried to believe it. I won't be afraid. But Jovilette, the woman who reclined on a living rug of lions, was very much afraid. What if he rejected her? I won't let him reject me, she told herself with a confident lift of her chin. *I'll seduce him.* She pressed her fingers to her temples. *I wouldn't know how to begin.* I've got to tell the driver to turn around.

But before she could form the words, the cab pulled up to a curb. With the precision of a robot, Jo paid the fare, overtipping in her agitation, and climbed out.

Long after the cab had pulled away, she stood staring up at the massive glass-girdled building. Snow waltzed around her, sprinkling her hair and shoulders. A jostle from a rushing pedestrian broke the spell. She picked up her suitcases and hurried through the front door of the apartment buildings.

The lobby was enormous, with smoked glass walls and a deep shag carpet. Not knowing she should give her name at the desk, Jo wandered toward the elevators, innocently avoiding detection by merging with a group of tenants. Once inside the car, Jo pushed the button for the penthouse with a nerveless forefinger. The chatter of those in the elevator with her registered only as a distant humming. She never noticed when the car stopped for their departure.

When it stopped a second time and the doors slid open, she

stared at the empty space for ten full seconds. Only as the automatic doors began to close did she snap out of her daze. Pushing them open again, she stepped through and into the hall. Her legs were wobbly, but she forced them to move forward in the direction of the penthouse. Panic sped up and down her spine until she set down her bags and leaned her brow against Keane's door. She urged air in and out of her lungs. She remembered that Rachael Loring had called her a fighter. Jo swallowed, lifted her chin and knocked. The wait was mercifully brief before Keane opened the door. She saw surprise light his eyes as he stared at her.

Her hair was dusted with snow as it lay over the shoulders of her coat. Her face glowed with the cold, and her eyes were bright, nearly feverish with her struggle for calm. Only once did her mouth tremble before she spoke.

"Hello, Keane."

He only stared, his eyes running over her in disbelief. He was leaner, she thought as she studied his face. As she filled herself with the sight of him, she saw he wore a sweatshirt and jeans. His feet were bare. He hadn't shaved, and her hand itched to test the roughness of his beard.

"What are you doing here?" Jo felt a resurgence of panic. His tone was harsh, and he had not answered her smile. She strained for poise.

"May I come in?" she asked, her smile cracking.

"What?" He seemed distracted by the question. His brows lowered into a frown.

"May I come in?" she repeated, barely defeating the urge to turn tail and run.

"Oh, yes, of course. I'm sorry." Running a hand through his hair, Keane stepped back and gestured her inside.

Instantly, Jo's shoes sank into the luxurious pile of the buff-colored carpet. For a moment she allowed herself to gaze around the room, using the time for the additional purpose of regaining her composure. It was an open, sweeping room with sharp, contrasting colors. There was a deep brown sectional sofa with a chrome and glass coffee table. There were high-backed chairs in soft creams and vivid slashes of blue in chunky floor pillows.

There were paintings, one she thought she recognized as a Picasso, and a sculpture she was certain was a Rodin.

On the far right of the room there was an elevation of two steps. Just beyond was a huge expanse of glass that featured a spreading view of Chicago. Jo moved toward it with undisguised curiosity. Now, unexplicably, fear had lessened. She found that once she had stepped over the threshold she had committed herself. She was no longer afraid.

"It's wonderful," she said, turning back to him. "How marvelous to have a whole city at your feet every day. You must feel like a king."

"I've never thought of it that way." With half the room between them, he studied her. She looked small and fragile with the bustling city at her back.

"I would," she said, and now her smile came easily. "I'd stand at the window and feel regal and pompous."

At last she saw his lips soften and curve. "Jovilette," he said quietly. "What are you doing in my world?"

"I needed to talk to you," she answered simply. "I had to come here to do it."

He moved to her then, but slowly, with his eyes on hers. "It must be important."

"I thought so."

His brow lifted, then he shrugged. "Well, then, we'll talk. But first, let's have your coat."

Jo's cold fingers fumbled with the buttons and caused Keane to frown again. "Good heavens, you're frozen." He captured her hands between his and swore. "Where are your gloves?" he demanded like an irate parent. "It must be all of twelve degrees outside."

"I forgot to buy any," Jo told him as she dealt with the heavenly feeling of his hands restoring warmth to hers.

"Idiot. Don't you know better than to come to Chicago in November without gloves?"

"No." Jo responded to his anger with a cheerful smile. "I've never been to Chicago in November before. It's wonderful."

His eyes lifted from her hands to her face. He watched her for a long moment, then she heard him sigh. "I'd nearly convinced myself I could be cured."

Jo's eyes clouded with concern. "Have you been ill?"

Keane laughed with a shake of his head, then he pushed away the question and became brisk again. "Here, let's have your coat. I'll get you some coffee."

"You needn't bother," she began as he undid the buttons on the coat himself and drew it from her shoulders.

"I'd feel better if I was certain your circulation was restored." He paused and looked down at her as he laid her coat over his arm. She wore a green angora sweater with pearl buttons and a gray skirt in thin wool. The soft fabric draped softly at her breasts and over her hips and thighs. Her shoes were dainty and impractical sling-back heels.

"Is something wrong?"

"I've never seen you wear anything but a costume or jeans."

"Oh." Jo laughed and combed her fingers through her damp hair. "I expect I look different."

"Yes, you do." His voice was low, and there was a frown in his eyes. "Right now you look as if you've come from college for the holidays." He touched the ends of her hair, then turned away. "Sit down. I'll get the coffee."

A bit puzzled by his mercurial moods, Jo wandered about the room, finally ignoring a chair to kneel beside one of the pillows near the picture window. Though the carpet swallowed Keane's footsteps, she sensed his return.

"How wonderful to have a real winter, if just for the snow." She turned a radiant face his way. "I've always wondered what Christmas is like with snow and icicles." Images of snowflakes danced in her eyes. Seeing he carried two mugs of coffee, she rose and took one. "Thank you."

"Are you warm enough?" he asked after a moment.

Jo nodded and sat in one of the two chairs opposite the sofa. The novelty of the city made her mission seem like a grand adventure. Keane sat beside her, and for a moment they drank in companionable silence.

"What did you want to talk to me about, Jo?"

Jo swallowed, ignoring the faint trembling in her chest. "A couple of things. The circus, for one." She shifted in her chair until she faced him. "I didn't write because I felt it too important. I didn't phone for the same reason. Keane..." All her carefully thought-out speeches deserted her. "You can't just give something like that away. I can't take it from you."

"Why not?" He shrugged and sipped his coffee. "We both know it's always been yours. A piece of paper doesn't change that one way or the other."

"Keane, Frank left it to you."

"And I gave it to you."

Jo made a small sound of frustration. "Perhaps if I could pay you for it..."

"Someone asked me once what was the value of a dream or the price of a human spirit." Jo shifted her eyes to his helplessly. "I didn't have an answer then. Do you have one now?"

She sighed and shook her head. "I don't know what to say to you. 'Thank you' is far from adequate."

"It's not necessary, either," Keane told her. "I simply gave back what was yours in any case. What else was there, Jo? You said there were a couple of things."

This was it, Jo's brain told her. Carefully, she set down the coffee and rose. Waiting for her stomach to settle, she walked a few feet out into the room, then turned. She allowed herself a deep breath before she met Keane's eyes.

"I want to be your mistress," she said with absolute calm.

"What?" Both Keane's face and voice registered utter shock.

Jo swallowed and repeated. "I want to be your mistress. That's still the right term, isn't it, or is it antiquated? Is *lover* right? I've never done this before."

Slowly, Keane set his mug beside hers and rose. He did not move toward her but watched her with probing eyes. "Jo, you don't know what you're saying."

"Oh, yes, I do," she cut him off and nodded. "I might not have the terminology exactly right, but I do know what I mean, and I'm sure you do, too. I want to be with you," she continued and took a step toward him. "I want you to make love to me. I want to live with you if you'll let me, or at least close by."

"Jo, you're not talking sensibly." Sharply, Keane broke into her speech. Turning away, he thrust his hands into his pockets and balled them into fists. "You don't know what you're asking."

"Don't I appeal to you anymore?"

Keane whirled, infuriated with the trace of curiosity in her voice. "How can you ask me that?" he demanded. "Of course you appeal to me! I'm not dead or in the throes of senility!"

She moved closer to him. "Then if I want you, and you want me, why can't we be lovers?"

Keane swore violently and grabbed her shoulders. "Do you think I could have you for a winter and then blithely let you go? Do you think I could untangle myself at the start of the season and watch you stroll out of my life? Haven't you the sense to see what you do to me?" He shook her hard with the question, stealing any breath she might have used to answer him.

"You make me crazy!" Abruptly, he dragged her against him. His mouth bruised hers, his fingers dug into her flesh. Jo's head spun with confusion and pain and ecstasy. It seemed centuries since she had tasted his mouth on hers. She heard him groan as he tore himself away. He turned, leaving her to find her own balance as the room swayed. "What do I have to do to be rid of you?" His words came in furious undertones.

Jo blew out a breath. "I don't think kissing me like that is a very good start."

"I'm aware of that," he murmured. She watched the rise and fall of his shoulders. "I've been trying to avoid doing it since I opened the door."

Quietly, Jo walked to him and put a hand on his arm. "You're tense," she discovered and automatically sought to soothe the muscles. "I'm sorry if I'm going about this the wrong way. I thought telling you outright would be better than trying to seduce you. I don't think I'd be very good at that."

Keane made a sound somewhere between a laugh and a moan. "Jovilette," he murmured before he turned and gathered her into his arms. "How do I resist you? How many times must I pull away before I'm free of you? Even the thought of you drives me mad."

"Keane." She sighed and shut her eyes. "I've wanted you to hold me for so long. I want to belong to you, even for just a little while."

"No." He pulled away, then forced her chin up with his thumb and forefinger. "Don't you see that once would be too much and a lifetime wouldn't be enough? I love you too much to let you go and enough to know I have to." Shock robbed her of speech. She only stared as he continued. "It was different when I didn't know, when I thought I was—how did you put it? 'Dazzled.'" He smiled briefly at the word. "I was certain if I could make love to you, I could get you out of my system. Then, the night Ari died, I held you while you slept. I realized I was in love with you, had been in love with you right from the beginning."

"But you..." Jo shook her head as if to clear it. "You never told me, and you seemed so cold, so distant."

"I couldn't touch you without wanting more." He pulled her close again and for a moment buried his face in her hair. "But I couldn't stay away. I knew if I wanted to have you, to really have you, one of us had to give up what we did, what we were. I wondered if I could give up the law; it was really all I ever wanted to do. I discovered I wanted you more."

"Oh, Keane." She shook her head, but he put her from him suddenly.

"Then I found out that wouldn't work, either." Keane turned, paced to the window and stared out. The snow was falling heavily. "Every time you walked into that cage, I walked into hell. I thought perhaps I'd get used to it, but it only got worse. I tried leaving, coming back here, but I could never shake you loose. I kept coming back. The day you were hurt..." Keane paused. Jo heard him draw in his breath, and when he continued, his voice was deeper. "I watched you step in front of that boy and take the blow. I can't tell you what I felt at that moment; there aren't words for it. All I could think of was getting to you. I wonder if Pete ever told you that I decked him before Buck got to me. He took it very well, considering. Then I had to—to just stand there and watch while that cat stalked you. I've never known that kind of fear before. The kind that empties you out, body and soul."

He lapsed into silence. "Then it was over," he continued, "and I got to you. You were so white, and you were bleeding in my arms." He muttered an oath, then was silent again. He shook his head. "I wanted to burn the place down, get you away, strangle the cats with my bare hands. Anything. I wanted to hold you, but I couldn't get past the fear and the unreasonable anger at having been helpless. Before my hands stopped shaking, you were making plans to go back into that damnable cage. I wanted to kill you myself then and be done with it.''

Slowly, Keane turned and walked back to her. ''I saw it happen again every time I closed my eyes for weeks afterward. I can show you exactly where the scars are.'' He lifted a finger and traced four lines on her upper arm precisely where the claws had ripped her skin. He dropped his hand and shook his head. ''I can't watch you go in the cage, Jo.'' He lifted his hand again and let it linger over her hair. ''If I let you stay with me now, I wouldn't be able to let you go back to your own life. And I can't ask you to give it up.''

''I wish you would.'' Solemn-eyed, Jo watched him. ''I very much wish you would.''

''Jo.'' Shaking his head, he turned away. ''I know what it means to you.''

''No more than the law means to you, I imagine,'' she said briskly. ''But you said you were willing to give that up.''

''Yes, but...''

''Oh, very well.'' She pushed back her hair. ''If you won't ask me, I'll have to ask you. Will you marry me?''

Keane turned back, giving her his lowered brow frown. ''Jo, you can't...''

''Of course I can. This is the twentieth century. If I want to ask you to marry me, then I will. I did,'' she pointed out.

''Jo, I don't...''

''Yes or no, please, counselor. This isn't an easy question.'' She stepped forward until they stood toe to toe. ''I'm in love with you, and I want to marry you and have several babies. Is that agreeable?''

Keane's mouth opened and closed. He gave her an odd smile and lifted his hands to her shoulders. ''This is rather sudden.''

Jo felt a wild surge of joy. ''Perhaps it is,'' she admitted. ''I'll give you a minute to think about it. But I might as well tell you, I won't take no for an answer.''

Keane's fingers traced the curve of her neck. ''It seems I have little choice.''

''None at all,'' she corrected. Boldly, she locked her arms around him and pulled his mouth down to hers. The kiss was instantly urgent, instantly searching. Joined, they lowered to the rug and clung. For a long, long moment, their lips were united in a language too complex for words. Then, as if to reassure himself she was real, Keane searched the familiar curves of her body, tasted the longed-for flavor of her skin.

"Why did I think I could live without you?" he whispered. His mouth came desperately back to hers. "Be sure, Jo, be sure." Roughened with emotion, his voice was low while the words were spoken against her lips. "I'll never be able to let you go. I'm asking you for everything."

"No. No, it's not like that. Hold me tighter. Kiss me again," she demanded as his lips roamed her face. "Kiss me." She wondered if the sound of pleasure she heard was his or her own. She had not known a kiss could be so intimate, so terrifyingly exciting. No, she thought as she soared with the knowledge that he loved her. He wasn't asking everything, he was giving it.

"I'm leaving something behind," she told him when their lips parted, "and replacing it with something infinitely more important." She buried her face in the curve of his neck. "When you realize how much I love you, you'll understand."

Keane drew away and stared down at her. At last he spoke, but it was only her name. It was a soft sigh of a sound. She smiled at it and lifted a hand to his cheek. "If there's a way to compromise..."

"No." She shook her head, remembering his mother's words. "Sometimes there can't be a compromise. We love each other enough not to need one. Please, don't think I'm making a sacrifice; I'm not." She smiled a little and rubbed her palm experimentally over the stubble of his neglected beard. "I don't regret one minute of my life in the circus, and I don't regret changing it. You've given me the circus, so I'll always be a part of it." Her smile faded, and her eyes grew serious. "Will you belong to me, Keane?"

He took her hand from his cheek and pressed it to his lips. "I already do. I love you, Jovilette. I'll spend a lifetime loving you."

"That's not long enough," she said as their lips met again. "I want more. I want forever."

With slow, building passion, his hands moved over her. Taking his time, he loosened the buttons on her sweater. "So beautiful," he murmured as his lips trailed down her throat and found the gentle swell. Jo's breath caught at the new intimacy. "You're trembling. I love knowing I can make your skin tremble under my hands." His lips roamed back to hers before he cradled her in his arms. "I've wanted to be with you, to hold you, just hold you, for so long. I can't remember not wanting it."

With a sigh washed with contentment, Jo snuggled against him. "Keane," she murmured.

"Hmm?"

"You never answered me."

"About what?" He kissed her closed lids, then tangled his fingers in her hair.

Jo opened her eyes. Her brows arched over them. "Are you going to marry me or not?"

Keane laughed, rolled her onto her back and planted a long, lingering kiss on her mouth. "Is tomorrow soon enough?"

*   *   *   *   *